THE DEVIL'S TOMBSTONE

THE DEVIL'S TOMBSTONE

Carolyn J. Rose

The Devil's Tombstone
Copyright © 2014 Carolyn J. Rose
ISBN: 978-0-9837359-8-4

www.deadlyduomysteries.com

All rights reserved. No part of this book may be used or reproduced by any means, graphic, electronic, or mechanical, including photocopying, recording, taping, or by any other means, without the written permission of the author, except in the case of brief quotations used in articles and reviews.

This novel is a work of fiction. Names, characters, places, incidents, and dialogues are products of the author's imagination and are not to be construed as real. Any resemblance to actual events or persons, living or dead, is entirely coincidental.

Cover design by Dorion D. Rose, Broken Cork Photography

Interior design for print edition by Boulevard Photografica/Patty G. Henderson

Digital editions (epub and mobi) produced by Booknook.biz

For Lorin and Shirley and Dorion and Jeanine

And for Chanel—don't let a pink collar stop you from rolling in the mud

Chapter 1

"Cold cases?" I shoved the stack of bulging file folders across Sheriff Clement North's rumpled desk calendar. "If this is your idea of an early April Fools' Day joke, it's all irony and no humor. I can't even handle *fresh* cases."

"I admit you thrash around a bit, Dan." North scratched a bristly eyebrow with his thumbnail. "And you take a few dead-end roads. But you get where you need to be."

"I get to where someone has to step in and save my sorry ass." I gave the files another shove. "And when I'm done, people don't go to trial, they go to their graves."

"Some might find fault with that form of justice, son. Others might say you're due a medal for saving on prosecution costs." North scratched the other eyebrow. "Appeals can go on for years. Never mind how cut-and-dried those two cases were."

Those cases. Two killers. Both deranged. Both convinced their actions were necessary and justified. One, the best friend from my childhood at Hemlock Lake, a man turned monster by anger and the need for control. The other driven by demons to demean and kill girls in the likeness of his mother.

"There are others more qualified, more experienced."

"They don't want this burden. Although for the price of a few drinks they'll give you plenty of advice." He tapped the files. "And you can call on a woman in records for computer stuff. Hired her part-time but she's here *all* the time. Likes a challenge. Knows you'll be along."

I groped for another excuse. "I'm a civilian."

"Take the job and you'll be a cold-case investigator."

I shook my head. "I can't be here 40 hours a week. Camille and I have plans for how things will work after the baby arrives."

North smiled. "Camille's a wonderful woman and I was happy as a hog in slop to pronounce you married, but you know what they say about mice and men and plans. And, hell, the budget only allows for 10 hours a week. Fifteen at the most."

He opened the top drawer of his desk and drew out a blackened pipe and a sack of tobacco. "You can work from home. In between walking the floor with a crying baby."

I imagined myself rocking a squalling lump of tiny human while considering the contents of those folders. It didn't seem the optimum way to focus on either task.

"Two murdered for sure. Three missing and probably dead. Read through the files." North packed tobacco into his pipe. It smelled like cherries and brandy. "That's all I'm asking."

I turned my gaze from the files and studied the chipped base of a bookshelf. "I see the hook you're trying to set."

He sealed the tobacco pouch and slid open a box of wooden kitchen matches. "If I remember right, you saw it two years ago, too."

I had. The bait on that hook was a string of anonymous letters threatening arson and more. Two years ago the lure of Hemlock Lake had been every bit as strong as my determination to stay away. A few months later the lake almost claimed my life.

And now I lived beside Hemlock Lake with Camille, the woman who pulled me from its dark water and drew me up into light and life.

North hit the switch for the exhaust fan that ventilated pipe smoke from his office, struck the match, and applied flame to fragrant tobacco. "Read through them, son," he mumbled around the stem. "Talk it over with Camille."

Setting the hook.

Camille wouldn't see that stack of files as a heap of lost causes. She'd see hope and the possibility of closure. She was a realist, but a realist with a soft heart and a strong desire to heal.

North sucked at the pipestem, making the tobacco glow. A fragment flamed and fell from the bowl, floating to the desk, landing on the wide paper calendar. North brushed at it twice with the edge of his free hand, leaving a faint X of ash across today's date, March 25th.

The day marked the final quarter of the Worm Moon and signaled the coming of April, traditionally a month of change and disruption in my life.

An omen?

Some around Hemlock Lake would say "Yes." And after Clarence Wolven's murder, I wouldn't argue with their beliefs and superstitions. Last April I'd been guided by his ghost, directed into the wild lands of the Catskill Mountains, to a serial killer's dump site.

I shuddered. This April would be different. This April Camille and I would have a child.

North prodded the stack of files. A photograph of a boy slipped free. I told myself to look away.

I couldn't.

He stood at center stage in a cone of light, barefoot, wearing a pair of ragged overalls, sporting a floppy straw hat, and carrying a bamboo fishing pole. Playing Tom Sawyer? Huckleberry Finn?

"That's Franklin Turner," North said. "Fourteen when he died. End of the summer three years ago. Stabbed. More than two dozen times."

Two dozen wounds spoke of rage, passion, vengeance. Someone had wanted Franklin Turner blotted out, obliterated.

How had he incited such violence? What had he done? And to whom?

His grin was broad and promised mischief and practical jokes. His eyes were brown and clear and without a glint of malice. His freckles were genuine, not stage makeup. He was the kid next door, friendly and naïve, helpful and hopeful.

I slid the photograph into the file, sighed, and drew the stack toward me, counting. The folders shed bits of paper, a staple, a gummy green rubber band. "Who's been working these?"

"No one with any serious intention." North stared out the window at bare branches transecting a swatch of sky. Cloudless, it was more white than blue, as if color had been swept south by winter winds. "Not since Harry Pallister ate his gun a few months before you signed on."

I recalled no one seemed surprised that Pallister drove to the end of a dirt road, drank a fifth of vodka, and checked out. His debts were mounting faster than his blood pressure and he'd found himself on the wrong side of the bars after his wife decided being slapped around wasn't what she'd agreed to in her wedding vows.

"You didn't assign the cases to someone else?"

"Of course I did." North sucked at the pipe and spewed smoke my way, then slumped. "Turned them over to Orville

Eakins. Thought with his experience he'd get traction, talk with family and friends, develop new leads. But all he did was poke at them while he counted down to retirement."

I had a dim memory of Orville—Orrie as he was called. Thanks to his seniority, he commanded a plum schedule. No one thought much of Orrie, and what they did think was that he came in late from breakfast and left early for lunch.

"Turns out his idea of progress meant moving the files to a cabinet in the basement."

Despite a cement floor, ventilation, and wallboard that hid the original stone foundation, the basement had all the ambience of a tomb. Given a choice between being locked in a cell or allowed to roam the basement, I'd pick the cell.

"You didn't assign anyone else?"

"Didn't *have* anyone else. Not with that serial killer and all. But now I got breathing room and a little grant money." He leveled the pipe at me. "And a man I know won't let go once he gets his teeth in."

I shuffled the folders, releasing dust and the scents of mold and misery. Anger swelled high in my chest, anger at Harry Pallister who abandoned his duty for death, anger at Orville Eakins who placed more importance on repast and retirement than on these lives cut short, and finally, anger at the killers.

The hook caught in my heart.

"The reports are in the system," North said. "But I figured you'd want the original files and notes. That's the way I'd do it."

As always, his approval—approval I'd never gotten from my father—gave me a jolt of pride. Still, I put up a semblance of a struggle. "I'll read through them. And I'll talk it over with Camille. No promises."

North smiled through a swirl of smoke. "Not a one."

Chapter 2

"I said I'd read through the cases," I told Camille that evening. "I didn't make any promises."

"I'm certain you didn't." She lowered herself into the rocker beside the fireplace with a soft grunt. "But the minute you touched those folders you were all in. You and Sheriff North both knew that."

She raised a hand before I could protest. "That's fine. In fact, it's more than fine. You need something beyond this." Her hand moved in an arc, taking in the high-ceilinged living room and settling on the tight swell of her belly beneath a faded blue T-shirt pilfered from my bureau. "I don't doubt that you can fill your days riding herd on this baby and keeping up the property and being a gofer at the store, but I also don't doubt that you'll need something more fulfilling."

I rested my hand beside hers, feeling tiny ripples of movement. "I'll cut brush. I'll plant a bigger garden. Nothing says 'fulfillment' like a bumper crop of zucchini."

Camille laughed, the deep, rich sound making the baby wiggle as if it shared her amusement. "Do you intend to can it, freeze it, or leave it on doorsteps in the dark of the moon?"

"The moon's only dark one night a month and that's hardly enough to keep from being overrun. I'll print off every recipe for zucchini bread on the Internet and work my way through them."

I struck a pose, shoulders back, chest out, and adopted the serious tone of network newscasters. "Zucchini bread will become synonymous with fruitcake in the annals of Hemlock Lake. It will be known as the gift that can't be forgiven."

She shook her head, the glow of the fire playing across her bronze hair and skin. "Spare me. Spare our friends and neighbors. Take the job. Please take the job."

"What job?"

Julie ambled in with a teenager's gawky grace. Nelson, our three-legged dog, followed, nails clicking on the wide stone hearth as he headed for his bed, a large cushion with a dog-sized indentation. Camille had covered it with a quilt pieced from triangles of red, orange, yellow, and brown, but Julie informed me last week that a summer quilt in blues and greens would soon appear. Apparently dog décor kept pace with changing seasons. But the question remained: Why did a dog that spent most of his sleeping hours on the ground, the sofa, or in Julie's bed, need a special cushion?

Anchoring his lone hind leg, Nelson executed a rolling flop, curling as he spun. He finished up with his muzzle resting against the white plume of his tail.

"Hard day?" I asked him.

Julie brushed aside a strand of hair. It was growing out after the pixie cut she'd endured to remove tape a killer had used to gag her. This week it was dyed a blondish red. "Hunting the first frog of the season."

"Followed by enduring the first bath of the season. In the master bathroom, I might add." Camille pointed at me. "And with *your* shampoo and towels."

"I couldn't use the hose like in summer." Julie went into teen argument position, feet apart, hands on hips, chin raised, chestnut brown eyes flashing. "The water out of the well is way too cold."

"And the water in the lake isn't?" Camille arched her back and rubbed her fist against her spine. "He was in and out all afternoon. Never mind slabs of ice thick enough to float polar bears."

"But the air's warm. Except when there's wind," Julie argued. "And Nelson doesn't notice the cold when he's chasing frogs."

"Nelson also doesn't obey commands when he's chasing frogs." I slipped a throw pillow behind Camille's back and kneaded her shoulders. "All that chasing and no catching. Reminds me of high school."

"You didn't have any dates in high school?" Julie abandoned her confrontational stance and sprawled on her belly on the brown leather sofa, her chin in her hands. "How come?"

"Because I couldn't get the words out. Every time a girl looked at me, I got tongue-tied with fear."

Camille chuckled. "And you already had a relationship. With books."

"Most of them were easier to understand than girls."

"But you should have had a lot of dates," Julie said. "You were handsome."

"Were?" I feigned shock. "You mean I'm not now?"

She rolled her eyes. "And you were on the football team."

I took a breath, framing my words while fighting my instincts. Camille and I promised Julie's counselor that—when we could work them into conversations naturally—we'd say positive things about her father. Our aim was to demonstrate that Ronny Miller had been more than a demented man who murdered her mother, shot local prankster Willie Dean Denton, and tried his best to kill me. "I played football, sure. But not the same way your father did."

Julie brushed that aside as if it wasn't relevant. "You were the quarterback."

"Mostly because our coach was big on designing plays no one else could remember. And because I always managed to get up one more time than I was knocked down."

"The secret of your success," Camille said with a smile. "And a prime reason to take this job."

"What job?" Julie kicked her feet against the armrest. "With Sheriff North? Will you wear a uniform? And carry a gun?"

Since the day last September when Jefferson Longyear put a bullet in the brain of the man holding her hostage, Julie had wanted a gun. Camille contended she'd feel safer and more in control if she learned to shoot, so we got her a rifle and nominated Jefferson to train her. He reported she had a good eye, a steady hand, no compunction about blowing away tin cans, but no desire to kill a living thing. As one of the few men in Hemlock Lake who didn't hunt, that was fine with me.

"No uniform," I told her. "And no gun. I'd work cold cases."

Julie squinched up her face.

"Old cases," Camille said. "Cases detectives haven't solved."

"You'll solve them, Uncle Dan." Julie sniffed the air, sprang to her feet, and bounded for the kitchen. "Yay. I smell tuna casserole with potato chips on top. I'll set the table."

"Ah, to be young again," I said. "And believe that all things are possible."

Camille levered herself from the rocker. "Ah, to be young again and able to bound instead of waddling like a duck."

"I was thinking you waddled more like a penguin."

"Not funny." She hit me with a burnt orange throw pillow. "You try carrying a bowling ball in your belly and see how graceful you are."

"Is this where I get the infamous it's-all-your-fault speech, or are you holding that in reserve until you go into labor?"

She put both hands under her belly and lifted, grunting and leaning to her left as she did. "I'm starting to wonder if labor is a myth and if I'll go on like this forever. My hair is brittle, my skin is oily, my ankles are swollen, and I feel like an overloaded blimp."

I turned her to me, smoothed her wiry cinnamon hair, and gazed into her eyes. In the dim light they seemed brown, but I knew better. There was a red flame deep in those eyes. I'd seen them coppery. Russet. Flashing fire. "You're beautiful," I told her. "Beautiful."

The next morning, after Camille headed for the general store with Julie on board to catch the school bus, I packed the files in a canvas satchel, grabbed a beat-up denim jacket, boosted Nelson into the passenger seat, and searched out Jefferson Longyear. It wasn't a lengthy search. I found him in the first place I looked—out behind the house he shared with his wife, Mary Louise Van Valkenberg. The last of a family stretching back generations in these mountains, Mary Lou had inherited the house, the general store, the old schoolhouse that was now an informal kids' club, and the church.

Despite a biting wind gusting off the lake, Jefferson had worked up a sweat scraping years of paint from a door laid across two sawhorses.

"They don't make doors like they used to, so I'm not tossing these out." He blotted his forehead with the sleeve of a green flannel shirt, settled his steel-rimmed glasses higher on his nose, and flexed his shoulders. "Could haul them to someone who strips paint for a living, but what else do I have going?"

He said that without regret. Jefferson didn't have a job, hadn't had one since his memory flamed out when he returned from the war in Vietnam. He'd wandered away from a hospital and continued wandering until a spark ignited recollections and he returned to Hemlock Lake. The doctors he checked in with every few months pronounced him in good physical condition and regularly proposed new theories to explain his mental break and reconnection. Meanwhile, he was content with little, his needs covered by money left by his mother and the hoarded coins and currency piled up by Mary Lou's sister, the woman he nearly married.

"Got coffee going?" I asked.

"Always. And for once Freeman and Evan haven't come by to drain the pot and bend my ear and generally get in the way." He hooked the scraper on the edge of the door and led me up the steps to the kitchen, Nelson hopping past us to snuffle beneath the table in search of crumbs. "Gonna wash up. You know where everything is."

That last wasn't a question. I'd been in and out of the Van Valkenberg home from the time I was able to walk. Fraternal twins Mary Lou and Louisa Marie babysat for me and my brother Nat. About the only thing Nat and I ever had in common was the hope that Lou Marie—mean-tempered and bent on following rules, especially those she made up on the spot—would get frustrated, go to her room, and slam the door.

Lou Marie slammed a lot of doors in her lifetime, maybe even the one Jefferson was scraping. She died of heart failure on the eve of her wedding, setting Jefferson free from a promise made before he went to war. When Camille and I tied the knot in February, he and Mary Lou took their vows with us.

The coffee machine sat on the corner of the counter, the glass pot half full. Jefferson rose early, so the brew would be strong and a little scorched. A healthy dose of cream and a splash of vanilla from the spice cabinet gave it a lift.

The designer-coffee trend hadn't reached Hemlock Lake. From 7:00 to 9:00 every weekday morning, Marcella Wilson served up sludgy stimulant and reheated pastries at the little shop tacked onto the side of Stub's garage. Camille had a pot of something far more fragrant at the store after 8:30, but otherwise you were on your own. Most of the older women drank tea. Their men preferred generic instant coffee because it was quick and easy. They often shoveled two or three heaping spoons of granules into their mugs, added hot water from the tap, and drank the mix down like a potion purchased from a traveling snake oil salesman.

I shuddered at the thought, set the satchel on a chair, and took a seat at the oval oak table I'd played under as a kid. Nelson licked a dribble of something from the floor beside the refrigerator, then curled up on a braided rug by a heat vent near the sink.

Jefferson emerged from the tiny downstairs bathroom, wiping his hands on a miniscule white towel with a yellow duckling embroidered in one corner.

"That's not a guest towel, is it?"

"Probably. House has more towels than a Turkish bath and every one of them has its own particular function." He blew his nose in the towel, grinned, and tossed it on top of the washer. "I tell Mary Lou, 'Put labels on them so I know what they're for. Put a sign up on the wall.' She says this isn't rocket science and I need to pay attention and be more civilized."

We both rolled our eyes, Jefferson because he'd lived in places where the term "civilized" didn't apply, me because I'd never come across a claim that one cornerstone of civilization was a supply of tiny towels.

Raising the lid of the washer, he tucked the towel inside. "At least I'm civilized enough to try to hide evidence of being uncivilized." He poured coffee, his gaze sliding to the satchel. "What brings you out of the woods?"

"Sheriff North thinks I need a job. Part-time. Investigating cold cases."

"A job would give you an excuse to get out. Might welcome that after the baby shows up." He sat and sipped coffee. "How cold are the cases?"

"Think Northern Greenland. In January." I stacked files on the table.

"Different killers?" He aligned the edges of the stack. "Or just one?"

The coffee in my throat turned to lead. I swallowed more to ram it down. "Can't be just one. I haven't looked hard at these cases, but there's no common thread. The victims are male *and* female, and the age spread is from 14 to 48."

Jefferson rubbed his brush cut. "Could be someone who doesn't operate like Colden Cornell did."

Cornell, the man Jefferson shot last fall, had targeted only young women with brown hair.

"He cast a long and bloody shadow," Jefferson said. "Wouldn't be wise to stand in it while we're considering. Better if we aim to shed light on these one at a time."

I noticed the plural pronoun and smiled. He was hooked.

He glanced away from the folders. "Provided I'm allowed."

"The sheriff knows you have my back and don't run off at the mouth."

"North's a lot of things." Jefferson slid the top folder from the stack and opened it. "Stupid's not one of them."

Chapter 3

By 11:00 we'd drained the coffeepot and skimmed the details of the cases. "Sandwich would be good about now," Jefferson said. "And then a walk to kick this around. What's Camille got on special at the store?"

I packed the files into the satchel. "Egg salad?"

"That's Friday."

"Roast beef?"

"Monday."

"Eat there a lot, do you?"

"My intention when I rise each day is to fend for myself." He carried our mugs to the sink. "But I lose momentum in the face of convenience and convivial company."

"Convivial company? Somebody whack you with a dictionary?"

He opened the door. "Trying to be civilized."

"Better get the hang of those towels, then."

I whistled Nelson awake and we walked over to the general store. Camille sat on a stool behind the counter, watching a shaggy-haired man plumping bags of corn curls and lining them up in the metal rack near the door. She shot Jefferson a warm smile. "I'm stocking a new type of barbecue chips. Thicker. Hickory smoked."

"Sold." He reached for a bag and winked at me. "She knows my weakness."

"That the best you can do in the way of a weakness?"

"Oh, he's got a few others." Mary Lou came through the door from the post office side of the building and snuggled against Jefferson, tucking her head beneath his chin. As always when I saw them together, I felt joy that they'd found each other and sadness because they'd lost so many years. Mary Lou was past 50 and Jefferson a few years older. How much time would they have together?

Mary Lou tipped her head and Jefferson kissed her forehead and then her lips. "You're my weakness."

Cheeks pink, Mary Lou slipped from his embrace, smoothed her white blouse and navy skirt, and headed for the refrigerated cases in the rear of the store, Nelson at her heels. "Turkey or ham?"

"Ham," we said together.

"There's sliced apple in the ham sandwiches," Camille advised.

She seldom made sandwiches the same way twice and last week layered turkey with roasted red pepper and onions and mixed chopped grapes into the tuna salad. A few older Hemlock Lake folks weren't happy with what they considered flights of culinary fancy. But then, the same few hadn't been happy with other changes Camille and Julie made after Lou Marie died and they took over the store.

"Apple works for me," Jefferson said. "As long as there's plenty of mustard."

"Julie squirted on the mustard." Camille's eyes sparkled. "You better take an extra napkin."

"Or three," I cautioned.

Mary Lou returned with two sandwiches wrapped in wax paper and two bottles of root beer. "You read my mind," Jefferson said.

"Huge challenge that was." Mary Lou smiled, plucked the chips from his hand, and packed our lunch in a paper sack Camille produced. "When you have a choice, you drink root beer with ham sandwiches, ginger ale with roast beef, lemon-lime with egg salad, birch beer with turkey, and cola with tuna."

I jabbed him with an elbow. "If she can figure that out, you can crack the code on those towels."

"And *you* can pay for lunch," Jefferson growled. "You're the one with a job."

Mary Lou handed me the sack. "A job? Doing what?"

"Investigating cold cases." Camille turned to me. "It's definite? You told the sheriff you'd take it?"

"Doesn't have to. North knew as soon as Dan saw those files he couldn't refuse. Probably has the paperwork filled out and waiting for his signature." Jefferson opened the door, letting in a gust of frigid air. "Let's head up on the ridge and eat."

"Up on the ridge" meant the town cemetery. I zipped my jacket. "Sure. It's bound to be balmy as Key West up there."

"At least you won't have to worry about keeping the drinks cold." Camille pulled a box of dog biscuits from a shelf beneath the counter. "Leave Nelson here. That climb is hard and I don't want him catching a chill."

Nelson had survived two attempts on his life and was about as likely to catch cold as he was to go to college, but Camille and Julie pampered him. Would that change when we had a real baby?

"Say hello to everyone," Mary Lou said as we went out the door. "And pull a few weeds while you're there."

"Women," Jefferson groused. "Always wanting to tack on another chore. Like a little relaxation is the first step on the road to ruin."

Not that Jefferson did much relaxing. The work ethic was a powerful force in Hemlock Lake, and he was more driven than most. In high school he'd memorized Longfellow's "A Psalm of Life" for extra credit. "Up and doing" was his motto, so I was prepared for the pace he set across the dam, past the church, and up the twisting road to the cemetery. There had been no recent funerals, so Stub hadn't plowed. Snow lingered where the dirt road lay in shadow, and the ruts were glossy with mud.

By the time we reached the gate, my breath came in sharp puffs. Jefferson breathed like he'd been lounging in an easy chair. A lesser man might have suggested I spent too many hours reading by the fire, but he said nothing as he led me behind the Sagendorf family monument and pointed at a couple of logs shaped by a chainsaw into rough chairs. "The Sagendorfs break the wind. And the Goodrich marker," Jefferson pointed at a broad monument a dozen feet away, "reflects sunlight this way in the spring and fall."

I noted a clump of snowdrops about to flower. "Thoughtful of them."

"Not the way they were in life. Not according to Mary Lou." He jerked a thumb toward a double row of lunchbox-sized granite grave markers flanking the monument. "Seems like if Samuel Goodrich loved his wives and kids he'd have drunk less and taken better care of them. Two wives. Seventeen children. Most dead within a week. Only two lived to be tall enough to see over the counter at the general store."

One of Mary Lou's passions was genealogy, so I wasn't surprised he knew this. And I wasn't surprised by his vehement tone. Despite the killing he did as a sniper, Jefferson had profound respect for life. And he had a deep admiration for women.

I crossed blighted grass, hunkered on a log seat, and found it more comfortable than it looked. Jefferson rolled another log from beneath an ancient maple and set it upright as a table. I stood the sack in the center and tore along the creases, making a tablecloth. "It appears you come here often."

"Probably more than some would say is healthy." He folded his lanky frame into the other seat and reached for his sandwich. "From here I can see Lou Marie."

I gazed at the pink marble stone atop her grave. Lou Marie had elevated frugality to a fine art. Had she seen death coming, she would have contracted for the cheapest possible marker, or made it clear she'd go without. Jefferson and Mary Lou acknowledged her character, then bought this stone and had it carved with the roses Lou Marie hadn't lived to carry down the aisle.

"I used to feel her around here. Last summer and into the fall." Jefferson opened his root beer and took a swallow. "But she's been gone since the first snow."

Probably a good thing. Lou Marie had been jealous and vindictive. If she knew the man she waited for all those years married her sister, and if she found a way here from whatever came after death, she'd bring a rain of misery on both of them.

"And Clarence is over there." Jefferson pointed the other way, at the place where we buried the old dog handler who had hoped to train Nelson as a search and rescue dog. Nelson lost a leg but survived the slaughter that killed Clarence and seven other dogs. I liked to think Nelson would have made Clarence proud—if only for his tenacity. "I could have sworn I felt him here the other day when I was working out how to run that new wiring inside the kitchen walls."

I nodded. Last summer I'd felt his spirit as an electric hum and buzz. It made sense he'd take an interest in wiring.

"You'd think this would be a lonely place." I opened the bag of chips and picked up a couple of pebbles to anchor our napkins. "But sometimes it feels crowded. And not all that quiet."

"Maybe they're talking among themselves." Jefferson took a bite of his sandwich. "Shame we can't ask them about those cases of yours."

"If the dead could speak there'd be a lot of lawyers out of work."

"Detectives, too." He took another bite and grunted. "Apple slices with ham and cheese. A stroke of culinary genius."

I nodded and we dedicated ourselves to our food for a few minutes. Then Jefferson wiped his hands. "Can't shake the feeling some of those cases might be linked somehow."

For a moment I thought he might be joking, but his eyes were flat. "I can't see it. They're all over the map. Franklin Turner was stabbed. Genevieve Graham was shot. In a phone booth. The other three might not be cases at all. Jeremy Yount might have run off. His father was strict and he could have wanted a different life. Angelina Vernon and Judy Arnold might have done the same."

"Angelina's parents were breaking up. She was 16. That's a volatile age. But Judy was older, had a steady job." Jefferson gazed at Lou Marie's gravestone and I recalled the rehearsal for his wedding and my conviction that he intended to abandon any hope of love and joy, shoulder obligation, and soldier through the years to come.

"Maybe Judy got sick of the job," I said. "Maybe running off was more attractive than going to work."

"Running off's not hard. Neither is dropping out of sight. Staying dropped is tougher."

Good point. Unless you went off the grid and didn't drive or vote or hold a conventional job or pay taxes or get legally married, sooner or later you needed documents. If you had the right contacts, you could establish a new identity. But had Angelina or Judy or Jeremy done that?

"Sounds like nobody dug too deep into these cases after the first few weeks," Jefferson said. "And it seems that with all kinds of information going onto computers and getting linked up, an investigator has a good chance of finding someone—if that someone is alive and isn't held prisoner."

"And if that someone slips up." I finished my sandwich and tipped my stump chair against the Sagendorf stone, basking in reflected sun and warmth.

Jefferson folded the potato chip bag and stuffed it in the paper sack. "I wonder if there are others."

"Other cases North didn't give me?"

"No, cases in other counties. But close by. And around the same time."

I sat up, stump thumping the ground, thinking about Colden Cornell. He'd dumped his victims not far from here, but hunted farther afield in several counties. A cloud passed in front of the sun and a bitter wind slipped past the Sagendorf monument and coiled around me.

North didn't attempt to hide a smile when I knocked on his half-open door the next morning. For my part, I didn't attempt explanation or pretense.

"These are from Julie." I set a foil-covered paper plate on the corner of his desk. "Oatmeal cookies with pecans and blueberries."

"Don't tease an old man, son. Pass those closer."

I did and he tore off the foil and snatched two cookies, stuffing one in his mouth. "These are good for me, right?"

"Camille tweaked the recipe. No butter. No egg yolk."

"Then no problem." North poked the second cookie between his lips and flipped a manila envelope my way. "Sign those. Get them to Jane."

As Jefferson predicted, the paperwork was ready for me. I put aside stirrings of resentment and picked up the envelope.

"If you want a desk or file cabinet, tell Jane."

"No need. I'll work from home. Do you have a list of contacts and numbers for law enforcement in surrounding counties?"

North's gaze flickered to the state map and he scowled. "You trying to put me off my feed, son?"

"I want to make sure these cases aren't—"

"Don't say it!"

North slapped the foil over the cookies, then yanked open the shallow center drawer of his desk. A welter of paperclips shot out, spattering against the wall behind him. He wrestled out an untidy stack of papers, shuffled through the heap, and flipped a stapled set of pages onto the blotter. "Copy that. Return it ASAP."

I plucked up the list of names and numbers and headed for the door.

"I can handle fact just fine," North called after me. "You know that. But my blood pressure doesn't need unfounded supposition and suspicion. Work up all the theories you want, but don't bring them to me until there's a foundation under them."

Serenity Brook, the part-time-all-the-time computer wizard, was nothing like her name. Her short, white hair, mangled into tufts, said she wasn't serene, and the way she pounded her keyboard reminded me more of the thunder of Niagara Falls than the babble of any brook I'd come across in the Catskills. I found her in the habitable part of the basement inside a bunker constructed of rusting file cabinets and a metal desk turned on its side. Two more desks formed an L and supported three wide computer screens, ergonomic keyboards, a can of diet cherry cola, and a sack of peanuts salted in the shell.

"Stone? The cold-case guy?"

"Guilty."

"North said you'd be along." She stood, shook bits of peanut shell from her denim shirt and sagging sweat pants, rolled shoulders as broad as mine and nearly on the same level, and got my hand in a grip that halted the blood flow to my fingers. "I scanned your cold files."

She released me, flung herself into a rump-sprung seat, and gestured at a folding chair leaning against a file cabinet. "Sit. Speak."

The chair fought to avoid its assignment, metal grinding on metal as I pried it open. One leg was bent, the seat had a sharp corner, and the whole thing wobbled and bucked. Serenity Brook was either oblivious to those issues, didn't care, didn't like visitors, or was testing me. Given that she'd applied no makeup to disguise lines, wrinkles, and age spots, sported no jewelry, and wore shoes even a tramp might cast aside, I went with "didn't care."

"How do you find someone who disappeared? Someone who might be alive?"

Making check marks in the air, she spouted a list. "Fingerprints, license, insurance, Social Security, public records, and blah blah blah." She jerked her head at the screen to the right. "Checked everything for Yount, Vernon, and Arnold yesterday morning. Got nothin'."

I blinked. If Serenity Brook accomplished that in a few hours and found no trace, what the hell could I do?

She cracked a peanut, tilted her head, shook kernels into her mouth, and tossed shells over her shoulder. They landed a foot from the wastebasket in a pile of discarded wrappers and crumpled paper sacks. "Doesn't mean there *is* nothin'. Might mean I haven't looked in the right place. I'll storm the brains of my friends out there and try again."

I guessed "out there" meant cyberspace, but didn't ask. I figured she already assumed I had the IQ of the chair I sat on.

"Bring me more." She spun her chair to the center computer and flung a command over her shoulder. "Bring me what *isn't* in the reports."

I almost laughed. How could I know what *wasn't* in the reports? Hold a séance and try to conjure the ghost of Harry Pallister? Ask his spirit what he didn't make a note of, what he discovered but discounted?

Parting words seemed unnecessary, so I folded the chair, leaned it against the file cabinet, and left. Any bit of confidence I'd felt at the start of the day was long gone. Never mind finding what wasn't in the reports, how could I determine the truthfulness of those interviewed and questioned?

Yeah, I'd talk with everyone again—everyone still alive and available—but if they lied in the past, they'd had a lot of years to practice and perfect those lies. On the other hand, time, like wind and rain, had a way of eroding lies. And truth, like stones heaved up by frost, had a way of coming to light.

Chapter 4

Friday evening, as was our custom, 12 of us gathered at the round table in the rear of the Shovel It Inn. Julie took the seat beside Jefferson—a seat once occupied by Lou Marie—and Justin sat beside her in the chair Priscilla Denton once claimed. Widowed when Ronny Miller killed her husband in an attempt to cast suspicion for a rash of arson fires, Priscilla had sold her house, boat dock, and bait shop, heading to Florida with winter on her heels. Camille and I bought the property for Justin and now, when he wasn't preparing for summer business, taking classes at the community college, or doing homework, he put sweat equity into the house.

"Gonna start on the roof this weekend?" Stub Wilson asked. "I could lend a hand."

"After you finish changing out those faucets," Marcella Wilson told him in a tone that made other husbands cringe.

Stub turtled his head into the open collar of his gray coverall. "Now, Marcella, it's a big job and the boy can use a little help. And it's not like our faucets are leaking *real* bad."

Beside me Evan Bonesteel sucked in a breath. "That's gonna fly like an anvil," he whispered.

For Evan, who spoke seldom and used few words when he did, the comment was on a par with a long-winded political speech.

While Marcella sputtered about Stub being eager to help everyone in town except his own wife, Julie leaned past Justin and patted her hand. "Jefferson let me install the new faucet in their kitchen sink and he only had to tighten one thing when I was done. I bet I could do yours. Stub could check my work."

"The kid could work for the United Nations," Camille said. "Watch."

As if drawn by a magnetic force, Freeman, Evan, and Jefferson leaned toward Marcella. Not to be out-manned by a girl, they swore allegiance to the faucet project, promising to get it done first thing the next morning. A beat behind the others by virtue of the fact that he was young and short on experience with women, Justin promised to pitch in.

Marcella ignored the others and beamed at him. "No, you need to get those old shingles torn off and replaced before there's more water damage in the attic. The faucets will keep for a bit."

Stub shook his head like a dazed man who had run full-tilt into a tree. Freeman Keefe leaned closer and spoke to him in a stage whisper. "Rule number one of marriage: It's only a good idea if it's your *wife's* idea."

Alda Keefe pinched Freeman's earlobe and Marcella shot him a glance sharp enough to skin a snake. Then Camille and Mary Lou laughed and everyone joined in.

"It shouldn't take long," Justin assured Marcella. "It's the original part of the roof that's leaking."

Like many older homes in Hemlock Lake, the Denton place had started as a box divided into smaller boxes: living room and dining area, kitchen, bedroom, and bath. When Priscilla and Willie Dean bought it from his father, they added a master bedroom suite and then a den, a small garage, and finally a carport.

"Better start early," Freeman said. "You can bet we'll find rot up in there. Willie Dean—rest his soul—wasn't keen on upkeep, and Priscilla had other interests." He stressed the last two words, reminding us about her love of spreading gossip as well as hinting at what she'd been up to behind closed doors with her handyman. "I'll be there at 8:00."

Stub, Jefferson, and Evan nodded their agreement.

"Works for me," Justin said.

"There's a stack of plywood in my garage," I told him. "It's yours for free and I'll haul it over, but you might have to piece it together like a jigsaw puzzle."

"If the price is right, piecing's not a problem," Justin assured me.

Since his father's death and the chaos that followed, Justin had learned a lot about prices and piecing—the price of bad decisions and the difficulty of piecing life together again. A high school football star with a future, he'd plummeted into a vortex of anger, refusing to acknowledge his father's guilt, blaming me for Ronny's death. His grandmother helped him enlist, but he went AWOL in no time. When Jefferson and I found him he was out of money and out of ideas, but still spoiling for a fight.

Jefferson gave it to him.

When it was over, we helped him up and helped him out. He'd paid his dues to the military but, so far, refused to go to counseling or talk about the past. Camille worried, but I argued that he had his head on straight and his eyes on the future. He'd talk when he was ready.

"Plywood piecing don't have to look good," Stub said, "seeing as how we'll slap tar paper and shingles over it."

"You better do that quick," Alda said. "Before that storm gets here."

Pattie Bonesteel nodded. "They say it will be a monster by the time it reaches us. The storm of the century."

Jefferson laughed. "The century is only three years old and this is the fourth storm with that title."

Pattie's cheeks flushed. "I'm just repeating what the weatherman said."

"Weather folks tend to talk about the worst that can happen." Mary Lou patted air, her way of saying "Calm down." "That's how they get us to tune in."

"Mountains usually deflect the storm pattern," Stub said.

"Except when they don't," Evan added.

Camille choked on a laugh, then let it loose, holding her belly with both hands.

"You're going to shake that baby right out of there," Alda warned.

"I wish." Camille sipped at her water. "I was ready to have this thing a week ago. Two weeks ago."

"It'll come when it's time," Pattie said.

I smiled, partly at the remark, and partly at the word "it." Julie had lobbied hard to be surprised and Camille and I decided it didn't matter whether our baby was male or female, as long as it was whole and healthy. And, despite relentless prodding, we had yet to draw up a list of possible names.

"As long as it doesn't come on April Fools' Day," Camille said. "Wednesday will be fine. Monday would be better. But not Tuesday."

"And not in the middle of a storm," Marcella said. "Not with you at the end of the lake miles from the main road."

"You got a plan worked out?" Stub asked me.

"Yep. I went to all the classes. Even took notes," I said with pride. "When the contractions get serious, we get in the car and drive to the hospital. If they speed up, I drive faster."

Camille rolled her eyes. "It's a little more complicated than that."

"But not much."

"Not for you," Marcella said. "All you have to do is drive. Camille has to do the real work."

"And there could be a lot of that," Alda said. "First babies usually take their time getting into the world."

"Except when they don't," Mary Lou added.

"Oil level is good. Hoses and belts are fine." Julie closed the hood of the SUV and gave me a mock salute. "Except that right front tire looks a little low."

"Then you may take your seat." I opened the driver's door and bowed with a flourish.

Julie giggled, climbed behind the wheel, adjusted the seat and mirrors, and checked to make sure we were all belted in. The ritual was one I learned before I tried for my driver's license and I wanted Julie to follow it faithfully until she had a year behind the wheel. So far she hadn't complained, but no doubt that would come once she had a license and more miles to her name. The license, however, was two months off. To avoid distraction, she'd decided to wait until school was out before she took her test.

Without a jolt or lurch she worked clutch and gas and pulled out of the parking lot and onto the road that ran along the east side of Hemlock Lake.

"I couldn't have done that better myself." Camille patted her belly. "The kid approves."

"I'll be glad when we know what's in there." I worked slack into the seatbelt and turned sideways on the rear seat. "I never thought I'd long to use a gender-specific pronoun."

"Alda says it's a girl," Julie said, "because you're carrying high."

Camille chuckled. "Pattie told me that means it's a boy."

"Maybe there are two babies, a boy *and* a girl."

"I hope not," I said. "If it's twins I'll have to beg the sheriff for a full-time job to feed us all."

"We can plant a bigger garden," Julie said. "And I don't have to eat so much."

Camille leaned forward and laid a hand on her shoulder. "Dan's kidding. There's plenty of money and the last thing we'll ever scrimp on is food. In fact, when we get home, I intend to bake a batch of gingersnaps with crystallized ginger chunks."

So far, Camille's cravings had been for foods I liked or at least didn't mind eating. No liver and onions or lentil soup or sauerkraut.

"Yum. Warm cookies. I'll chop the ginger." Julie pressed on the gas, then slowed as we passed the road that snaked into Bobcat Hollow where she once lived and where her mother died. "I'm glad you took that job, Uncle Dan. Those poor people need somebody to find out who killed them or where they went. And you'll do it. You don't give up and you never walk away."

Camille's stretched her arm and patted my knee.

"I'm glad you found out all my father did. I'm glad I know about my mother even though . . ." Julie's voice cracked and she hunched over the wheel. "Alda says we all have a cross to bear and Mary Lou says that means everyone has a burden and accepting it can make you work harder and be a better person."

Mary Lou should know. She toted the burden of her disagreeable twin through the years, leaning the other way, toward the bright side, the kind side.

Camille glanced at me, tears glimmering in her eyes.

Before either of us could speak, Julie went on. "That's why I want to go into law enforcement and maybe work for Sheriff North. Except I really like being out in the woods, and I love birds and animals, so maybe I'll be a game warden."

"That would be interesting," Camille said.

"Especially if you were assigned to this area. Half the men up here hunt year-round."

"Jefferson says that's because they came from big families and had to hunt so they didn't starve. He says it's more necessity and tradition than sport. And he says that when it comes to deer, this area has exceeded its carrying capacity."

I smiled at Julie's new knowledge and at her quoting Mary Lou and Jefferson as if they handed down the gospel in Hemlock Lake. "Does that mean you can suspend the rules? What if it was a month after deer season closed and you found Freeman standing over a buck on state land? Or what if you spotted Evan with two fish over the limit? Would you turn your back?"

Julie thought for a few moments. "If I saw them, I'd have to do what I had to do. But if I *didn't* see them . . ." She shot me a smile. "Jefferson says once a game warden phoned Freeman and told him he heard he had a deer and was coming out to check his shed and Freeman moved the deer before he saw it and Alda made a venison roast and the warden stayed to dinner."

I didn't doubt the story was true. Tradition often trumped law in these hills.

"You have to admit there are a lot of deer," Camille said. "I planted five dozen tulip bulbs last fall and Marcella says soap and garlic and hot sauce won't keep deer away. Unless I fence in the flowerbed, I won't see a single petal."

"We'll pick up a roll of chicken wire at the hardware store," I said. "And the future wildlife officer can help me build a tulip cage. But no more planting unless it's something wildlife doesn't have a taste for."

"Like Lima beans." Julie giggled. "Nobody likes them."

Sunday was warm and dry by March standards with a light but steady wind—perfect for tearing off Justin's roof. Julie helped me load scraps of plywood into the battered metal trailer and promised to remind Camille about the chicken wire when they went to Ashokan City later. I figured Stub, Freeman, and Evan had all the tools we'd need, so I took only my hammer and a pair of gloves.

Camille hustled from the house with an insulated jug of coffee and a paper sack. "Take the rest of the cookies and they'll forgive you for being late."

I stowed the bag on the passenger seat and checked the clock on the dashboard. 7:45. "I'm not late yet."

She cocked her head toward the lake. "It sounds like everyone else is early. I hear hammers. And I can't make out the words, but I bet that's Stub swearing."

Julie laughed. "He better hope the wind keeps blowing this way or Marcella will hear and give him a lecture."

"Stub gets a lecture most days," I said. "That's how he and Marcella relate."

"Another reason I'm glad I live with you," Julie said.

Camille smacked the side of the SUV. "You better get going or Stub will work your name into the next round of cursing."

I obeyed, plywood thumping against the sides of the trailer as it shimmied in the ruts of the driveway. No point in filling them, not with more frost and melt to come.

Herded by wind funneled through Bluestone Hollow on the west side of Hemlock Lake, slabs of ice scudded east, scraping and clacking, riding up on each other in the coves. Soon those slabs would be only mounds of floating slush, fishermen would launch boats, and anglers would wade into icy streams and cast for trout. Soon I'd turn over the garden soil and plant peas and onions. Soon I'd hold a baby, be a father.

Would I do a decent job?

My father had favored Nat and disapproved of my choices, especially my decision to leave Hemlock Lake. My mother tried to soften his verbal blows, but there were days when I felt every one of them strike my heart.

I reached Bobcat Hollow and stopped. Ronny Miller hadn't handled fatherhood well, either. He'd favored Justin and belittled Julie for her dreams and desire to see more of the world. Perhaps that needling helped her develop the mental toughness she needed to cope with the horror of her mother's murder and the long afternoon a serial killer held her captive. And perhaps it was favored treatment that hampered Justin when he left Hemlock Lake.

He was getting past that now.

And so was I.

But would either of us ever stop peering into life's rearview mirror and wondering about roads not taken?

Chapter 5

I rolled on, past Stub's garage and the Shovel It Inn, across the dam, past the post office and general store, and past intersections of narrow streets leading to a cluster of homes. Then I was on the west side of the lake and Evan stepped into the road, motioning me to get the trailer close to the house. I jockeyed it into position, Evan and Freeman unloading even as it rolled. We stacked plywood near a couple of sawhorses and a battered plastic table laden with circular saws and tape measures.

I climbed out, shading my eyes to watch Jefferson and Justin tearing off layers of shingles and shoveling them into the bed of the dump truck snugged under the eaves.

"Appears we gotta rip off more than we thought," Stub said. "The truck won't hold it all. We'll need your trailer."

"Had to junk the gutters," Freeman said.

"Gutters, hell," Stub groused. "Had so many holes they were strainers."

"Dead leaves were all that was holding them together," Evan added.

"Let's hope we don't find too much worse," I said, "or Justin will blow the whole renovation budget before he gets to the kitchen."

"That's what happens when you make a budget." Freeman grabbed the last piece of plywood. "But the boy should make money this summer. He's got that bait shop cleaned up and organized to the last hook. And he's got a better way with people than Priscilla."

"A copperhead has a better way with people than that witch." Stub kicked the front tire on the SUV. "You need air. Come by and let me check that for leaks when we're not burning daylight."

We got the last gutter in place shortly after 11:00 Sunday morning and then packed up our tools and sipped coffee gone cold.

"Could have put the gutters and downspouts off until next weekend," Freeman admitted, "but then we woulda been out an excuse for skipping church."

Jefferson grinned as he raked up scraps of metal and broken bits of shingle. "I noticed how slow you and Evan were moving the last hour."

"Any slower and you would have been taken for dead," Justin said.

"A man does what a man has to do to avoid torture. Especially torture that requires wearing your best pants."

"And a clean shirt," Evan added.

"Reverend Balforth is a good man and he means well," Stub said. "He'd throw himself between any of us and a demon out of hell, but—"

"His services have the appeal of a root canal without anything to numb the pain?" Jefferson asked.

"Well, yeah." Freeman kicked at a ragged clump of grass. "Seems like a man committed to his religion could work up more enthusiasm."

We all nodded our agreement. Reverend James Balforth droned his sermons and often lapsed into the singsong phrasing of a child reciting a rhyming poem. The sermons themselves were rehashed and recycled. Or so Alda and Pattie claimed. In the past two decades I'd skipped Sunday services and heard Balforth preach only at funerals—and far too many of those.

Like Stub said, Balforth was a good man, and he did his best for the congregations of the three tiny churches he served. But those congregations were shrinking and Balforth—never without a black suit and starched white shirt—didn't have the charisma to draw new members.

"But he's loyal," Freeman said. "When he retires, the board will have a tough row to hoe finding a replacement. And with my luck, I'll still be serving and saddled with the project. Every time my term is up, Alda signs me up for another. This time around I ended up being chairman."

"Wonder if Mary Lou will sell off the church when he retires," Evan mused.

Justin plucked a roofing nail from the grass. "I know change comes, but I'd hate to see that building torn down or converted. When I was a kid, I thought of that steeple as a point on a compass."

Evan frowned, turned, and gazed in the direction of the church. "It's south. What was the north point?"

"East was my grandmother's house. And west was the sandpit. I think north was one of those boulders up in Dark Moon Hollow. The erratics."

Jefferson stopped raking and faced north, his eyes dark with something I couldn't read.

Stub scratched his head "Er-what-ics?"

"Rocks brought from somewhere else by a glacier." Justin flashed me a shy smile. "I learned that in geology class."

"So ice picked them up and carried them along?" Freeman asked. "And dropped them off when it melted?"

"Pretty much."

"Where?" Evan asked. "Where'd they come from?"

"North. Northeast. Maybe I'll look into that for my final paper."

"Don't use a lot of fancy words when you tell us what you find out," Stub cautioned. "Some of us didn't go to college."

Freeman rolled his eyes. "And *some* of us wouldn't crack a dictionary unless there was money inside."

I spent the early afternoon pretending I didn't ache all over, building a cage over the flowerbed, and taking care of a few other chores on Camille's list of things to be done before the baby arrived. I understood the logic behind taking inventory of the items packed into the huge chest freezer in the garage, so I didn't quibble about that, but when it came to rearranging the supplies in the pantry, I cited the necessity of paying bills and got out of the way.

Julie cooked up a feast of a dinner—roast chicken, scalloped potatoes, salad, and blackberry cobbler. While she and Camille mixed salad dressing and filled the pepper grinder, Justin joined me at the table. His left thumb was bruised and swollen and his right hand bore a dozen nicks and cuts, but he smiled as he bragged about the roof. "It's tight as a drum. Once I replace the old insulation and seal and paint the ceiling in the den, you'll never know there were 15 water stains on it."

"That many?" Camille gasped. "I knew the roof was in bad shape, but I had no idea."

"We would have known if we had a full-bore inspection," I reminded her. "But that might have held up the deal or made Priscilla think twice about selling."

"I hated her," Julie said. "She was so mean to me when I started working in the store. If she hadn't left town, I would have moved."

"To where?" Justin asked.

"Antarctica. The moon. Anywhere she wouldn't be. I hope she never comes back, not even for a visit."

"Who would she visit? Nobody up here liked her."

"I doubt she has friends anywhere," Camille said in a voice tinged with sadness. "She doesn't know how to go about being a friend."

"And I bet she doesn't want to learn." Julie opened the oven and hoisted out the roasting pan and then a deep casserole dish layered with potatoes, cream, and butter, bubbling around the edges and golden brown on top. "Let's not talk about her. Change the subject."

"Fine with me," Justin said. "Freeman put a weather station on the bait shop this afternoon."

Camille sliced a loaf of bread, the crust flaking and crackling beneath the blade. "Doesn't he have one at his house?"

"Sure. And one at Evan's. And another at Stub's garage." Justin set a trivet in the center of the long oak table and carried over the casserole, inhaling its aroma and grunting approval. "He's single-handedly keeping the folks who make those things in business. Alda told him no more unless he can figure out how to deduct them from their taxes." He smiled and lowered his voice to a conspiratorial whisper. "I don't think she knows about the one at the bait shop."

"Why does he need so many?" Julie carved chicken, her knife flashing. "The weather won't be any different at his house than at Evan's just down the road."

"But it might be different at the bait shop on the lake, or over at Stub's," Justin said. "More wind or less rain. He's interested in how the mountains and valleys channel storms."

Julie shrugged. "Okay."

"He said to tell you that storm coming up the Appalachians is getting stronger." Justin glanced at Camille. "Maybe you should wait it out close to the hospital."

Camille laughed and got the salad from the refrigerator. "The weatherman on the radio says the storm will slide by east of us, like that one in November."

"That storm was weaker and there wasn't a system pushing down from Canada."

Julie set the platter of chicken beside the steaming casserole. "What does that have to do with anything?"

"Two things can't occupy the same space at the same time, right?"

"Yes." Julie flounced to her chair. "Everyone knows that, Mr. College Student. But we're talking about air."

"Right, but the same rule applies." Justin used his fists to demonstrate. "When those two systems collide, one of them has to give way, go up, or go around. That will change their courses."

One hand gripping the table, Camille lowered herself into her chair. "Well, if the storm is moving as fast as they say, it won't be over us for long."

"But if the storm rides up over colder air, we could get a heck of a lot of snow."

"Uncle Dan will put the chains on," Julie said, "and drive faster than the snow can fall."

Justin frowned, but didn't argue. I recalled the snowstorms I'd seen in my years at Hemlock Lake, snow as fine as sand and flakes like feathers, ice coating trees and shearing off limbs, screaming wind and mounting drifts. I wasn't worried about whether the house could stand up to the storm or whether we could survive a few days without power. But if the baby came while we were cut off and if something went wrong . . . "Maybe we should stay with Mary Lou and Jefferson."

"Or at my place," Justin offered.

"Thanks." Camille patted his hand. "But a few miles won't make a difference."

I knew by the set of her jaw that she'd made up her mind, and it was pointless to suggest anything else, but then I thought of those tiny grave markers in the cemetery, those children who didn't live long enough to be diapered. "We could check into a hotel near the hospital and stay for a couple of days. It would be an adventure."

"Oooohhh." Julie hugged herself. "Can we get one with an indoor pool? Can I order from room service?"

Justin and I laughed. Camille didn't. "I'm not going to squat in a sterile room and worry about what's going on here."

"The house will be fine," I said.

"And Dither can run the store," Justin added.

"Yeah," Julie agreed. "But she's gonna need a new nickname. She hardly dithers at all anymore."

True. I'd had misgivings when Camille hired Meredith Bonesteel. Dubbed Dither for her inability to make decisions, she'd spent years deciding among her suitors and more years planning her wedding. When her marriage went sour, she dithered on, blaming herself. But when she felt her baby was in danger, she moved home to Evan and Pattie. Camille, patient but precise about tasks and timetables, had managed to turn dithering into doing. But no one ever got a new nickname in Hemlock Lake. Meredith would be Dither for the rest of her life.

"I'll get the snow off the parking lot," Justin said. "And if the power goes out I'll bring over Willie Dean's old generator and hook it up to the freezer case so you don't lose any stock."

"I appreciate that. But there's another reason for staying here." Camille pointed at Nelson who had his head in Julie's lap, waiting for a sliver of chicken or a chunk of bread. "I doubt those hotels take dogs."

"I bet they will if I put down a deposit," I said.

"Or he can stay with me," Justin offered.

"If they won't let Nelson in, I'm not going." Julie patted his head and bent to kiss his muzzle.

"Then that's settled," Camille said. "Besides, I told you before, if I have to stand on my head, I won't have this baby on April Fools' Day."

Chapter 6

Monday, the last day of March, was clear and dry with a gentle downslope breeze out of Dark Moon Hollow on the north end of the lake. After Camille and Julie took off, I filled a mug with the dregs of the coffee, commandeered the kitchen table, and spread out a map of New York, my files, a stack of index cards, and several legal pads. I started by phoning through the list I'd gotten from Sheriff North, working in spiraling circles out from Ashokan county. I called small town police chiefs, county sheriffs, and detectives. Mostly I left messages and collected e-mail addresses. When I got a live body I sketched my assignment and asked about unsolved cases in their jurisdictions.

The first round of calls netted me three cases. Number one was an elderly woman who appeared to have died in an accidental fall but was probably pushed by a son with a gambling habit. He had a shaky alibi, but they couldn't put him at the scene. Number two was a suicide made up to look like murder; the man was dying of cancer and angling for an insurance payout for his widow. Number three, though, had possibilities. Number three was 18-year-old Micah Thielman from Buckingham County. He'd gone missing a year ago.

I put notes on the first two in a manila folder labeled "Probably Not." Notes on Micah Thielman, went into a different folder. I labeled it "Possible" and hoped I wouldn't have to add an *S* to that word. The sheriff's assistant promised she'd get the file copied and sent over to Ashokan County as soon as possible and seemed glad to make that offer. She said the original investigator on the case had taken a job in Ohio and the sheriff was short on bodies with badges and long on a string of burglaries that had a citizens' committee calling for his resignation unless he made an arrest soon.

After moving the files to my desk in the corner of the library, I demolished a plate of leftovers, and whistled Nelson out of his bed on the hearth. While he nosed through flowerbeds in search of moles, I carried firewood, building a stack on the front porch and covering it with a heavy tarp. The latest from the weather experts was that the storm would veer off, but if they were wrong, I wanted dry wood close by.

That done, I found the chains for the SUV, laid them out on the garage floor, and made sure all the links were intact. I started up the chainsaw to make sure it would run, then tucked it under the tarp with the firewood. After that I dug out the instructions for the generator I bought last fall and housed in a hut built from scrap lumber out beyond the hot tub. If the storm took down power lines, a lone house at the end of a long road wouldn't be a priority. With the generator, I could keep us fed and flushing. Without it, we'd have no way to power the pump to provide water, and no juice for the refrigerator.

Back in the kitchen I made a list: fuel for the generator and the grill, candles, matches, extra flashlight batteries, coffee, cocoa, and a sack of tiny marshmallows. The kitchen stove ran on propane, so we could heat milk, and nothing said "snowbound" like a cup of hot cocoa smothered in a blanket of melting marshmallows.

With Nelson riding shotgun, I headed for Stub's garage to top off the tank on the SUV and fill three gas cans. After he charged my account, Stub kicked the front tire, pronounced that it didn't look any lower, shot in a little air, and told me to watch it. "Weather like this, it's hard to believe we're gonna get hammered."

"The noon report said the storm will pass by."

"Freeman says not." Stub glanced toward the house beside his garage and lowered his voice. "Want to bet five bucks?"

"Nope. I like my skin." I climbed into my rig. "And I don't like thinking about what Marcella will do to it if she finds out I took your bet."

Stub glanced at the house again. "It's only five bucks."

"To you, maybe. To Marcella it's the rim of a slippery slope leading to financial ruin."

"Beer's fine with her. Whiskey now and then is okay." Stub slapped the fender as he talked. "A little cussing is all right. But she grew up with nothing because her father loved poker and the ponies. If I bet even a nickel she cries or lectures or both."

"We all have things we fear and loathe."

"Wish it was something else that lit her fuse. Having a few dollars in play now and then makes things interesting."

"Then pretend we made the bet. If you win, I'll pretend to pay you."

"Ain't the same," he grumbled.

"Never thought it was."

I fired up the engine and drove to the general store and post office. Cars crammed the lot and lined the shoulders of the road. I eased behind the building, jammed into a space between Camille's car and a lilac bush, and told Nelson to stay.

Eyes wide with amazement, Mary Lou leaned against the post office counter, peering into the store at a milling mass of customers. Their baskets overflowed with jugs of water, batteries, sacks of charcoal, cans of tuna and fruit, loaves of bread, packages of cheese and sandwich meat, bags of chips and cookies, jars of peanut butter and jelly. "That cash register will overheat if this keeps up. Thanks to Freeman's weather predictions, everyone is laying in enough supplies to wait out a war. This will be the best day the store ever had."

Counter to her nickname, Dither Bonesteel raced from the rear of the store, arms loaded with packages of toilet paper. Her fair hair drifted around her head and her eyes were wide. Hands snatched at her supply and in a moment she gave a squeak and trotted back for more.

Mary Lou lifted her glasses with her left thumb and blotted her eyes with a tissue. "Lou Marie would have been in hog heaven."

I remembered the cash box we discovered in the storeroom after Lou Marie died, and the silver coins and bills squirreled away over the years. "She probably would have marked everything up 10 percent."

Mary Lou winced, then chuckled. "More like 20. She loved a bargain if she was the one driving it. Camille's the opposite."

"Don't tell me she marked things down."

"A little. She's selling batteries and bread and milk at cost and giving away a bag of chips to anyone who spends more than $50.00."

"Good for her." I grinned. "If I thought I could get to her through that crowd I'd give her a kiss the town would talk about until summer."

Mary Lou blotted her eyes again. "This town has never been accepting of outsiders, but she has a way. I don't know how she does it—she doesn't beg or flatter or push—she naturally does the right thing at the right time and two days later folks realize they dropped their defenses and invited her over for coffee. She's special, Dan. But you know that."

I did now. The day we met, the day she thought I was an intruder and hit me with a pail of water followed by the pail itself, you couldn't have convinced me if you talked all night.

The door swung open behind me and Denny Balmer shoved past. He had a list in his hand and an expression of panic on his face. He sucked in a breath, braced his hands in front of him, and thrust himself into the melee.

I patted the list in my pocket. "At this rate the shelves will be empty before the school bus pulls in. Maybe I better make a run to Ashokan City for what we need."

"Camille got a big order in this morning—batteries and charcoal and candles and camp stove fuel. The storeroom is packed to the ceiling and it's all stuff she'll need for summer. It will keep if it doesn't sell before the storm hits."

"Sounds like you're betting on Freeman and against the experts."

"Experts can be wrong." Mary Lou shrugged. "Better safe than sorry."

"Exactly why I want to check Camille into a hotel by the hospital. But she's as stubborn as anyone born and raised in these hills." I jingled my ring of keys. "Think I'll use the rear door to the storeroom so I don't get trampled."

"List anything you don't find and I'll slip a note to Camille when there's a lull."

"When might that be? After the storm?"

Mary Lou didn't have an answer.

Howls of pain woke me the next morning.

I kicked at the sheet tangled around my feet. "Is it time?"

"No. That's Julie!" Camille threw aside the comforter and struggled to rise. I offered her a hand and, when she was stable, raced for the staircase, my bare feet thudding on the cold floor.

The stairs rose to a narrow loft above the living room. Three doors opened off it, a bath and two bedrooms. Julie's was the one farthest along. Her howls were now shrieks and Nelson joined in, yelping like a young coyote. I stumbled over Julie's backpack, slammed my knee against the corner of a cedar chest, and flung myself at the door.

Nelson stood at the foot of the bed, teeth bared, hair on his neck raised. Julie huddled against the maple headboard, knees drawn to her chest, a pillow clamped against one leg. Her fingers, pale blue nightgown, and flowered sheets were smeared with blood.

"It hurts so bad, Uncle Dan," she sobbed. "There's a screw sticking out of the dresser and I tore my leg open on it."

"Lie back." I snatched another pillow and folded it in half. "See if you can get your foot on this pillow to elevate it."

"Is she okay?" Camille called from the staircase.

"She cut her leg."

"There's a first aid kit in the bathroom. And extra gauze and tape."

Moaning and whimpering, Julie planted her heel on the pillow. "I can't look. I'll be sick."

"Put your arms around Nelson, close your eyes, and take a deep breath."

She buried her face against Nelson's chest and sucked air. I lifted the pillow. It was heavy, sodden with blood.

I swallowed fear and bile and kept my face still as I studied the wound. It started at her knee and sliced diagonally across her shin. She twitched and blood welled from it.

"How bad is it?" Camille's voice crackled with anxiety.

"It's not spurting, but it's long and deep. She'll need stitches. A lot of stitches."

Julie moaned and clutched Nelson so hard he yipped.

"You're doing great," I told her. "You did the right thing when you pressed the pillow against the wound. That slowed the bleeding."

"I'll call an ambulance!" Camille called.

"We can drive to the emergency clinic faster. Get a glass of juice for her and bring the SUV around. I'll put on a pressure bandage and carry her down."

Another glance at the wound told me gauze pads supplied with the average first aid kit wouldn't be enough. I headed for the bathroom and a supply of washcloths, but spotted a basket filled with clean laundry and snatched a white tank top from the top of the stack.

"Not that one," Julie said. "It's my favorite."

Only a teenage girl would worry about her wardrobe at a time like this. I tossed the tank top aside and grabbed the gray T-shirt beneath it.

"I need that for gym today."

"You'll be out of gym for a week." I leaned over the bed to press the folded shirt against the wound. "Bleeders can't be choosers."

With a shriek of laughter, Julie rolled away. "April Fool!"

"What?"

"April Fool. It's a fake wound."

She sat up, picked at the side of her leg, and peeled off a strip of skin-toned material with a gaping wound in the center. Nelson sniffed at it, then snorted and jumped from the bed. Julie squeezed the wound and red liquid dribbled onto the sheet. "Isn't it cool?"

"I've got the juice," Camille wheezed. "I'm almost there."

"You can turn around," I called. "It's an April Fools' Day prank."

"I got it from a guy at school." Julie hugged herself and giggled. "You should have seen your face, Uncle Dan. You were really freaked. I almost laughed too soon and ruined everything."

Camille trudged through the doorway with a glass of orange juice. Her gaze swept the fake wound, the smeared sheets, the soaking pillow, and my hands knotting the T-shirt. "I see."

Her right eye closed and she set the juice on the dresser. "Well, I guess I better go downstairs and start break—"

She gasped, clutched the doorjamb, and hunched over.

"What's wrong?" I dropped the T-shirt and put my arms around her. "Are you having contractions?"

"Pain," she wailed. "Stabbing pain."

She sagged against me. "I can't stand."

I lowered Camille to the carpet and she turned on her side and drew her knees up. Julie knelt beside her and rubbed her back.

"Don't," Camille said. "That hurts. I hurt all over. Shouldn't have climbed those stairs so fast."

I made for the door. "I'll call an ambulance."

"Don't leave me. I feel like I'm sinking. Don't leave me, Dan, hold me, don't leave me."

I stroked her springy hair, and kissed her forehead. "I'll never leave you."

"Falling," Camille whispered. "Falling down a long tunnel. It's so dark."

Her face pale, Julie lunged for the nightstand and her cell phone. "I'll call the ambulance. You'll be okay."

"Gotcha," Camille said. "April Fool."

Julie froze. "That's not funny." She dropped the phone on the bed. "I thought you were gonna lose the baby. I thought you were dying."

"And I thought your leg would be scarred for life," I said in a tight voice.

Julie rolled her eyes. "It's not the same."

"Close enough." Camille clutched my arm and hoisted herself upright. "Clean up your mess, Miss April Fool, and get ready for school. When you get there, give that nasty wound to the nasty boy you borrowed it from and tell him he owes me a pillow. And don't try that stunt with your teachers."

"He's not nasty, just kind of geeky." Julie pulled the sheets from her bed. "And it was an old pillow from the garage. And two of my teachers are so out-to-lunch they wouldn't notice if blood squirted from the top of my head like a geyser."

In the interest of ending a discussion bound to go nowhere, I took Camille's hand. "How about banana and blueberry pancakes?"

"With whipped cream?" Julie asked.

"If we have it in a can. I'm not whipping cream for someone who almost gave me a heart attack."

"Well you scared me, too. I think we're even."

"Only if you take out the garbage before you go to school," Camille said.

"Ick." Julie shook her hands as if they were covered with slime, then withered under Camille's glare. "Okay, I'll do it."

Forty-five minutes later they were ready to roll. "I don't know why you need to open the store," I told Camille. "There can't be much left to sell except hot sauce and pimiento in those little jars. And nobody ever buys that."

Camille laughed. "Denny Balmer bought two jars yesterday. He brought them back an hour later. Said he thought they were strawberries."

"Would have been worth a week's profit to have been there when his wife set him straight."

"We should totally stop stocking them," Julie said. "Other stuff too. And make more room for chips and candy bars."

"Or fresh fruit and vegetables." Camille stood on tiptoe and kissed the point of my chin. "At least having the shelves cleared out gives me a chance to clean. And at least I didn't let Freeman stampede me into ordering snow shovels and ice axes." She nodded at the small TV tucked into a corner of the counter. "The latest report says the storm will miss us."

Julie slipped on a jacket and shrugged into her backpack. "We gotta go. Right after I pet Nelson."

She headed for the living room but halted in the doorway. "There are lights on at the Brocktons' house."

"Ha." I poured myself another cup of coffee. "The Brocktons are still wintering in the south. I'm not falling for that."

"Me, neither." Camille struggled to snap a denim jacket across her belly. "Darn it. Even this doesn't fit and I got it from your closet."

"Really," Julie called from deeper in the living room. "I see lights. And a car in the driveway."

Camille touched my arm. "You don't suppose someone broke in, do you?"

"Only the world's dumbest burglar parks out front and turns on the lights." I ruffled her hair. "More likely they hired a handyman to get the place ready. I'll go around and check in a bit."

"Let me know what's what. And be sure to tell Mary Lou." She kissed my chin again. "Come on, Julie. You'll miss the bus."

Nelson barked, Julie raced past, and then the house was silent except for the hum of the refrigerator and the chatter of the icemaker releasing a load of cubes. I cleaned up the breakfast dishes, wiped the counters, and got out the cold files and a roll of brown wrapping paper. I unrolled about six feet and went to work marking off years and writing in the names of the dead and missing. I was placing Franklin Turner when my cell phone rang.

"Dan Stone?" a faint and rasping voice asked.

"Right."

"Jonah Umhey. Quarry County. Retired. Heard you're working cold cases."

"Tryin' to."

"Good. Got one stuck in my craw."

Chapter 7

"Her name was Theresa Gilligan."

Jonah Umhey lapsed into a damp cough that rumbled and sputtered. "I used to call cigarettes coffin nails. Didn't know how true that was. Doctor says I won't see the first frost of autumn. Doubt I'll prove him a liar."

"Sorry to hear that."

"No need for sympathy. It's my own damn fault."

I liked that. There were plenty who never took responsibility for misfortune of their own making.

"If I have to cross to the other side to find out what happened to that girl, so be it, but I'd rather know before they bury me." He coughed and spat. "Seems like it would be more fitting to set me afire and toss my ashes to the wind, but my daughter has other ideas, and my son says this is no time for me to pick a fight with her."

"Especially if you won't be around to see if you won."

"That's what he says." He unleashed another torrent of coughing followed by a string of gasps that made my chest ache. "Better get to the point," he wheezed, "while I still can. Theresa Gilligan. Twenty years ago. Strangled. Dumped in a hollow behind an abandoned house. If it wasn't for kids looking for Indian pipes for a science project, she might be there still."

Indian pipes. Spectral plants, white and spindly, turning darker as they died. They grew deep in the woods, grew without sunlight. Indian pipes went by other names—Fairy Smoke, Death Plant, Ghost Flower, and Corpse Plant.

I shook off those thoughts. "Any suspects?"

"She had a boyfriend, but he was in the Coast Guard, off in Alaska. Been there a few months when she disappeared. One of her friends said she might have been seeing someone on the sly, but didn't have a name to go with that feeling."

"When was she found?"

"March 30th. But she disappeared February 12th. She intended to spend the night with a friend—same one who had a feeling she was stepping out—but she never turned up."

I jotted the dates and the year two decades in the past. As I did, I glanced at the timeline. Genevieve Graham died the same year. On February 13th.

Coincidence?

I said nothing to Umhey. Even if the cases were connected, that connection might not yield new information, might not help solve either of them.

A gust of wind herded last year's leaves across the patio and tumbled them against the low stone wall that surrounded it. Another gust funneled them into the air and out of view. I peered at the sky. Still clear and blue except for a few feathery wisps of cloud to the south.

"She was a nice kid," Umhey said. "Lots of friends. Training to be a legal secretary and already working in a law office. Maybe she *was* stepping out on her boyfriend, but—"

He coughed again, fighting for breath, for life. I waited him out, penciling Theresa's name on the timeline beside Genevieve's. "Who's got the case now?"

"No one official," he gasped. "Only me."

"I'll request a copy of the file," I told him. "Is it all there?"

"Everything. And I keep a duplicate. Call me if you find anything. Call me even if you don't. I'm here." He coughed once more. "Until I'm not."

I thought about that as another gust—this one from the opposite direction—sent leaves skittering. They collided with the tarp-covered barbecue, lapped against the thick plastic and then, like water loosed from a dam, spilled over the wall.

I turned my gaze to the stack of files, to the folders for Genevieve Graham and Franklin Turner, the two cases I knew were homicides. They had been on this earth. Now they weren't. And someone, somewhere, knew why.

I called Quarry County, got shuffled around a bit, and finally left a message for the sheriff requesting the file on Theresa Gilligan. Then, the weight of those lost lives on my shoulders, I walked through the house and, with Nelson by my side, crossed the front porch and went to the lake where I could get a better view of the sky. The pale sun had cleared the mountains and leafless trees along the path cast stark shadows on the frost-split earth. The clouds to the south seemed like plumes of an exotic bird stitched to the stratosphere.

I stepped onto the dock, taking wide strides as it pitched and rolled beneath my feet. The dock wasn't long and beyond it the lake bed dropped off fast. Slabs of ice thrashed and crashed at the whim of a fitful wind and one slammed into the dock, the thud booming across the water. Nelson barked out a warning, retreated to the shore, and sat on a flat rock, lifting his muzzle to the sun.

A flash of light caught my eye—a car backing out of the Brocktons' driveway.

Damn it!

I'd intended to drive over there after I cleaned up the breakfast mess.

The car, a dust-colored compact that blended with banks of dirty snow plowed up over the winter, eased onto the road and rolled away. At this distance, I couldn't make out the license plate.

Another slab of ice hit the dock. It bucked beneath me and I shot my arms out for balance. Some investigator I was. Forgetful. Distracted. As observant as the planks beneath my feet. I hadn't noticed anyone get into the car, hadn't even noticed the car until it moved. And the snow banks blocked my view of the driver.

"At least it was a small car," I told Nelson. "They couldn't make off with the big stuff."

Not that the Brocktons had big stuff—at least not big stuff that would be of interest to the average burglar. Because they went south every winter, they'd handed the family silver off to their daughter along with knickknacks of sentimental or financial value. Their furnishings were good quality but worn, their television old and small, and their laptop traveled with them. Angela Brockton never wore jewelry other than tiny diamond earrings and her engagement and wedding rings, and the coin collection William joked about consisted of small change he tossed into a coffee can and handed out to kids for ice cream.

Still, there were things of value in the Brocktons' house—dozens of oils by area artists, their own stunning watercolors, shelves packed with books, handmade pottery, and small ceramic pieces. Those could be sold, but the process would involve more work than most thieves wanted to go to.

Probably the car belonged to a handyman or someone with a cleaning service. In the past, Camille readied the place for the Brocktons' return and helped them with occasional chores, but with the store and the baby, that wasn't on the calendar this year. Julie had talked about taking over the tasks to earn money toward a car, but so far hadn't called the Brocktons to present her plan. Perhaps their daughter, an impatient, take-charge woman, had made a plan of her own.

In any case, someone should check on the house and the visitor, and that someone was me. Hemlock Lake—little more than a wide spot in the road—lacked a police force or mayor. After Ronny Miller died trying to kill me, Stub Wilson hoped to be the one folks turned to for help and advice. But, despite my lack of desire and what I saw as many failures, responsibility fell to me.

I shuffled my files together, locked up, lifted Nelson into my rig, and headed out.

Wind sluicing through Silver Leaf and Bobcat Hollows sent ragged brown leaves tumbling along the road and whirling into the woods. A few robins hunted for worms in a grassy spot near Stub's garage, cocking their heads and darting forward to peck here and there. I took another look at the southern sky as I crossed the dam. Half the dome was laced with high clouds. Mares' tails. Signs a storm was out there.

But the rush for provisions was over. The parking lot in front of the store was empty. Except for a dust-colored car.

I braked hard and angled in beside it, then noted the license number on the receipt for the crib I'd yet to put together. Nelson whined when I slid out and snorted when I told him to stay. Nose pressed against the window, he watched me check out the car. It was old, but clean outside and in. A stack of paper bags lay on the rear seat, and gray knit gloves were folded into a slot in the console. But that was it. If the driver had taken something from the Brocktons' house, it was in the trunk.

I opened the bright blue door and entered the store, heralded by a jangling bell. "Be right there," Camille called. "We're cleaning shelves."

"Don't stop on my account. I'm not a customer."

"If you were, you'd be the first today. There's not much left to sell unless you want cocktail onions or those pimientos Denny Balmer returned."

Dither laughed from the vicinity of the dairy case. "We can make you a deal on a carton of buttermilk. That's all that's left in the cooler."

"Sold," I said. It had been years since I drank a glass of buttermilk. Not that this would be anything like the buttermilk my grandmother bought in glass jugs from a farmer in Silver Leaf Hollow. She used it for biscuits and pancakes and drank it on hot afternoons with a little salt stirred in. "Set it aside for me."

Hunting the driver of that car, I crossed to the post office. She was there, but for a long moment, I didn't see her. Dressed in gray slacks and a tan and white coat with a muted pattern, she blended with the wall and the dozens of bulletins stuck to a cork board. Urban camouflage.

Mary Lou waggled her fingers, beckoning me to the counter. "Dan, this is your new neighbor. She and her family are renting the Brocktons' house for the summer. I'm giving them Priscilla's old mailbox."

The woman glanced up from filling out a form. If she'd ordered up a top-of-the-line forgettable face, she couldn't have gotten a better model. Her light brown hair was short and fine and lay flat against her head. Her eyes were blue, paler than a winter sky, and almost without lashes. Her nose was small and her lips narrow. She wore no lipstick or blush or mascara and her features seemed to blend into each other. She was hunched and bunched, like a rabbit at the edge of a field alert to the snap of a twig or the shadow of a hawk.

"Hannah Falton, meet Dan Stone," Mary Lou said. "You must have seen his house when you were getting acquainted with the Brocktons' place."

The woman's eyes clouded. "Did I?"

"It's right across the lake. Cedar siding. And a dock," Mary Lou added.

"I suppose I must have." Hannah's voice was an uneven whisper, like leather-soled shoes scuffing a carpet.

Mary Lou frowned, then patted air the way she did to smooth things over. "Well, you were probably too busy checking to see if there were enough pots and pans and all. Anyway, that's where Dan lives and he's a good one to call if you need help."

A darker shadow flickered across her eyes. "Thank you," she said in a voice louder and stronger, "but we never ask for help. We pray for guidance."

She shoved the form and a few rumpled bills across the counter as if punctuating that sentence, then turned to study a notice about income tax assistance. Without a word, Mary Lou gathered in the form, made change, and laid a pair of small worn brass keys on the counter. Hannah scraped coins and keys into a battered purse without making eye contact and, neck bowed, hurried out the door.

"Something's not right with a woman who never asks for help and scurries like a frightened hamster." Mary Lou shook her head and tucked the form into a folder. "But she seems like a tidy sort. Should take good care of the place."

"I'm behind the curve. The Brocktons are staying in Texas?"

"For a time. He took a fall and she had a bad case of the flu. Their daughter decided the drive would be too much for them so they've got a place in the hill country out there for the summer." She wagged a finger at me. "And before you get your nose out of joint, I didn't know about that *or* her plans to rent the house until she called me last night."

I raised my hands signaling surrender. "I'm not carping. I'm curious."

"About what?" Stub ambled in from the store.

"The folks renting the Brocktons' house," Mary Lou told him. "The Faltons."

Stub frowned. Like many born and bred around Hemlock Lake, he didn't greet newcomers with a wide smile and open arms. "City folks?"

"She didn't say."

"And you didn't ask?"

I smiled as Mary Lou's wagging finger targeted Stub. "I'm not a busybody, Stub Wilson. I don't spend every waking hour prying into everyone's lives."

As I had moments before, Stub raised his hands in surrender.

"It just so happens that folks tell me things." Mary Lou glanced at the dust-colored car pulling away. "Most folks, that is."

Stub shifted from foot to foot and cleared his throat. "Um, well, I came to tell, er, ask you to help spread the word. The plow's on my truck, but folks need to know to be careful when the power goes out and they light candles. Especially folks up in the hollows. As fast as Freeman says snow will fall, the fire engine might not make it through."

I thought of those high clouds, harbingers of a storm—a storm experts said would slip by. "Freeman's still saying we'll be walloped?"

"Says when it's over we'll hold the snowfall record. Says it could be days before we get power."

Freeman the weather prophet. Predicting a plague of precipitation.

Mary Lou rubbed her arms. "I sure wish Camille would get a room near the hospital, or at least stay with us."

"I'll give it another shot. But I have a feeling I might as well try to persuade her to name the baby after a celebrity in the news for doing stupid stuff."

"Freeman's not wrong about this storm," Stub said. "I can feel it."

"Like you felt the restaurant stock you bought would go through the roof," Mary Lou teased.

"It should have! Everyone said so."

Mary Lou and I exchanged a knowing look. "Everyone" was likely someone involved with the restaurant chain.

"Marcella says putting money in the stock market is about the same as putting it on a horse race or taking it to a casino. But I bet that chain will bounce back. I'll double my money. You'll see."

Mary Lou shot me another knowing glance. Neither of us mentioned that Stub used the words "I bet" in defense of his economic venture.

"Gotta go," he said. "Gotta get the word out. You best put your chains on when you get home."

"I'm not one to bet," Mary Lou said when he was gone, "but I'd be tempted to put money on Freeman. I never knew him to be so certain about anything."

She reached across the counter and gripped my arm. "Talk to Camille again. Please. She's got to go to Ashokan City until the storm passes."

Chapter 8

Recognizing the futility of my mission, I trudged to the store, passed Dither swabbing out the bottom of the dairy case, and found Camille bellied up against the rear shelves, scrubbing with a sponge dipped in vinegar. "The place smells like a pickle factory," she said with a laugh, "but everything else made me gag. Must be my body's way of saying commercial products aren't good for me."

"You feeling okay otherwise?"

"Sure. My back aches, my feet are swollen, my ankles wobble, my knees feel like jelly, and I haven't been able to take a deep breath for three months or have a glass of wine for three times longer than that." She gave the shelf a vicious swipe. "I can't remember when I felt better."

Dither made a sound like a mouse squeezing through a knothole and retreated to the front of the store. I trotted out my signal for surrender once again. "So, if we have another baby I'll be the one carrying it?"

"This is not a good time to use the words 'another baby' within ten miles of me, Dan Stone."

"I love it when you talk like my second grade teacher."

"I'm glad one of us is amused."

She jammed the sponge into a plastic bowl balanced on the shelf below. Vinegar splashed out. Trying to avoid it, I stumbled against a rack of laundry products, dislodging a jug of detergent. It caught me on the shoulder and then on the knee before it hit the floor and spun to a stop.

"I'm ready to be myself again." Camille spread her hands across her belly. "Not myself plus whoever this is. I feel like a science experiment gone wrong."

I groped for words, got nothing, tried the surrender sign one more time.

"Oh, stop it. I'm not angry." She squeezed the sponge. "I'm cranky. Irritable. Tired."

I kicked the detergent aside and drew her against me, dripping sponge and all. "Let's collect Nelson and Julie and get a hotel room with a soft bed, an enormous bathtub, and a huge TV with mindless movies on demand."

"I have all that at home." She kissed my neck. "And home's where I'm staying."

"I'll rub your back."

"No."

"Your feet?"

Forget it. No wild-eyed talk about a snowstorm is going to drive me out of my home." She tossed the sponge into the bowl, gripped my hand, and led me outside. "I don't see a storm. Do you?"

I tipped my head. The feathery clouds had retreated to the southeast quadrant of the sky. The gusting wind had died to a fretful breeze.

"It's not cold enough for snow. In fact, it's warm enough to take this off." She tugged at the sleeve of the padded flannel shirt I'd layered on over a T-shirt to combat the morning chill.

I unbuttoned the shirt. "But what—?"

"If the storm comes, we'll toast marshmallows in the fireplace. And if the baby comes, you'll deliver it. You did that once beside a freeway in Arizona."

"I had a lot of help. And I never want to do it again."

She patted her bulge. "You won't have to. This kid isn't coming tonight."

She sounded as certain as Freeman was that the storm would clobber us. Caught between the proverbial rock and hard spot, I drove to the house and laid the cold case files out on the table. But concentration eluded me, so I spent the rest of the day stacking more wood, putting the chains on the SUV, and parking so it faced out of the garage. I loaded shovels, a small chainsaw, two flashlights, and a sack of sand into the back, then checked that I had an ice scraper.

Back in the house, I filled several gallon jugs with water, did two loads of wash, piled firewood on the hearth, stacked kindling in the fireplace, wadded newspaper beneath it, and set a box of kitchen matches on the mantel. We'd installed a small woodstove in the corner of the bedroom and I got it ready as well. There was plenty of cardboard in the garage and I carted a bunch to the pantry along with a few boards, a box of nails, a roll of heavy plastic, and all the tape I could find. If a window broke, I'd be ready to patch the hole.

In case snow drifted against the doors, I stashed a snow shovel in the kitchen and another in the living room. In these mountains, folks generally had at least one spare snow shovel, and my father had accumulated half a dozen before he died. Alongside the shovels, I parked boots and wool socks.

In between tasks, I checked the weather forecasts on several different websites and noted the experts were still calling for the storm to scrape by the Catskills. I walked out to the edge of the lake and studied the southern sky. Those wispy clouds hovered, but weren't advancing.

Not long before 5:00, Camille and Julie came home. Exhausted, Camille flopped on the sofa and dozed while Julie, complaining all the while about the snow day it appeared she wouldn't get, made macaroni and cheese and a spinach salad. Glad of an excuse to test the grill, I removed the tarp and charred a few pork chops.

Camille turned her nose up at those and ate only tiny helpings of macaroni and salad. "I feel like there's a band around my stomach, the kid must be pushing on it with both feet."

"That might mean he's standing on his head the way he's supposed to." Julie frowned and laid her fork aside. "What happens if he turns around?"

"He won't." Camille shoved away from the table and carried her plate to the counter.

Julie asked the question looming in my mind. "How do you know?"

"I just know." Camille rubbed her belly. "He's wedged in tight. I'm going to sit outside and enjoy the evening."

Still complaining about the fickle weather and the book report she had to write, Julie cleaned the kitchen and stomped upstairs. I checked the weather reports once more, then scraped the grill, covered it, and used extra cords to secure the tarp. With throw pillows and a comforter from the cedar chest, I joined Camille on one of our two porch swings—the one facing south toward town.

Those filmy clouds seemed pasted to the darkening sky and the fitful breeze raised small ripples and rocked dwindling slabs of slushy ice, but gave no evidence of growing to a gale. Nelson hopped along the path to the water, muzzle held high, tasting the air. Camille pointed to a glint of light on the rim of the mountains to the east. "The first star. Make a secret wish."

I didn't mention that her first star was likely a planet, but wished the storm would swing by and Freeman would have to eat crow.

"It's so beautiful. I could stay out here all night." Camille closed her eyes and leaned against my shoulder. "Let's sleep out here with the baby this summer."

I grunted, thinking about the wandering creatures of the night—raccoons and possums, bears and coyotes. What would a baby smell like to a nocturnal predator? How could I secure the porch without sacrificing the experience of being outdoors?

Considering electric fence and motion detectors, I rocked the swing and watched the stars emerge. Nelson returned to the porch, muzzle wet, paws muddy, and whined at the door. Camille thrust herself from the swaddle of the comforter and ran her hands over the swell of her belly. "Feels like he might have bent his knees to give me room for ice cream and chocolate sauce. I'm going for it before he changes his mind."

"He? You've been using that pronoun all evening."

"Have I?" She paused at the door and gazed out across the starlit lake. "Have I?"

"It's snowing."

Julie's voice sliced into my sleep and set me clawing air, rising from my nest of quilts, and stumbling to the living room in the long underwear I'd put on to fight the chill from our time in the porch swing. Wrapped in a blanket, she rested her forehead against one of the wide windows that looked out over the lake, her breath making a ragged circle of condensation. The glow of the lamps along the path to the dock revealed huge fat flakes slipping from the darkness, drifting among the bare branches of oaks and maples, and coating hemlock boughs with icy lace.

"I spent a whole hour on that book report," Julie mourned. "And now school will be cancelled."

"Don't be so sure. There's no wind, and flakes this size usually mean the air is getting warmer and the storm is ending."

"Ending?" Her bare feet stamped the oak floor. "It's not fair. Freeman promised."

"Take it up with him tomorrow when you get home from school."

Dragging her feet, Julie trudged up the stairs. I snapped off the outside lights and headed to the bedroom. "Snow?" Camille asked. "Or another prank?"

I glanced at the clock on the nightstand. "We're eight minutes into April Second and the flakes are real. Big ones, though, and not many. That usually means the snow will turn to rain."

"Ah." Camille tugged the quilt tighter around her shoulders and snuffled her way to sleep.

The phone roused us. It was Stub, his voice high, his breath short. "Storm's here. It's hitting hard. Power's out in Bluestone Hollow."

I clicked on the bedside lamp. "We've still got juice."

"Doubt you will for long."

"Who is it?" Camille mumbled.

"Stub. The storm's here."

"What time is it?"

"1:33."

She grunted and pulled the pillow over her ears.

"Coming down harder than I've ever seen," Stub said.

I slid from bed, carried the phone to the glass door that opened to the patio, and snapped on the outside lights. The air was a blur of white, pellets of ice swirling, pelting the side of the house, bouncing, sliding, shifting. Areas of the patio were clear, but a sloping drift crept up the low stone wall. Twigs and bits of bark jittered and jumbled. Despite my efforts to tie it to the grill, a corner of the tarp had come loose and flapped like a wounded bird.

"I, uh, I can come get you with the plow truck," Stub offered.

"I put chains on. I can get out through this."

"You oughta make a run for it. Freeman says it will blow itself out around dawn but we'll have a ton by then. Gonna take down trees, too."

I lifted the pillow and bent close to Camille. "Stub wants to come get us."

"I haven't had even a twinge of a contraction." She tugged the pillow from my fingers. "And we're safe and warm here. Who knows what could happen out on an icy road? We might end up in a ditch. Or a tree might come down on us."

Good point. "Camille's fine. She doesn't want to risk the roads."

Stub sighed. "I'll check again in a bit."

I clicked the phone off, but before I get it into the cradle, it rang again. "Are you all okay?" Mary Lou asked.

"We're fine. We still have power."

"You're lucky. Evan's blocked in by a couple of birches. Denny has a tree on his garage. And Jefferson says shingles are tearing loose on the old schoolhouse."

Was everyone in Hemlock Lake awake and comparing notes?

"I wish you'd bundle up Camille and Julie and come to us."

I studied the lump beneath the pile of quilts on the bed. "Camille says we're safer here than on the road with trees falling."

"All right. Call me now and then to let me know how you're doing. I won't be asleep."

Something thudded along the slope of the roof and the metal gutter squealed in protest. The light beside the bed flickered. A branch as thick as my arm crashed on top of the grill, slid off, and lodged against the flapping tarp, pinning it fast.

"What was that?" Julie called from upstairs.

"A branch hit the roof and fell to the patio." I tucked the phone into its cradle and dug in the dresser for my heaviest socks. Two pairs. "It must have snagged the power line."

Feet thudded on the stairs. Nelson at her side, Julie appeared in the doorway with a comforter wrapped tight around her. "Are we gonna be okay?"

"We'll be fine."

She shuffled to the glass door and peered out. "But what if a window breaks?"

I pulled on the jeans I'd kicked into the closet and reached for a flannel shirt. "If a window breaks, there's cardboard and wood in the pantry to patch the hole."

"What if a tree crashes on the house?"

"I cut all the trees close by except small ones. We won't take much of a blow."

"But that branch. It's huge."

"Probably dead." I pulled on socks. "Sheared off a tree up the hill."

A blast of ice pellets struck the window. Nelson growled. Julie shivered. "But what if—?"

"What if you let me sleep?" Camille mumbled from beneath the pillow. "Go make cookies. Work a jigsaw puzzle. Write a novel."

Julie gaped. "How can you sleep through this?"

Camille sat up, a process that involved much grunting and one mild swear word. "I don't know, but I was managing until you two decided to hold a meeting in here."

"I can't help it," Julie said in a tiny voice. "I got scared. I'm *still* scared."

"It's only a storm." Camille stood and trundled to the bathroom. "We had plenty of storms this winter."

"Not like this one," Julie said. "This—"

The phone rang.

"Probably Stub planning an airlift," Camille muttered as she closed the bathroom door.

I scooped up the receiver. "You still have power over there?" Justin asked.

"Yes, but I expect that won't last. You doing okay?"

"Yep. Lost the lights half an hour ago, there's at least one tree down and the ice slamming into the dock sounds like mortar fire. Temperature is dropping like a rock and the wind is something else. Good thing we got that new roof on when we did. Camille feeling okay?"

"Except for being pissed off about Stub and Mary Lou waking us up to tell us to come to town."

He laughed. "Is Julie wetting her pants?"

"Getting close. Want to talk to her?"

"Sure."

I held out the phone. "It's your brother."

Julie seized the receiver. "It's scary over here. The wind sounds like wolves and—"

The light went out.

Chapter 9

Julie screamed.

I fumbled for the flashlight I'd set next to the clock and clicked it on. "We're okay. We knew we'd lose power and the landline." I navigated to Camille's nightstand and retrieved a second flashlight.

"I'm scared," Julie whimpered. "I thought this would be fun, but it's not. It's loud and spooky and I want it to stop."

"It won't stop until it blows itself out. You know that." I traded the flashlight for the dead phone and set it in the cradle. "Let's go light the fire."

"Will the chimney draw with wind whipping like this?" Camille made her way to the bed.

"Good point." With all my overthinking, I hadn't considered that. I aimed the flashlight at the glass doors on the squatty woodstove in the corner. "How about we light that little guy? Or I can go out and power up the generator."

"No," Julie said. "Don't go out there. It's dangerous."

"It's only wind and snow." I shone the light through the glass door. The patio wore a shroud and the drift against the stone wall was already wider and deeper. If Freeman was right about how much we'd get, even Stub's truck might not chew through the drifts.

"Where do you suppose the line snapped?" Camille asked.

I swung the flashlight beam around the perimeter of the patio. "Probably up the road by that stand of old birches."

Julie lifted Nelson to the bed and huddled beneath the comforter with him, the flashlight beam creating an eerie glow. "How long will it take them to fix it?"

"Days. Maybe a week."

She moaned. "A week in the dark. A week without TV."

"Maybe we should have gone to a hotel." Camille's voice quavered. "At least gone to stay with Mary Lou and Jefferson."

"I put the chains on this afternoon. I think I can get us that far."

"What if you can't get through?" Julie asked the questions in my mind. "What if we get stuck?"

"Stub will plow his way to us." Camille stood and plucked clothing from the closet—leggings, one of my shirts, and a bulky sweater that reached almost to her knees. "Call him on the cell and tell him we're on the way. And Julie, you should call your brother so he doesn't worry. And get dressed to go outside."

Julie emerged from her comforter cocoon and bolted upstairs. I took my cell phone to the living room. Reception was always iffy in the mountains, but I'd found that a spot in the corner gave me a connection. Until tonight.

I tried by the kitchen door, my second most reliable spot, but got nothing.

"I can't get a signal," Julie called. "Can you?"

"No. And I'm not going out to that spot at the end of the dock that almost always works. Not while the wind is blowing so hard."

I returned to the bedroom where Camille balanced against the wall, struggling to jam her right foot into a boot. Tears ran down her cheeks and she pounded the wall with one fist. "My feet are so puffed up they won't fit in my shoes. My back hurts, my head hurts, and I'm tired of being the size of a whale."

Over the last few months, I'd learned not to deny her feelings or argue with statements as extreme as that last one. But I hadn't learned what to say instead. I went with a more immediate topic.

"We don't have cell service. We can't reach Stub. Or anyone. I think we should stay here."

"No. I was wrong. We should go. We'll get a connection along the way."

That had been my first thought, but then I'd recognized the flaw. "If we don't link up, no one will know we're on the road. If we get stuck, we could be stuck a long time."

Camille waved that aside. "They'll come looking for us."

"They will. As soon as they can. But if snow keeps falling at this pace and if the road is clogged with fallen trees, we—"

"We'll take food and blankets."

"We're better off here."

"Then we'll come back here if we get stuck!"

She kicked the boot.

It slammed into my shin. I swallowed a yelp and waited for her to understand that we might not be able to make it back.

After a long moment she sobbed and collapsed against me. "This is my fault. Julie's scared and you're mad and Mary Lou's probably worrying herself sick. I was stubborn and stupid and wrong, wrong, wrong."

I rubbed her back, the sweater rough beneath my hand. "I'm not mad."

"You should be."

"That's a waste of energy. How about I see if I can get up the driveway and get a look at the road? It's got a bit of elevation. Maybe conditions aren't as bad."

"And maybe they're worse."

I stood. "I won't know until I take a look. Then we can make a decision based on facts. Put on a couple of pairs of socks and those new boots of mine in the box at the rear of the closet. Wad newspaper in the toes so they fit. Then get Julie ready and round up everything we need to take with us."

I tipped her head and kissed her lips, salty from tears. "I'll be back in no time."

The first part of "no time" stretched to a good five minutes spent in the mudroom lacing up my waterproof boots, layering on a fleece, jacket, wool stocking cap, and scarf, then sorting through a plastic tub of outdoor gear to find the insulated gloves Julie gave me for Christmas. Even with all that as a barrier, the screaming wind knifed through and chilled me in seconds. Ice pellets blasted my face, coming from all angles, tearing at my skin like tiny claws. Head lowered, I plunged across the driveway, the flashlight beam blotted out by swirling snow before it scanned the ground. I slammed into the garage and felt my way along the wall to the side door.

The SUV stood ready, but with the power off, I struggled with the chain release on the automatic opener, then struggled again to raise the overhead door. A drift more than a foot deep sloped between me and the drive. Not good.

For a few seconds I reveled in the comparative silence inside the SUV, then I fired up the engine, revved it, and took a run at the drift. The chains bit. The engine whined. I backed up, took another run, and broke through. In low gear I churned toward the top of drive, defroster fan turned up all the way and wipers on high.

Even with chains, the SUV slipped and slid on a shifting bed of ice pellets. I wrestled the rig into the first turn and felt the front wheels sink into another drift and the rear end shimmy. I backed up a few feet and plowed forward. The wheels spun, then gripped, and I was up and over.

But the toughest part came next. The final turn crimped left around a stand of maples. Snow spilled from among them and mounded in the ditches on either side of the road, in the ruts, and on a long pile of stones pushed aside the last time the road was graded. The road, smoothed out and glazed white, had lost definition. There was no way to gauge the depth of the snow except to goose the gas and plow into it.

Within a few feet the wheels ground to a stop.

I reversed and saw the snow was a good eight inches deep. Still possible.

I trod on the gas and rammed forward, attempting to make the bend in a series of slants. My rig shook and strained, but I gained another few feet and reached the tightest angle of the turn.

If the rear wheels went into the ditch, I doubted I'd get out, so I reversed by inches. When the headlights revealed a few feet of rutted snow ahead, I hit the gas again.

I plowed another yard into the drift. Then the left wheel hit something with a thud audible over the shriek of the wind and the whine of the engine.

A rock? Was I off the road?

I backed up, straining to peer through roiling surges of snow. The headlights revealed the arc of a smooth log and, crossing it, a snaking length of wire.

Power line.

Heart pounding, I braked.

Was it live?

I felt the kind of chill that has nothing to do with temperature—the chill that comes with a sudden recognition of mortality.

Everything I ever heard or read about downed power lines pinged through my mind. The gaps in my general knowledge were huge. So were the gaps in what I knew about this particular line.

It lay across what must be a fallen power pole, but which way did the line run beneath the snow? Did snow conduct electricity? Was the wire in contact with the SUV's bumper or undercarriage? Worse, was it wrapped around the axle? Did I dare touch the key to turn off the engine?

As a rookie patrol officer, I'd directed traffic in the aftermath of a storm in Flagstaff while linemen made repairs. I remembered one saying the safest thing was to avoid downed power lines. The second safest was to stay in the vehicle until expert help arrived.

I couldn't do that. If I didn't return soon, Camille and Julie would worry. And anxiety—especially the kind a pregnant woman and a stressed-out teenager could work up—might prompt them to come out and search for me. Then all kinds of things could go wrong.

I closed my eyes, and brought up a mental picture of the power company guy complete with heavy boots, canvas pants, and the meatloaf sandwich in his right hand that balanced the cup of coffee in the left. Then I tried for what he'd told me. "Hold your hands at your sides and jump clear. Land on both feet. Then shuffle. Don't run."

I blinked and squeezed my eyes shut again, wondering if I remembered that correctly and trying not to think about what could happen if I had it wrong.

Clicking on the flashlight, I studied the dashboard and the key. If electricity was coursing through the metal around me, would the rubbery casing on the key be enough insulation to allow me to turn off the engine?

I didn't want to find out the hard way, so I borrowed a move from the bad-drivers' handbook and took my foot off the clutch. The engine died with a shudder.

No point in speculating about getting zapped by the knobs. The lights and wipers could stay on.

That left the door.

I beamed the flashlight at the latch. Not metal. So far so good.

I flipped the latch and used the plastic flashlight as a battering ram to shove the door wide. Ice pellets sifted into my coat. The wind shrieked.

I slid my foot from the brake, pulled my knees up, and angled my body toward the opening.

The seatbelt held me in place.

Cursing, I aimed the beam at the buckle. Metal gleamed. Not good. Recessed plastic button. Good. But small.

I flashed the beam around the interior, spotted a pencil wedged into a crease of the passenger seat, took off my heavy glove, and stretched for it. Using the eraser end, I punched myself out of the belt, wiggled stiff fingers into the glove, drew my knees up once more, and concentrated on the leap.

Given the size of the opening, the width of my shoulders, and layers of clothing, a clean leap would be close to impossible. I was bound to hit the door.

I set the flashlight on the passenger seat, the beam shining toward the open door. Shivering from cold and fear, I stripped off my jacket, fleece, and scarf, and tossed them into the storm. The jacket and fleece fell a few feet away, but the scarf rode the wind out of sight, fringe waving farewell.

I picked up the light again. Could I hold onto it while I made the jump? Or would it be better to leave it shining on the opening?

I'd packed other flashlights, but they were all in the rear compartment.

Leaving the flashlight where it was, and without taking time to think and rethink, I threw myself into the storm.

Chapter 10

I landed on my shoulder with a bone-jarring thud that blasted the breath from my lungs.

For a moment I lay there like a mummy. Then involuntary reflex took over and my lungs drew in membrane-searing air.

I eased onto my back, gathered the jacket and fleece against my chest, and flexed my shoulders. No stabbing pain. Then, afraid that getting upright and shuffling my boots would drive them deep into the snow and into contact with the wire, I rolled.

Snow packed around my neck, up my sleeves, under my hat, and into my ears. Letting the slope guide my slow progress, I rolled until I could no longer see the flashlight beam.

Stiff with cold, I got into the fleece and jacket, but couldn't manage zipper or buttons without taking off my gloves. Left arm tight across my chest and right outstretched and groping in the darkness for trees and branches, I followed the fall of the terrain.

Before long I realized I'd lost the road.

My panicked mind recalled reading about pioneers swallowed by blizzards on the prairie. Some went only as far as the barn to check on their cows, lost their grip on a rope strung to guide them, missed the house, and wandered onto a vast open plain.

I crashed through an ice-crusted thicket of hemlock. There were no plains here. Just the lake.

Branches whipped my face and I rubbed at my eyes. The house was large. And the garage was long. Surely I'd run into one of them. But at least if I went as far as the lake, I'd know where I was. I could follow the shoreline to the dock and find the house from there.

If I recognized the feel of the shore through what was now a foot of snow. If I didn't stumble into icy water, lose my footing, and go down.

I forced my thoughts to hot cocoa and a crackling fire in the stove. I thought of Camille and Julie and Nelson. He wasn't always obedient, but he was as loyal as dogs come. And he was a fine tracker. Perhaps Camille would send him to find me. Perhaps she'd tie a bottle of brandy and a flashlight to his collar. She'd give him the scent from one of my shirts and then, in spite of his missing leg, he'd make it through the drifts and lead me home.

My foot caught on a root or rock and I fell, my stocking cap peeling from my head. Crimped beneath me, the fingers of my left hand twisted in ways they shouldn't. I felt pain for a few seconds, felt cold for a few more, then felt nothing much.

Get up!

Get up now!

I groaned, got to my knees, and thought of all I had to live for, all I *wanted* to live for. Growing old with Camille. Watching our baby grow up. Seeing Julie graduate from college. Solving those cold cases.

I laughed at my arrogance, the presumption that I would uncover leads no one else had.

Laughter provided a shot of energy and determination. I searched in vain for my hat, then wobbled to my feet, wind tearing at my jacket and fleece, wrapping around my core like an icy steel belt. The fingers of my left hand had no sensation, but I managed to anchor the flaps of my jacket with my forearm and the icy belt loosened a notch.

My feet seemed longer, wider, and heavier than usual. Snow reached my knees and, although I was sure I wasn't climbing, I was no longer certain whether I was heading down the slope.

I thought about the stove again and cocoa and a slug of something to pep it up. I thought about the soft pillows and comforter on my bed, about warm socks, and a deep sleep. Although I knew I shouldn't think about stopping to rest, I no longer knew why that was a bad idea.

My right hand found the trunk of a tree. I hugged it, knees bending, eyes closing.

And then I saw a faint light wavering off to my left.

"Hello," I shouted. "Over here."

Julie cried out, her words tattered by the wind. "Uncle Dan. Where are you? Uncle Dan."

"Here!" I shouted. "I'm here. I'm coming."

Eyes on her light and shouting all the while, I crashed through another thicket, felt rock shift beneath me, floundered into a ditch where snow rose to my thighs, and staggered onto the road. The ruts I'd made on the way up were now only faint impressions.

"I was scared I wouldn't find you." Julie hugged me, shivering despite her puffy coat. "And then I was scared I'd never find the house again."

"It's okay. Don't cry. Your tears will freeze." I turned her around. "Follow your footprints. We'll get there."

She beamed the light at the ground, gripped my arm, and plunged along the ragged trail she'd made.

"We heard something smash upstairs," she gasped. "And Camille and I went to see and while we were patching the window her water broke."

No! Not now!

I stumbled to a halt. "Is she having contractions?"

"Yes. I didn't want to leave her, but she said . . . she said she was scared for you because you'd try to do more than you should and it was her fault you went out. So I knew I had to go."

"I'm glad you did. I got off the road."

"Why are you walking? Where's—?"

"That's a long story. For later. Let's get home."

Julie moved a little ahead of me, breaking a better trail. In a few moments we spotted a glimmer of light. Then we were on the patio, the grill nothing more than a hump in the snow. In the light of a flickering candle I saw Nelson, his nose pressed to the glass.

Julie shoved the kitchen door open and pushed me inside. The warmer air burned my cheeks and Nelson whined and nuzzled my legs. Julie worked the door closed again, kicking snow from the track. "We're home," she called.

Hands pressed to her belly, Camille came to join us, eyes widening as her gaze passed over me.

"What happened? Are you okay?"

"Most of me." I tugged the glove from my left hand. My skin was blue and red and white. "I fell once or twice. Hurt a couple of fingers. But at least I'm not having a baby."

Camille laughed, then burst into tears, wiping at her face with the sleeves of a bright yellow padded bathrobe she'd received from Alda and Pattie at a baby shower three weeks ago. She hated both the color and the padding. Was wearing it a gesture of solidarity with women who had given birth? "I'm sorry," she sobbed. "I'm so sorry I sent you out there."

"It's not your fault."

"It is. I'm a stubborn idiot."

"And I'm the idiot who should have tied you across the hood like a trophy deer and driven you to a hotel."

"And *I'm* the idiot who thought it would be fun to be snowbound." Julie pulled off my other glove and pushed me into a chair. "What happened out there?"

"There's a power pole across that last turn in the driveway. I ran into it."

"And I bet that tire blew." Grunting with each step, Camille got a dish towel from a drawer and dried my hair. "The one you were worried about the other day."

"Tire's fine."

"My turn." Julie tugged at my left boot. "I bet you had to jump out because there was an electric line in the road."

"You win. I don't know if it was live, but I decided to abandon ship and let the experts find out."

Camille sucked in a breath and kissed my forehead. "I'm sorry."

"It's okay. Thanks to Julie I found my way. And at least we know what caused the outage." I flexed my foot to help Julie free the boot. My bare toes were a bluish tint, but I didn't see the suspicious patches of white or yellow that signaled frostbite and every toe wiggled on command.

"We have the stove going in the bedroom." Camille dropped the towel in my lap. "I'll get dry clothes for you."

"And I'll make cocoa. As soon as I get the laces loose on this boot."

"Cut them."

Julie didn't have to be told twice, and in another minute my right toes were free. She filled a pan with milk and I hustled to the bedroom with Nelson at my heels. Fat candles burned on the nightstands and dresser, releasing the scents of vanilla and cinnamon. Fire blazed behind the glass door of the woodstove, light glittering on flecks of mica in the granite hearth. I held my hands toward the heat, skin tingling, injured fingers throbbing, shirt cuffs steaming. Camille stepped close, unbuttoned my shirt, and helped me out of it, pausing once to groan and huff a few short breaths.

Using my right hand, I shucked my jeans and long underwear. "How close are your contractions?"

"A lot closer than they're supposed to be this early in the game."

A spatter of ice pellets hit the door. "Freeman predicted this would blow itself out around dawn." I stepped into fresh underwear and jeans, wrestling right-handed with the button and zipper. "When it does, I'll get the boat out. Without the wind, we'll be able to get around those chunks of ice and—"

Camille laughed, then winced and clutched her belly. "I'm not leaving a warm room to give birth in an open boat, Dan Stone. Besides, I have a feeling this baby's coming before the storm leaves this valley."

How long had I been out in the storm? What time was it now? I scrabbled through my nightstand for the wristwatch I seldom wore. "But they say first babies—"

"I know what they say, but this baby has other ideas." Her eyes clouded. "And you know it's not my first."

Halting my search, I snugged her against my chest with my right arm. Years before she'd been pregnant with a baby girl, seven months along when her husband killed her mother and beat Camille. She lost her daughter, and lost out on any real justice—until she got it for herself with a bullet.

"She would have been about Julie's age," Camille said.

"She would have been a wonderful girl." I kissed the top of her head. "Smart, talented, beautiful. As brave and strong as her mother."

Camille grunted and I pulled her closer, felt the contraction that rocked her. "Wow. That one packed a punch."

"Yeah. We're having fun now," she panted. "I can hardly wait for the next one."

"Cocoa delivery." Julie came through the door balancing a tray with three huge mugs and a plate of oatmeal cookies. "I put 20 marshmallows in each mug, Uncle Dan, and the same amount of cocoa. They're all exactly the same."

"You sure?"

"Yes." She set the tray on a low table beside one of the easy chairs flanking the woodstove, put her hands on her hips, and gave me full-bore teen-girl attitude. "You have too much other stuff to do to waste time seeing who has the most. We have to read the birthing books and make sure we have everything we need, like towels and stuff."

"Yes, ma'am."

"Ooooh. Your fingers look like those hot dogs Marcella sells at the garage. They're all red and nasty."

"Let me see." Camille gripped my wrist and raised it into a circle of candlelight.

Like Julie said, my index and middle fingers were swollen, the skin tight and bright.

"Tell me where it hurts." Camille ran her fingers along mine.

I contained a whimper and tried for a real-man voice. "There. That one. And that one."

She studied the fingers. "Hmmm."

Julie peered over Camille's shoulder and asked the question I wasn't sure I wanted an answer to. "What does that mean?"

"There's no way to tell without an X-ray," Camille said. "But I don't think they're broken or dislocated. We'll splint them and see if that helps."

"I'll get tape and stuff." Julie dashed for the bathroom.

"Take your wedding ring off," Camille told me, "in case your finger swells more."

I tugged at the ring, then let it slide into place. "The ring stays."

"We'll see. When that finger turns blue and Julie goes for the hacksaw, you might wish you'd made a different choice."

"Won't happen. You gave me this ring. It would never hurt me."

Camille shook her head. "Then you must have the world's highest threshold of pain. It's my fault you went out into that storm and ran into the power pole and fell and jammed your fingers. You're lucky you didn't knock yourself out and freeze—"

"Are we going to have another pity party?" Julie set the basket of first-aid supplies on the table and picked up a mug of cocoa. "Or are we going to drink this before it gets cold?"

Camille knuckled tears from her eyes. "I vote for cocoa."

I grabbed a cup and handed it to her. "And I vote for no more talk about things we should have done."

The cocoa was just the right temperature, and I drank most of it without pausing, feeling a rush of warmth to my core. I followed it up with two cookies and fed a third to Nelson. "As soon as you get my fingers taped, I'll fire the generator."

"No," Camille said. "Don't go out again."

"But—"

"We're fine with the woodstove for now. And the oven will put heat into the kitchen and keep the pipes open." Camille gripped my arms. "Don't go out there."

"But the generator is—"

"Please. I thought I'd lost you." Camille put her hands on her belly. "I thought *we'd* lost you. Please don't go out again."

I abandoned my argument, but felt obligated to get in a few words to stake out my male territory. "All right. But the minute the wind drops we'll get the fireplace going. And as soon as it's light I'll get the generator fired up."

Camille nodded and lowered herself to the bed as if exhausted by the discussion. "I can't remember what I'm supposed to do when. All I know is that I shouldn't push until later. Where are those books?"

Julie scurried around searching for them while I rubbed Camille's back with my good hand. "I can do this," she said, her tone a mix of confidence and fear. "I know I can. Women have been having babies for thousands and thousands of years."

I thought of those tiny stones in the Goodrich plot up at the cemetery, then made myself imagine *this* baby, healthy, smiling, holding Nelson's collar and toddling along the edge of the lake. "You can do this. *We* can do this."

We have to do this.

Chapter 11

Camille gripped my shoulder, fingers biting to the bone, and rode out another contraction. "I wish *we* could share the pain," she said when it subsided. "If men had to go through this, I bet the population of the world would be a whole lot smaller."

"There's stuff in these books about making it hurt less." Julie plunked into the chair by the stove, and flipped through the pages. "This one says to put heat on your back and this one says cold. This one says you should walk or climb stairs or get on your hands and knees."

Camille shook her head. "No crawling."

"Right." Julie opened a brochure and waved it. "This says you should dance. Slow," she added, "with Uncle Dan."

"I have the proverbial two left feet but I can manage a slow dance." I helped Camille to her feet. "If you lead."

"What about music?" Julie asked. "There's that emergency radio, but it only works if you keep cranking, and I bet they won't have music."

"You can sing," Camille said.

Julie laughed. "Remember last week when I was raking leaves behind the store? And Nelson started howling? That's why. I was singing."

"Maybe it was your choice of songs." I slid my right hand around Camille's waist and offered her my bandaged left. She gripped my thumb and rested her head against my shoulder. "Nelson prefers the classics."

Julie wrinkled her nose. "Like Beethoven and all that old stuff?"

"No, songs from the 60s."

I spun Camille gently, singing the opening lines of "My Girl" in a low voice.

"I know that one. I saw a video." Julie stood and executed a few backup singer moves. Nelson raised his head from the spot he'd claimed in front of the stove, barked once, and lowered it again.

"Apparently he likes The Temptations," Camille said.

"Nelson has good taste," Julie informed us.

"Extraordinary taste," I agreed. "He nibbles only the finest roadkill."

Camille laughed, then broke from my arms and turned in a circle on her own, eyes closed, breathing in and out through her mouth. "Okay, you two," she said when the contraction ended, "we sing, we dance, but we don't make me laugh too hard or this baby will think I'm pushing before it's time."

"Deal." I held out my arms and started the song from the top.

Pausing only for Camille to dance to the rhythm of her contractions, or to stoke the fire, check the weather, consult birthing information booklets, or brew more cocoa, we sang our way through every tune that lent itself to slow dancing. When we couldn't remember the words, we hummed. I concentrated on recalling where I was the first time I heard each of the songs, concentrated on good times in the past, not on what could go wrong tonight.

Finally, Camille shuffled to the bed and curled up on her side. "I need to rest for a few minutes."

Julie glanced at me, her eyes dark with worry. "Is that a good thing?" I asked Camille.

"I think so. What do the experts say?"

Julie riffled through booklets, then smiled and shoved one into my hands. "We're almost to the pushing part."

"Stop using the word 'we' or I'll push you," Camille muttered.

Julie slapped a hand over her mouth, then collected dirty mugs and plates and hustled to the kitchen. I took a flashlight to the window and checked on the storm. Snow, now coming in flakes instead of pellets, fell at a slant, but no longer swirled and slapped at the door. "The wind's dying. I'll bring in more wood and light the fire in the living room."

"When you're finished, grab the stack of old towels from the top shelf in the laundry room. Then put on your thickest skin. If the baby is the size Mary Lou says you were when you were born, this won't be the most relaxing night of my life. I'll be taking your name in vain and I won't be mincing words when I do."

"Yes, ma'am." I bundled myself into a parka, and went out onto the front porch.

I expected to find a tall drift of snow, but the wind that drove it against the rear doors swept it from the front, and there was only an inch or two. The wind no longer howled and I heard the soft hiss of drifting snowflakes. Using my good hand, I freed a dozen small logs from beneath the stiff tarp, shoved them against the door, then opened it and let them fall inside where Julie scooped them up. Leaving the fire to her, I found the towels and put a few pans of water on the stove to heat.

Freeman, Evan, and Stub had regaled me with tales of women in labor cursing the men who got them in a family way. I'd laughed and assured them Camille, sensible and even stoic, would never do that.

Now I ate my words.

Camille was calm and patient with Julie, speaking in a low and courteous voice. But that vanished when she addressed me. I piled pillows on the bed the wrong way. I let the fire get too low or built it too high. She wanted a green towel instead of the blue one. The tea was too strong and the coffee not strong enough.

As Freeman might say, she rode me like a rented mule.

Nelson whimpered and made himself small in a corner until Camille let out a string of curses that would make a pirate proud. Then he hopped into the closet and squeezed behind a shoe rack.

When Camille complained that I couldn't rub her shoulders the way I should because of the bandage on my hand, Julie pulled me into the kitchen under the pretense of finding more candles. "Maybe you should take a few more aspirin and wait here until she calls for you."

Much as I wanted to be the guy who was there for the whole process, I grasped at the straw Julie offered and slumped into a chair. Somehow, despite Camille's grunts, moans, and cries—and despite my fears—I fell asleep.

When I woke up, I heard a different kind of cry, a halting, hiccupping, wail of distress and surprise and confusion.

I blinked, taking in the foggy gray light outside the windows, then bolted to the bedroom.

Camille, naked and slick with sweat, reclined against a mound of pillows, holding a baby on her chest. A crest of brown hair stood up from the baby's head. Its skin was mottled pink and red and its face was clenched like a fist. It gulped and snuffled and jerked thin arms and legs, twitching the white umbilical cord tied with a green ribbon.

"It's a boy." Julie wiped Camille's brow with a washcloth. "Like Camille said."

Camille flashed me a thousand-watt smile. "Look how long his back is. He's going to be taller than you."

I inched to the edge of the bed, stretched out my hand, and stroked his arm with one trembling finger. "He's okay? You're okay?"

"We're both fine." She flashed that smile again. "Julie's a champ."

"No argument there. But I should have been here."

Julie flushed and ducked her head. "I yelled for you, Uncle Dan, but I guess you didn't hear. And I was gonna come get you, but then he popped out so fast and . . . I'm sorry."

"Don't be. It's my fault. What kind of a man sleeps through his son's birth?"

"The kind of man who could have died in the storm," Camille said in a soft voice. "That's on me, so we're even. And from what I've heard from this little guy so far, I'd say that sleep is something you're not going to get much of for the next few months."

I bent and kissed her. "You're sure you're okay?"

"I'm fine. But Julie will be scarred for life. She'll probably never have kids. She may even enter a convent."

"Good. Then I won't have to train Nelson to attack hormone-happy teenage boys when they descend on our home like the horde of Attila the Hun."

Julie made the gag-me sign. "Can we change the subject?"

"Sure." I stroked Camille's damp hair. "How about a name for our son?"

Camille glanced at Julie. "I thought I'd let Julie decide."

"Nice." Julie pumped a fist in the air, then bit her lower lip. "But if Uncle Dan—"

"No, go ahead. But don't name him after my father or brother or me. And don't come up with anything weird."

"Define weird," Camille ordered.

"Naming him after a planet or a vintage car." I shrugged. "Or a cartoon character or brand of beer or snack food."

"Darn." Julie pouted. "Those were my first picks."

Camille chuckled and my son flailed his arms. Julie smiled, then gazed at me and the smile faded. "I want to name him after Jefferson. Because he saved my life. And yours."

"Works for me. What about a middle name?"

"Chancellor. Because Camille saved you, too. And that was her last name until you got married."

"Jefferson Chancellor Stone," Camille mused.

"Chance for short," Julie said. "Because all those names will be too much for him to say until he's way older."

"Chance," I repeated. It fit. Chance brought Camille to Hemlock Lake two years ago. And chance brought her back the night Ronny Miller tried to kill me. "Chance it is."

Julie checked a booklet open on the nightstand, then gathered up a couple of fresh towels and brought them to the bed. "It's time to cut the cord and push out the placenta."

Camille nodded. I sucked in a breath, swallowed, and tried to look like there was no place I'd rather be. Apparently I didn't succeed. Julie rolled her eyes and hooked a thumb toward the kitchen. "Uncle Dan, you go get hot water and ginger ale and cranberry juice and—"

"Potato chips," Camille said. "Then make a grilled cheese sandwich with tomato and avocado. I'm hungry."

"Me too," Julie said. "Make lots."

Reprieved.

I told myself I should stay and attempt to help—emphasis on "attempt" because I felt as useless as a handle on a bowling ball. "You sure?"

"Positive," Camille said. "Go."

I went, delivered the hot water, then rustled up sandwiches, slaw, chips, and cold drinks.

Camille and Julie were ready when I returned and ate like soldiers at the end of a long march. I tried to ignore the plastic sack Julie warned Nelson to stay away from and pretended I had a say in where we'd bury the placenta after the snow melted. They were polishing off the last of the chips when a shaft of sunlight struck flakes lingering on their way to the snow-covered patio and created a shower of tiny rainbows.

Julie ran to the door. "It's so beautiful."

"Not as beautiful as you," I whispered to Camille.

She gave me a sleepy smile and I tucked the sheet and comforter around her and my son and called for Nelson. "It's time you went outside."

The last word in that sentence set him hopping to the front door, whining as I shrugged into my jacket and wedged my feet into a fresh pair of boots. There were a few inches of snow on the porch and I used the shovel like a plow to scrape a path down the steps, then excavated a short trail with a wide spot at the end. Nelson barked once, raced along the trail, and took care of business.

I was covering the yellow snow when I heard a shout from the lake.

Chapter 12

Squinting against sunlight dazzling off snow, I spotted Justin threading an aluminum fishing boat around chunks of ice.

I waved, then cleared a path to the dock and along the planks to the end, Nelson hopping behind.

"I started out as soon as it was light enough to see." Justin tied the boat to a cleat and clambered out, his feet slipping on the icy planks, his jacket flapping open to reveal a life vest. A year ago stubborn pride would have kept him from taking that precaution. "Is everyone okay?"

I held up my injured hand. "Except for a few jammed fingers and bruises, all five of us are fine."

Justin's gaze swept past me, past Nelson, to the house. He held up a gloved hand, fingers spread, and frowned. "Five?"

"Camille had the baby."

Justin let out a whoop that echoed across the ice-choked lake.

"A boy. Julie delivered him."

He whooped again, yanked off a glove, dug his cell phone from an inside pocket, turned to the east, and keyed in a number. "It's a boy," he shouted and held the phone up for me to speak.

"Jefferson Chancellor," I said. "Chance for short."

"Get that?" Justin asked the person on the other end. "How far off are you?" He frowned, shook his head, and kicked at the dock. "I'll start at this end." He stashed the phone and headed for the house, feet sliding, arms swinging for balance. "They're cutting their way in. Freeman and Evan and Stub and Jefferson. And anyone else who turned out."

I cupped my ear to the southerly wind, heard the snarl of chainsaws, and called after him. "The lines might be—"

"Stub's on it. All the juice in this valley is off so they can clear the roads."

Stub, head of the volunteer fire department, apparently had enough clout to get that done.

"I'll round up my gear." I headed for the garage where water already dripped from the eaves. Nelson followed, nails scrabbling on the slick dock. Somewhere out on the lake a goose honked a complaint and up the hill a woodpecker pounded away in search of breakfast. Clouds tumbled in the distance and the sky took on the depth and color of a sapphire. Nelson lifted his muzzle to the breeze and wagged his tail.

In a few minutes I was loaded up with rope, axes, another spare snow shovel, and a chainsaw. Justin emerged from the house munching on a sandwich and sipping from a tall cup of coffee. "Julie says your rig is up the hill against a downed power pole. If that was the first pole to go, that line might have been hot."

"Tell me about it." I gave a nod of thanks to that Arizona lineman and we headed up the drive, slogging through snow to our knees.

Snow packed the driver's seat of my rig and the battery was stone dead. We pulled the chainsaw and a shovel from the rear, scraped the seat and floor clear, and moved on.

Neatness didn't count, so we stripped the task to the essentials—slice off branches, saw fallen trees into lengths, drag or toss big pieces aside, and trudge on to the next obstacle. Thanks to my injured hand, Justin outworked me two to one. On another day, I might have felt guilty, but today pain and exhaustion trumped remorse.

"Storm really slammed this side of the lake." Justin dug his shovel into the drift shrouding a fallen birch a few yards beyond where the driveway fed in to the road. "There's three times as much snow over here."

"Lucky us," I panted. "Must be retribution for ignoring the weather prophet."

Justin guffawed, then turned serious. "He called it, though, didn't he? He was right and the experts were wrong."

I thought of something my grandmother used to say, "Even a blind squirrel finds a nut now and then." But I kept my mouth shut. After all, if I'd taken Freeman seriously, I might have spent last night in a hotel instead of battling the elements. So I'd let him revel in the accuracy of his prognostication. I'd even pick up his next tab at the Shovel It Inn.

Justin flung a mammoth branch like a javelin and cocked his head. "They're close. This side of Silver Leaf Hollow." He jerked a thumb toward the house. "I'll keep going. You go tell Camille and Julie to expect company."

My swollen fingers urged me not to argue, so I didn't.

"Yay!" Julie squealed as if we'd been snowbound for weeks. "I'll make coffee. And sandwiches. And get more cookies from the freezer."

She scurried about, stowing dirty plates and glasses in the dishwasher, wiping counters, and swabbing wet spots on the floor. I set bottles of rum and whiskey and brandy on the table, then stood in the doorway to the bedroom, gazing at my wife and son. Camille slept on her side, the baby tucked against her chest. His face had unclenched, but his features seemed flattened and compressed. I had no sense of what he might look like in a week or a year.

Before two hours passed, Stub had the driveway plowed, my rig was back in the garage, and the house was filled with men smelling of sweat and smoke and fresh sawdust. They laced their coffee with liquor, filled their plates, and took turns leaning in the doorway and studying Hemlock Lake's newest resident. They trucked out on the porch, called their wives, and then returned to grill me with questions I couldn't answer but that Julie fielded easily—questions about weight and length and the exact amount of time Camille had been in hard labor. Then they called their wives again and huddled in the corner of the kitchen.

"Be best to take him to the hospital," Stub said when the huddle broke. "Get him checked out."

"Camille too," Freeman added.

"And you." Jefferson nodded at my bloated fingers. "Might be you did more than jam those fingers."

"County roads should be clear by now," Evan said.

"And if I put the seats down, there's enough room in my rig for Camille to stretch out." Freeman handed his nearly full coffee cup to me. "Make me a fresh one with just sugar. Don't want my senses impaired if I'm gonna be driving such precious cargo."

Julie darted for the stairs. "I'll get quilts and pillows. And I'll keep the fires going while you're gone."

"I'll stay and help her get the crib set up," Justin offered. "Then start your generator."

I dumped out Freeman's cup, spooned in sugar, and filled it with fresh coffee. "Looks like you've made up your minds."

"It's the women who made the decision," Jefferson said.

The others nodded.

"We don't get Camille and that baby to the hospital and put their minds at ease," Stub said, "I'll be sleeping in the garage and eating cold sandwiches for a month."

The others nodded again.

"Well, I don't want to be the one standing between you and soft beds and hot meals. I'll get us ready to roll."

When we returned that evening, the trees were bare of snow thanks to a steady breeze from the south. Silvery streams of water swept from beneath drifts, filled ditches, and spilled across the road. Freeman's rig rocked as his tires alternately skidded and stuck.

"Mud season," he groused. "I hate mud season."

"At least Chance is too young to track it in," Camille offered.

I glanced at my wife and son, swaddled in comforters and pronounced strong and healthy by the same doctor who X-rayed my hand, wrapped it in a tight bandage, and told me to rest and ice it. But I had work to do—brush to chip, logs to cut, fires to tend. And after my time out in the storm, I'd had enough of ice.

After so much disruption, Camille was anxious to establish a routine—or as much of a routine as Chance would allow. But the women of Hemlock Lake had their own ideas. Mary Lou and Alda were at the house when we returned and, after bustling Camille into the rocker by the fire, took turns cradling Chance and presenting the schedule they'd worked out to cover cooking, cleaning, and baby rocking.

Julie, standing behind them, rolled her eyes, and I suspected Camille longed to do the same, but she was gracious and accepted each suggestion and offer, although with a caveat. "I worked hard all my life, so I doubt I'll be good at lounging around while you wait on me, but I'll give it a shot."

"At least for a few days," she told me after they'd gone and she slid between clean sheets with a long sigh. "Until we get power. And get the hang of being parents."

I pointed at the crib near the stove and at Nelson curled beneath it with one eye open. "Nelson seems to have decided on his role."

Camille smiled, plumped her pillow, and was asleep before I blew out the candle.

By rights a single dwelling at the end of the road shouldn't have been a priority, but Stub made a few calls and the next day trucks rolled in and men in hardhats went to work replacing broken poles and stringing line. At sunset I returned from chipping and chopping to find the lights on, the dishwasher running, a chicken pot pie bubbling in the oven, and Pattie and Alda locked in shrill debate in the laundry room.

Julie looked up from the book open on the dining room table. "Regular bleach or the other kind. Cold water or warm. It's almost as good as a TV reality show."

"Glad you think so." I ruffled her hair. "Because the cable guys might not get here for days."

"That's okay. I don't have time for TV. I have a book report due Monday for extra credit."

I got a bottle of beer from the refrigerator. "What book?"

"*Pride and Prejudice.*" She riffled the pages. "Nothing much is happening."

"Ah. Well, life had a whole different pace then." And it was no surprise that a girl with Julie's experience would find that pace too slow. "Can you switch?"

"Yeah. We have a whole long list to pick from. I got this one because of the prejudice stuff. But it's not prejudice like I thought it would be."

"Well, let's check the other choices."

Julie dashed to her room for the list and we settled on *The Shipping News* because I'd read it, liked it, and kept it to read again.

The argument in the laundry room simmered to a halt and Pattie emerged muttering about stains setting for good and sheets being ruined for no reason except stubborn ignorance. Jamming her arms into her coat, she gave us each a curt nod. "Don't let her touch that chicken pie or it won't be fit to feed to your dog."

"Maybe I should have told them those were old sheets," Julie whispered. "Camille planned to tear them up for rags."

"That would have spoiled the show."

Muffling a giggle with one hand, she opened the book with the other. I retreated to the bedroom and found Camille standing beside the crib, dressed in one of my shirts, a pair of sweat pants, and moccasins.

"I feel like such a fool—watching him breathe in and out, counting his fingers and toes, memorizing every little sound. Is this what all mothers do with their first child?"

I wrapped her in a hug. "Does it matter what anyone else does?"

"I suppose not." She kissed my chin and then chuckled. "You missed the battle of the bleach."

"Caught the end of it. Alda won. Pattie left in a huff."

"They've known each other all their lives. They'll be best friends again tomorrow. Or the day after."

That's the way it worked in small towns. Sometimes issues couldn't be resolved and relationships eroded to single-syllable acknowledgements or mere nods that recognized existence. But mostly folks put arguments aside and went on because that was the example set by parents and grandparents. I doubted any of them would admit it, but I guessed they feared loneliness and isolation and craved companionship—in spite of its imperfections.

"Could be they'll clear out sooner if they can't play nice," I said.

"If only. Not that I don't appreciate the help, because I do, but it's exhausting answering questions about where I keep things and then seeing that expression that says, 'Really? That can't be right.' I mean, what does it matter which drawer I keep the silverware in or whether the bowls are to the left of the plates or to the right?"

"It doesn't matter at all." I stroked her hair. "The way you think isn't the way they think."

"I doubt there's much *thinking* involved. It's simply the way they always do it." She pulled from my embrace and yanked at her hair. "Crap. Listen to me. I'm possessed by the princess of postpartum prissiness. I'm everything I didn't want to be."

"And no one knows but me." I grinned. "And I know better than to leak a syllable of this conversation. But if I hinted to Mary Lou that the battle of the bleach upset you and Chance, well . . ."

She widened her eyes and put a hand over her heart. "Why, Dan Stone. Are you saying you'd lie to Mary Lou?"

"For you, and for peace and tranquility at home, I'd lie like a rug."

"Then get to it."

I did, and after they dropped by another few casseroles and offered another dozen bits of advice, the women of Hemlock Lake put a second plan in place—one that had them providing more help for Dither at the store and being on stand-by status for Camille, available if and when she called. "Which I won't," she told me when I returned from another day of chopping and chipping, "unless there's a dire emergency. We need to establish a routine and we can't if they're underfoot."

"Right." I snagged a beer and limped toward the sofa, Camille trailing with Chance cradled in one arm. He wore a pale yellow sleep outfit with a green turtle embroidered on one shoulder.

"This little guy's going to dictate the schedule, so we have to be flexible."

"Right," I repeated, rubbing the small of my back, feeling an ache in every muscle, and thinking flexibility—at least of the physical kind—was a thing of the past. "Tell me what you need me to do."

"Right now I need you to hold your son. You haven't done that yet."

"I couldn't get through the line of women waiting to hold him. There was no shortage of arms for him to lounge in."

"He needs *your* arms. Bond with him. Let him get used to your touch and smell."

"Maybe we should wait until I shower. I smell like sweat." I took a long pull from the bottle. "And beer."

"You often do," she said with a chuckle.

"Point taken." I set the bottle on the side table, then sat and stretched out my arms. "Hand him over."

"You look like you're about to catch someone jumping from a roof." She laughed. "Or miss someone. Lie back and I'll put him on your chest."

I brushed sawdust from my shirt and followed her instructions. She lowered Chance to my chest and, putting aside fears that I'd snap his tiny spine, I patted his bottom and breathed in his sweet, warm baby smell. He burped, a faint burst of sound, and kicked like a frog. I patted him again and he snuffled and was still.

"That's what I need you to do." Camille dropped into the rocker. "Hold him, rock him, change his diapers, walk the floor when he's fitful and I'm exhausted, talk to him."

"Got it."

"And get to those cold cases. Get out of the house every day and bring stories to tell and progress to report."

"And if there's no progress?"

"There will be. Not right away, but there will be. I feel it."

"I wish I had your mother's confidence," I told Chance.

He opened his lips and blew a bubble of spit.

Chapter 13

I woke Saturday morning to the sound of a jay scolding a squirrel and the flutter of a flock of robins. Camille rocked in a puddle of sunshine by the open sliding glass door, nursing Chance, pointing to chipmunks playing on the low wall and murmuring about their antics. Watchful, Nelson sat beside the chair.

I glanced at the clock. 7:12 "Sorry."

"For what?"

"For not getting up when he cried in the night. I never heard him."

"That's because he didn't cry. Whimpered a little, sucked up a late-night snack, burped, and went back to sleep." She tapped his nose. "He's the best little guy in the world. He knows his mother needs her rest."

"Don't jinx it." I knocked on the wooden nightstand, flung aside the comforter, swung my feet to the floor, and stood on the second try. Every muscle and tendon screamed at me to lie down again or shoot myself.

"I'm glad that tree cutting is done," Camille said. "Your joints sound like popcorn."

"They feel like I've been stretched on a rack."

"It's the pace you set that did it. All you men trying to out-work each other." She tapped Chance's nose again. "You're not going to be like that, are you?"

I laughed and went to shower. Of course he'd be like that. It was in his blood.

That afternoon the thermometer eased into the 70s. Camille took Chance for his first ride in his new car seat and his first visit to the post office. Julie, home from a morning working with Dither at the store, slipped into shorts and a halter top, then carried a lounge chair and her book to the dock. I checked for a message from computer queen Serenity Brook, found nothing, and lugged my cold case files to the table on the porch. Nelson hopped to the edge of the lake and nosed along the shallows in an attempt to get his mouth around a bullfrog. I doubted he'd succeed and suspected he'd be sorry if he did.

Up the hill near the spring, peepers sang their repetitive froggy mating songs. Two woodpeckers beat out call-and-answer rhythms, and a turkey vulture circled, black against the sky, towing its shadow across the placid lake.

A door closed with a dull whomp. Then two more. Shading my eyes I gazed across the water. Three people walked from a car—an old model, long, low, and as white as white gets—to the Brocktons' house. The last in line was Hannah Falton. Even at this distance I knew her by the tension in her body, and the way she scuttled.

The man at the head of the line was a study in contrast. Tall and thin, pale and stiff, he sported a silvery white suit and a shirt the purple color once reserved for royalty and power. His head seemed too small for his height and his hair, clipped close, did nothing to change that impression.

He strode to the porch and took the steps two at a time, sunlight reflecting off a watch or ring as he extended his hand to open the screen door.

With them, like a single volume between a pair of bookends, was a younger man, a faint carbon of the man at the door, slightly shorter, even thinner, and moving with a sideways shuffle that reminded me of a crab. Like his mother, he wore bland colors.

Julie sat up on her lounge chair and watched the trio enter the house. Then she ambled to the porch. "Who are *they*?"

"The woman is Hannah Falton. She's renting the house for the summer. I'm guessing that's her husband and son."

"How old is he?"

"I don't know. He looks like he's around Justin's age."

I could almost see her doing the math, computing the difference between her age and his. She'd reached the time when girls start to picture themselves going through life with a particular man, when they start to guess who would fit into that picture and who wouldn't. Although I worried about where this would lead, and especially about jolts and heartache, I was also glad events in her past hadn't closed off this aspect of her future. I hoped she'd be cautious, but not afraid.

"That's it?" She put her hands on her hips. "That's all you know?"

"Until Camille gets home from the post office and delivers some fresh talk of the town, that's the sum total."

She huffed out a sigh that indicated I was of no use, then returned to her lounge chair and lowered the back rest. Flopping on her belly, she propped her chin in her hands and stared at the house across the lake.

The shadow of the turkey vulture intersected the dock, crossed the planks, and traced her spine.

I shivered and turned my attention to my timeline and the 20 years marked off on it. Theresa Gilligan and Genevieve Graham were on one end of the line, Micah Thielman—with a question mark beside his name—on the other. Franklin Turner's name appeared two years before Micah's, and Angelina Vernon and Judy Arnold a year before Franklin's. Jeremy Yount's name appeared a year before Angelina and Judy. The years in the center of the timeline were empty.

For me that was the strongest argument against Jefferson's feeling that some of these cases were connected. Why had almost 15 years passed without another killing, another disappearance? Had the killer been in jail or restrained? Had he stopped for other reasons? Or were there cases I hadn't come across yet?

I wished I had the Gilligan file in my hands. It felt vital. But maybe that was because I didn't have it or because it was the first case on my timeline and my mind worked in linear ways.

Feeling like I was chasing my tail, I watched the Brocktons' house for a few minutes, seeing curtains twitch and windows open. Like Julie, I was intrigued. Except for the families that bought homes in a cluster built two years ago farther up the lake, the population had changed little over the years. Newcomers brought a different energy and were both feared and fascinating. They changed what Camille called the weave of the community's social fabric. Even those who came for a few months, like the Faltons, could affect the pattern.

As a cover for my surveillance, I got a rake from the garage, and went to work clearing twigs and leaves from the stone path to the lake. The task needed to be done and it allowed me to watch the Faltons and draw conclusions I could test later.

The man I assumed was Hannah's husband emerged and marched around the house, lifting his feet high and setting them down with care, then surveyed the shore and the short, narrow dock poking out into the lake. The Brocktons often set up their easels on the dock. Sometimes they went out in an aging rowboat. Would the Faltons use that? Would they fish?

I shook my head. The father didn't look like the outdoor type. Not that a man had to be sturdy, rugged, and tanned to hike or hunt or fish, but Falton's edgy movements suggested he wasn't comfortable with the outdoors. And there was little stillness about him.

Hannah Falton came out, closed the door, and approached the man, her head lowered. She reminded me of a whipped dog, hungry and crawling to its abusive owner. The tall man turned to her, pointing at the car, the road, the muddy shore. She nodded without lifting her head, pointed at the house, the road, and the lake, then went inside.

Windows closed and curtains twitched again. Hannah ushered the boy out and turned to lock the door. Julie sat up and primped at her hair, but he didn't gaze in her direction. Instead he stared at the road to town, then kicked the ground, folded himself into the car's rear seat, and slammed the door.

The sound echoed across the lake. The man turned and advanced on the car. Hannah scurried along the walk and intercepted him as he reached for the handle. He raised his hand as if to strike, then lowered it by inches. Hannah opened the passenger door and slipped inside. The man stalked to the driver's door, jerked it wide, shook a finger at the boy, then thrust himself inside and slammed the door. For at least a minute the car was still, then the engine roared and it took off.

"Not a happy family," I muttered. "Or at least not today."

But what did I know about the Faltons and the long-term state of their happiness? This might be the worst day of the past decade. On the other hand, it might be the best.

And what would they make of us? They couldn't help but see our comings and goings, even hear fragments of conversations on sultry summer nights when the breeze blew in their direction.

"Camille's back." Julie bolted from the lounger and trotted to collect a sack of groceries. Peering inside, she crowed with joy. "Ice cream on a stick. The really expensive kind. Four boxes!"

"I had Dither order them for you." Camille winked. "Maybe you better try one right now."

Julie tore into the top box, peeled the wrapper from an ice cream bar, bit off a chunk, hugged herself, and twirled to the kitchen door with the bag.

"I think she likes them." Camille freed Chance from his car seat and carried him to the porch.

I leaned the rake against a tree and followed. "Was he a hit?"

"Of course. He's as charming as his father."

"Hmmm. Are you trying to tell me I'm not his father?"

Camille chuckled, plopped into the swing, and unbuttoned her shirt. Chance latched onto her breast like a leech.

I winced and took a chair a few feet away. What I'd seen of motherhood so far seemed to involve discomfort, pain, and sacrifice. Not to mention anxiety, stress, and a lot of additional work. No wonder some women snapped under the strain. "I don't care what anyone says, that looks painful."

"Compared to the other night, this is nothing. Did you see our new neighbors?"

"Yeah. Looked like they were inspecting the house and he didn't think it passed."

"From what I hear, he's that way about everything."

"Who's what way?" Still dancing and licking her ice cream bar, Julie came through the door and perched on the railing.

"Mr. Falton. Evan says he's the kind of man who measures others by his standards and finds everyone wanting."

Which explained his wife's timid manner. "Evan said that? *All* that?"

"Evan was Lieutenant Loquacious this morning."

"Loquacious? Throw around words like that and Julie will have you writing her book report," I warned. "What prompted Evan, master of the single-syllable response, to string so many words together?"

"He has previous knowledge of Wesley Falton. He saw him last summer. At a revival."

I blinked again. "Evan was at a revival?"

Camille laid Chance over her shoulder and patted his bottom. "Yes, but it wasn't a destination of choice. He and Pattie drove up to the Adirondacks for a weekend. She wanted to poke through antique stores. He thought they had plenty of antiques already so he took a walk. They were giving away lemonade and cookies in the revival tent, so he loaded up with free snacks, took a seat in the shade and, in his words, 'Here came this guy, tall and skinny as a whipsnake. Got in the pulpit and bellowed like a bull, his eyes all fiery.'"

Chance released a burp and Camille smiled and cradled him against her breast once more. "Evan said that under all the ranting and posturing, it was the same old message about sin and damnation, but he felt like Brother Elijah could reach in and shake the soul in his body."

"You're sure Evan said that? You're not embellishing?"

"Not a bit. Evan was fascinated by the man. But *not* by his message." She smiled. "When Brother Elijah started in on all the temptations of the flesh they should put behind them, Evan got another cookie and left. He said life is too short to live it without beer."

Nelson wandered up from the lake, paws caked with mud. Julie held the ice cream stick out for him to lick. "So that guy's a minister? Like Reverend Balforth?"

Camille shook her head. "According to Evan he's *nothing* like Reverend Balforth. Evan says Balforth is a minister but this guy is a preacher."

Julie frowned. "Isn't that the same thing?"

"Not according to Evan."

"It sounds like Evan means this guy puts a lot more energy and spirit into his sermons than Reverend Balforth does," I speculated. "Could be that Evan thinks he's more focused on saving souls than ministering to them."

"Where's his church?"

"He doesn't have one." Camille laid Chance across her shoulder again. "He rents halls and theaters in the winter and in the summer he sets up tents."

I hummed a few bars from "Brother Love's Traveling Salvation Show."

"Like that," Camille said.

"Like what?" Julie tucked the stick in the pocket of her shorts and pointed at me. "You didn't say anything. All you did was hum."

"A song about a tent revival preacher," Camille said. "We'll play it for you later."

Julie nodded toward the house across the lake. "Will he set up a tent there?"

"No. He paid Evan to use that empty field where the road starts up to the cemetery. He plans to preach there a few days a month."

"So, Evan doesn't like his message," I mused, "but he likes his money."

"Pattie's been talking about new carpet for a year now. I think she tipped the scales in the decision-making process." Camille stood, settled Chance in my arms, and stretched. "*We* may not have heard of him, but apparently Brother Elijah is quite well-known in some circles. He'll draw a crowd. But I wonder how many local folks will go."

"Evan will go for the cookies," Julie said. "He won't care if they're any good, as long as they're free and there are lots of them."

I smiled, liking that she recognized that about Evan, and really liking the implication that she felt quality trumped price and quantity.

Chapter 14

Monday morning I got on the horn to Sheriff North who said a copy of the Gilligan file was on the way and should be on his desk by afternoon. "And I got one here from Buckingham County. You intending to work cold cases for the entire state?"

"Only if I think there's a connection to ours."

He snorted. "Well, keep track of your time. I might want to bill it out. Or use the threat of a bill to call in favors."

He hung up and I passed the morning reading through Genevieve Graham's file once more. What struck me this time was that it contained a wealth of information about the crime scene and autopsy, but darn little about her. Either investigators hadn't made a study of how her life might have contributed to her death, or they hadn't recorded details. They didn't come right out and chalk her death up to a random shooting or thrill kill, but they leaned hard in that direction. Harry Pallister's notes indicated he didn't agree with that theory, but had discovered nothing with which to knit another.

I made a list of things I wanted to know about Genevieve and the others, all the details of daily living from childhood on. Previous addresses. The routes they took to school and work. Places they shopped. Where they'd traveled for vacations.

Associations and groups they'd joined. Schools they'd attended. Repairmen they'd hired. Doctors, lawyers, hairdressers, paper and mail carriers, neighbors, relatives.

After lunch I took the list with me to the sheriff's office, picked up the Gilligan and Thielman files, made copies of both, and paid a visit to Serenity Brook in her basement lair. Today she was snacking on sunflower seeds, but her attitude was the same.

"More cases to add to my workload?" she asked without looking up.

"If I don't keep you busy you'll be straightening Sheriff North's office."

She muttered something about Hercules and the Augean stables, flipped to the final page of the document beside her keyboard, pounded for another moment, dumped the document in a cardboard box beside her desk, and reached for the files. "Another old one," she noted after a quick riffle through the Gilligan file. "Strangled. Same month as the Graham woman was shot. What are the odds they're connected?"

"Math isn't my strong suit. I was an English major."

She shook her head as if to say that even that field of education had been wasted on me "Let's just say the odds are long."

"What about the odds that they're connected to the other cases."

"Longer than winter in Alaska."

"That's my thinking, too. But spring has a way of coming, even in Alaska. Which is where Theresa Gilligan's fiancé was serving in the Coast Guard when she died. Think you can find him?"

"Can a pig find a truffle?" She flipped through the file, tapped a few keys, and spit sunflower hulls into a cracked coffee cup. "Ketchikan. Runs a fishing charter service."

She jabbed two more keys and a printer on the second desk groaned to life. She handed over the paper it spit out. "Anything else?"

"Yes. Start with the Gilligan and Graham cases and do the same thing for every name in every file—get me numbers and addresses. I'm going back to square one. *We're* going back to square one."

I laid a copy of the list of what I wanted to know about each victim in front of her. "I'm hoping that between us we can fill in these blanks. You with your keyboard, and me working the phone and knocking on doors."

She ran her finger down the list, nodding.

"There's nothing to suggest the victims had anything in common. I want to work the cases separately, but not in a vacuum."

She beamed. "Who said you were a slow learner?"

"So, you can do that?"

"Can a melon roll downhill?"

I took that to mean it was not only possible, but relatively simple.

"Don't let the door hit you in the butt on the way out." She pinched sunflower seeds from the bag and stuffed them in her mouth, flipped to the first page of the Gilligan file, and went to work.

When I checked my e-mail after dinner, I had three messages from her, one titled "Gilligan," one titled "Graham," and one titled "Cold Cases: General." The Gilligan and Graham e-mails were loaded with names, addresses, and phone numbers. The general message was brief. "More to come. You're going to be a very busy boy."

The next morning I made preliminary phone calls on the Graham and Gilligan cases, introducing myself, telling friends and relatives I was looking into the case, and warning them not to get their hopes up. I told them I was casting a wide net, hoping to discover more details about the women's lives, habits, interests, or friends. I stressed the amount of time that had passed and told them it was normal to try to protect reputations, but even a small secret kept to shield a friend might be the key to finding a killer. I urged them to think back and call me if they remembered anything they hadn't shared with investigators before.

I called Fred Maddox, Theresa's boyfriend, last, figuring with the time difference I'd catch him just getting up. I had to settle for his machine and left a brief message, delivered in a tone designed to discourage false hope.

When I finished, I felt wrung out, exhausted. But tense, anxious with wanting, and knowing I had no control.

That evening Chance had his second road trip and his first dinner out.

"Not that he'll be able to eat anything on the table," Mary Lou had said when she issued the invitation, "but I want to be in his baby book for a first of some kind."

As we prepared to leave, I surveyed the mound of items necessary to take along with a newborn for even a few hours. "Does he *have* a baby book?"

Camille narrowed her eyes and shot me an expression that indicated I was in the running for world's worst new father.

Julie came to my rescue. Behind Camille's back she pointed to a padded yellow book half buried by a pile of baby gear on our long kitchen table.

I excavated it from beneath packages of wipes, tissues, and diapers. "What I meant was: does this baby book have a place for his first meal out?" I thumbed it open and saw Camille had already recorded details of Chance's birth in the storm.

"We'll make a place." Julie took the book from my hands and tucked it into a small duffel bag. "I picked this one because it has lots of blank pages so we don't have to write exactly the same stuff everyone else would. Lots of room for pictures, too. It's way better than all the others we looked at."

I followed them out the door, thinking of the book my mother kept for me—a book burned to ash when Ronny Miller torched the lodge. I remembered my mother's hands—pale and skeletal then—paging through it a few days before she died. I recalled pictures of me cradled in her arms and one where, eyes and mouth wide, arms flailing, I appeared to be trying to fly from my father's grip. Had he held me more than that one time? He hadn't been a warm man. And I hadn't been the son he loved.

"Where's your baby book?" Julie asked Camille as I navigated across a channel carved by snowmelt in the winter-ravaged driveway.

"I don't think I had one. My mother wasn't married and my father took off before I was born." Camille's voice trembled. "She didn't have a lot of money. Or education."

I squeezed Camille's knee, then gripped the wheel, easing over a plow gouge and across a ridge of rock. "She had a lot of love. Your mother set you on course to be an amazing, beautiful, strong, intelligent woman."

And gave her life to help set Camille free from a man who didn't want her to be any of those things—wanted only a servant, a possession. That ultimate maternal sacrifice made all others pale by comparison. And it lit a spark of courage in Camille that the man who abused her didn't see or didn't acknowledge until the moment she ended his miserable life.

Camille sniffed and fished a tissue from the pocket of another of my shirts—a green and black check that looked better on her.

"I'm sorry," Julie whispered. "I forgot all about . . . I'm sorry."

"Don't be." Camille turned in her seat and patted Julie's cheek. "Dan's right. My mother was a good woman. I hope I'm even half the mother to Chance that she was to me."

"And I hope I'm half as good as my mother," Julie said in a faltering voice.

Except for an occasional sniffle, we rode the rest of the way in silence, bound together by what we'd lost.

Mary Lou bustled out to meet us with Jefferson and Justin on her heels. "I made pot roast," she said. "Because that's Dan's favorite. And candied carrots for Julie. And broccoli with cheese sauce for Camille. And ten pounds of mashed potatoes and a gallon of gravy for Justin because I'm worried he's losing too much meat off his bones working so hard at school and on the house."

"I guess that leaves all the pies for me." Jefferson eyed Justin. "Unless you want to fight for them."

"Did that once." Justin laughed and reached for a couple of the sacks we'd loaded into the SUV. "Didn't care much for the outcome."

"Jefferson's got to be slowing," I told him. "He's almost a year older."

"And a year smarter," Justin answered. "He could be blind as a bat and down to one arm and one leg and I wouldn't be wild about my odds of winning."

Jefferson clapped him on the shoulder. "Keep thinking like that, son, and you and I will never need to fight again."

"Enough talking." Camille handed Chance to Mary Lou and headed for the house. "I'm not eating for two anymore, but I'm hungry. Is there whipped cream to go on that pie?"

"She bought enough to subsidize a small dairy," Jefferson said.

Mary Lou rolled her eyes, but smiled at him in a way that seemed to create a golden glow around both of them.

I thought back to a year ago, to the numb and haunted look in Jefferson's eyes in the weeks leading up to the date Louisa Marie set for their wedding. There would have been no golden glow in that marriage, only endless attempts to please a woman who derived satisfaction and warped happiness from the misery of others. Perhaps, along with heart disease, it was her harsh nature that carried Lou Marie off the night before they wed. Or perhaps it was cosmic justice.

Karma?

Fate?

Luck?

Events of the past two years made me believe in forces—both good and evil—that I couldn't put a name to. Like the mountains around Hemlock Lake, they just were.

After we demolished all but a few slices of pie, we adjourned to what had once been called the parlor. Previously the domain of Mary Lou's sister, it had housed furniture handed down through generations—a horsehair loveseat, a pair of prim rockers, a braided rag rug smelling of a cat long departed, and a host of rickety tables and wobbling lamps with fly-specked shades. Doilies had covered every flat surface and dark green drapes prevented even a single beam of sunlight from fading family photographs on walls the color of dried mud.

Now that the house was no longer divided, this room belonged to Mary Lou. Over the winter she and Jefferson expanded it, knocking down the wall to what had been her father's den. They painted it a soft yellow, laid honey-colored carpet, replaced family mug shots with colorful landscapes, and filled the room with a sofa long enough for napping, comfortable chairs, fresh lamps and tables, and a big-screen television. I found it ironic that Mary Lou paid for it all with her sister's hoarded cache of bills and coins.

Jefferson lit a fire and Chance fell asleep inside a corral of cushions on the sofa between Camille and Mary Lou. When talk turned to the Falton family, and Justin said he hadn't seen them, Julie described Wesley and Hannah Falton and their son.

"He's 18," Mary Lou supplied. "His name is Isaac."

Julie slumped lower in the puffy armchair and wrinkled her nose. "Isaac?"

"I thought names from the Bible were in style," Camille said.

"I guess. I wonder if he has a nickname."

"And I wonder if he wants a part-time job." Justin snagged a throw pillow from the sofa and stretched out on the broad hearth. "There are two classes I want to take over the summer."

Isaac Falton's body language and behavior hadn't struck me as that of someone who could manage the dock and bait shop even for a few hours a day. But he had the advantages of being close by and being the son of a man who seemed to inspire fear. My father had been the same type. That fear made me meet most expectations.

"If you can't find anyone to fill in, I'll lend a hand," I offered.

"So will I," Jefferson said. "I know which side of a boat goes in the water."

Justin laughed. "Thanks. I appreciate that. But, Dan, you have enough with the baby and those investigations and Jefferson has more remodeling to do over the summer."

He pointed to the ceiling, indicating the three rooms and bath upstairs. Mary Lou had plans—wide windows, an enormous shower, and even a balcony. "Besides, I think I should figure this out on my own. If I can't find someone, then I'll put off the classes. No law says I have to take chemistry this summer."

Julie laughed. "I hope I don't have to take chemistry in college at all. High school chem is hard enough."

Justin beamed. "Is that why you have an A instead of an A+?"

Julie tossed a pillow at him. He laughed and snatched it from the air.

Camille and I exchanged a glance filled with joy. Two years ago there had been little love between these two. Their father had done all he could to push them apart, favoring Justin and belittling Julie and her dreams of college and travel. A year ago Justin was AWOL and on the run, a boy with attitude and little else. It took a beating from life in general and Jefferson in particular to make him acknowledge the truth about his father and return to the family that remained.

"Where did they live before?" Julie asked. "The Faltons?"

"Most recently in Ashokan City." Mary Lou took her glasses off and pinched the bridge of her nose. "But I got the impression they move often. She said she'd filled out a lot of change-of-address forms over the years. And Evan heard him preach that people should limit their possessions and shouldn't become attached to property so they'll be ready to go when they're called."

"Like you have a choice about being ready," Justin said with a sharp laugh. "Like someone would say, 'Hold on, Grim Reaper, I have to sell my house and have a yard sale.'"

Julie snorted into her cola. "Isaac might be bored out of his mind here in the sticks. There's way less to do than in the city. Unless you like outdoor stuff or have a car." She looked at Mary Lou. "Does he?"

"I don't know. I saw Hannah's car, and that old white boat Wesley drives, but that's it."

"They'll drive those cars into the ground," Jefferson mused, "getting out of this valley and around to summer revivals."

"He's only preaching on weekends this summer," Mary Lou said. "Taking time off to write a book about his life and his calling."

"Exactly what the world needs." Jefferson shook his head. "Another book by a Bible thumper."

"Well, it could be some time before you see it for sale. Hannah says his editor likes the middle, but wants more from the beginning."

"Probably wants to fictionalize the facts," I said, "to make him look better."

"Or worse," Camille said. "So it appears he was a minute from being damned for all eternity before he saw the light."

"Either way, I won't buy a copy," Jefferson said. "Although I expect plenty will, especially if he peddles them at revivals. People get worked up and filled with the spirit and they're more likely to part with good sense *and* the price of a book."

"I won't buy one, although if the library gets a copy I might take a peek." Mary Lou stroked Chance's head. "It's ironic that with all the places he could have found to rent for the summer, a man who claims to have such a close relationship with God winds up so near the Devil's Tombstone."

Chapter 15

"The Devil's Tombstone?" Julie leaned toward Mary Lou, eyes bright with interest. "Is it a real tombstone? Is the devil really—?"

Mary Lou waved that off. "It's not a tombstone. And nobody's buried under it. It's one of those boulders at the end of the lake."

Jefferson sucked in a breath. His eyes glittered. I recalled a similar reaction when Justin mentioned the rocks the day we put on his roof.

Camille glanced at me and I shrugged. "Never heard of it."

"I bet it's an erratic," Justin said. "A boulder left behind by the glacier."

"Mr. Geology thinks he knows everything." Julie stuck out her tongue. "I bet it's way more than a rock if it has a name. I bet there's a story about it. An old story. Right, Mary Lou?"

"Yes," Mary Lou said, her voice low and hesitant, "there's a story."

Julie plumped the throw pillow and settled against it. "Well?"

Mary Lou glanced at Camille. "It's . . . it's not a story with a happy ending. It's dark."

"And spooky?" Julie's eyes sparkled. "Is it spooky, Uncle Dan?"

"I don't know. I never heard it."

"How could you not?" Mary Lou asked. "I listened to it lots of times when I was a girl. After summer picnics when night fell and the bats swooped over us, our grandfathers would talk about hunting and our grandmothers would tell stories from way before."

"I was probably catching fireflies."

"More likely you were reading a book by the light of the fire," Mary Lou said. "You were always reading, always had a book in your hand."

"The story," Julie prompted. "Tell the story."

Camille sighed. "You'd better tell it, Mary Lou, or Julie will pester you for the rest of your life."

Mary Lou chewed at her lower lip, then nodded. "It happened long ago. Almost two centuries. There weren't many people living around Hemlock Lake then, only a few dozen, and one was a mean man with a black, black heart. He called himself Mr. Smith, but no one believed that was his name. Never had a good word to say. Never lent a hand to his neighbors. He had a little farm near where the Brocktons' house is now, and he lived there alone for years until he took a wife."

She gazed at Julie for a long moment. "She was a pretty girl, with sky-blue eyes and curling blond hair. And she was young. Younger than you."

"That's too young to get married."

"It is now. But things were different then. Girls grew up faster and married younger."

"They died younger, too," Camille added.

I thought again of those markers in the cemetery, of short lives and mothers' sacrifices.

"Was the girl from here?" Julie asked. "From Hemlock Lake?"

"No. No one knew where she came from or how he arranged to marry her. No one even knew her name because she never spoke. Some folks claimed he won her in a game of cards, and others believed he bought her like a slave because that's the way he treated her."

Julie shivered and moved to the hearth beside Justin.

"The story goes that one day in the dead of winter he rode off and the next he rode in with her behind him on his horse. White that horse was. Pale as the belly of a fish from the deepest and darkest part of the lake."

Death. Death rode a pale horse. And hell followed.

I glanced at Camille. She pointed her chin toward Julie and shrugged as if to say that halting the story now would only make her more determined to hear the rest of it.

"He set tasks for her every day," Mary Lou continued, "and she worked from sunup to sundown, tending the garden, milking the cow, churning butter, cooking, and scrubbing. Folks out fishing would sometimes hear him yelling, finding fault, threatening to whip her until she did her chores faster and better."

Justin sat up, eyes flashing. "Somebody should have called the sheriff."

"Sheriff—if there was one—couldn't have done much then," Jefferson said. "Women had damn few rights and men pretty much called the shots, especially on their own property."

I leaned over and twined my fingers with Camille's. "Sometimes, even now, there isn't much a law officer can do. Or *will* do."

"But somebody should have helped her. I would have."

I had no doubt that the person he was now would have intervened. But two years ago he hadn't seemed to notice or care about the many ways in which his father dominated and verbally abused his mother. Two years ago, however, he'd also been controlled by Ronny Miller. I wondered if he'd ever talk about it.

"People were frightened of this man," Mary Lou said. "He was a crack shot and he had a rifle with him always, even when he slept."

"And women had a hard lot in those days. Unless they were rich enough to have servants, they did housework, had babies, and got pregnant again." Camille wiped a dribble from the corner of Chance's mouth. "And in most marriages the man gave the orders and the woman followed without question. If she didn't, she suffered."

"I'm glad I didn't live then," Julie told Camille. "I like now way better. And when I get married—not until after I go to college and travel all over the world—we're gonna be partners, like you and Uncle Dan." She turned her gaze to Mary Lou. "What happened? What's the rest of the story?"

"Well, the man with the black heart had no use for church," Mary Lou said, "but one Sunday in the summer he rode off at dawn. Later that morning she came to the service—walked all the way to the very same church where Reverend Balforth is minister now. Because she never talked, everyone was surprised when she sang with the congregation and folks said she had a voice like an angel. They invited her to stay for the picnic dinner and she played tag and waded in the lake with the boys and girls, because, after all, she was a girl herself."

"Then the man with the black heart came back?" Julie whispered.

"Yes, at dusk. He bellowed like a mad bull, spurred that white horse into the lake, and chased her down the road, slicing strips from her dress with his whip."

"And nobody tried to stop him?" Justin asked.

"Oh, men followed, yelling at him to stop. But he turned and pointed his rifle and told them to stay out of his business or he'd kill them all."

Julie sucked in a breath. "And then what happened?"

"And then no one knows for sure." Mary Lou spread her hands. "A summer thunderstorm rolled in and everyone ran for shelter. The next day a couple of men heard the cow bawling the way cows do when they haven't been milked. After a time they took their guns and rode to his place. There wasn't a sign of anyone around the house. Not the man. Not the girl. Not the horse."

Julie gripped her brother's hand. "Where were they?"

"No one knew, not until they heard the horse whinny off in the woods. They found him, still saddled, chomping grass beside one of those rocks near where the stream comes in from Dark Moon Hollow. He wouldn't let anyone near him—he reared up and his eyes sparked. When they grabbed for his reins, he galloped into the woods and was never seen again."

"And the girl?"

"They found her on top of the rock, curled in a shallow depression."

"Was she alive?"

Mary Lou shook her head. "They carried her to town and made a coffin and held a service and buried her on the hill. No one knew her name, and while they were debating what to put on her stone, a white birch sprouted from her grave. It grew six feet before the snow fell and they let that be her marker. Birches are symbols of new beginnings."

"What about the man?"

"They never found him. They never found his whip or his gun, either. There was nothing but a burned spot on the ground in front of the rock. They say the earth there stayed hot for a year, so hot you couldn't hold your hand on it for more than minute."

Here, I thought, is where fact leaves off and legend takes over.

"The scorch mark could have been caused by lightning. But a hot spot . . ." Justin shook his head. "I've never heard of anything like that in the Catskills. I'll have to ask my professor."

"Sounds like someone had a good imagination," Camille said. "Or along the line they added a little fiction to make it sound like something Washington Irving might have written."

"I didn't add to it," Mary Lou insisted. "I'm simply repeating what I heard. My grandmother swore that sometimes, when thunderstorms rolled through, the spot got hot again. And sometimes lightning cracked like a whip and people heard the girl scream. And sometimes they heard the horse whinny."

Justin rolled his eyes. "The scream is probably the wind whistling through a crack in the rock. So is the whinny. But the hot spot—that's gotta be imagination."

"Coupled with the power of suggestion," I added.

"Maybe," Mary Lou agreed, "but these hills are thick with ghosts, Dan. As you and Jefferson well know."

Jefferson held my gaze and I knew he was thinking about the ghost of Clarence Wolven, the electrical hum and sizzle that goaded us to find his killer.

"There are lots of things that go on in these hills no one can explain," Mary Lou continued in a near whisper. "I heard it said that if you go to that rock right after a storm, you'll find blood on it."

Justin laughed. "That's definitely a myth. I bet there's red lichen on that rock. On a dark day, when it's wet, it might look like blood—from a distance."

"I want to see the rock. But I don't want to go by myself." Julie's gaze swept the group. "Who wants to come with me tomorrow after school?"

Camille and Mary Lou shook their heads. Justin muttered that he had too much work to do. Julie turned her pleading gaze on me. Before I could cave, Jefferson spoke up. "I'll go. Come to the house when you get off the school bus."

"Better take your rifle," Justin taunted. "In case you come across the man with the whip or the ghost of that fire-breathing horse or Bigfoot or a lake monster."

"I'm more worried about living men than monsters and ghosts," Jefferson said. "But I've made it a policy to stay out of these woods unless I'm armed. So Miss Julie and I will examine that rock and then seize the opportunity to take a little target practice."

The next morning I found a string of e-mails from Serenity, each one packed with phone numbers and addresses for those named in the files for the remaining cold cases. I printed them out and was about to pick up the phone when Camille announced she was taking off for a few hours to check on the store, leaving me in charge.

All went well until Chance woke up from a nap and seemed to sense that he was at my mercy—and vice versa. He cried, hiccupped, refused the bottle Camille left, then sucked at it exactly twice, spit up, and soiled two diapers. After that he refused all efforts to calm him except those that involved me walking, rocking, and singing simultaneously.

Nelson trailed me from room to room. I assumed he was offering canine moral support, but his anxious whining got old fast. I ordered him to be quiet, and he lifted his lips in a snarl and hopped up the stairs to Julie's room.

When Camille returned I practically hurled Chance into her arms. "According to this little guy, I'm not fit to be a father."

"Of course you are." Her fingers brushed a patch of dried puke on my shirt. "He gave you the badge to prove it."

"I did everything I've seen you do. He hated being with me."

"He's a guy." Camille kissed his head and carried him to the porch swing. "He was challenging you for the position of alpha male."

"Challenge over." I followed her, unbuttoning my soiled shirt. "I give up. He can be the alpha. I'll be a lowly member of the pack."

Camille settled into the swing with Chance clamped to her breast. "Your father was an alpha. Ronny Miller was an alpha. Were you content being a lowly member of their packs?"

"No. That's why I left Hemlock Lake. " I tossed the shirt over the porch rail and stretched my arms to the warm breeze. "Does a pack have to have an alpha? Do alpha wanna-bes have to posture and fight?"

"It seems that's the way nature is set up." She curled a strand of Chance's hair around her finger. In the sunlight streaming in from the west the lock appeared a lighter brown and his coppery skin was no longer mottled. "The alpha will try to keep members of the pack in line by fear or force and keep interlopers from claiming territory," she told our son. "But pack members or interlopers often try to claim the alpha spot so they can breed and pass on their characteristics."

I gazed across the lake. The front door of the Brocktons' house was propped open and Hannah Falton lugged a brown suitcase up the steps. Legs braced, both hands gripping the handle, she scraped it across a step and then heaved it. I considered driving over to help, then remembered what she said the day we met: "We never ask for help. We pray for guidance."

Did that mean she wouldn't accept help if it was offered?

It was a 12-mile drive to come to her aid. If the canoe was in the water instead of stowed in the rafters of the garage, I could paddle across in a few minutes.

Hannah heaved the suitcase up the final step, dragged it across the porch, and closed the door.

Camille hummed, Chance made tiny sucking sounds, and I rehashed Hannah Falton's words: "We never ask for help."

Did she use the word "we" because she'd contributed to the development of the policy and agreed with it? Or did she use it because it had been decreed, because Wesley Falton was the alpha of their pack and she followed his rules because there would be consequences if she didn't?

Nelson emerged from the house, slunk past me to the steps, and scurried down, tail tucked.

What would happen, I wondered, if Wesley Falton and Reverend Balforth, alphas in the realm of religion, crossed paths?

"Are you planning to take flight?" Camille asked. "Or is that a meditation pose?"

I lowered my arms. "Neither. Got lost in thought."

"Well, you need a break. Why don't you get lost in the woods with Jefferson and Julie? Take Nelson with you."

Chapter 16

An hour later we left my rig beside the padlocked chain strung between metal posts to keep unauthorized vehicles off an old logging road. Rutted and overgrown with brush, the road crossed a tongue of state-owned land and joined the east and west sections of pavement to complete a circuit of the lake. As chief of the volunteer fire department, Stub had a key to the padlock. If we'd decided against walking, he would have handed it over without argument because we had history at Hemlock Lake. To Stub, ancestry gave us a right to use the road, no matter what state regulations said.

Besides, boundaries were vague in the folds of land on either side of Dark Moon Hollow. Deeds went back generations and made vague mention of water courses, stone walls, marked trees, and other landmarks. Estimates of acreage were rough at best. I'd heard of families inheriting 200 acres of ridge and ravine, surveying and selling off 250, and having more than 40 left.

My property butted up against state land on the east, and the Brocktons' met it on the west. Both of our holdings ran from crumbling ledges of red shale beside the lake up steep-sloped ridges thick with hemlock. With the only natural building sites taken, and construction restrictions described by one builder as "oppressive," developers weren't lining up to ask me to sell chunks of view property.

Jefferson got the rifles, handed Julie's to her, stepped over the chain, and set off along the track without a word. Julie followed a few yards behind, leaving enough space so bent branches wouldn't whip her eyes when Jefferson released them. Nelson trailed her, and I slung my camera strap around my neck and brought up the rear.

When my ancestors quarried and logged this land, trees never had a chance to do more than sprout on this track before they were crushed by draft horses and the loads they hauled. But no one worked the quarries now—unless you counted the scavenging I'd done for slabs of stone to build the patio. Discards from the days when stone was hauled for city sidewalks worked fine for me. And the price was right.

A boulder loomed from a thicket and Julie left the road to examine it. "Justin was right about the red lichen." She stretched and placed her hand over a patch. "Most of what I've seen is greeny gray, but this is rusty. Somebody might mistake it for blood."

"If that somebody was standing far off and not wearing glasses," I said.

Julie rolled her eyes and returned to the trail. "How will we know which rock is the one?"

"We'll know." Jefferson's voice was flinty, his face grim. Two years ago, he'd haunted these woods, trying to connect his memories after years of wandering. He'd camped near a spring above the quarries. He'd fished in the lake. He knew this road. He knew that rock. And he didn't like what he knew.

Dark Moon Creek was running hard and high. The banks were steep and slick with hemlock needles. "When you see this creek in the summer and it's only a foot or two wide," Jefferson said, "you can't imagine it carrying enough water to fill that lake."

"Bobcat and Bluestone Creeks spill into the lake, too," Julie pointed out. "And Bobcat's bigger."

"Still, it's 14 miles around the lake, and who knows how deep it is. I can't do the math, but it's a lot of water."

"I bet Mr. Geology could figure it out," Julie said with a grin. "Especially if a glacier made the lake."

"I expect it scoured out the valley a good deal," I said. "It may have pushed along that pile of rock that forms the natural dam at the south end. All early settlers had to do was plug a few holes, make a spillway, and build a road across it."

Jefferson turned north into the hollow and led us to a spot where a flat-topped rock the size of a school desk sat in the middle of the stream.

"You put that there?" I asked.

He nodded. "Got tired of getting my feet wet. Levered that out of the ground and rolled it from the ridge, then cleared the bank on both sides so I could get a run at it when the creek was up. Took the best part of a day."

"Who'd you borrow the pry bar from?"

"You." He ducked his head and shot me a sheepish grin. "Returned it as quick as I could."

"I never noticed it was gone."

"Didn't think you would. You had three of them in your garage. Don't think you touched them until last spring when you tore down the chimney."

He checked his rifle to make sure the safety was on, then took three long strides, leaped to the rock, and sprang to the other side of the creek.

Julie checked her rifle, then glanced at Nelson. "What about him?"

"He's in and out of the lake every day. Cold water won't hurt him. You go across and I'll nudge him in."

"But the water's so fast." Julie beamed on a pleading expression. "And he only has three legs. What if he gets banged up on the rocks?"

Nelson barked as if to say, "Yeah. What about that?"

"Can't you carry him across?"

Nelson barked again.

"He weighs 35 pounds. Or more. How about he and I stay here?"

"But he wants to come."

"A wise man admits when he's beat," Jefferson called.

With a sigh, I picked Nelson up and slung him over my left shoulder. "You better not wiggle or we're both going in the creek."

He whined and braced himself by digging the claws of his lone hind leg through my shirt and beneath my belt, then gripping my collar in his teeth.

Jefferson backed up a few steps and leaned his rifle against a tree. "Don't stop or you'll lose momentum. I'll steady you when you hit this side."

"*If* I hit that side."

I retreated a dozen steps, studied the approach, and decided this was one of those times when it was better not to think. Keeping my gaze locked on the flat rock in the center of the stream, I broke into a wobbling run, launched myself, hit the rock close to the near side, breast-stroked air with my right arm, took a short step, and leaped again.

My feet hit the lip of the bank and Jefferson gripped my wrist. With force that made my shoulder socket scream for mercy, he swung me to solid ground, leaving Julie space for a far more graceful landing.

"We'll go home the long way," he said as he peeled Nelson from my chest. "Up past where the creek splits there's easier crossing."

"Now you tell me. After I ruin another shirt."

"Camille says you need new shirts anyway," Julie said.

"And she should know," I groused as I fell in line, "she's been wearing them more than I have."

We paralleled the watercourse toward the lake, found the old road again, and followed it for a few minutes. "That's the rock." Jefferson pointed through a shroud of hemlock at a boulder not far from the shore.

It seemed little different from the boulder we'd seen earlier. A little taller and broader. Crusted with more lichen. Pocked with more crevices. I tried to remember if I'd climbed on top when I was a kid, claiming it as Ronny and I did when we came across an old foundation, or an unusually large tree. We'd explored the woods for miles around the lake, but this rock wasn't familiar.

Odd.

And even more odd that I'd never heard the story behind it. Or that Ronny hadn't, either. Because if he had, he would have been intent on finding the rock, feeling the ground, coming here during a thunderstorm to hear the horse whinny, and searching for blood when the storm passed.

Had Mary Lou made up the tale? Was she even now chuckling softly, imagining us tromping through the underbrush?

Julie gazed at the rock through the binoculars she'd brought, took a step toward it, then gripped my arm. "Come on, Uncle Dan, let's check it out."

"Afraid to get up close on your own?"

"No." She fingered the safety on her rifle.

"Bullets won't do any good against what's not of this world." Jefferson's eyes narrowed, his lips set in a grim line.

"You two are trying to freak me out." Julie managed a tight laugh. "Well, it's not working. I'm going to write an extra-credit report about the rock for English class and you're going to take pictures for me. Come on, Nelson."

She plunged off the road into a gully, stepped over a fallen tree, skirted a wide slab of rock leaning against another in an easy slant, and threaded her way between two young oaks. Nelson tipped his head toward me, whined, then followed.

I wondered why she was so intent on coming here. Was it because the girl who died had been about her age? Because she'd been brutalized and controlled? What did Julie hope to accomplish? To inoculate herself with this ancient horror and gain some kind of immunity?

"This story isn't just myth and legend, is it?"

"Never heard it until last night," Jefferson replied, "but I'm not inclined to disbelieve it."

"That's not the same as saying you believe it."

"Don't know *what* I believe about that rock. There's something . . . well, you'll see."

We bushwhacked to it and found Julie standing on the side toward the lake staring at an area clear of vegetation—an area about the size of a grave. "Nothing's growing here."

"Nothing did last year, either," Jefferson said. "Or the year before. It's like that piece of ground is poisoned."

"Maybe somebody does that. Somebody who knows the story comes out here and sprays the ground." Julie forced a squeaky laugh. "For a joke."

"Long way to come for a joke no one will get unless they also come a long way," I observed. "But it's possible." Given what I'd seen of human nature over the past few years, plenty of weird or outlandish things were possible.

Nelson sniffed the edge of the barren area and Julie snatched at his collar and pulled him away. "What if it's not a joke?" Her voice quavered.

I put my arm around her. "Could be lots of reasons nothing grows there. Maybe there's a fungus or a mineral in the soil. See, there are hardly any trees between here and the lake. And most of those are broken or blighted."

"Could be something on the rock," Jefferson said. "Or in it. Water could sluice across it and spill off at that spot."

"There's stuff growing on the other sides, moss and grapevines and pines." She knelt and lowered her hand until it was an inch above the ground. "It's not hot." She swung her hand across the area. "In fact, it feels colder than the ground around it."

"Maybe there's a spring," I suggested.

"The ground's dry."

"Maybe the spring is under a slab of rock and feeds out farther downhill."

Julie made a face, not buying that, and set her rifle on a fallen tree. "I'll lie on the spot so we can tell how big it is and you take a picture."

"No." Jefferson gripped her arm and pulled her away. "You take the pictures. I'll lie next to that spot and Dan will stand by the rock so you can see how tall it is."

I handed over the camera and took a position a foot from the bare spot and another foot away from the rock that loomed nearly twice my height. Gripping his rifle, Jefferson stretched out, teeth clenched. Julie circled, taking shots from several angles.

"Enough." Jefferson lurched to his feet. "Let's go."

"Not yet." Julie pointed to the top of the rock. "Boost me up. I want to see where they found her."

Jefferson sucked in a breath and glanced over his shoulder. Odd behavior for a man who seemed to fear nothing except his own failings. "Getting late."

"It's not even 6:00. There's plenty of light and I'll only be up there for a few minutes." Julie swung the binoculars around so they dangled down her back. "Make a step with your hands."

"Okay." I bent and laced my fingers together. "But be careful you don't fall."

"It's not *that* high."

"It's high enough to hurt you bad if you landed on your head. And look before you stick your fingers in crevices. Watch for snakes and spiders."

"And squirrels with shotguns," Julie taunted. "Or chipmunks with cutlasses."

Having told me off, she stepped into my hands. When I lifted, she felt with fingers and toes for indentations, then swarmed up the rock.

Nelson whined and I patted his head. Part of raising a child, I told myself, is caring but not controlling, laying a foundation of common sense, then letting the child loose—within limits—to take risks and learn lessons. I got that. What I didn't get was how to keep worry from gnawing a hole in my gut. Given that Julie wasn't my child and had been with us for less than a year, I figured my insides would be nothing but scar tissue by the time Chance was her age.

"Hand me the camera." Julie leaned over the edge and stretched. I held the camera high.

"Six inches shy," Jefferson said. "Jump."

"You'd better write a hell of a report and you better get an A+." I gathered the strap so a few inches poked from my grip, bent my knees, and sprang.

"Got it." Julie drew away from the edge.

I stepped back and craned my neck. "You ever been up there?"

Jefferson shook his head. "Never wanted to."

"There's a place where I can hang over the edge of the rock and see the end of our dock through the binoculars," Julie called. "And if I look the other way I can see the top part of the Brocktons' house, the little window in the attic. There's somebody looking out. It's Isaac. I wonder if he can see me."

I felt a jab of annoyance and anger. I didn't like the idea of a stranger watching Julie.

"Oh, he turned away. Now he's gone."

"We should be gone, too."

"Okay, but you know what? This is weird. The hollowed-out place in the top of the rock is bare."

Odd. Concave surfaces accumulated debris. Especially concave surfaces in a forest. "Maybe the snow slid off fast and swept out twigs and needles."

"There's no moss, either." Julie's voice faded, then grew stronger. "And no lichen."

Jefferson tapped his watch and pointed to the trail.

"Let's go," I called. "Ask your brother about that when we get home."

"Okay. I'll climb down myself. There's a tree leaning against the other side. But I'm not calling Justin. He'll say the glacier did it."

"Maybe it did." I headed around to watch her descend. "Maybe the ice sheet dragged that rock along and scoured it."

"And the glacier comes back to keep it clean?" Julie laughed. "You'll have to do better than that, Uncle Dan."

I glanced over my shoulder at Jefferson. "Any ideas?"

"Nothing that doesn't sound like the plot for a movie. There's something here that feels like a magnet for bad energy.

Maybe because of what happened to that girl. Maybe something more."

I halted and turned to face him. "Like what?"

He shrugged. "I don't know. I feel . . ." He stretched his hand toward the rock, but didn't touch it. "I feel something dark. Evil. A long way off, but coming."

I felt a chill. "Evil we'll know, or evil we won't suspect? Like Colden Cornell?"

"I don't know."

"What happens when it gets here?"

"We fight it." He stroked the stock of his rifle. "Any way we can."

Chapter 17

Over the next few days Chance and I worked out an uneasy truce that held while Camille went off to the store for part of each day. If she fed him right before she left and wasn't away much over three hours, and if I rocked or walked with him, he tolerated the situation and didn't resort to full-scale bawling or holding his breath until I was certain he'd never breathe again. As soon as she returned and he filled his belly, he put on a show of smiling and gurgling that made her question my description of how he behaved for me.

In between spurts of baby bonding and helping Justin chip away rotted sills and install new windows, I worked through the list of names and numbers Serenity sent my way, making preliminary contact and asking those I talked with to do what I supposed many of them did every day—take a painful mental excursion into the past. The task took every bit of patience and compassion I could summon and left me as numb and exhausted as I'd been when I spotted Julie's light in the storm.

Sunday morning, while I worked on getting the canoe cleaned and into the water, Camille brought Chance out to the garage. She was wearing a pair of her own sweat pants and a loose cotton blouse and I felt hope that I might soon be reacquainted with my entire wardrobe.

"You're right," she said without preamble. "He won't take milk from the bottle. Even for me."

I restrained myself from saying, "I told you so," or allowing my lips to lift in a smug smile. "He's a smart guy. He wants the real thing or nothing."

She rewarded me with a lingering kiss that promised more. "It's a long way to drive home to nurse him or for you to drive him to the store when I need to stay more than a few hours. And with summer coming, I will."

"I don't mind the drive."

"It's not just the drive, it's the preparation and then waiting to take him home again. That's time you could be spending on those cases."

"It's not like I have a deadline. They've been on hold a long time."

Camille gazed out over the lake. "I know, but I have a feeling . . ." She shook her head and rocked Chance. "Probably wishful thinking. I want *you* to be the one to solve them."

She sat on a lawn chair destined to be pressure washed once I got the canoe in the water. "That's selfish and prideful, isn't it? It shouldn't matter who solves them as long as justice is done, but I guess it's human nature. Like it or not, there's a part of me that wants to feel important, special, a cut above the herd."

I wiped my hands on my jeans. "And if I solve the cases you'll feel that way?"

"Sure. It will show that I made a good choice of a mate, that I selected a man who is as smart as he is strong and handsome and kind and patient."

"Sounds like I'm being buttered up." Leering, I pulled up my T-shirt. "I'm not complicated. If you want to have sex, just say so."

"Not in front of the baby." Camille blushed, shielded Chance against her shoulder, and lowered her voice. "Later. After dinner. When he's asleep."

I yanked my shirt down. My leer morphed into a grin.

Camille shot me a wicked smile. "Maybe you better take a nap. You're going to need a lot of energy."

"No problem. I've been saving up."

"Well, if I don't wear you out, we'll go to baby-minding Plan B tomorrow."

"And that involves . . . ?"

"Leaving him with Pattie or Alda."

"But I thought you had enough of—"

"I had enough of them in my house. But they want to help, they love babies, and they have a knack."

"And I don't?"

"Yes, but not a knack of the same caliber," she said in a diplomatic tone. "And they're so much closer to the store. Much as I try to be rational about it, I don't want him more than five minutes away."

One of the prime mottos of surviving marriage is to step aside if a woman admits to not being rational. "If that's what you want, then let's do it. I'll bond with him in the evenings, after he eats and he's feeling mellow. And I'll change more diapers."

She smiled. "Now who's buttering someone up?"

As it turned out, baby-minding Plan B came at an opportune time because Fred Maddox called that afternoon. He was in Quarry County for his mother's birthday, but was leaving on Tuesday. "I don't know anything I didn't know then, but I'd like to meet you," he told me. "I want to know who has the case now, who's looking out for my Theresa."

He said that last as if she were still alive, said it in a hollow voice that echoed in my mind long after I agreed to meet him the next morning. He suggested a bakery in a town on the far side of Quarry County where he contended the coffee was slightly more passable than the muffins.

True to her word, Camille tested my endurance that evening, but I dragged myself out of bed at dawn, showered, shaved twice, and put on my newest pair of jeans, a gray blazer, and a crisp white shirt with the collar unbuttoned.

"No tie?" Julie asked when I poured a cup of coffee for the road.

"And what about slacks?" Camille chimed in. "Or your black suit?"

I felt like a kid on the first day of school, a kid who wasn't passing inspection. "I'm trying to look competent, not like I'm there to check his tax returns."

"You know best," Camille said in a tone that implied I didn't.

I snapped the lid on the insulated cup, folded a piece of wheat toast into a square small enough to fit in my mouth, scooped up the satchel with the Gilligan file, and made my escape.

Quarry County lay to the west of Ashokan County and the two-lane road over, around, and through the mountains twisted on itself often enough to make me wonder if I was coming or going. Not a road I'd want to take in a storm or in pursuit of a suspect or with a baby on board.

Picking out Fred Maddox in the bakery required no great powers of deduction. He had a few years on me and the squint of a man who spends his days gazing across open water into a low sun. A tan line above his eyebrows indicated he wore a hat much of the time, and his hands were nicked and gouged by hooks and knives and maybe even teeth.

He was also the only man in the place.

"Apple muffins are edible," he said after we shook. "Tell Alice to heat one up, butter it, and put it on my tab along with your coffee."

"I'll—"

He raised a hand to cut me off. "Alice is my cousin. I get a deep discount. And I promise not to turn you in for taking a bribe."

"Fair enough." I set my satchel on a chair and headed for the display case.

"I heard him." Alice tucked a strand of graying hair into her topknot and shoved a thick sand-colored mug filled with coffee across the top of the case. She pointed to a small table where cream and milk containers clustered around a bowl filled with packets of sugar and sweetener. "Edible, my ass. The muffins are damn good. I made them myself. Taste-tested them, too."

Before I could respond, she laughed. "Freddy and I have been teasing each other all our lives. Don't know what I'd do if he didn't turn up once a year to top off the insult tank. I'll bring your muffin when it's hot."

I thanked her, sloshed milk into my coffee, and returned to the table.

Fred Maddox nodded toward the satchel. "Her file in there?"

"Yes."

"Doesn't look like there's much."

"There isn't." I sipped coffee, strong and rich, far better than he'd led me to expect. That boded well for the muffin.

"Didn't expect there would be. I'm not faulting Jonah Umhey. He chased down every lead, even followed up on all the kooks who called in about space aliens and cults. He worked it hard and he never let it go, even when he retired."

"He still hasn't."

"I heard he's dying."

"Lung cancer."

"How long's he got?"

"End of the summer."

Alice set a carafe of coffee on the table and slid a plate in front of me. Two muffins, oozing melted butter, steamed with the scents of cinnamon and apples. She patted my cheek. "You look like my kind of man, one with an appetite."

"Go fill your creampuffs." Fred topped off his mug. "You'll be flirting with the undertaker when he screws the lid on your coffin."

"Won't be able to help myself." Alice chuckled as she returned to the counter. "He's a fine-looking man."

"He's also her husband. They've been together forever." Fred's voice thickened and cracked. "I'm happy for her. I am. But I wish . . ."

He stared into his coffee.

I did the same, thinking of the losses in my life and the people I wished with me still—Lisa Miller, Clarence Wolven, my mother, and even Willie Dean Denton. Then I thought about the ones I hoped wouldn't return—Colden Cornell, Ronny Miller, Louisa Marie Van Valkenberg, and my father. Finally I thought of those I once wished to have with me, but no longer did. My first wife, Susanna, was one of those. I'd thought the love we shared was deep and pure, but discovered it was mainly a figment of my need and desire. She and my brother were together now. He was the one who couldn't go on without her and who proved it with a bullet to his brain. They had their forever, side by side in the Hemlock Lake cemetery. And I had

Camille and a love that was—more than anything else—real. And realistic.

Fred raised his mug, sipped, and lowered it to the table again. "We weren't going to get married until the fall or even later, depending on the kind of wedding she settled on and what was available for the party, but she was full of plans. Every day she wrote a long letter—I got them in clumps because we didn't get mail delivered often. They started off about the same, with something about the weather or work or a movie or advice her girlfriends gave her. And then she'd have something about our wedding. Big stuff like ideas about her wedding dress and how many bridesmaids she'd have and where we'd hold the ceremony and what we'd say to each other and where we'd go on the honeymoon. Small stuff like the color of the invitations and flowers and napkins and what friends and co-workers thought."

He sipped coffee, lines creasing his forehead. "To tell the truth, I kind of skimmed them. I'm not much of a reader, and she wrote so much—other guys would get one a week, just a few pages. And the wedding details didn't matter to me. I wanted her to have it all her way."

His hands curled into fists and he pressed them against the sides of his head. "After she died I couldn't look at those letters without feeling the hole in my heart. But I couldn't throw them away either."

I did a mental review of the file on Theresa Gilligan, but recalled no mention of correspondence. Those letters were a potential gold mine of information about her character, activities, acquaintances, and whether her path crossed that of Genevieve Graham.

I gave Fred Maddox another moment, then asked, "Did you ever tell Jonah Umhey about those letters?"

"No, I don't think I did." He reached for his coffee, then slapped his hands on the table. "Damn it. I should have. There might—"

"And there might not. Don't beat up on yourself."

"Right." He flexed his fingers. "Right. And even if . . . It's been 20 years."

"I'd like to see those letters."

"There must be 200 of them."

"That's okay."

"I could look through and send the ones—"

"I'd like to have all of them. And as soon as possible."

He thought for a few seconds. "You're the expert."

If only.

"I'll be a week in Wyoming, but I'll ship them out as soon as I get back. Well, as soon as I clear a day to get up to Sitka. Used to live there and never emptied out the storage unit."

I dug a business card from the satchel and printed my Hemlock Lake address on the back. "Send them here instead of the sheriff's office. I'll get them quicker."

"Will do." He pocketed the card. "I shouldn't hope, should I?"

"A little hope can't hurt. Just don't believe."

Chapter 18

In an attempt to ignore the itch to get hold of those letters, I decided to work the cases from the other end, backward from Micah Thielman. His file was thin and, although all the correct steps had been taken, I could almost feel the lack of commitment behind the written reports. There had been no signs of suicide or foul play and Micah was no longer a child. He was old enough to disappear if he wanted to. He'd driven off, headed for a math class at a community college ten miles away. Neither he nor his car had turned up.

I'd made a preliminary call to his mother and given her my canned speech about looking into the case along with investigators in Buckingham County and hoping she'd phone if she thought of anything she hadn't mentioned before. Next to Margaret Thielman's name I'd written the words "vague, depressed, needy" and "husband dead for a decade" and "talks in circles." I'd expected to hear from her at least once—not because she had new information, but because she wanted to talk about her son. I was surprised she hadn't called.

That bothered me.

It could be the dog that didn't bark in the night.

Or it could be nothing.

Preparing myself for a long and meandering conversation, I sharpened two pencils, found a doodle pad, got a fresh cup of coffee, and dialed. Jennifer Thielman, Micah's sister, answered. "Mom's upstairs," she said after I introduced myself, "cleaning Micah's room. She does it every day. She'll be finished in an hour or so if you want to call back."

She passed that along in a sad but matter-of-fact voice, then asked, "Can I help you?" She paused for a second before rushing on in a whisper. "The thing is, well, Mom's in denial about Micah. She always has been."

My fingers tightened on the handle of my mug. "What do you mean?"

"I mean . . . Can I meet you someplace? Someplace not here? Tomorrow's a light day at college. I'm free after 11:00."

"Name the time and place. I'll be there."

She named a diner in Buckingham County and said 12:30 would be good. I said lunch was on me and she said if I got there early I should order a vanilla malted milkshake with extra malt and a grilled cheese and tomato sandwich on sourdough, with fries, a side of slaw, and a slice of pickle. Before she disconnected, she told me I'd know her by her hair.

The waitress was setting my coffee and a tall shake on the table when a slender girl with spiky pink hair and a diamond stud in her nose slid into the booth across from me. She wore a glittery tank top that revealed the tattoo of a parrot on her left shoulder and a vine twining around her right arm.

I caught myself thinking like a father, hoping Julie never announced she "had to have" a nose piercing or a tattoo the size of that parrot. "Jennifer?"

"That's me." She shucked the paper wrapper, plunged her straw into the milkshake, and sucked. "Yum. Lots of malt. They must think you're a big tipper."

"I am."

"Good. I hate cheap people. Waitresses work hard and the pay is crappy." She smiled, her bright blue eyes sparkling beneath eyelids smeared with fuchsia shadow. "Maybe she'll bring *two* slices of pickle."

"I'll get a side order of dills if you like."

"Nah." She sucked at her shake again. "I'll need a doggie bag as it is."

The waitress, a middle-aged woman with faded red hair and a pained smile, returned with two oval platters. My burger sat on an oversized bun and came with lettuce, tomatoes, pickles, onions, and enough fries to make me doubt there were more than three potatoes left in Idaho. "I may need a bag myself."

"Sometimes I wonder how this place stays in business." Jennifer nibbled at cheese melting from between thick slices of bread. "They give you so much food for not much money."

I saw no point in a discussion of sales volume, loss leaders, overhead costs, customer goodwill, or possible money laundering.

She ate the pickle slice first, then opened one half of her sandwich, forked on slaw, and bit into it as if she was intent on building up a layer of fat to survive a famine. After licking her fingers and using two napkins plucked from a silver container, she salted her fries and went to work on them, easing each one from the stack as if she were involved in a game of pick-up sticks. Meanwhile, I devoted myself to the burger. It was as good as any I ever had, and I ate until my stomach cried out for mercy and ordered my mouth to stop sending food down the pipe.

"So . . ." Jennifer shoved her plate to the side. "My brother." She stirred her shake, shifted on the red plastic bench, and rested her hands on the table. The nails were ragged and chewed to the quick. "My brother was different."

Past tense. Why? And how would a girl with pink hair define "different"? "In what way?"

"Different as in not like most other guys. Not like my father would have wanted or my mother hoped he would be. Micah was too sensitive. Too soft and quiet and sweet."

Was she trying to tell me Micah was gay? Why not come out and say it? Was she in denial? Or was she used to skirting the issue because her mother did?

She gnawed at the nail on her right thumb. "He didn't fit in at high school. Or much of anywhere. He was unhappy and Mom wasn't helping. That's why I got inked and dyed my hair."

I waited a beat, but she didn't elaborate. "I don't understand."

"To take the pressure off him. If Mom wore herself out lecturing me, she wouldn't pick at him so much." She shrugged and the parrot tattoo seemed to fluff green feathers. "I didn't mind the lectures or being grounded. It gave me an excuse to stay in my room and read."

She folded the paper from her straw in half and in half again. "I don't have to get done up like this now that he's gone, but it makes me feel close to him."

"Where do you think Micah is?"

"Dead." She dropped the straw and bit off a chunk of cuticle, drawing blood. "Mom cleans his room every day and prays for him an hour every evening and keeps his favorite foods in the freezer. I think she does that half in penance because she knows picking and poking at him was wrong, and half because it lets her believe he's coming home. But I think he's dead."

"Why?"

"Because he loved me. And he loved Mom. He knew she'd go crazy and fall apart if he left because that's what happened when Dad died. It was years before she got it sort of together again. If Micah scraped up the courage to get away, he would have had the courage to let us know he was going and he would have helped her get used to the idea. And he would have called her every day."

Maybe. Or maybe, he just ran. Then, having gotten out from under a crushing burden of expectation and guilt, he wanted time to decide he wasn't a failure, time to rebuild his strength, define himself. Having felt the freedom of being on my own when I left Hemlock Lake for college, I understood the desire to delay a return—perhaps permanently. Unlike me, Micah Thielman had taken nothing with him except his car and what he was wearing—a pair of black loafers, gray slacks, a pale yellow shirt with a button-down collar, and a black sweater. Was that symbolic? Had he meant to make a statement that he wanted nothing more from the life he'd lived up until that day? "When did you see him last?"

She studied her bleeding thumb as if it belonged to someone else. "It must have been at breakfast the last day he was home. He was in college and I was finishing high school, so we had different schedules, but we always got up early so we could have breakfast together. Mom doesn't cook anymore and mostly I have to remind her to eat and lots of times she doesn't. But then she always made breakfast for us and she always made way too much—pancakes and eggs and sausage or waffles and fruit or fried potatoes with bacon and cheese. Micah said it was how she showed she loved us, and we should show her we got it by cleaning our plates and sometimes asking for seconds."

"He sounds like he was a good son. And a good brother." Not the kind who would leave his mother to grieve, leave his sister to watch her death spiral.

"He was the best." She rubbed at her eyes, smearing mascara. "I miss him so much. I loved him the way he was. I wish he could have been happy being himself instead of trying so hard to understand why he was different and why some people thought he should change."

"Change in what way?"

"Be normal." She drew air quotation marks. "Find a nice girl and get a good job and make Mom happy. That's why he was going to counseling."

I couldn't recall anything about counseling in the file. "Do you know who he was seeing?"

"No. A guy he met somewhere. Maybe through his job at the college. He worked in the registration office." She dipped a fresh napkin in her water glass and scrubbed at the skin below her eyes, feathering smeared mascara onto her cheeks. "I guess it wasn't really counseling—the guy had issues of his own. They'd have coffee and talk."

Talk about going away together? "Do you know his name? Or where they met?"

"Micah never told me. And I never asked—partly because I respected his privacy, but mostly because what I didn't know Mom couldn't try to nag out of me."

She crumpled the napkin and tossed it aside. "Mom can't help being like she is. It's not because of religion. She stopped going to church after Dad died. It's because of how she was brought up and because it's what Dad might have wanted and because she thought Micah would have been happier if . . ."

She shook her head. "I gotta go." She waved to the waitress and pointed to her plate. "Thanks for lunch. Don't forget that giant tip."

"I won't. Thanks for talking with me."

"Too bad I wasn't any help."

"You never know." I handed her my card. "Talking about Micah might have joggled something loose deep in your mind."

"If it floats to the surface, I'll call you."

"Any time. Day or night."

As I drove away, I wondered why the Micah Thielman case had tugged at me from the first moment I heard his name, why I thought he'd been killed. Had the man he met with been toying with him, setting him up for murder?

Or was I wrong? Had their relationship been about life instead of death? Had he and the man he met to commiserate with become lovers and run off together? If that was the case, how well had he covered his tracks? Could a deeper and wider computer search locate him?

Having no doubt I'd find Serenity Brook in her basement lair, I stopped by the sheriff's office on the way home. She saluted me with a carrot the length and circumference of her forearm. "Doctor told me I need more of something that isn't salted or processed. Figured if I eat one of these every day, it should do the trick."

"Sure. What's that old saying? A carrot a day—"

"And you'd rather eat hay." She tossed the carrot into a drawer where it landed on top of a bag of corn chips. "Those are the reward for choking down the carrot."

"Whatever you say. Find anything new on Micah Thielman?"

"Not a thing. You think he's alive?"

"Nope. I'm 75% convinced he's dead."

"Ooooh. A percentage. I thought you didn't do math."

"Only on Tuesdays. Anything turn up on Vernon, Arnold, or Yount?"

"Did you bring me new data?"

"No, but you said you'd check with your friends for fresh ideas on where to look."

"Did I send you an e-mail?"

"No."

"Then that's your answer."

"You're taking crustiness to new levels today."

"Talk to the carrot," she snarled. "I'm not listening."

Chapter 19

When I got home, Camille was in the kitchen feeding Chance while Julie made macaroni salad and bubbled with news. "I got an A+ on my project on that rock. And someone messed up in chemistry lab and the custodians had to bring in a bunch of fans. And there's chicken *and* pork chops for you to grill. And Nelson and I went out on the lake in the canoe and guess what?"

"The canoe sank and Nelson rescued you and towed you to shore and gave you mouth-to-mouth?"

"Yuck."

I winked at Camille and snagged a beer from the refrigerator. "A monster rose from the waves, stomped on the canoe, and went off to terrorize Tokyo?"

Ignoring her "get real" expression, I scratched Nelson's head, popped the beer, and sat beside Camille. "A snapping turtle attached itself to your paddle and you brought it home and it's in the laundry sink?"

Camille snickered. Chance burped. Julie blew a raspberry. "You are the worst guesser in the history of the world."

I stroked Chance's downy head. "And yet you keep asking."

"Apparently she doesn't get enough aggravation from everyday life." Camille pointed to the stove. "Like that pot of macaroni that's about to boil over."

"Eeek." Julie lowered the heat and stirred the frothing pot. "Just in time."

"Just in time is still a good time." Camille smiled. "When I was a kid we had a neighbor who yelled that when she saw me running for the school bus."

"Were you late a lot?" Julie asked.

"Every other day." Camille patted her springy hair. "Trying to get my hair to lie down and look like everybody else's. Trying to fit in."

"I'm glad you gave up on that." I kissed her ear.

"Because you like me the way I am?"

"No, because you'd spend half the day in front of a mirror and I'd never get in the bathroom."

"You're a guy." Julie carried the pot to the sink and poured steaming macaroni into the colander. "You can go out in the woods."

"And when he's older," Camille said, "you can take Chance with you. Maybe that's what we'll do instead of toilet training."

"Tree training." Julie dumped the macaroni into a bowl of chopped vegetables. "You can teach him the names of the trees while he's watering them."

"Ha. Ha. Ha. How long before you go off to college?"

"Another year." She glopped on mayonnaise dressing. "And three months."

"Let's not think about it until we're down to those three months," Camille said. "I can't imagine what a day would be like without you here."

"Quieter?" I suggested.

"He meant quiet as in dull," Camille corrected. "Now tell us what happened on the lake."

"Okay, so Nelson and I went out in the canoe and I put on my life jacket and took an extra paddle and my phone in case Camille needed me." She set the pot in the sink and attacked it with a scrubber. "And I paddled way over so I could look through the binoculars and check if there's a spring that feeds into the lake that would make the ground so cold by the rock."

My hand tightened on the beer bottle. "You didn't go to the rock, did you?"

"No." She halted her assault on the ring left by the cooking macaroni. "I didn't want to admit it when we were out there, but that place creeped me out. I told Justin I'd take him, but I wouldn't go there alone."

I let out air in a silent sigh.

"Anyway, I didn't see a spring and Nelson was getting whiny and sticking his head over the side and I was afraid he'd jump, so I started home, and that's when I met Isaac Falton."

"The boy from across the lake?" Camille asked.

"Yeah. Only he's kind of not a boy because he's about as old as Justin. And he's growing a beard but it's all scraggly. And he's tall, but real skinny and not very strong." She laughed. "Or coordinated. He couldn't keep his rowboat straight or go very fast and he dropped an oar and I got it for him."

I let out another silent sigh. Isaac Falton was interesting because he was new. But to Julie, raised among strong and muscular men who grew thick beards and could pull an oar equally hard with either hand, Isaac Falton might not have the right stuff for a summer romance.

I wanted Julie to date and experience young love. But I wanted . . . well, I wanted her to find a boy who wasn't the son of a bombastic preacher and whose mother didn't appear to be afraid of the man she married.

"And he can't swim, but he wasn't wearing a life jacket." Julie rinsed the pot and upended it in the dish drainer. "So I told him he should even if he was a good swimmer and he said he didn't have one and I told him we had a bunch of extras and I could maybe loan him one but he said he didn't want one because if he drowned nobody would care, not even him."

Camille's gaze locked on mine for a second, her eyes flashing concern. Then she turned to Julie. "How do you feel about that?"

"Well, kind of sad. He seemed really depressed and maybe he meant it or thought he did. Sometimes kids at school say stuff like that." Julie wedged the macaroni salad into the refrigerator. "And mostly it's drama. But you can't always tell, can you?"

"No," Camille said. "Sometimes it's a cry for attention and sometimes it's a cry for help. And sometimes there's nothing you can do to change their thinking *or* their plans."

She didn't look at me, but I knew she was recalling the night she found me drunk, sucking on the barrel of a gun, moments from pulling the trigger. Her rational objections to my intention to follow my brother to hell and seek vengeance transferred my anger to her. And that saved my life.

I doubted anything or anyone could have stopped my brother from killing himself. Nat made his plan and followed through within moments of losing the woman he loved—the woman I was married to.

"In our health class we learned that when we hear kids talk that way we should tell the school nurse or a teacher." Julie sat on the other side of Camille and ran a finger along Chance's toes. "But Isaac's not in school."

"I'll talk with his mother," Camille said. "Next time I see her in the store."

I recalled Hannah Falton's statement the first time we met: "We never ask for help. We pray for guidance." I doubted Camille would get more than a blank stare or a cold shoulder, but often she made progress where it appeared none was possible. No point in discouraging her from the attempt.

The next morning, after unloading the dishwasher, catching up on the laundry, and shoving the vacuum cleaner around the living room, I set aside the files for Theresa Gilligan and Micah Thielman and spread the others on the kitchen table. Yount, Vernon, and Arnold had disappeared and Serenity was casting a net in cyberspace to see what she could find. Graham's case was not only cold, it was frozen solid, but it *was* a clear homicide. And so was that of Franklin Turner.

I flipped a coin.

It came up Graham.

I poured a fresh cup of coffee, opened the file, and considered the next round of calls. That didn't take long. Graham's parents, ex-husband, and former in-laws were dead. That left a vitriolic sister-in-law who, when I made my first round of calls, had implied Genevieve's death was no loss and advised me not to bother her again. So, I was down to Genevieve's children, teenagers then, and now in their 30s. Chuck Graham was in Arkansas working on a drilling rig. His phone message told me he'd gone fishing and would return calls after he caught his limit. Helene Graham, now Helene Cooper, managed a specialty grocery store in Ashokan City.

"I've thought about it since you called before," she told me. "But I can't remember anything I didn't tell the first detectives or Mr. Pallister. I wish I could, but it's like there's a black hole in my head. Every time I go over the day Mom died it seems there's less I remember. And less I'm sure about."

"I understand. It's been a long time and you were only 15 then."

"Sixteen. Barely."

An age when most girls paid more attention to boys and fashion and TV shows than to their mothers' friends or feelings. Still . . . "If you're willing, I'd like to take one more run at this. I could buy you lunch. Or dinner."

"I'm on a diet. Lunch is six celery sticks and a quarter of a cup of tofu salad. Followed by a three-mile walk."

"We could talk while you walk."

"All right. But you'll be wasting your time."

"Won't be a waste if I'm burning calories."

She laughed. "Be here at 12:45."

I tightened the laces on my running shoes and rounded up a spare T-shirt, water bottle, and ball cap. I thought about taking along a recorder, but decided that might make her feel pressured and have a negative effect. If a more casual conversation turned up something I recognized as a clue, I'd remember it.

The store stood on a corner at the edge of the oldest part of Ashokan City. The small lot was full and I wasn't fool enough to hunt for space on the narrow streets within the original boundaries of the county seat—not when there was a hospital parking garage a few blocks the other way. Others apparently had the same idea because I hit the top level before I found a spot, then jogged to make my appointment.

If Helene Cooper carried excess body weight, I couldn't see it. Short brown hair framed a pixie face that, coupled with her jeans and an official store T-shirt, made her seem far younger than 36.

Genetics. Her mother had also appeared younger than her years.

"Thanks for being on time." She tipped a thumb up to a white-haired man with a red bow tie. "Back in an hour, Henry. Don't worry about the asparagus. I'll take care of it."

Henry adopted the panicked look of a possum on a freeway, then nodded hard enough to loosen a few molars. I doubted he'd given any thought to the asparagus before Helene mentioned it.

When we turned the corner, she confirmed my suspicions. "Henry's a sweetheart and older women are wild about him. That's a good chunk of our customer base. If I take up the slack and keep him on, he keeps them coming in."

Setting a brisk pace, she led me along a sidewalk of bluestone slabs that might have come from the quarries above Hemlock Lake. Every year I read about a citizens' committee lobbying for funds to remove roots or add sand to level the slabs. Every year that story was followed by another about a second citizens' committee lobbying to keep the tilted slabs as they were because they added to the charm of the old part of the city.

"I guess I could walk on the track by the high school," Helene said. "But these sidewalks make it more challenging. And I like to think about people who walked here over the years—where they were coming from and going to."

"And why," I added.

"I hadn't thought about that. But I guess you ask the question all the time. Because of your job."

Or maybe I'd wound up with the job *because* I asked that question.

She opened an iron gate and led me along a walkway that cut through a cemetery beside a massive stone church. Gravestones—some leaning, a few fallen, all worn—crowded beneath ancient trees and up to the walls of the church.

"Mom's buried over near Rhinebeck," Helene said. "That's where Grandma and Grandpa wanted her because that's where they planned to be—where they are now."

"Pretty town," I said.

"Yes." She opened the gate on the opposite side of the cemetery and we trucked through what I always thought of as the legal district—sloping, twisting streets around the courthouse, lined with houses set right up against the sidewalk, their doors adorned with brass numbers and plaques with attorneys' names. "I guess Mom would have wanted to be with her parents. But I don't know for sure."

"Most mothers don't discuss funeral arrangements with their teenage children unless they know they don't have long to live."

She kicked at a dandelion sprouting between slabs of stone. "I wish I had it to do over. I wish I'd paid more attention." She slowed and walked backwards. "I bet you hear that all the time."

"Pretty much. I've said it myself more times than I can count."

She nodded. "I read the stories in the paper from last summer, and the summer before. The stories about you and those killers."

My turn to nod.

She gazed into my eyes for the time it took to take three more steps, then turned and picked up the pace. "After the divorce, Chuck and I stayed with Mom during the week and with Dad on weekends. So for a couple of years I have no idea what she did on Saturday and Sunday or who she did it with. But the last few weeks before she was killed Chuck and Dad had been all about squirrel hunting and stalking wild turkeys so they'd know their habits when the season opened. Are you a hunter?"

"No."

"I don't object, as long as hunters eat what they shoot—and Dad and Chuck always did. But even then I didn't have a taste for meat, and now I don't eat anything with a face. So, after I whined a bunch and made enough noise in the woods to scare off any creature within a mile, Dad let me stay with Mom if they were headed into the hills."

We reached a corner where slabs of stone gave way to a concrete sidewalk that sloped to the river. A breeze rising from the water brought the scent of life and death, rotting wood and green growth. "Like I said, though, I didn't pay much attention and I spent a lot of time in my room on the phone with friends."

"Would there have been issues if she was seeing anyone?"

"If you mean would Dad have been angry, then no. He and Mom were friends. I think they'd always been friends—but they didn't set off sparks against each other. Does that make sense?"

"Yes."

"I don't know if she was trying to meet someone. I do know she didn't go out in the evening—not on dates, anyway. Sometimes she had choir practice."

I didn't remember mention of that in Genevieve Graham's file, didn't recall interviews with anyone involved with a church or choir. "What church did she go to?"

Helene shrugged. "I don't know. She went real early on Sunday morning and she didn't push me to get up and go with her."

"Methodist? Presbyterian?"

"I don't know." She leaped across a metal delivery door set in the sidewalk outside a tavern. "We never went to church when she and Dad were together, so she must have started going after the divorce. But, like I said, we were with Dad on weekends and—" She smacked a parking meter with the flat of her hand. "I wish I could remember more."

"You're doing great. When she went out to choir practice, did she drive, or did someone pick her up?"

"She drove."

"How long was she gone?"

"A couple of hours."

If choir practice ran a set time and if she didn't linger afterward or stop on the way back to pick up a quart of milk, or drive a friend home, that might help me figure out where the church was. But I'd need more than a vague sense of how long she was gone. I tried another approach. "Did you ever hear her singing? Singing hymns?"

Helene shook her head. "No. Sometimes she sang along with the radio, but I never heard her sing anything that sounded like a hymn."

When I was growing up, Rachel Miller, Julie's grandmother, sang in the church choir. Most every morning she'd warm up with scales, in the afternoon she'd sing show tunes, and in the evening she'd sit on the porch and sing hymns while she mended clothes or shucked peas. Singing lit her with joy. But perhaps Genevieve Graham didn't have the same experience. Perhaps she sang for companionship or because she'd been asked and felt obliged.

At any rate, identifying a particular hymn and then linking it to a specific church was a long shot. I took another tack. "Was the phone in your house working the day your mother died?"

"Yes. Grandma called while Mom was making dinner. And after dinner the phone rang, but it was a wrong number. And then I called a friend. I was talking to her when Mom told me she was going out."

"To choir practice?"

"She didn't say."

We crossed the street that ran beside the river and Helene picked up the pace, putting a couple of yards between us as we strode through a long and narrow park. Was she wishing she'd never agreed to speak with me? "Halfway point," she said.

We emerged from the park and faced another long hill. I sucked in a few deep breaths and closed the distance.

Genevieve Graham had driven past two other phone booths before she picked one next to a gas station closed for the night. The gas station faced a side street; traffic on the main drag had no view of the booth. That told me she wanted privacy.

She'd spread change on the shelf and lifted the phone from its cradle. Shotgun pellets tore into her before she dialed even one number. Either she'd never closed the door and triggered the dome light, or the killer opened it and shot her in the dark.

Her fingerprints weren't on the phone book, so Harry Pallister assumed she knew the number she intended to call. From the amount of change, he theorized the number was long distance. But what if she'd dug the coins from a pocket and spread them out to find the ones she needed? What if she intended to call someone who lived close? Someone she didn't want others to know about? A lover? Someone she hoped might become a lover?

But why hide the relationship? Was he married?

"Have you ever wondered why she went to a phone booth?"

"Only every day." She kicked a crumpled aluminum can to the gutter. "Maybe if I hadn't been hogging the phone, she wouldn't have—"

"It's not your fault. Think about the way things were before that night. If you were on the phone and she wanted to use it, what did she do?"

Helene stopped and faced me, her eyes widening. "She gave me a sign. Like a referee." She made a time-out sign with her hands. "Like this."

"But that night she didn't."

"No."

"When that wrong number call came after dinner, who answered?"

"Mom. We were doing the dishes and I reached for the phone on the wall in the kitchen and Mom said she'd get it."

Helene frowned. "And she said 'Hello' and listened for a minute and then . . . And then she didn't say, 'You have a wrong number.' She said something like 'No. Not at all. It's all right. Yes.'"

Helene gazed off across the river. "You know, I asked her why she said that. She told me the person on the other end realized right away it was a wrong number and kept apologizing and she didn't know what to say because usually people insisted they didn't misdial and didn't say they were sorry."

Had that person asked Genevieve if she was alone, asked if she could call back from a phone booth?

Helene checked her watch, faced the slope again, and hit it double time. "I'm running late. Can't leave Henry too long or he takes it upon himself to make decisions—not always good ones. Did . . . Do you think this was any help?"

Leery of offering false hope, I gave her a string of vague phrases peppered with the words "we'll have to see."

Chapter 20

Wesley Falton held his first revival Saturday evening. Although everyone claimed to have no interest, almost everyone found an excuse to be in the vicinity as the huge tent went up.

My excuse was that Julie wanted more practice parallel parking before she tackled her driver's test. We cruised downtown Hemlock Lake—all six blocks of it—sliding the SUV among the few cars parked on the street. That accomplished, we headed up the hill to the cemetery to practice three-point turns.

"I thought the tent would be white," she said as we passed the crew spreading canvas on the newly mowed field.

"It probably was when it was new." Now it was splotched with mildew and stained by leaves that had lain on it too long. The corners were mended with brown and green patches and the seams on top treated with a yellow substance.

"It will look better after dark." Julie stopped and crimped the wheel. "When they plug in the twinkle lights and light the candles."

"How do you know they'll do that?"

She eased the front wheels to the edge of the gravel. "Isaac told me."

I felt a prickle of concern at the back of my brain. "When you met him out on the lake the other day?"

"No, when he came to the clubhouse yesterday."

The clubhouse was the old school building. Once Mary Lou had intended it to become a museum, but last year when a serial killer picked off teenage girls, she turned it into a gathering place for kids, a place of safety in numbers. Colden Cornell was gone now, but kids still used the building to study, play games, or hang out.

"Isaac's mother got his father to say it's okay, so he's going to work for Justin." Julie spun the wheel the other way and backed up, working the clutch like a pro. "Two days a week. More if Justin needs him."

I had reservations, but vowed to stay out of the mix. If Isaac worked out, great. And if he didn't, Justin would learn a lesson in hiring and firing.

"Isaac's excited. It's his first job ever. He's gonna save up to buy a car." Julie completed the turn. "But he has to give a lot of his money to his parents, so I'll have mine first."

"Got one picked out?"

"Not yet, but Jefferson and Freeman and Evan and Stub are checking the ads on the Internet and in a bunch of papers." She stopped at the bottom of the hill and peered both ways along the main road. "They want to come along to make the deal when we find the right car."

I grinned, pitying the owner or used-car-lot salesman who found himself dealing with her posse of honorary uncles.

Smooth and steady, Julie pulled out and accelerated. "I told them I'd have to check with you first because I didn't want to hurt your feelings if you wanted to be the one to do that."

"I'd love to go with you." I tousled her hair. "But it sounds like those guys have a lot of time invested in this project and I'd hate to see them disappointed."

She thought about that as we rolled across the dam and pulled behind the store. "Okay, but what if Alda and Pattie and Mary Lou and Marcella want to come, too? We'll have to charter a bus."

"How about one of those stretch limousines? Camille and Chance and Nelson won't want to miss out."

Julie giggled. "And Justin and Dither."

"Right. And the guys who deliver to the store. And the deputies who patrol up here. And Sheriff North."

Her giggle morphed to a series of snorts, then rose to a gasping shriek and gave way to hiccups.

Take that, Isaac. Unless you can make her laugh, you'll never be her number-one guy.

When twilight seeped from the hollows and ribbons of mist twined on the lake, Camille and I wandered out to the dock, listening for faint snatches of song carried on the wind.

"You'd think that all the years I lived in the South I would have been to a tent meeting," Camille said. "For curiosity's sake if for no other reason."

"You could go now. I'll go with you," Julie offered.

To see what went on under the tent? Or to see Isaac?

Camille gave me the old we-need-to-talk-later glance. "All right. Let's all take a spin. You need a little more night-driving experience anyway."

"Yay!" Julie darted into the house. "I gotta change my clothes. Be there in a minute."

"More like half an hour," I groused. "She must change her clothes three times a day."

"That's what teenage girls do. Why don't you change your son's diaper while you're waiting?"

It's a wise man who knows that what might appear to be a suggestion offered in a soft, sweet voice should be treated as an order barked by a drill sergeant. Proud of myself for placing my hands in the right position, I lifted Chance from his blanket on the swing, carried him to the changing table in our bedroom, and went to work.

And so did he, sending out a stream that hit my Adam's apple and splashed my T-shirt.

Camille chuckled. "*Now* who has to change his clothes?"

Mopping up with a handful of wipes, I mumbled about conspiracies and told Chance that in the not-so-distant future I expected more male solidarity.

"He's smiling." Camille passed me a fresh diaper. "He thinks you're funny."

"He has gas," I informed her. "What he thinks is that you should burp him while I put on a fresh shirt."

Thirty minutes later we rolled into town along a road narrowed by cars and trucks parked on both sides. Stub, clad in an orange vest and wearing a helmet with a light attached to the front, stood on the main road, directing traffic. "Back up and park behind the garage," he shouted. "I saved a space."

"How did he know we were coming?" Julie asked.

"It's a major event in a small town," Camille told her. "Everybody's coming."

In fact, everybody was already there, clustered in groups under the budding branches of trees surrounding the field, close enough to see and hear, far enough away to make it clear they were spectators, not participants. And, perhaps, far enough so they wouldn't be affected by Wesley Falton's magnetism.

Dozens of people sat on camp chairs facing a raised platform and a tall pulpit painted silver. The canopy glowed, stains and mended spots barely visible in the soft light of candles and the twinkle of tiny white bulbs strung from tent pole to tent pole.

"It's so pretty," Julie breathed. "Like starlight on the grass."

Camille shot me another let's-talk-later glance. "I suppose it's symbolic of salvation. The light in the darkness. The star that leads the way."

The image in my mind wasn't that of wise men making their way to Bethlehem, but of moths drawn to a flame.

"There's Isaac." Julie pointed to the tall boy moving among those beneath the canopy, indicating open spots for chairs and passing out papers. Hannah Falton, a bucket clutched in both hands and a smile glued in place, bobbed along behind him, accepting contributions. Wesley Falton, I suspected, was inside a small tent off to one side. I assumed he timed his entrance, letting his audience anticipate, letting his wife and son take care of the mundane work of organizing and collecting coins and bills.

Julie tucked her hair behind her ears, then pulled it loose. "I'm gonna go say hi."

"He looks busy," Camille said. "Maybe you should wait."

Until the last day of never.

I bent to check my shoelace so Julie wouldn't see aversion written on my face.

"Okay." Julie tugged the zipper of her jacket up and down for a few seconds while she scanned the crowd. "There's Justin. With Jefferson and Mary Lou."

Camille sighed as Julie darted off. "We need to talk."

"About Isaac? You bet. The sooner the better."

"Not that I'm worried she'll rush into anything," she said as we strolled along behind Julie, "but we need to be on the same page. And careful not to say anything to make her want to prove we're wrong."

"Right. Same page. Careful. Got it."

"I hope so, because we could be walking an emotional tightrope. Without a safety net."

"Do I get to wear spangled tights?"

Camille shifted Chance to the opposite shoulder, leaving one hand free to punch my arm. "Only in the bedroom."

"Should have kept the store open," Jefferson called as we approached the rise on which they'd planted their chairs. "Could have done a ton of business."

"Merle and Shirley at the Shovel It Inn ran out of cash register tape and they're down to their last dozen take-out boxes," Mary Lou added.

"Maybe we should open the store next time," Julie said. "When it gets hotter we could stock extra ice cream and cold drinks and chips."

"And make a banner with a slogan," Justin said in a teasing voice. "Fill your belly with chips while Brother Elijah fills your heart with the spirit."

"I'm not sure how I feel about capitalizing on this." Camille frowned and gazed toward the tent. "These people may come because they're sick or worried or in doubt about where their lives are headed."

"That's true," Mary Lou agreed. "Just because it's not what Reverend Balforth delivers, doesn't mean it's not worship."

Justin wore a chastised expression for a few seconds. "I bet Marcella will be out here for the next one selling stale doughnuts and reheated pastries. And those wrinkly hot dogs that she's had boiling since I was a kid. Folks will go home thinking Hemlock Lake is the heartburn capital of the state."

"The boy makes a point," Jefferson said. "Might be you should call a merchants' meeting and see how everyone wants to handle this. 'Everyone' being a small group."

"Stub and Marcella and Merle and Shirley and us." Julie ticked off names on her fingers.

"And me. I have chips and pop at the bait shop." Justin nudged her. "And I could make up sandwiches. Worms on whole wheat. Crickets on a croissant."

"Stop." She stuck her fingers in her ears. "Stop right now."

"Perhaps we should hold a general town meeting," Mary Lou said. "There are issues we never thought about, like parking and security. We can't expect Stub to direct traffic every time the tent goes up, and what would happen if somebody was picking pockets or stealing from the collection plate or if a fight broke out?"

"What would folks fight about at a revival?" Justin asked. "Which wise man rode into town first? How many lions were in the den with Daniel?"

As Mary Lou wound up to fling a tart reply, Jefferson tapped my shoulder and pulled me aside. "I need to stretch my legs and spine. Been on my knees all day wrestling with baseboards."

We fell in step, circling the field, then tackling the road to the cemetery. There were no streetlights here. There was, after all, no need to illuminate the road. Funerals were held during daylight hours. Those who remained on the hill when services were over and mourners gone, had—with the exception of restless ghosts—already reached final destinations.

I told Jefferson about the interviews I'd conducted that week and the little I'd gleaned from Fred, Jennifer, and Helene.

"Sounds like two of your victims had secrets."

The road curved, leading us to an overlook with a view of the town and the lake. "Yeah. And they'll remain secrets unless

I find out who Genevieve Graham was about to call and who Micah Thielman met with."

"If no one knew then, it's not likely they'll know now."

"Who needs the bluebird of happiness? I've got the partridge of pessimism."

Jefferson snickered.

"Good evening, Dan. Jefferson. I see you came to watch the show."

The toneless voice bled from the darkness ahead of us.

Chapter 21

"Evening, Reverend Balforth," Jefferson said. "Appears you're doing your viewing from a distance."

Balforth took shape at the edge of the road, his suit darker than the night, his white shirt like the flare of a falling star, his face gray as dust.

"I don't mean this to seem that I am in any way judging Mr. Falton, but I feared my presence would be a disruption. Not for Mr. Falton, but for those who came to listen to his message."

"Meaning folks in your congregation who may be embarrassed to show their faces in church tomorrow?" I asked.

"I imagine there are several of those." Balforth gestured toward lengths of log braced by posts, designed both as a resting spot for those walking to the cemetery and as a makeshift guardrail. "And I have no complaint. It's their right to search for paths to salvation. In fact, it's their duty."

We sat and peered into the valley. The tent was a bright smudge casting a faint glow onto the trees at the edge of the field. The knots of people gathered beneath those trees weren't visible from here, but I was certain no one had left. Those who had never seen Wesley Falton wanted to check out the man now living among them.

Gossip claimed Falton had style, energy, charisma, and a strong speaking voice. In contrast, Balforth favored severe clothing, flat delivery, and age-worn sermons. Those who turned out for his services did so because it was the only game in town. In fact, it was the only game in three tiny towns where he delivered sermons, performed marriage ceremonies, baptized, and buried the dead.

The sound of a trumpet drifted up from the valley and Wesley Falton, wearing a white suit and a crimson shirt, bounded from the small tent and onto the stage beneath the canopy. The trumpet sounded once more. Heads bowed.

"Trumpet's a nice bit of showmanship," Jefferson said.

"If that's what you want with your ration of religion," I added.

Balforth coughed twice, dry sounds from high in his throat. "What do you gentlemen want with *your* rations?"

"Nothing above my head except sky," Jefferson said. "And no one getting between me and whatever keeps the world turning and the stars shining. No one trying to explain what can't be explained."

"And there's a hell of a lot of that," I added. "Not only how things came to be, but why they are as they are. The works-in-mysterious-ways theory doesn't hold water for me. Not after what I've seen in the past two years. And not after what shows up on the news."

"All these folks fighting evil, and no one seeming to get the upper hand." Jefferson gestured toward the tent below. "Hell, they can't even agree on what evil is and where it comes from."

An ironic cry of "Amen" rose from the tent below.

I expected Balforth to launch into a chapter-and-verse rebuttal and defense of his calling, but he said only, "You men have seen more horror than most. And more sudden loss. If I had lived your lives . . ."

His voice seemed to evaporate, then he coughed and went on. "I've concluded that I believe because I think I should, because my father did and his father before him, and back two more generations, all educated and trained to guide their flocks. But when I look into my soul instead of at that legacy, I don't know if I was ever called. And I don't know what I truly believe. Wesley Falton doesn't have my training, but he has the force of belief. He has fire."

"A minister doesn't need fire to counsel and care for his flock," I told him. "In my mind it's about steadiness and devotion and commitment. You have all that. You're not a one-night wonder."

"And yet you didn't come to me to marry you." He said it without accusing, but as a statement of fact.

There were a lot of reasons we hadn't asked him. I went for the one that was least hurtful and easiest for him to accept. "How many times did you stand by an open grave at the top of this hill in the past two years?"

"Far too many."

"Yes. And that's what burns in my brain when I see you—those needless deaths, tragedy, and pain. It would have cast a shadow on the day Camille and I married."

"And when I see you, I think of Louisa Marie practicing for our wedding right before she died," Jefferson said. "It didn't feel right to ask Mary Lou to marry me where her sister intended to be my wife."

"I see," Balforth said.

I almost thought he did—or at least wanted to.

The ride home featured long descriptions of Julie's impressions of the revival: Wesley Falton's clothing and energy, the two boys who played their guitars and sang a song she thought was "way too rock and roll to be a hymn," and the message about baptism and a fresh start.

Later, with Chance asleep, and the bedroom door closed, Camille asked, "Am I the only one who wishes kids came with operating instructions?"

"Nope. I have no idea what to say about Isaac or his father or baptism. I feel like I'm walking into a minefield wearing a blindfold and snowshoes."

"And carrying a backpack full of grenades with loose pins." Camille plumped her pillow. "I understand the interest in baptism. Who could blame her for wanting to wash away bad things in the past and start over? What we need to know is whether she believes that's possible. And if she does, then what?"

"Yeah, then what? Julie's practical and logical, but she has wounds that may never heal, even with time and age and the support she gets from her psychologist and the rest of us."

Camille gave her pillow another thump. "If she thinks what Wesley Falton is peddling will give her peace, then I guess we stand aside and let her try it out."

"Even if we think it's a load of crap?"

"Even if."

"What if she wants to gut her college fund and give it all to Brother Elijah? Or shave her head and become his spiritual slave? Do we stand aside then?"

"No, then we hold an intervention, send her to Iceland for a month, and ride him out of town on a rail."

I laughed. "I was hoping you'd say that. I'll cut a rail and have it ready. Now, let's move on to the Isaac issue. Another minefield."

"But we're not alone in it." She flopped onto her back. "Justin picked up on the vibes and took me aside. He's been worried Julie would be afraid to get involved with a guy, so he's encouraged by her interest, but he wants to know more about Isaac and his family."

"As do we all."

"I told him what Isaac said about drowning and that I was worried first that he meant it and might follow through, and second that he'd use his depression as a way of manipulating Julie. Justin said he'd sound him out."

"A year ago he wouldn't have cared whether Julie was put on the block and sold into bondage."

"He wasn't that bad." Camille tugged at my hair. "And now I worry that he's driving himself too hard with that house and the bait shop and school."

"He's trying to fill the void. Like all the rest of us." I pulled her against me and eased up the long T-shirt she wore to bed. "He wouldn't work so many hours if he had someone like you."

"Are you saying you're lazy and I'm to blame?"

I slid my hands along her spine and hips. "No, I'm saying you can be a little distracting."

"Only a *little* distracting?" She nibbled my earlobe. "That will have to be remedied before this night is over."

Phone lines buzzed Sunday as people compared notes about the revival, Wesley Falton's style, Reverend Balforth's lack of style, and the impact more revivals would have. In the afternoon, Stub, Jefferson, Freeman, and Evan rolled up to present Julie with photographs and fact sheets on used cars. Once they stated their opinions, they stayed on, sipping my beer, eating my potato chips, passing my son from shoulder to shoulder, and discussing what Freeman referred to as "filthy lucre," and the issue of making money off the revivals.

"I'm already feeding at the trough," Evan said. "So I can't throw stones."

"Or slop. Wouldn't want to mix metaphors," Jefferson said. "I don't have a financial interest, so I'll play devil's advocate."

"Devil's advocate." Freeman laughed. "The way Wesley Falton gets worked up, the devil might be scared to set foot around here whether he had an attorney or not."

"Huh?" Julie looked up from the stack of car specs. "I don't get it."

Jefferson explained the meaning of the term "devil's advocate" and added that Freeman had been making a joke. Julie snorted and returned to the stack of papers. "Next time tell me when I'm supposed to laugh."

That drew a round of guffaws at Freeman's expense and another round when he abandoned efforts to appear insulted and joined in.

"Hemlock Lake is in the U. S. of A." Stub tugged at the collar of his Sunday coveralls, ones yet unstained by oil and grease. "And that means we're free to pursue happiness—and money—so I propose we let everyone make independent decisions about selling stuff or letting people park on their lawns. If there's blowback, let them deal with it individually."

Freeman nodded. "I second that. The folks who settled these hills and hollows figured they could live the way they wanted—because that was their right, and because damn few would come this far to mess with them."

"Except tax collectors," Evan added.

"Yeah, it's never too far for those sons of bitches." Freeman slapped a hand over his mouth. "Sorry, Julie. Pardon my language."

"Like I never hear swearing at school." Julie grinned. "I bet I know as many bad words as you do."

"And I bet we don't need a contest." I covered Chance's ears. "Not while there's an impressionable young man among us."

"He can't understand what we're saying."

"Are you sure?" Jefferson aimed his beer bottle at her.

"The baby books say—"

"How do they know for sure? Were they written by babies?"

"No, but . . ." Julie narrowed her eyes. "Are you being a devil's advocate?"

Jefferson grinned. "It's an annoying talent, but one that might serve you well. Especially when you go off to college and you're out in the world beyond Hemlock Lake."

"Are you telling me I should start questioning everyone?" Julie glanced at me and then at the others. "And everything? Including the advice you're giving me right now?"

"She's got you there," Freeman said.

Julie drew a check mark in the air, awarding herself a point. All eyes turned to Jefferson. Evan tapped his watch. "You have ten seconds to answer."

"Nine," Stub said.

"Eight," Freeman noted.

"Seven," Julie informed him.

Jefferson waited until they reached one. "Don't question so much that you bring your life to a standstill. Question enough to make your life your own."

"Deep," Freeman said.

When Julie nodded and pulled another paper from the stack of car specs, Jefferson tipped a thumb up in my direction, telling me he had my back.

Monday I turned to another cold case I knew was a homicide: Franklin Turner.

I hadn't spoken to his mother when I made my initial round of calls, only to her answering machine. An aunt, Eleanor Lovett, told me not to expect Natalie Turner to call. "Frankie's killing wrecked her, cut the heart from her chest. She gets out of bed and she gets through the days. Still makes the best pastries around as far as I'm concerned, but if she walked in front of a bus, it would be fine with her."

My knowledge of bakeries was limited. I knew the air was usually warm and sweet with the scents of sugar, vanilla, cinnamon, and chocolate. I knew the crusty chewiness of fresh rye bread and the bite of sourdough. And, even at my age, I knew the feeling of being a kid on Christmas morning when I gazed into the showcase at streusel-topped muffins, flaky pastries oozing fruit filling, and rows of cookies, brownies, and cream puffs. I couldn't imagine mixing batter, rolling dough, and spreading icing after suffering a loss like Natalie Turner's. I wondered if she kept the job because it was familiar or because it filled the hours.

Remembering one more thing about bakeries—that bakers' days usually started well before dawn—I waited until afternoon to call. Natalie Turner answered in a voice so weary it made me think each word would be her last.

I introduced myself, reminded her I'd left a message earlier, and explained that I was reviewing a number of cases, including her son's.

"What's the point? It won't bring Frankie back."

I had nothing to say that wouldn't sound like the same old pap about justice and closure. And after I was done talking, Franklin Turner would still be dead.

"I'm sorry, but that's the way I feel."

"No need to apologize. Some pain never passes, never heals."

"Yes. You understand. That other man, Eakins, had no sense of it, no feeling. It was just a job for him."

But understanding and feeling didn't guarantee I'd have more success than a man who was simply killing time until retirement.

"How many cases are you looking into?"

No one else had asked that and I found it interesting that the question came from a woman deep in an abyss of grief. "Seven. Five of them here in Ashokan County. Two others nearby."

"Seven," she repeated.

Did she think her son's case would be lost in the shuffle?

"Seven cases." Her voice lost a little of its weariness. "Seven families torn apart. Dreams shattered. Friends falling away. It must be hard for you, carrying the burden of all that loss and ruin."

I hadn't thought of it that way, but now I could almost feel it bow my shoulders. I braced my elbows on the kitchen table.

"Saturday," she said. "Come see me Saturday morning. At eight. I'll make cinnamon rolls and coffee."

She hung up and I passed the remainder of the week thinking about her pain—pain for which there was no relief in this life.

Not that I had all that much time to think. That night Chance developed colic.

Chapter 22

By Wednesday Camille and I were bleary-eyed and short-tempered. Our quiet, happy baby seemed possessed by a wailing demon. Nothing we tried—and we tried every remedy listed on websites or phoned in after word got around—reduced the volume or intensity of his screams. He rejected my efforts to soothe him, but he rejected Camille's and Julie's with equal force and conviction. My job and hours were more flexible so, once we learned we were in for three weeks or more of nightly misery, I offered to take the brunt of it.

"I feel so guilty," Camille said when I showed her the earplugs I bought for her and Julie. "There must be something I can do to make him stop."

"There's nothing," Julie told her for the tenth time. "And there's nothing you did wrong."

Whispering having proven to have no positive effect, we spoke in voices raised a few notches above a level marked "Normal Indoor." On occasion, to be heard above his relentless bawling, we resorted to shouting.

"The books and websites say a lot of babies do this," Julie said.

"Then it must be true." I took my squalling son from Camille. "Go to sleep."

"How can I?" She stroked his cheeks, fiery red and streaked with tears. "What mother can sleep when her baby is in such a state?"

"A mother who needs her rest."

"A mother who told Dither she could take tomorrow morning off." Julie took Camille's arm and led her toward the bedroom.

"It's too early to go to sleep," Camille objected. "It's only 8:30."

"So, soak in the hot tub," I suggested. "Make lists of things you want me to do. Read a book. Watch something mindless on TV."

"Paint your toenails," Julie said with a laugh. "You can reach them again."

"All right. But I won't sleep. I know I won't."

"Then close your eyes and relax." I laid Chance across my shoulder. "He's safe with me."

"Don't put him down. He cries more then."

Julie rolled her eyes and I gave her a microscopic nod. Neither of us had noted that any position produced a change in pitch or ferocity. "I won't put him down until he stops crying. Promise."

With one more backward glance, Camille went into the bedroom and closed the door. Julie turned a thumb up, told Nelson to stay with me, and trotted upstairs, earplugs in hand. Nelson watched her go, whined for a few seconds, then curled into his bed on the hearth.

"Guess it's you and me," I told Chance. "And we might as well get a little work done, so let's pay a few bills."

Opening envelopes with one hand was difficult, but not impossible. Writing checks, however, proved to be more than I could master with Chance arching his back and sliding from my grip. I scraped the bills into a pile and abandoned the project in favor of a pattern of walking and rocking. When my walk took me into the kitchen, I sometimes sipped beer or ate a potato chip. I also checked the progress of the minute hand on the clock, progress best described as "excruciatingly slow." To ease the monotony, I talked to Chance and Nelson.

My comments to Nelson were along these lines: "We can send a man to the moon but nobody knows what causes colic. I bet putting a colicky baby in the room with a hung jury would make someone change his vote in less than five minutes. If you'd been like this when you were a three-week-old puppy, your mother would have carried you into the wood and left you for the coyotes."

Nelson's comments were all body language: lifted lips, paws over his ears, and an emission of gas.

My comments to Chance went like this: "You're a peeing, pooping, yowling ad for birth control. I should have Julie walk the floor with you, then I wouldn't worry about her getting involved with Isaac or any other male. I love you, but I believe I'll love you more when you get past the colic and I get past wanting to glue your lips shut."

A few minutes before 2:00 he stopped crying as suddenly as he'd started, and made the soft slupping sound we'd come to know meant he wanted to nurse. With great relief, I carried him to the bedroom, turned on the lamp by the crib, and saw that Camille lay on her side, hugging a pillow and breathing in a deep and regular manner. So much for "I know I won't sleep."

Sliding the pillow from her grip, I slipped Chance into her arms and shook her.

Camille didn't budge.

I shook her again and popped out an earplug. "Your son is hungry."

She opened her eyes, blinked, and tugged up her T-shirt. "I wasn't asleep. I'm not asleep."

"Of course not." I flopped onto the bed beside her. "But I will be in about three seconds."

Saturday morning Camille shook me awake at 7:00. "There's a note on the calendar in your handwriting. It says 8:00. Is that tonight or this morning?"

My sleep-deprived mind grappled for an answer. "This morning?"

She shook me again. "That's what I'm asking you."

"That's all it says?"

"If there was more, don't you think I'd tell you?" Her tone had the warmth and sweetness of vinegar on the rocks.

I sat up on the second attempt and tried to think beyond the fact that late this afternoon Chance would haul in a breath, clench his tiny fists, and empty the silos again.

"I'll bring coffee. Then I've got to run."

Coffee. Something about coffee.

I thumped the sides of my head with the heels of my hands.

Coffee. Coffee and something. Somewhere.

With a gurgling Chance slung over one shoulder and his travel bag on the other, Camille brought coffee in the largest mug we owned, kissed my forehead, and left. Sipping scalding stimulant, I listened to the sound of her car fade, to the scream of a hawk, the caw of a crow, and then to a few seconds of a rare sound—silence broken only by a breeze sifting through the window.

I set the coffee on the nightstand and lay back, sinking into the absence of dissonance and discord, soaking in it.

And then I remembered Natalie Turner who would never hear her son's voice again.

I considering calling and asking if we could reschedule. Then I recalled her reluctance. This opportunity might not come again.

I splashed cold water on my face and chest, scrubbed with a washcloth, and yanked on a red T-shirt, jeans, and moccasins. That left me enough time to gulp more coffee, stuff the file in my satchel, and make it to Ashokan City and Natalie Turner's apartment with two minutes to spare.

She opened the door before I knocked and, without a word, stood aside. I entered a room that made me think of a surgical suite. The walls were white and without a single picture, poster, or bulletin board. A white futon sofa, flanked by cubes of clear plastic, faced a white bookcase holding a few dozen paperbacks, their covers providing the only touches of color. No towels or potholders hung from hooks above the stove. No decorative magnets clustered on the refrigerator. A round glass-topped table marked the division between living room and kitchen. It was set with white plates, white mugs, a white carafe, and white-handled cutlery.

Natalie, who wore washed out jeans and a gray sweatshirt, waved me toward the table and the nearest of two white chairs. "The rolls are about done. Do you take cream and sugar?"

"Cream. But black is fine."

I dug out my notepad, pen, and recorder and tucked them in my pockets, then set the satchel by the door and crossed to the table in three strides and filled my mug.

She plucked a white towel from a drawer, pulled a glass pan of rolls from the oven, and set them on top of the stove. The aroma made my head spin and saliva filled my mouth. I hadn't eaten since lunch yesterday and I'd probably walked ten miles with Chance last night. "Smells great."

"These were Frankie's favorites." She got out a white butter dish and removed the top. "He liked extra butter although there's half a pound in those rolls already."

"I was always a fan of extra butter." I patted my stomach. "Until I got to the downhill side of 35."

"Frankie could eat that whole pan and never gain an ounce." She cut the rolls apart with a wide knife and used the blade to lift two loose and slide them onto a plate for me. "You look hungry."

"I am."

"And tired."

"That too." I almost told her about Chance, but a woman who'd lost her son didn't need to hear about a baby—even a cranky baby with colic. I forked off a bit of cinnamon roll and didn't so much taste as feel flavors explode in my mouth. I held back an animal grunt of pleasure.

She poured coffee for herself, took a sip, and sat across from me, her plate bare. Her face was all angles and planes, her neck so thin I felt I could wrap one hand around it. When she shoved up the sleeves of her sweatshirt, I saw her forearms were muscle and bone, close beneath the skin. I had the feeling she ate only for fuel and never for taste and texture and pleasure.

Self-conscious about my hunger, I forked off another bit about the size of a dental filling.

"You don't like it?"

"It's delicious."

"Then eat. Please. Eat."

Hunger overrode all and I ate, washing it down with rich, strong coffee that did little to erase my exhaustion.

"This is the reason I don't give up baking. It's like salve on a cut, seeing someone enjoy what I created. Especially children. And hungry men. For a moment or two the pain tapers off." She sipped coffee. "But then it returns. Like you said, some wounds never heal."

I raised my head and gazed into her gray eyes. They seemed at first cold and lifeless, but then I had the sense of heat, of glowing embers. I thought of those coal fires that burn deep, hundreds of feet under the ground, burn for weeks, months, even years. There was fire like that inside Natalie Turner, flames of pain consuming her flesh, her energy, and her will to live. It would burn until she was no more than ash.

She filled my cup and I stalled, scraping the edge of my fork across the plate, getting up the last of a fusion of cinnamon, sugar, and butter. Having seen the depth of her pain, it seemed even more wrong to probe her wound in the name of possible justice that would provide no relief.

"Franklin." She said his name as if it were a prayer, or perhaps a mantra. "Franklin was a delight from the moment he was born, the moment he was conceived."

A blush bloomed high on her cheeks and she ducked her head. "He had a father, of course, but he never knew I was pregnant, and I told the hospital I didn't know his name. I didn't care what they thought of me. I had Franklin. I didn't need anyone else."

I laid my fork on the edge of my plate, pushed it aside, slipped the recorder from my pocket and clicked it on. "There's a picture in the file. Maybe from a play. He seemed happy."

"Thrilled. He was thrilled to the core." She almost smiled and the pain in her eyes flickered for a second. "From the time he was tiny, he loved acting. He'd put on shows for me. Shows with three or four characters. He'd play them all. When he got a part in the church summer camp play he was over the moon. He loved making believe he was someone else."

She gripped my hand, her fingers like talons. "Not that he wasn't happy being himself. But that was harder than a part in a play where he knew how it would turn out. Franklin wasn't like most other boys."

I remembered what Jennifer Thielman said about Micah. "Not like them in what way?"

"He was too kind. Too sweet and sensitive."

Another echo of Jennifer's words. What was behind those words? Something Natalie didn't want to say, perhaps because then she'd have to admit it to herself?

"How did he feel about that? About being different?"

She frowned, sipped at her coffee. "I never asked. And he never told me. When he was younger he would sometimes wonder why *everyone* was different, why we didn't all like the same TV shows or foods, or why all kids weren't smart or strong or have curly hair."

I waited, hoping for something more specific.

"Franklin didn't like sports except for swimming and tennis. He liked to watch baseball, but he hated football and he didn't like to hunt or fish."

"I fished growing up—still do, sometimes—but my father and I almost came to blows because I wouldn't shoot a deer. I know how tough it can be when you won't go along with the others—especially when you're a teenager."

"Yes. They can be cruel. And he didn't have a group of friends to stick up for him." Her fingers dug into my wrist and then she released me. "I'm sure a lot went on at school that he never told me about. And he made jokes about what he did tell me. I don't think anyone ever hurt him—not physically—but they bullied him and said hateful things."

"How did he handle that?"

"He tried to avoid it when he could. When he couldn't, he'd shrug it off."

"What kinds of things did they say?"

"That he was weird. That his father knew he would turn out to be a sissy and left him. That I dressed him up like a girl when he was little."

"Do you think it's possible that one of them . . . ?"

She shook her head. "I think about that every day. And every day I decide it wasn't one of the kids from school. I don't think those boys treated him the way they did because they hated him. I think they did it because it made them feel better about themselves, because they enjoyed it and it entertained others."

I didn't say what was in my mind—that kids who tormented other kids with words sometimes moved on to more brutal forms of torture, even to murder.

"Besides," she said, "the boy who bullied him the most moved away when school let out. To California. The other boys—the ones who went along with the bully—lived miles away and they were too young to drive. Frankie hadn't seen them for two months."

She didn't say that was a long time in the life of a teenager. I didn't say that two dozen stab wounds in Franklin's face and chest spoke more of white-hot, right-then rage than of amorphous anger nursed during summer vacation. Franklin had gotten under someone's skin. Deep under. Why? How?

Chapter 23

We talked on until my coffee was cold in the cup, but all I came home with was a sack of cinnamon rolls. I intended to take a short nap and type up notes from the recording, but the nap became a solid four hours of sleep. I never heard Camille and Julie come home and I snored on through the call to dinner.

I woke feeling refreshed.

Then Chance cranked up once more.

And that's the way it went for the next four weeks. A few evenings were better than others and a few were worse. But all of them left me drained—by the physical demands of walking and rocking, and by the mental strain of feeling helpless, of fighting frustration and simmering anger.

Every few minutes I'd remind myself to stay calm and gentle. "It could be worse," I'd tell Nelson several times a night. "It could be an incurable disease. I could do all of this and then lose him."

Meanwhile, we tried every remedy passed along. Camille gave up anything containing milk or butter, sat him up while nursing, didn't let him gorge himself, and burped him often. We turned off all the lights we could and dimmed others, swaddled him, and rubbed his back. I set up fans, played soft music, and bought a white-noise machine.

Nothing worked.

And no matter how much he screamed in the dark hours, he woke up bright eyed and cheerful.

Camille grew frantic, then resigned, crossing off the days until July when Chance would be three months old. That was the magic number, the point at which most experts claimed colic stopped.

"Maybe he'll stop before that," Julie said one evening during the second week of May as Chance warmed up for a symphony of screeches. "He cries longer every night than they say other babies do."

"That's my boy!" I scooped him from Camille's arms. "Going for a world record. Going to out-scream every baby on the planet."

"I'll stay up with him tonight," she volunteered. "You look like a zombie."

"And you don't find that attractive?" I leered and shuffled around the living room with Chance in my outstretched arms. "Admit it. You've had fantasies about—"

"Not in front of the children!"

Julie laughed. "Probably nothing I haven't heard at school."

"I'll be glad when you go off to college," I told her. "They talk about serious stuff at college—stuff like who will break into a prof's office and steal the final and where to hold the next keg party."

"Justin says beer at college parties is cheap and tastes like donkey—"

"Not in front of Chance," Camille said. "Seriously, we need to start controlling our language now so we don't let something slip when he's learning to talk."

"Mom doesn't want you dropping the F-bomb," I told Chance.

For ten long seconds he stopped squalling and stared at me with wide eyes. Then he unleashed a howl to make all others seems like whispers.

"I guess we know what he thinks about that," Julie said.

"Probably intended it to be the centerpiece of his first sentence," I agreed.

Julie snorted apple juice on her blouse and mopped at it with one of the hand towels that, like the antimacassars of Victorian times, lay on the back of the sofa and every chair. Not a day went by when I didn't use at least ten of them to wipe drool and dribble from Chance's chin and milk spit from my shirts. At night, when we were walking the floor, I washed and dried towels, first in an attempt to soothe him with sounds, but then because it needed to be done.

"You two won't be laughing when he toddles into the post office and utters that sentence to Mary Lou," Camille snapped.

"Homework," Julie said in a bright voice. "I just remembered I have homework."

"Don't leave me," I wailed.

Julie took the stairs two at a time and thumped her door closed.

"Now," Camille said, "let me have him and you get a good night's sleep."

"Bad idea." I laid Chance over my shoulder. "The Scream Machine and I have a rhythm. We have bonded. We are as one, floating through the darkness."

"But he's wearing you out."

"I'm a big guy. I can take it. And if we disrupt his routine, he might be worse."

"Give him to me."

Camille's jaw set and her mouth pressed into a hard line. Having read up on a lot more than colic recently, I sensed this was not about whether I needed a break. This had to do with hormones and maternal instinct and an irrational fear that I was usurping her role.

I handed Chance over.

"Now, go to bed."

"In a minute. Got a few chores to take care of."

I collected soiled towels, carried them to the laundry room, dumped them into the washer on top of a dozen of their tribe, added soap, turned the dial to the usual setting, and got the wash underway. After that I snapped on the floodlights and escorted Nelson outside. This was the season young bears came around searching for food and territory. I figured Nelson had as many lives as a cat, but he'd already run through a bunch of them and there was no point in pushing it—especially because Julie would skin me alive if anything happened to him.

When I returned with a fresh deck of towels to deal around the room, Chance had added hiccupping to his routine, using it to punctuate each shriek.

"Get out of here," Camille snapped. "Go to bed."

She laid Chance across her shoulder and patted his bottom. He never missed a beat. In fact, he seemed to pick up the pace and increase his volume. A childish part of my brain felt the joy of vindication.

"I can't go to bed yet. My body's used to being upright. My legs are used to walking. If I lie down they'll twitch."

"Then take a drink. Or a pill. Rest so you can work on those cold cases tomorrow. You haven't touched them for weeks."

"I've been a shade distracted." I nodded at Chance. "Sheriff North's secretary explained colic to him. He knows what I'm up against."

"But I know you want to be working on them."

"You're right. I do. But those cases will be there when Chance gets past this and I can focus. In the meantime I've been cutting brush, getting the garden going, and cleaning up those piles of crap behind the garage."

"If the heaps are still there next year, so what? Those cases are impor—"

"Yes, they are. But no one expects me to solve them."

"No one? Including you?"

"Yes, including me. I have no expectations. All I have is hope." I tossed the last towel. "Listen, if I had even a glimmer of a lead, a bit of a thread and an idea about how to pull on it, then I wouldn't argue with you. But so far—"

Halting his screams for only a second or two, Chance spit up. Yellowish liquid poured across Camille's shoulder and down her back. She hunched. "Tell me he didn't do that."

"I'd be lying." I snatched a fresh towel from the sofa and sopped up the worst of it. "I should have warned you. He does that every night about this time. I'll take him."

"No." Camille clutched him tighter, triggering a wail that rose to the rafters and seemed to drive all the oxygen from the room. "I can do this."

"I know you can."

"I'm his mother."

"And you're a wonderful mother."

"I'm not." Her wail blended with his. "If I was any kind of a mother I could make him stop crying."

"A presidential order backed up by ground troops and air support couldn't make him stop."

"Stop joking," she screamed.

I spread my hands. "That wasn't a joke, Camille, it was a fact. And you need to face it. He'll cry every night until he gets through this stage."

Her eyes sparked and she pointed at the bedroom.

Being sane—or as sane as a man can be who has walked the floor for nights untold with a crying baby—I shrugged and headed that way without another word.

I was almost to the door when Chance pulled the pin on another howl. And then another. Like steps in an escalator, they rose higher and higher.

Without a backward glance, I passed through the doorway and stripped off my shirt. I made it to the bathroom door before Camille caught up.

"Take him. Please take him."

She thrust Chance into my arms and collapsed on the bed. Sobbing, she curled into a fetal position.

I got Chance against my shoulder where I could hold him in place and pat him with my fingertips. Then I sat beside her, rubbing her back and shoulders with my free hand. Chance's screams subsided. So did Camille's sobs.

"It's okay," I told them. "We'll all get through this."

"I was afraid I . . . I was so frustrated I . . . What if I hurt him?"

"You wouldn't. You couldn't."

"You don't know that."

"I know you brought him to me when that was the last thing on earth you wanted to do."

Her body went stiff and for a moment I wished I could bite that back. And then she laughed. "It was. I hated that you were right."

I thought of that joke: If a man says something in the forest and there's no woman around to hear him, is he still wrong?

Probably not a good time to tell that one.

"It's not that I'm any better at walking the floor, but I'm what he's used to. I could be a robot for all he cares. I could be a trained seal or a kangaroo."

She rolled over and delivered a light punch to my arm that let me know we were good. "Then hop out of here so I can sleep."

And so the routine continued.

And because of the routine, I found a thread to pull to untangle one mystery.

Bit by bit I'd sorted through the stacks behind the garage, the "heirlooms" left by my grandfather, the "priceless pieces" dumped by my father, the "one-of-a-kinds" contributed by my brother. I'd hauled a trailer-load of pipe, vent covers, railing, and even a circular staircase to a metal recycling center and gleaned a chunk of cash to start Chance's college fund. Removing big pieces cleared the way for the rake work, turning over leaf-covered mounds to reveal rusted shovel blades and dull hatchet heads, hinges and knobs, saw blades and drill bits, paint cans and coils of wire.

If it was up to me, I would have raked the ground level and covered it with wood chips, then let the earth reclaim the junk. But Camille and Julie had plans for the space, plans that involved junk-free soil and shade-loving plants. If they were happy, then my happiness quotient was higher. So I brought a wheelbarrow around and shoveled, sifted, and sorted.

Well, to be honest, I made a pretense of sorting. The hours I'd invested hauling away junk from the interior of the garage—and from the house before it burned—had inoculated me against the hoarding virus. I didn't pause to consider whether this trash might become another man's treasure years down the road.

The wheelbarrow was nearly full when I came across the license plate. Bent into an elongated V, it dated from before my birth. I thumped it against the wheelbarrow handle until I could make out letters and numbers and the slogan "Empire State."

Leaning against the garage, I remembered an essay I'd written for history class. "The Many Things that Make New York the Empire State." The assignment called for us to write about one stand-out New York landmark or accomplishment, but I wanted extra points and wrote a whopping ten pages featuring Niagara Falls, the Statue of Liberty, the Erie Canal, the Stock Exchange, dairy farms, apple crops, the Adirondacks and the Catskills, and on and on.

Smiling at my youthful enthusiasm, I pitched the license plate in the wheelbarrow. My teacher must have loathed me for sucking away so much of her time, but she read it all—I knew that because she corrected two egregious spelling errors—and gave me an A+.

With a grunt, I raised the handles and aimed the wheel at the driveway. The load was heavy and uneven and I was sorely in need of a nap. The wheelbarrow wobbled. The license plate slid from the heap, struck my leg, and bounced aside.

"Damn it."

Nelson, who'd been digging along a mole tunnel beneath a laurel bush, hopped over to investigate. He sniffed the plate, then crisscrossed raked-over ground and returned to his mission.

The day was warm and humid, and I rested for another minute before I wiped sweat from my forehead, retrieved the plate, and wedged it in among other junk. The one-design-for-all license plate was once the only show in town. And now it was a thing of the past. Sure, most old-timers I knew stuck with the basic plate, but when Julie got her car she might order a customized plate and make a statement. A first car was more than a mode of transportation. It was a symbol, a rite of passage, a means of escape, and a mini home on wheels tricked out with seat covers, bumper stickers, and doodads hanging from rearview mirrors.

I thought of Micah Thielman, driving off on the day he disappeared, driving into oblivion. Serenity Brook had combed data bases across the country searching for tickets or citations connected to his driver's license. She'd searched accident reports for his car. She'd found nothing.

And that nothing made me more certain that Micah was dead, that he and his car were at the bottom of a lake or deep in a hollow. Perhaps this fall a hunter would find him.

And perhaps not.

I shoved the wheelbarrow around to the front of the garage and up a makeshift ramp to the trailer. Metal rattled and scraped as I dumped it. That damn license plate slid off, bounced against my leg again, and clattered along the ramp to the ground.

What about the other cars?

Genevieve Graham's was accounted for. So was Theresa Gilligan's. Judy Arnold's car was on the street near the men's clothing shop where she'd worked. Angelina Vernon, only 16 when she disappeared, hadn't owned a car or had a license. Ditto for Franklin Turner. And Jeremy Yount . . .

Had he owned a vehicle?

Chapter 24

I retrieved the bent plate, jammed it into the heap of scrap, shoved the wheelbarrow behind the garage, and headed in for a shower and a nap. As water beat against the outside of my skull, questions about Jeremy Yount beat against the inside.

Had he owned a car?

He was 19 when he disappeared. By that age, most young men who lived in this part of the world had their own wheels.

Had Harry Pallister mentioned a car in his notes?

I couldn't remember.

Why?

"Because you've got seven cases and a son with the colic," I told myself as I toweled off. "It's a good day if you remember your name and phone number."

Excuses.

I made an egg salad sandwich, fetched a rawhide chew from the closet for Nelson and a beer from the refrigerator for me, and took Jeremy Yount's file to the porch. For the first few minutes I flipped through the pages, hoping to spot a reference to a vehicle. When that didn't pay off, I finished the sandwich and settled in the swing to read the entire file again.

Jeremy Yount's mother had died when he was 12. He was tall, had a crew cut, a job stocking shelves at a market a few blocks from his house, and a father Harry Pallister noted was a "strong disciplinarian." Jeremy Yount had chores and duties, responsibilities and obligations. What he didn't have were friends.

Or at least Harry Pallister hadn't interviewed them.

Odd.

Was Jeremy Yount friendless?

In high school I'd known plenty of kids who were loners by choice or because they were ostracized by others. But most made a connection with at least one other. And most made an impression on a teacher or school administrator, co-worker, or boss.

But Harry Pallister made no mention of that except to write that Jeremy's employers, Floyd and Belle Poole, said he was a good worker, respectful and quiet.

That led me to wonder whether Harry Pallister, like Orville Eakins, went through the motions but didn't do the job. Or didn't do it right.

Checking the file again, I followed the course of the original investigation and Pallister's follow-up. The first round made extensive use of area media sources and included radio interviews and newspaper reports. A hotline received only two tips, and those were noted as being from "the usual cranks" claiming Jeremy Yount had been beamed up by aliens. Having no leads on where else to look—the dog they brought in circled the parking lot and sniffed its way to the Yount home—they hadn't done more than search the house, the market, and the general vicinity.

When Pallister took over the case, he talked again with Paul Yount, sent out fresh news releases, and made another request for information. The same two cranks called, one claiming he'd sighted Jeremy Yount in a crowd of extras in a low-budget slasher movie, and the second insisting she'd had a dream that he was locked in a shed behind an abandoned house. A third caller claimed he'd spotted Jeremy mounting a motorcycle at a rest stop 50 miles south of Ashokan County.

Pallister followed up on the shed tip but found nothing.

I flipped to my own notes. I'd called Paul Yount several weeks ago and left a message on his machine introducing myself. I didn't ask him to return the call, but now I was mildly surprised that he hadn't. Angelina Vernon's mother and Judy Arnold's aunt called the same day in response to similar messages. They were encouraged that someone was working the case, but discouraged because there was nothing new. Still, they appreciated the opportunity to talk.

Perhaps Paul Yount found talking too painful. Perhaps he held his emotions close. Or . . .

I shook off darker thoughts, dug out my cell phone, punched in his number, and left another message on his machine. "This is Dan Stone with the Ashokan County Sheriff's Department. I'm reviewing the file on your son's disappearance and I have a few questions. I'd appreciate it if you'd call me as soon as you have the opportunity."

The opportunity came as we sat down to the roasted vegetable lasagna Julie concocted from produce Camille pulled from the display case that morning.

"The carrots and zucchini and stuff weren't bad," Julie informed me. "They had a few spots or were a little soft."

"Soft" was one of the words Paul Yount used a few minutes later when I asked him to describe his son. "Lazy, forgetful, sullen. Didn't do his chores right and didn't care."

The implication was that Paul Yount cared about the quality of Jeremy's chore performance—cared a lot.

"I didn't see any mention of friends in the file and I'm wondering if that's an oversight or if the file is incomplete. Can you think of any of Jeremy's friends?"

"Not a one."

"Any neighbors he might have hung out with?"

"None."

"Classmates?"

"No."

He snapped off the word in a way that told me he was finished with that line of questioning.

"How long had he worked at the market?"

"A couple of years. And before you ask, he didn't have any friends there, either. And if he worked for the owners like he worked for me, it's a wonder they didn't fire him the first day."

So much for that. I moved on. "Did Jeremy own a car?"

Paul Yount responded with a derisive laugh. "No. He didn't make squat at that market and after he paid room and board, he was broke. He never got a license. Couldn't be trusted behind the wheel."

"Why was that?"

"Too jumpy. Didn't pay attention."

I asked a follow-up question, pretty sure I already knew the answer. "Did he take lessons or did you teach him?"

"I taught him. Until he admitted he'd never get it."

He didn't say, "Any other stupid questions?" But I heard that loud and clear. Paul Yount had standards and Jeremy couldn't meet them. He was a disappointment, a failure, a sorry excuse for a human being.

Still, I lobbed in one more question. "I realize that Harry Pallister asked you if you had any idea where Jeremy might have gone, and you said you didn't. Has anything occurred to you?"

"No."

The line went dead.

I wandered out to the porch, my appetite gone.

After my long nights with Chance, I was well aware that kids had a way of trying a father's patience. But from experience with my own father, I also knew some men were short on patience and long on expectations, discipline, and control. Like me, Jeremy Yount may have faced the impossible task of trying to be "the right son."

I'd recognized the impossibility early on and focused on what it would take to get away to college—good grades, savings, and the support of my mother. Without maternal support to balance paternal criticism, Jeremy might have felt college was impossible and marked time through high school.

That left money. He didn't have enough for a car. Did he have enough for a bus ticket, cheap meals, and a room at a Y?

Beyond that, he needed inner steel, belief in himself. If he hadn't mustered that, he might have chosen another form of escape—suicide.

Or, had he scraped up the nerve and the money and told his father he was leaving. Had Paul Yount flown into a rage and—

I shook that off and gazed across the lake, to the ridges and mountaintops. I wanted Jeremy Yount to be alive. And I wanted him to be living far away from his father. Most of all, I wanted to find him.

Chance didn't put on as much of a show that night, and he drew the curtain on his performance at least an hour earlier than usual.

"It's a trick," I told Camille when I tucked him beside her for his late-night snack. "He's trying to get me off guard."

"But maybe—"

She slapped both hands across her mouth.

"Right," I said. "Don't jinx it."

In the morning I was rested enough for rational thought. Paul Yount hadn't used the word "sensitive" as others had to describe Franklin Turner and Micah Thielman. But in his language, "soft" could mean the same thing. If Jeremy Yount was dead, was his death linked to the murder of Franklin Turner and the disappearance of Micah Thielman?

Telling myself to be objective, I drove across the county to the market where Jeremy Yount had worked. It was twice the size of the store in Hemlock Lake, but had half the charm. Fluorescent lights flickered, cans staggered across sagging shelves, and the soles of my shoes stuck to the floor and came loose with a ripping sound as I approached the elderly woman slumped on a stool behind the lone cash register. She wore a red apron over a pink turtleneck, and bright blue clips in her white hair. "Mrs. Poole?"

"Yes." She laid aside a paper folded to the crossword puzzle and looked up, her eyes appearing huge behind thick glasses. "Can I help you?"

The left side of her mouth drooped and her voice quavered, making it sound as if she doubted she'd be able to help anyone ever again.

I introduced myself and told her I'd been assigned to cold cases. "I'm wondering if you remember Jeremy Yount."

"Of course I remember Jeremy. My stroke didn't wipe the whole slate clean." She tapped the right side of her head. "Such a hard worker. Always doing more than he had to. Why, this store sparkled when he worked here."

Not the story I'd gotten from Jeremy's father. "You didn't have any problems with him, say, not paying attention to details or goofing off."

"Never. He took care of things Floyd and I didn't notice. Bulbs getting dim, freezer doors not closing like they should. And never a bit of argument."

She raised her glasses and knuckled tears from her eyes. "I wish I had him with me now. Since Floyd passed it's been an uphill struggle. But if I don't keep moving I might as well lie down and pull the sod over top of me."

"Would you say he was sensitive? Soft?"

Belle Poole rubbed the drooping corner of her mouth. "Sensitive? Yes, I suppose you could say that. He cared about people. He was kind and helpful."

"And soft? Was he soft?"

Her eyes narrowed. "Only according to his father. I don't know what that man expected of Jeremy. I don't know if he knew!"

She smacked her paper against the counter. "Paul Yount made that poor kid a nervous wreck. Jimmy asked him all the time why he put up with it. And Jeremy—here's how kind he was—said he felt he owed his father a little more to make up for the time and money he'd spent raising him. And he said if he left, his father would be all alone and that made him sad."

"Jimmy?" The file on Jeremy Yount made no mention of anyone by that name. "Who's Jimmy?"

"Jimmy Forester. Delivered bread and chips and such. Tall guy, red hair, two thousand freckles. He's in Miami now. Used to go there on vacation. Liked the heat, he claimed. Wouldn't suit me, but—"

"And he was friendly with Jeremy?" I reached for a granola bar from a display beside the counter and dug a handful of change from my pocket.

She picked through the coins on my palm. "Rode motorcycles together now and then. Jeremy had a blue helmet."

Something else that hadn't been in the file—except for the motorcycle mentioned in that tip from the caller Harry Pallister dismissed as another crank. "I understood Jeremy didn't have a license."

She flushed. "Well, that was a secret. Jimmy took him to take the test. And bought the motorcycle for him, too. Well, I mean Jeremy paid for it, but Jimmy put the title in his name and stored it in his garage so Paul Yount wouldn't know."

By now I suspected there was a whole lot Paul Yount didn't know.

I bit into the granola bar. It was stale and sticky, but I forced a smile as I chewed and swallowed. "Were there other secrets?"

She flushed again, then sighed. "Well, maybe the tax men will take pity on an old widow. The thing is, we paid Jeremy the bare minimum, but we gave him more under the table. The store was doing good then and we had it to spare. And Floyd said it wasn't right that he had next to nothing after paying rent to his father."

"The tax men won't hear a word from me." I stuffed the rest of the granola bar in my pocket. "When was the last time you saw Jeremy?"

"Let me see." She rubbed the drooping side of her mouth again, wiping a spot of saliva. "Must have been a Saturday. That's right. Saturday. Five years ago just about. Jimmy came by at closing and Jeremy got up behind him on his bike and off they went."

Another fact—a major fact—that wasn't in the file. The original investigator noted that Jeremy Yount walked away from the market and Pallister hadn't amended that. "Did you tell investigators?"

"No." She shook her head. "No, I didn't."

Chapter 25

She raised her hands, cutting off my question. "But they never asked."

I drew in a long breath and let it out, counting to five. "But you must have known that was critical. You must have realized the investigation would get nowhere without that information. Why did you hold it back, Mrs. Poole?"

"Call me Belle." She smoothed her apron. "Mrs. Poole was my mother-in-law."

"All right, Belle, why did you keep that to yourself?"

"I didn't intend to, but . . . See, Floyd and I took off to Albany that evening. Had a niece getting married Sunday afternoon over in Buffalo. Got a brand new dress but it had this silly bow in the back and since Jeremy had young eyes, I gave him my nail scissors and he picked out the stitches and you couldn't tell that bow had ever been there."

She smiled at a distant memory, then shook her head and patted my arm. "But you want to know why I never said anything. Well, you see, the story going around when we came home Monday evening was that Jeremy walked away. And he did. He walked to Jimmy's bike. And Floyd said he bet Jeremy finally got up the gumption to get out and maybe we shouldn't volunteer answers to questions no one took the trouble to ask us."

My opinion of previous investigators slipped another notch. "Do you remember an investigator named Harry Pallister?"

She shot me a sly smile from the good corner of her mouth. "I remember he had his mind made up that Jeremy wasn't too bright. Told me Jeremy must have stuck out his thumb along the highway and got picked up by a psychopath. Had himself convinced Jeremy was dead in a ditch."

"Pallister rubbed you the wrong way?"

"That man didn't rub, he scoured."

"So you didn't tell *him* about the motorcycle, either."

She slid off the stool and put her fists on her narrow hips. "He didn't ask. He told me and Floyd that the report said Jeremy walked away from here and never made it home. Well, I looked at Floyd and he looked at me and then Floyd gave a little shrug and—"

"And you went on keeping that secret for Jeremy?"

"Yes. Floyd and I talked it over later and I said maybe we were messing up the investigation and he said it didn't seem like there *was* much of an investigation and hadn't been from the start. And then we decided that if Mr. Pallister came around and asked more questions, why we'd answer them. And if he didn't come we'd keep our lips zipped. And I guess you've figured out we didn't see him again."

I swallowed a smile. "Where do you think Jeremy is?"

She spread her hands on the counter, the knuckles thickened by years of work, the skin thin, bruised and scarred, the nails blunt. "I don't know. I wonder about that every day."

For a long moment she said nothing more, then she leaned across the counter in a conspiratorial manner. "I don't suppose it matters now if I tell you what I *do* know. The day he left he came back from his lunch break with a paper sack. Inside was a box of hair dye. Red. Like Jimmy Forester's hair."

On the way home I swung by Serenity Brook's basement lair. The stacks of files around her desk were higher and she'd abandoned the carrot in favor of a bowl of grapes.

"You look like death riding a camel."

"Thank you." I unfolded my usual chair. "You're as lovely as always."

She tossed a grape into the air, tipped her head to the left, and caught it between her teeth. "And you're not worth crap as a liar."

"So I've been told." I laid a slip of paper beside her keyboard. "I want to know everything about Jimmy Forester, formerly of Ashokan County, now believed to be living in Miami."

"Everything down to the number of fillings in his molars?"

"Everything short of that." I plucked a couple of grapes from the bowl. "Specifically where he is now and what he's doing, whether he had a passport five years ago, and what happened to the motorcycles he owned at the time Jeremy Yount disappeared."

Her fingers flew across the keyboard. "Jimmy Forester's name wasn't in the Yount file."

I chomped a grape. "It should have been."

She patted me on the head. "Who said you couldn't find sand in the desert?"

"I'll try not to let your endless praise go to my head."

"Got any other grist for my mill?"

"Not yet. Had to take a couple of weeks off due to lack of concentration."

"I heard about the colic." She tossed another grape and snapped it from the air. "Sheriff was in here wanting me to look up cures. Told him that would be a fool's errand and sent him packing. Didn't know the man had a heart until I saw him frettin' about you and your son."

I was touched by North's concern, but made light of it. "If I wasn't around he'd have to get a dog to kick. And he's allergic to dog dander."

She snorted a laugh and spun her chair to face the monitor. "Watch for my e-mail."

It arrived before dinner. Jimmy Forester was living in Miami, working as a bartender. He'd sold one of the motorcycles there, the one he'd bought a few months before Jeremy Yount went missing. Forester's passport was used around the same time to enter Belize.

I knew next to nothing about Belize, but a little surfing online told me the official language was English and I figured that's why Jeremy Yount picked it. I wondered if he'd assumed a new identity, continued passing himself off as Jimmy Forester, or found ways to live and work without documentation.

Over dinner—creamed tuna with peas on scratch biscuits—I told Julie and Camille about my discovery.

"Congratulations." Camille popped from her chair and kissed me. "I knew you'd find something nobody else had."

"That was more due to Mrs. Poole than my investigative technique."

"But your investigative technique led you to her." Camille sat and forked a chunk of steaming biscuit. "And you let her talk. Take credit for that."

"The credit belongs to you and Julie," I said with a grin. "The way you two go on, a man can't get a word in edgewise."

"Ha. Ha. Ha."

"Are you going to Miami?" Julie asked. "Can I come?"

"I'm not going anywhere until Chance is past the colic. Besides, I'm pretty sure if I get Jimmy Forester on the phone I can shake him enough to find out where Jeremy Yount is now."

"And then you'll go Belize or wherever and bring him home, right?"

I shook my head. "As far as I'm concerned, once I know he's alive and well, my job is done. If others have issues about the way he left and how he got out of the country, it's not my problem."

"Good." Camille mashed a biscuit with the tines of her fork and sopped up cream sauce. "I hope he gets to stay wherever he is. That father doesn't deserve a child."

"Yeah, he's pretty grim. But he makes me look good."

"So does Mr. Falton," Julie said. "Isaac says he picks on him all the time."

Camille raised her head. "Picks on him how?"

"Telling him he's lazy and not using his brain. He makes Isaac study religious stuff for three hours every day and then he quizzes him on it. And on weekends Isaac has to teach stuff to little kids. And in the summer it will be Bible camp and more lessons at home."

Julie plopped another biscuit on her plate, split it, and spooned on a huge helping of creamed tuna. She wasn't one to obsess about her weight and I was glad of it. "He has to memorize stories from the Bible and explain how to use them to make good choices and be more, uh, virtuous."

"Ah." Camille shot me another we'll-talk-later glance. "There's nothing wrong with a little more virtue. And I'm in favor of good choices."

"Me, too." Julie sliced her saturated biscuit with the edge of her fork. "But Mr. Falton doesn't want Isaac to have any fun at all. He unplugged the TV and they don't have a computer to play games on. They don't even get the newspaper or any magazines. Isaac says his father believes if you like something a lot then it's a temptation and your soul is in jeopardy and you should cast the thing aside and be done with it forever."

She forked tuna into her mouth and talked around it. "If I joined his church, I'd have to give up lots of stuff. Like creamed tuna."

"If we had to give up every food we like," I observed, "we'd be eating those beans you hate so much. And beets. And liver."

"And canned spinach." Camille shuddered. "And prunes."

"And those little oily fish in the can that's kind of square and flat," Julie added. "The ones Stub eats on rye bread with onions."

"Sardines," Camille said. "If it wasn't for Stub, I wouldn't stock them, but he's good for a can a week."

"Isaac has to eat stuff he thinks is icky—fish cakes and squash and lentil soup. He says even though his mom tries to make stuff taste good, it's still disgusting."

"Well, those things are good for him." Camille stood to clear the table. "And Isaac's old enough to start thinking about leaving home. When he's on his own, he can eat whatever he wants."

"If you don't want to live under a bridge, you have to have money to leave home," Julie said. "And you need a car."

"Didn't you tell us Isaac was going to save up over the summer for a car?" Camille asked.

"He was. But he has to pay rent and now his father says he has to give half of all he has left to charity. And he doesn't even get to pick the charity." She scraped the last bits of biscuit from her plate. "Jeremy Yount was lucky he had a friend like Jimmy Forester to help him. Will he get in trouble for letting Jeremy use his passport?"

"That's not my department."

"I'm glad." Julie licked her fork. "Maybe he'll say Jeremy stole it."

Which was about the same thing Sheriff North said when I ran it by him the next day. "Holding that boy accountable for whatever laws he broke getting out of this country doesn't seem like my problem." He slapped his palms on his desk blotter. "Sounds like Harry Pallister dropped the ball—if he ever *had* the damn thing. And I thought he was dedicated to those cases."

"Maybe this case was an anomaly. From what I know of Pallister—the way they say he treated his wife—he could have identified with Paul Yount and concluded that Jeremy wasn't worth looking for. Or maybe this case marked his entry into burn-out territory."

North smiled. "Bet you're thinking we should take a closer look at every case he touched."

"I hate it when people read my mind."

"You're married now, son. You should be used to that." He tipped his chair and laughed. "Hell, I expect you haven't had a private thought for the past year."

I drove home thinking he was right, first about taking a hard look at Pallister's cases, and second about my mind being an open book for Camille. When we found a few minutes to talk about Julie and Isaac later that evening, she commented on the relief she'd seen on my face when Julie shared her take on Wesley Falton's brand of religion.

"We may have to worry about her trying to be too good a friend to Isaac because she feels sorry for him. But I doubt she'll become a handmaiden to Brother Elijah."

"Or a regular at the Falton dinner table. By the way, did you ever talk with Hannah about Isaac's depression?"

Camille shook her head. "I tried a couple of times, but it's a one-way street. The woman keeps her head down and her lips tight."

"And you're more of an observer than an interrogator. But Julie hasn't mentioned it again, so maybe Isaac is in a different place."

Chance cranked up and Camille rolled her eyes. "Speaking of being in a different place, don't you wish you were right now?"

"Nope." I scooped my squawking son from his crib and headed for the living room. "I'd rather be with my boy. Paul Yount didn't appreciate what he had, but I'm going to make the most of every minute I have with this guy."

That Saturday Wesley Falton held another tent revival.

Camille debated whether we should both go or if one of us should stay behind with Chance. "He's so loud when he gets going. If he uncorks, people won't be able to hear the preaching."

"Falton's got a loud voice. If one baby drowns him out, he better invest in a set of speakers. Or a bullhorn."

That's all it took in the way of persuasion. We threw a bag of provisions and a couple of lawn chairs in the SUV and grabbed Chance's bag.

The show drew twice as many as the previous one, but this time Hemlock Lake residents were prepared for the crowd. Kids waving hand-lettered signs directed visitors to parking spots on lawns where homeowners collected five dollars a vehicle.

"Looks like everyone got over those qualms about profiting from this," Camille observed as I parked behind the store. Jefferson had posted the tiny lot with signs reading NO PARKING. That made space for Freeman, Evan, and Justin.

We strolled toward the field, passing kids manning lemonade stands. Others sold candy bars and sacks of chips from their backpacks, and one enterprising youngster rented out seat cushions borrowed from his mother's dining room chairs. Marcella sold hot dogs off a portable grill, and signs advertising box dinners pointed to the Shovel It Inn. Using tall stakes and yellow plastic rope, Julie and a few of the other teens had strung up a corral of sorts on the grounds of the old schoolhouse and offered to entertain toddlers—for a fee, of course—with a collection of toys, puppets, and dress-up clothes.

No one seemed concerned about love of money being the root of evil, but I wondered if Wesley Falton was concerned about commerce cutting into the contributions dropped into Hannah's bucket.

"Everybody for miles around is here to check it out and visit. It reminds me of those community picnics we had when I was a girl." Mary Lou stretched out her arms for Chance, and we set up our chairs in the space they'd saved for us.

"I could get behind a good old-fashioned picnic with potato salad and ribs and pie," Jefferson said. "Lots of pie."

"Maybe we'll do that next time. Set up tables and chairs in our yard. Figure out ahead of time who will bring what."

"Put up a fence," Jefferson said, "so strangers don't think our feed is part of the revival and elbow their way in."

I offered him a beer from the bag of provisions. "Sounds like you're fed up with this already."

"I'm not much for crowds, although I have to admit this is an interesting mix. All ages and shapes and sizes." He pointed off to the left. "Looks like Reverend Balforth is undercover."

Camille shaded her eyes. "I've never seen him without a black suit."

"Black slacks and a gray shirt aren't all that different." Mary Lou leaned forward, squinting. "Am I the only one who finds it odd that he wears black and Falton wears white?"

"No," Jefferson said with a laugh, "I'm sure Dan noticed and is casting his mind over all the books he's read looking for connections and symbolic meanings. Probably going to start expounding about *The Scarlet Letter* any time now."

"Like you don't crack a book or dig beneath the surface of just about everything." I twisted the cap off my beer. "The more interesting questions might be whether they've always worn those colors and how they came to choose them."

"Well, let's ask when he gets here," Mary Lou said. "He's walking this way."

Chapter 26

Like kids caught with their hands in a cookie jar, we ducked our heads and pretended great interest in the contents of Chance's bag or the tufts of grass at our feet.

"Good evening."

At the sound of Balforth's dental-drill voice even Chance looked up.

"This must be the young Mister Stone."

Balforth bent in a stiff manner that reminded me of those drinking bird toys, and chucked Chance under the chin. Chance's eyes grew round and he opened his mouth for what I was certain would be a record-setting screech, but Mary Lou jiggled him and he released a crowing gurgle instead.

"I understand he had quite an entrance into the world," Balforth said.

I waited for him to add that the man upstairs had been watching over us that night but, although he glanced toward the church, he said nothing more. Nor did he ask if we intended to have Chance baptized.

The answer was that we weren't sure. We'd talked around the issue, citing Pascal's wager and wondering what baptism could hurt. "Other than our ears while Balforth drones on and on?" Camille had asked. After that, we'd put further discussion aside until the colic ran its course.

"Wesley Falton draws quite a crowd," Balforth observed.

"We're not here for the preaching," Jefferson said. "When he gets going, so will we."

"A few of your neighbors are under the tent, though."

"Well, not much happens around Hemlock Lake. You can't blame people for wanting to check out something different." Mary Lou patted Chance's back. "Doesn't mean they'll keep coming after tonight."

Jefferson patted the bulge in his hip pocket. "And it sure doesn't mean they'll open their wallets far enough to slide out more than a single bill with a portrait of Washington on it."

Camille chuckled. "Folks around here aren't prone to throw money away on anything they can't eat, wear, drive, or live in."

"I'm not concerned about the money," Balforth said. "I'm concerned about the message."

I set my beer on the ground beside my chair. "What I heard of it seems pretty simple—give up anything you like too much."

"Yes, it seems simple. But man is not a simple creature. And we are made in His image."

Balforth inclined his head and walked off.

"I wanted to know what he meant by that," Jefferson said after a moment, "but I was afraid if I asked he'd deliver a sermon."

"I know." Camille dug out a sack of cookies. "It's a shame, because he has the welfare of the community at heart, but . . ."

"He can't connect," Mary Lou said. "He *knows*, but he doesn't seem to *feel*."

Pretty much what he'd said to me and Jefferson a few weeks ago.

"And if a message is too complicated, some people don't want to do the work to understand it. Or live it." Mary Lou pointed at the tent. "I wonder if that's why they're here."

The trumpet sounded and Wesley Falton bounded from his tent and onto the raised platform.

"Time to go." Jefferson stood and folded his chair. "Before he convinces me to give up the things that tempt me the most—beer and peach pie and the woman I married."

Mary Lou giggled like a teenager and they walked away with their arms around each other. Camille moved her chair closer to mine and I assured her that I would never subscribe to Falton's teaching and give her up. She assured me of the same and suggested we act on our mutual attraction when we got home.

Later, pacing the porch with Chance, I saw the Faltons return from the revival and trudge up the lamplit walk to the house, Wesley in the lead, Hannah and Isaac lagging. If Wesley Falton lived true to his message, then he couldn't love Hannah—at least not in the consuming way I loved Camille.

"That might get him into heaven when he's dead," I told Chance, "but it seems like a sad and lonely way to live until that day."

Sunday morning I resisted the urge to sleep in, drank two cups of coffee to jumpstart my mind, and called the number Serenity found for Jimmy Forester.

As I hoped, his voice was thick with sleep and his sentences slurred with whatever he imbibed after closing time at the bar. I got to the point before he was fully awake. "I know you registered a motorcycle in your name for Jeremy Yount. I know he used your passport to get to Belize. I'm willing to listen to you say he stole your ID, if you're willing to tell me where he is now."

"So you can tell his father?"

"No, so I can close a five-year-old case and get on to solving a few murders."

I heard the flick of a lighter and a long inhale.

"His father doesn't seem to care what became of him," I said, "but Belle Poole thinks about him every day."

And that was the key.

"He's still in Belize." Jimmy exhaled on the last word, stretching it out. "Got married and had a kid. Named him after me."

"Why not? You were a good friend."

"Yeah, well, he had to get away from his father." He inhaled again. "I didn't realize how far he intended to go until we got on the road. And then, well, I went along with it. Probably shouldn't have, but . . ."

"All right. Here's what you're going to do. Call Jeremy and give him this number." I reeled off the number of the Ashokan County Sheriff's Office. "Tell him to ask for Sheriff Clement North and not to settle for anyone else. Tell him to be prepared to prove who he is and tell the sheriff his story. Tell him he's got three days to do it."

Jimmy Forester didn't ask what would happen after three days. I didn't elaborate because I had no idea. What I did know is that when you set an imminent deadline, things had a way of happening.

"And tell him if he's as good a friend to you as you were to him, since he's in Belize, he'll take responsibility for where the chips fall."

"Meaning . . . ?"

"Think about it."

I hung up, second-guessing myself. Then I went to my desk and came up with three questions Sheriff North could ask the man who called, three questions that would determine whether that man was indeed Jeremy Yount. 1) What did you buy at the pharmacy shortly before you left town? 2) What color was your motorcycle helmet? 3) What did you do to Mrs. Poole's dress before you left?

I sent those along with the answers in an e-mail to the sheriff and said I'd add my report to the Jeremy Yount file and have it on his desk Monday afternoon.

Later that morning a soaking rain discouraged any but hardcore fishermen with their own boats and bait, so Justin came by and helped me put the boat in the water and get the motor on. After we were certain it would start, we tied the boat to the dock, opened a couple of camp chairs and an equal number of beers, and settled in the garage with the overhead door open to watch squalls sweep across the lake.

"No charge for the service," he said. "As long as I'm invited to dinner."

"Camille would be rigid with rage if you left without eating. And Julie would throw that banana cream pie she's making at your head."

"If it turns out half as good as the lemon meringue one, I wouldn't half mind." Justin wiped his hands on a rag and licked his lips. "But I'd rather have it in my stomach. I love pie. Cake, too."

He'd have to give that up if he followed Brother Elijah—something he showed no signs of doing.

I thought of Isaac, eating squash and lentil soup. "How's Isaac doing?"

"Fine. I mean, he does his work, does it right and never argues or complains. But he never makes jokes, either. Doesn't talk much at all." Justin tossed the rag in a bucket. "Not that silence is a problem. Some guys seem to think my dock is a forum for debating everything from the gravitational pull of a grapefruit to whether you could write a letter with squid ink. It's . . . well, I guess you could say it's the quality of Isaac's silence that's weird. It's almost like he doesn't know how to make conversation—or he's afraid to."

My vote was for both of those theories. I doubted there was much in the way of conversation in the Falton house that didn't center on the Bible.

"He's polite with folks who come to rent boats and buy bait," Justin said. "And he's helpful. But it's like he's figured out how to appear friendly, but he's sort of a beat behind. Does that make sense?"

Given what I'd seen from across the lake and what I'd heard from Julie, it made perfect sense. "Other than that he's doing okay?"

"Yeah. Rides an old bicycle, but gets there when he's supposed to, prints so I can read the names in the reservation book, takes great notes if someone calls to leave a message, doesn't mind cleaning up." Justin sipped at his beer. "When he's not working he's watching."

"Watching the way you do things?"

"I guess." He shrugged. "But he doesn't ask me why I do things certain ways. You know, keep stuff where I do, like that. Seems like if you ask questions, you understand the system better."

I nodded and we drank beer for a time while wind whipped the lake and the boat bobbed by the dock.

"Maybe his father raised him not to question things," Justin mused. "Because he's a preacher and all."

"Possible."

"Maybe his father's worried that if he gets in the habit of asking questions he'll start wondering about bigger issues than why I like one brand of lures more than another. Maybe Wesley

Falton's afraid he'll lose his live-in laborer if Isaac asks more questions than he has answers."

"Could be."

"And I kind of . . . I think that when it comes to why we're here and why bad things happen, the guys in the pulpits don't have answers that seem right to me."

I laughed. "Sounds like someone's been studying too much science."

"Yeah, according to some. I put up a chart up with the divisions of geologic time so I could memorize them. Isaac looked at it one day and the next he told me Wesley said I was wasting my time, and all I need to know about how the earth came to be is in the Bible."

"Lots of folks feel that way. What do you think?"

"Well, I'm not sure about what got the universe going, and I'm not convinced *everything* in the science books is right. But if you're asking me whether I'm giving up on geology, the answer is 'No.'"

"Okay. What if I asked if you're as hungry as I am?"

"I'd say I was hungrier."

I folded my chair and leaned it against the wall. "Enough philosophy. Let's fire up the grill and burn a few steaks."

When we'd filled up on pie and settled in the living room with a fire going, I brought up a subject that had to be addressed—the future of the property Julie and Justin inherited from their father and grandmother. Ronny's house, damaged by fire and mostly repaired, had been empty since the night he died. Rachel's had been rented, but the renters recently bought a place of their own.

There was no way to ease into the topic, so I cleared my throat and went for it. "There's something we need to discuss."

Julie froze, one hand on Nelson's ear as they sprawled on the hearth.

"The houses?" Justin asked.

"Yes. It's painful, but you both know it's bad for them to stand empty too long. And property and school taxes and insurance have to be paid whether they're empty or not."

"You don't have to sell them right this minute," Camille added. "But down the road you're going to need money for college . . . and other things."

One of those "other things" being paying back funds Camille and I fronted for a down payment on Priscilla's house and the dock and bait shop.

"If you decide to rent your grandmother's house again, that's fine," I said. "But we'll have to get it painted, put out ads, decide whether we want to manage it ourselves or hire a company."

"That all takes time we don't have. I vote we sell. Sell them both." Justin leaned forward and patted Julie's hair. "Grandma was way more practical than sentimental. She'd understand. And Mom . . . Mom really wanted you to go away to college. You'll get scholarships, but they might not cover everything."

"I know." Julie sniffled and buried her face in the thick hair on Nelson's neck.

"Why don't we go up there tomorrow afternoon when you get home from school," Justin continued. "Just you and me. We'll walk around and talk about it."

Julie nodded, her face still hidden.

As far as I knew, she hadn't been inside the house she grew up in for nearly two years, not since the night of the fire, the night her mother died. Walking through those rooms would dredge up a lot of memories—some horrifying. As Justin said, Lisa had wanted Julie to go to college, to travel, to go far beyond this valley. But her father had made it clear he didn't support those dreams.

"If you decide we should hold onto one or both of the houses," I said, "then we will. I have a chunk of land up above the Birchkill I've thought about selling. It should pay for a couple of years of college."

"I don't want you to do that." Julie raised her head and wiped her eyes with the heels of her hands. "You already did so much."

"Then what's a little more?" Camille asked. "Besides, thanks to you we have a healthy baby."

"With a really healthy pair of lungs," I joked. "Which he'll start using in about half an hour."

"I don't have earplugs, so color me out of here," Justin said with a laugh. "Dan, after the deal you worked with Priscilla you're considered the real estate guru of Hemlock Lake and vicinity, can you crunch numbers for us?"

"Be happy to. If Camille promises to double-check my work. Walking the floor with Chance tends to addle my brain."

Chapter 27

I spent the next afternoon comparing prices for comparable properties and figuring up the cost of paint and cleaning services as well as finish work, fresh carpet, and kitchen appliances for Ronny's house. Basic landscaping we could handle in a few long days of pruning and trimming and edging.

Camille checked my figures and pronounced them sound—and a little frightening. "We're running out of well to dip into. You might have to sell that land sooner than later."

"Then that's what I'll do. I don't want Julie to feel pressured to part with more pieces of her past until she's ready."

"You're a good man." Camille gave me a long kiss. "And you shall be rewarded later. Right now I have to make pulled pork, a giant pan of macaroni and cheese, a pot of candied carrots, and two loaves of garlic bread."

"Ah, comfort food. I'll hit the spare freezer in the garage and liberate the chocolate cake and caramel ice cream."

"Get those mini cheesecakes, too," she advised.

But when Julie and Justin returned, it was clear we could have made do with far less sugar and fat. Julie was sad, but certain the houses should be sold.

"Grandma's house was never really 'my' house. We didn't live there very long before we moved to the apartment, and then the renter people lived in it, so it feels like just a house to me."

"Same here." Justin dug into the bubbling pan of macaroni and cheese. "Especially since my room was in the garage."

"I would have slept out there."

"Then I would have had the sewing room. The bed in there was about a foot too short."

"And it wobbled." Julie spooned enough candied carrots from the bowl to cover half her plate. "I'd wake up feeling seasick."

"Good practice in case you decide to sail across the Pacific," I said. "So, the consensus is that we sell. When?"

"Whenever." Julie popped a carrot chunk into her mouth. "Yum."

"I don't see any reason to put it off," Justin said. "And it doesn't need much except paint and yard work."

"Instead of painting," Camille suggested, "maybe we could offer cash to the buyers. Then they can pick their own colors."

"I'll check on that." I got a notepad from the counter. "What about the other house?"

Justin looked at Julie. "That's up to the kid."

Julie shoved carrots around the rim of her plate, then sighed. "There were places where Mom was happy, but they mostly weren't inside the house. She loved hunting for acorns and twigs and bark to make little creatures."

"And taking care of her roses." Justin frowned. "But a lot of them are dead."

Crushed by the fire truck the night she died, and neglected ever since.

I felt heartsick. Lisa had deserved so much better. I should have—

"I have an idea." Camille gripped my arm, grounding me in the present. "Why don't we dig up the roses and move them here?"

"Here" meant the rose garden my mother had tended faithfully until her death, the garden Camille cared for as a tribute to her.

"Is there room?" Julie asked.

"Sure. There's plenty of space for a dozen roses or more."

Justin took seconds on macaroni. "If it's quiet at the dock, I can help."

Julie flashed him a dazzling smile.

"We'll bring in a load of good soil and plant your mom's roses all together in case you want to move them again. If the tags are gone we'll get Alda and Pattie to tell us what they are." Camille slid the notepad and pen across the table and made a note on a fresh page. "And we'll brush up on how to care for them. I haven't done more than shake on a little fertilizer since Chance came along."

"I can build a bench." Justin touched Julie's hand. "So you can sit out there if you want."

Julie flashed him another smile. "Could you build me a set of shelves for my room, too? Grandma saved a whole box of Mom's little creatures and I'd like to be able to see them when I wake up in the morning."

"Better make that a display case with a heavy glass door and a lock." I tipped my head toward Chance snoozing in a basket. "When he starts walking he'll be in everything. Those acorn creatures won't have a chance. He'll tear their little eyes off."

"What if he tries to swallow one? He could choke." Camille glanced out at the patio and beyond. "The woods are full of acorns. And pebbles. And mushrooms."

This wasn't the time to bring up the fact that the woods were also full of other hazards. As a kid, I'd been forced to throw up after eating laurel leaves. Ronny had acquired world-class cases of poison ivy and others had scars and stories about broken bones and dislocated fingers. As far as I knew, no one had choked on an acorn. But Camille wanted reassurance, not recollection.

"We'll watch him," I told her. "We'll keep him safe."

Her lips curved into a smile, but in her eyes I saw she knew there were no guarantees.

I spent the next day calling real estate agents, telling them about the properties, and asking pointed questions about pricing and marketing. "Get someone we can live with," Camille had instructed. "Not too hard-charging, but not too laid-back. Knowledgeable, but not a know-it-all."

"Call me Goldilocks," I'd joked. "I'll find one that's just right."

My sense of humor vanished fast. I talked to the eager, the hungry, the pleasant, and the pushy. I talked to agents starting out and those who sounded like they'd been around when the waters receded and Noah found enough dry ground to lay a foundation. I was told new paint was mandatory and I was instructed not to bother, I heard pre-sale kitchen upgrades were a must and that buyers would want to do their own. Three agents said no one wanted a place so far out and four others swore everyone was looking for a getaway near Hemlock Lake.

Mary Lou made the decision for us when I stopped by the store to update Camille on my lack of progress. "Martha Cutter's who you want. Great sense of humor, although she hasn't had much to laugh about lately. Her husband walked out on her over the winter. Moved to Kona with the heating oil delivery man. Martha never saw it coming."

"And that makes her the perfect person to negotiate for us?"

"Sure. She's as suspicious as a turkey in November. She'll check people out seven ways from Sunday so you won't waste your time."

I was all for signing her up immediately, but Camille put one more hurdle in the path. "I think the kids should meet her and make the decision."

The next evening Martha Cutter, a birdlike woman in her early fifties, met us in Bobcat Hollow. She wore jeans, a long white blouse, and a striped scarf with fluttering fringe. Her silvery hair shone in the sunlight and lifted and fell like feathers in the breeze. Despite her size, she had a deep voice and a grip like a set of locking pliers. She didn't gush and she didn't mince words after she walked through the properties. "Plenty of potential. You should get a good price if you don't scare off the prospects."

Julie winced and slid her hand into mine. "You mean, like, tell them what happened here?"

Martha Cutter patted Julie's shoulder. "Mary Lou brought me up to speed and I'll do what the law requires on that front. I was talking about the price. You don't want to scare off buyers by asking for the stars when you know all along that what you're willing to take is the moon."

"Then let's ask for the moon and an asteroid or two," Justin said.

Julie rolled her eyes. "Mr. Science means let's not ask too much. I want people to live here." She gazed up at the second-floor windows. "I want kids to play here like we did. I want them to be happy like we were, before . . ."

"I do, too." Justin took her arm and led her across the yard. "Let's count up how many roses we'll need to move. We'll leave Dan to sort out the details."

Friday morning the trilling of the phone woke me. "Your name is in the paper," Camille said. "There's a picture, too, but it's kind of fuzzy."

"Huh?" I sat up, checking bright sunlight streaming through the sliding glass door, then checking the clock. 10:00 AM. I'd slept for seven hours. And felt as if I'd put my head on the pillow less than ten minutes ago. Chance, after several days of tapering off, had started wailing early and continued until late.

"Front page. Article about Jeremy Yount. I'll set a copy aside and you can pick it up later."

I checked the clock again. 10:01. "Bring it home when you come. I'm not going anywhere that isn't back to sleep."

"Sheriff North says you displayed perseverance and determination."

"Does he say he's giving me a raise?"

"No, but he says that Jeremy Yount offered to reimburse the county for the cost of the original investigation and follow-up work and he's taken that under consideration."

"Hmmm."

Paper rustled and she said, "And . . . well, you'll see it later. Go to sleep."

Which is what I intended to do, but the phone kept ringing. Half of Hemlock Lake called to congratulate me. Belle Poole called to tell me how delighted she was that Jeremy was alive, well, and willing to make such a gesture. Helene Cooper said she didn't believe in omens, but if she did, solving this case could mean I'd discover who killed her mother. Jennifer Thielman congratulated me and said she was sure I'd find out what happened to Micah.

Natalie Turner didn't call, but I hadn't expected her to.

237

The final call of the morning came from Jonah Umhey, the retired detective who sent me the Theresa Gilligan case. He didn't identify himself, but got right to it, his voice raw, serrated.

"You getting' anywhere on the Gilligan case?"

"Not yet. Met with the boyfriend a few weeks ago."

No, longer than a few weeks. Five weeks. Six. More? Since Chance got the colic, time had warped.

"Anything come of that?"

"Not yet. But there might be something in the letters she wrote to him in the months before she was killed. He said he'd send them when he had time to dig them out of storage."

"Light a fire under him. I won't be around forever."

I made a note to call Fred Maddox.

"Maybe publicity will shake something loose on the other cases," Umhey said. "The fresh ones."

"I'll take any help I can get."

"Wish I could do more for you. For her." He coughed, a damp and nasty sound. "But I'm getting to the point where I can't even help myself."

His call left me with both a sense of urgency and a feeling of inadequacy and hopelessness that sapped my energy. Passing on a shower, I trudged to the porch and spent the afternoon rocking in the swing, watching Nelson pursue frogs, thinking his quest was as futile as my own. When Camille and Julie suggested we celebrate my five minutes of fame with dinner out at the Shovel It Inn, I begged off.

Chance seemed to pick up on my mood and was crankier than ever.

At midnight, stumbling with emotional and physical exhaustion, I decided to suck it up, get a better attitude, and get on with the job and with life in general. "I knew the odds were against me when I took on those cases," I told Chance. "I knew no one expected me to solve any of them. Yeah, the sheriff gave me a pep talk, but I bet he didn't think I'd get anywhere, especially in two months."

Had it been only two months?

Bouncing Chance against my shoulder, I walked to the kitchen and checked the calendar. May 23rd going on May 24th. I felt pleased with myself. I'd made progress where Pallister and Eakins hadn't. Granted, Eakins hadn't done more than push paper and Pallister went at things with his mind made up, but still.

Something on the left side of the calendar caught my eye. "Uh oh."

I held Chance so the square marked Mother's Day was six inches from his nose. "You missed it, buddy. But you've got such a good mother. She never mentioned it so you wouldn't feel guilty."

Knowing Camille, I bet she'd been proactive and had a talk with Julie, making it clear she didn't expect to be treated as a replacement for Lisa, didn't expect a card or bouquet.

"But we have no excuse, Chance. We better get busy tomorrow. I'm thinking a trip to that candy store where they make those dark chocolate truffles. We'll get a two-pound box. Then we'll pick up special soil and fertilizer for the rose garden."

Chance pulled in a long breath and I braced myself for another round, but instead he burped, twitched his arms and legs, and burped again.

I turned him so we were face to face. "Say 'Excuse me' when you do that. It's time you learned a few manners."

He burped once more and smiled. A smile at this age was probably a sign he had gas, but I took it as genuine and meant for me.

"You're going to be a big boy. When you have size, it's easier to be a bully, so it's important you learn to ask politely for things, and thank people who help you, and be kind. Except when you absolutely have to be tough. And you better share your toys. I don't want you to grow up as mean and miserly as Louisa Marie."

Chance gave a little squawk and rolled his head on the stem of his neck.

"I wasn't much bigger than you when I encountered her the first time. And I'm not ashamed to admit that I was scared of her all my life."

His eyes widened.

"Maybe not exactly scared, but I kept my distance and didn't push my luck."

He brought his hands together as if he was clapping.

I inclined my head in a bow. "No applause necessary. You would have done the same thing. Now, back to that calendar."

I cradled him in my left arm, scavenged a pen from a cracked mug on the counter, and wrote in the square for the next day "Chance and Dan shape up."

"Now, shaping up is a process, so that doesn't mean we have to turn it around in one day." I put the pen in the mug and sat so we faced the calendar. "But it *does* mean we have to start. It wouldn't kill you to take a bottle now and then. And if you can manage to cry for hours on end, I don't see why you can't manage to stop."

Chance blew a spit bubble and clapped his hands again.

"I'll take that to mean you'll think it over. Good. Because I need my rest. Starting Tuesday I'm getting to work on those cold cases. I'll check with Fred Maddox, I'll type up my notes from the interviews with Natalie Turner and Jennifer Thielman and Helene Cooper, and then I'll focus on Angelina Vernon."

Chance rolled his head and blinked at me.

"Why? Because her life was messed up and she thought no one loved her. That's a lot like Jeremy Yount, right? So maybe she ran off too. And maybe I can find her."

I stroked Chance's downy head. "You're way too young to understand, but it's nice of you to listen. See, you're already getting with that 'being polite' part of the program. It's not so tough, is it?"

Chance gave me a scowling look of concentration. Probably gas, but I decided to take it as a sign he was considering the shape-up program.

"I won't be mad if you backslide now and then. We all do. But the important thing is to take more steps forward.

He blinked.

"I didn't mean literal steps. I know you can't walk yet, but it won't be long before you can. In the meantime, I'll do the walking. Now, let's go to bed. Lots of chores coming up. Gotta move those rose bushes. And Monday we all go up to the cemetery and pull weeds and cut brush and then we have a picnic up there on the grass. You'll love it. Plenty of people to coo over you, so you've got to get your rest. Don't want bags under your eyes."

Chapter 28

Saturday afternoon I was unloading sacks of garden soil when Jefferson turned up in Justin's truck with a tiller in the bed. "Heard you had earth to turn."

"And you don't have enough projects of your own?"

"This is for Julie. Takes precedence." He slid a couple of planks across the tailgate to make a ramp and rolled the tiller off. "Besides, Mary Lou told me if I knew what was good for me I'd see this got done before the day was out."

He laughed in a way that told me he was happy to have Mary Lou order him around. I gave him a welcome-to-the-club high-five and, after time out to grab a couple of beers—purely for the purpose of rehydration—we got to work.

The first order of business was to study the existing layout, determine how much space was required between the bushes, and pace out the ground to be tilled for the nine bushes we planned to move. "And a bench," I told him. "Justin's building a bench."

"Boy's come a long way." He rubbed his chin, paced again, then dug an L with the heel of his work boot along the south and east sides of the plot. "Roses along there and there, bench up here in the corner."

"Works for me. Of course, that might mean it won't work for the women."

"Good point. You calling or am I?"

"Coin flip?"

"My coin?"

He'd carried that coin in his pocket for nearly 30 years and insisted he could tell heads from tails even though everyone else agreed it was worn smooth on both sides. I knew I'd already lost the toss. "I'll call Camille."

He grinned. "And I'll cool my heels on the patio."

After I explained the situation, Camille said she'd think about it, check with Julie, and get back to me in a few minutes. "Don't look at your watch," Jefferson advised. "That only makes time move slower."

I watched a cloud shaped like a lopsided doughnut cross the sky. I watched a breeze ruffle the water. I watched a hawk close a circle in the air and begin another. "It's ten minutes since I called. How tough can this be? It isn't brain surgery."

"Nah, it's way more complicated than that." Jefferson tipped his face to the sun. "First they have to find something wrong with our idea. Then they have to come up with an idea of their own. Then they have to figure out a reason why their plan is better, so they can shut down any arguments we muster. Give it another five minutes and they'll call and say south and west."

"Why not north and west? Why not the complete opposite of what we decided?"

"That'll be their first impulse, but Mary Lou will vote against the north side. Just saying the word makes her cold. Then she'll feel bad about not siding with the idea Camille and Julie had, so she'll come up with a frill that will mean more work for us."

"For a man who spent half his life wandering the hinterland alone, you know a lot about male-female dynamics. Or you're full of crap."

The phone rang and I punched it on. "Stone's gardening service."

"South and west sides," Camille said. "With the bench at the corner. And Mary Lou says a border of rocks would look nice if you have time."

Meaning we should plan to make time.

"It shall be done."

And it was, thanks to Freeman and Evan who got wind of our Herculean labor and turned out with shovels, burlap sacks, and their wives. Once the ground was prepped, holes dug for the bushes, and rocks stacked for a border to be laid later, we adjourned to the Miller house where Pattie and Alda supervised the digging.

"As if we couldn't manage without them yelling 'Careful!' and 'Don't cut that root!'" Freeman groused. "We're not stupid."

"Speak for yourself," Jefferson said. "You're the one who spent ten minutes digging up a sticker bush."

"It looked like a rose. It had thorns and everything."

Evan snickered. I held to silence. The brier looked nothing like a rose bush, but friends didn't pile on humiliation—at least not at *every* opportunity and certainly not when a man's wife had already questioned his lack of gray cells. Jefferson put a positive spin on things. "Good practice for you. We'll have a crop of briers to hack at the cemetery Monday."

And we did.

Tradition called for the men to "beat back the forest," chopping encroaching brush and pulling vines. Women and children took charge of weeding, scrubbing gravestones, and planting marigolds here and there. "I don't much care for them," Mary Lou said as she unloaded a crate, "but they're colorful, they survive the summer, and it's hard for the kids to get them in the ground wrong unless they plant them upside down."

"Hear that?" Evan asked Freeman. "They go in flower-side up."

Freeman shot him a scowl, grabbed his gloves and loppers, and headed for the far side of the cemetery. With a shrug, Evan grabbed a saw and tagged along.

I lingered for a minute with Camille and Julie at the marble dog that sat atop Clarence Wolven's grave. As if he knew that the man who'd intended to train him was buried here, Nelson sat beside the marker and hung his head. Julie knelt beside him, stroking his ears and whispering. I felt tears burn my eyes and heard Camille sniff and swallow.

In a moment Julie lifted her head. "Does Mary Lou know where that girl is buried? The one who died at the Devil's Tombstone?"

"Probably. Ask her."

Julie stood and trotted off, Nelson at her side.

"No lifting your leg on the gravestones," I warned him before I headed for the perimeter with a shovel and a hoe.

Jefferson settled an ax on his shoulder and fell in beside me as I passed Louisa Marie's grave. "One day we'll know more people up here than in town."

"And appreciate their silence." I nodded toward Freeman and Evan.

"Those two have been sniping at each other since they were knee-high to a grasshopper. Could be what keeps them close."

He glanced at Louisa Marie's marker again and I knew he was thinking that her sniping—spiteful and filled with venom—hadn't brought anyone closer.

"About time you got here with that ax." Stub waved a pruning saw. "I wanted to bring the chainsaw but Marcella lit into me about it being too noisy and this being a day of remembering. I told her some of the people I'd be remembering owned first-rate chainsaws when they were alive, but that didn't cut it. I'll be in the doghouse for a week."

Freeman grinned, then he and Evan banded together to needle Stub. Since Willie Dean Denton's death two summers ago, Stub was the butt of many jokes and in recent months had accepted the role thrust upon him with good humor.

I turned toward Ronny's grave. On the far side of the hill it was, at the request of his mother, a good distance from the others, and the stone lay flat on the ground. The expression "beyond the pale" came to mind. In his attempts to thwart change, Ronny had crossed boundaries, broken laws, trampled trust. He'd killed his wife, killed a friend, tried to kill me. Now, in death, he was cast out.

A lone figure worked around the marker.

Justin.

"Think the kid wants to talk about his father?" Jefferson asked.

"Maybe. But where the hell do I start?"

"*You* don't." Jefferson took the shovel and hoe.

Tugging on my work gloves, I walked to Ronny's grave, stomach tight. Justin was on his knees, digging out weeds with a trowel. His gray T-shirt was dark with sweat around his neck and along his spine. "Need a hand?"

"Thanks. Almost finished." His voice broke on the final word.

I knelt beside him, laid a hand on his shoulder, and kept still. The granite marker was rough, the surface unpolished. Only Ronny's name and the dates of his birth and death were chipped into it. No mention of him being a husband and father. No use of the word "beloved" or intimation that he was resting in the arms of angels.

"I still don't get it." Justin said after a moment. "Why he . . . why he thought he had to . . . I don't get it."

This was the place where some folks might plug in the moves-in-mysterious-ways explanation, but I went with admitting ignorance. "Neither do I."

He tipped his head to study me, his eyes bright with tears. "Do you wonder if I'll—"

"No." I tightened my grip on his shoulder, fingers biting into dense muscle. "You're on the right path. And you've come a long way along it."

He hung his head and stabbed at a weed. "That doesn't mean I'll stay on it."

"No, it doesn't. But I see you with your sister and I see empathy and patience and selfless generosity I didn't see in you before. Those qualities will keep you headed the right way when the path splits."

He stabbed the weed again, but with less conviction.

"Your father was my best friend for a lot of years. He loved Hemlock Lake, loved being the one people turned to. When you came down the lake after the storm, I saw his strength and determination and sense of responsibility—the qualities I admired so much in him."

Justin gave the weed a vicious stab and wrenched it loose. "He had so much. But he broke faith. He betrayed us, all of us."

"I don't think he meant to. Not at the start. But his thoughts got twisted."

He looked at me again, his eyes haunted, pleading. "And mine won't?"

"I can't guarantee that. No one can."

"But you'll say something if . . ."

"I will if Jefferson doesn't beat me to it."

He nodded, lowered his head, and traced his father's name on the stone. "A lot of people were afraid of him. Mom and Julie especially. But plenty of others." He nodded toward the men chopping brush. "Even them. Everyone but you. Julie says you fought him the night of the fireworks. She says you both lied and said you weren't fighting but she knew you were."

"It wasn't much of a fight. It was more like he threw punches and I ducked and hoped I wouldn't puke when he connected."

"Still, you stood up to him."

There was pride in his voice, enough that I squared my shoulders a bit. "And I'll stand up to you if I have to. But I doubt it will ever come to that. Like I said, you're on a good road. And when he gets old enough to get into trouble, I'm counting on you to watch out for Chance." I held my hand out. "Deal?"

"Deal." He stood, winced, and rubbed his right knee.

"I'll root out a few weeds if you want."

"Yeah? I wouldn't mind a cold drink."

"Camille brought a jug of lemonade. And I bet you could find a beer in that cooler in Jefferson's car."

He tipped his head to the sun, two hours from its high point. "It's not too early?"

"I like that you asked that question. But on a day as hot as this one will be, I think we can set the rules aside for one beer."

He dropped the trowel and headed off, leaving me with Ronny.

I studied his marker for a moment, glanced over my shoulder to make sure I was alone, then spoke. "The last time it was just you and me, I thought I'd be the one lying under a stone."

I hammered the handle of the trowel with the heel of my hand, getting the point under a dandelion and popping it loose. "I wonder if you'd be weeding at my grave if you got away with killing me. Or would you be pissing on my stone and planning to put someone else in the ground?"

I tapped the trowel on his marker. "When I was drowning, I thought I deserved to die for not seeing what I should have and stopping you."

A shadow fell across the granite slab and a dull voice proclaimed, "It is not for us on this earth to determine whether anyone deserves to die before the allotted time."

"I won't argue with you, Reverend Balforth." I attacked the last of the weeds. "Although if someone does great harm to innocent people, I would have no qualms about deciding they shouldn't continue to draw breath."

"There are certainly cases where there seems no other way." Balforth knelt beside me and laid his hands on the stone. "When we come up against evil so dark that purity and prayer cannot change its course."

Evil like that in Ronny Miller. Or Colden Cornell. Or the person or persons who killed Genevieve Graham and Theresa Gilligan and Franklin Turner.

Balforth bent his head and his lips moved.

"What are you praying for? Ronny's immortal soul?"

"That is my duty."

I pried another dandelion from the ground. "But is it your desire?"

"I pray for everyone on this hill."

Not an answer.

And I wanted one.

"In a one-prayer-fits-all way? Do you offer the same prayer for Ronny as you do for Willie Dean? The same for Lisa and Louisa Marie?"

He raised his head and looked me in the eye. "I am not the man I'd like to be. When I come to this grave, I also pray for myself. I pray that I will be forgiven for my failings in the past and I pray that in the future I will recognize evil even if it has been with us all of our lives and is as familiar as the sunrise. I pray that I will know it when it comes among us even though it may be disguised as succor or salvation. And I pray that I shall have the strength to put myself in its path."

He spoke with force and conviction I'd never heard from him before. "Familiar" was clearly a reference to Ronny. Was the other a reference to Wesley Falton? Were Balforth's words prompted by jealousy and fear of being squeezed out of his place in the community? Or . . .?

"If you're trying to tell me something, Reverend, you'll have to spell it out."

"My sins may be of lesser magnitude, but I am not without sin."

"So you won't cast stones?"

He didn't answer, but got to his feet and stood for a second, arms spread, casting the shadow of the cross on Ronny's grave. Then he walked away.

Chapter 29

That evening Chance pushed the start of his squalling back by an hour. "Nice going," I told him in a soft voice. "If you put a cork in it earlier, I'll consider that you took our discussion seriously and you're easing into the shape-up program. I don't mind if you hit the crying with all you've got, as long as you shut the show down at a reasonable hour."

Sticking to my theory that I could change his mood by changing my own, I hummed "Mr. Bojangles" and even danced a little as I carried him to the kitchen. "See, this is the calendar and this is what we wrote." I traced the words "shape up" with his tiny forefinger.

He stopped crying long enough to make a noise like a half-hearted growl and I traced the letters again. "I won't be mad if you're crying because you're hurt or scared. I'm not that kind of guy. I'm the kind of guy who wants to make it better. Not that I always can. A lot of things are out of my control. But I want you to know I'll always try."

Cradling him in my left arm, I strolled to my desk in the library and showed him the stack of files. "Now, I don't want you to feel guilty, but tomorrow I'd really like to work on the Angelina Vernon case that I told you about the other night. The thing is, though, I can't work if I can't concentrate, and I can't concentrate if I can't get enough sleep."

He squawked and flailed his arms.

"Don't get upset. If I can't work on the case tomorrow, there's always the next day or the day after that."

He gulped and did the growl thing again.

I held him up so we were eye to eye. "No pressure, kid." I kissed the tip of his nose. "No pressure."

Camille glanced at the kitchen clock and joggled Chance against her shoulder. "You're up early. And you never woke me last night."

"When he stopped howling he didn't act like he was hungry so I stuck him in the crib and he fell asleep."

"He was still asleep when I got up at 6:00." She took a bite of an English muffin slathered with almond butter. "Is it my imagination, or is he getting past the colic?"

"Don't jinx progress." I knocked on wood, tapping a cabinet door, a cutting board, and the table. "If it *is* progress. Might be a lull before another storm."

"Are you doing anything different?"

"Positive thinking." I poured coffee in the biggest mug I could find. "An upbeat voice and body language. And goal-setting. For both of us."

"Goal-setting for an eight-week-old baby." Camille laughed. "What kind of goals? Sit-ups? Learning the alphabet?"

"Less caterwauling and some bottle feeding." I sipped coffee. "We had a discussion and I'm pretty sure he agreed to work on his shortcomings."

She rolled her eyes. "And I'm pretty sure you've reached the end of the rope called sanity. No more walking the floor for you. I'll take over."

I didn't remind her of what happened when she tried that before. First thing in the morning wasn't the ideal time to negotiate with Camille. Her mind was on too many other things. "All right. If he refuses a bottle again today, you take over."

She rolled her eyes again, but then handed Chance to me and got a bottle from the refrigerator.

When the house was quiet, I made cheese toast, poured a second cup of coffee, and took Angelina Vernon's file, my cell phone, and a notepad out to the porch. Unlike Jeremy Yount's father, Angelina's parents—although involved in what Harry Pallister described as "a vicious divorce"—expressed their love and spoke of her in glowing terms. They'd participated in the search, tacking up posters, passing out fliers, opening their home to the media. All of that, Angelina's mother told me, brought reconciliation. They went to counseling, worked out differences, and "made themselves into better people" to be worthy of her when she returned. A newspaper clipping from 18 months ago updated Angelina's disappearance and reported on a stranger-danger awareness program her parents participated in.

One thing I learned from Jeremy Yount's case was that teenagers could be adept at showing parents what they want them to see, and at misdirection. Jeremy had demonstrated little skill behind the wheel, so his father believed he couldn't drive. Jeremy hadn't met his father's standards, so he was labeled incompetent.

I hoped Camille and I would be open and supportive enough that Julie wouldn't baffle us with BS, but I knew it was complicated. There were lines Julie might feel she had to cross as a rite of passage or to assert her individuality or for a dozen other reasons. Knowing that we couldn't support some of those crossings, she might lie. Or she might leave us.

I put that painful thought aside and went to the file. Like Jeremy, Angelina may have had a friend who kept her secrets. The trick was to find that friend.

Harry Pallister had talked to six of Angelina's friends, four girls and two boys, and Serenity Brook had provided current phone numbers. I went to work, calling them all again and this time asking for the names of anyone else she was close to. That got me a few more names, mostly girls who told me Angelina liked boys, but didn't like the drama of high school romances. When I asked them to describe Angelina's state of mind in the weeks before she disappeared, they gave me this: shy, nervous, confused, angry, frustrated, sick of the fights at home, feeling stuck in the middle, and lonely.

One girl told me something else—Angelina's dog had died over the winter. "He was really old and he had cancer and they operated but they couldn't get it all and Angie had him put to sleep and then her mother and father said they didn't want another dog because they were splitting up and she was really sad, so she volunteered at an animal clinic."

The girl didn't know the name of the clinic, but remembered it was next to a place that fixed shoes.

"Probably nothing," I told Nelson. "Probably another dead end."

He thumped his tail on the planks and favored me with a doggie grin.

"You're telling me it's an omen if there are dogs involved?"

Nelson thumped his tail again.

The phone rang in the house and I got up, stiff with sitting for what I noted had been three hours, and hobbled to a small table by the hearth. "Hear that?" Camille asked. "That's the sound of our son sucking on a bottle. The next sound you hear will be me bowing to your superior knowledge of baby psychology."

I mumbled that it was probably coincidence and he would have taken the bottle anyway, but when she hung up I high-fived air and did an end-zone victory dance that included spiking a throw pillow.

After lunch and a consultation with the phone book and a map, I found the vet's office where Angelina had volunteered. "Of course I remember her," the receptionist told me. "Everybody here does. Come tomorrow morning around 9:00. We'll all be here."

"We" turned out to be two assistants in scrubs patterned with parrots and jungle foliage, and two doctors, a lean and weathered man in his 60s who specialized in large animals and livestock, and a cheerful woman in her 40s who treated companion animals. "But not snakes," she informed me. "If a snake comes in that door, it waits for Dad."

As the receptionist predicted, they all remembered Angelina and added more to descriptions of her mental state: anxious, withdrawn, loving, thoughtful, wishing to be part of a family.

"She hated going home because she said it *wasn't* a home," Ed recalled. "One Saturday we went to a farm up in a hollow at the back of beyond. Goats, cows, chickens, you name it. One of those self-sufficient operations. Twenty folks or so—all shapes and sizes—living in one house, growing a garden, spinning yarn, weaving blankets. Back to the land stuff. She talked about it for days, about how everyone was involved and important."

A commune.

An instant family.

And perhaps a magnet for a girl who wanted to belong.

"Got an address?"

Ed scratched his head and looked to the receptionist, a woman about his age. Now that I focused on her nameplate I saw they shared a last name. "A post office box is all we have," she said. "And who knows if the farm's still running. They haven't called us in more than three years."

"That long, huh?" Ed frowned and then his eyes did a slow roll. I could almost see the synapses firing deep in his brain. "Come to think of it, they had a young guy out there who used to give me a hand. No formal training, mind you, but he had a way with animals and read a few books from the library. If they haven't called, he must be doing okay."

"Or they didn't like your barnside manner," the receptionist said in a voice I could use to scour a griddle.

Ed shrugged and spread his hands. "If you want things sugar-coated, you don't want me."

Ed and Sheriff North could have been brothers.

"And if you want things filed in any kind of order you also don't want him." The receptionist rolled her chair to a row of filing cabinets, pulled out a drawer, flicked through tabs and found a manila folder. "The person you want is me."

She slapped the file on the counter. "Galloway Hollow Farm. Directions are right there."

I bent over the file and the neat lines of writing detailing roads and landmarks.

"Want a copy?"

I flashed a smile. "Does a sheepdog shed on the carpet?"

"A communal farm! Up in the Blackhead Mountains!" Serenity Brook set aside the raw sweet potato she'd been gnawing on. "Sounds more like a cult compound to me. Better wear a vest. They're probably armed to the teeth. And alert the feds so you don't screw up an undercover operation."

I laughed, but felt an anxious tingle at the base of my brain. "You've been surfing too many conspiracy sites."

"And apparently you haven't. Those guys may have let Ed the vet in to tend to their cows, but it might be a different story when you flash your badge."

"I was planning on a more subtle approach."

"Like what? Call and say Angelina Vernon won a drawing for cruise and you have papers for her to sign?"

I smacked my forehead. "Why didn't I think of that?"

"This isn't a joke. And don't tell me you're going to pretend to be lost. They'll see right through that!"

"Yeah, if they're paranoid, meth-cooking, gun-trading, bomb-building whackoids. But if they're actual farmers—"

She slammed the sweet potato on the edge of her desk. "This root has more sense than you do! Don't go up there alone."

"Does this show of concern mean you're starting to like me?" I brushed a chunk of potato from my shoulder and another from my wrist.

"Arrgggh. Let me see what I can find." She squinted at the copy of the directions, turned to her computer, hammered at the keyboard, and brought up an aerial image. "Get me coffee. Not the crap from upstairs. Drinkable brew. With chocolate and hazelnut flavoring and whipped cream."

"Because your doctor prescribed designer coffee? Or because the latest foodie magazine claims it goes well with raw sweet potato?"

"No, because you owe me. And if you don't return from this fool's errand, this might be my last chance to ding you. And, finally, because I told you to."

Hiding a grin, and taking my time so she wouldn't think I had no will of my own where strong women were concerned, I got to my feet, stretched, flicked another chunk of potato from my jeans, and ambled to the door.

When I returned, she had a sheaf of printouts and a frown. "Well, I give them credit for one thing, it looks like a legitimate farm. They filed papers, paid taxes, jumped through the hoops to sell at farmers' markets and health stores."

I set the coffee—extra large with double whipped cream and chocolate shavings—on the desk beside the beleaguered sweet potato. "But you think they have another agenda?"

"Most people do." She popped the lid off the coffee, studied the topping, then replaced the lid and sipped. "Not bad."

I riffled through the papers. "So this Mark Galloway inherited the land ten years ago and put his degree in agriculture to work. Sounds more like a farmer than a cult leader."

"If you do a little research you'll see the two aren't mutually exclusive." She shoved the sweet potato into a metal wastebasket. "I hope you don't find that out the hard way."

"Because you like me?"

"Because I like this coffee and I'm counting on another dose next time you need something."

Chapter 30

In the words of old-time Hemlock Lake residents, "I'm not as green as I am cabbage looking." That's why I invited Jefferson to ride along the next day.

As I drove, he studied aerial pictures of the layout of Galloway Hollow Farm, Angelina Vernon's file, and a glossy picture of her taken four years ago with the word "MISSING" printed at the top and physical details and phone numbers listed at the bottom. When he finished, he concentrated on the scenery as I turned onto roads leading into the slope-shouldered Blackhead Mountains.

"Haven't been up this way for years. If we don't find Angelina Vernon, at least we got our eyes full of nature. Been spending too much time indoors on Mary Lou's projects and I'm feeling depleted." He reclined the seat a bit and stretched his legs. "Remodeling does make her happy, though, and that has a way of making me happy. Speaking of that, how's Chance doing?"

"Cried for only two hours last night."

"Only?"

"Yeah, never thought I'd say two hours of screaming was a good thing."

"Bet he'll bellow with a vengeance tonight."

"Maybe. If I plan for full-bore torture, I'll be happy with medium-grade misery."

We took the final turn listed on the sheet of directions, rumbled over a cattle guard, and crept along a lane that wound through birches and pines and opened on a sweeping strip of green meadow sprinkled with wildflowers. Beyond lay pastures and plowed fields, two barns painted the traditional red, several outbuildings painted white with green trim, and a two-story gray farmhouse with yellow shutters.

A collection of vehicles surrounded the house. Two men worked on a fence at the far edge of an upper pasture and a woman paced a plowed field, a child ahead of her poking a broom handle into the ground to make holes for the seeds she dropped. Another child, trailing, kicked soil into the holes.

"Well-kept place. Goats look fat and happy," Jefferson said. "No armed guards. Not that I can see. Nobody running for cover or a cache of weapons. Any chance of a signal in here?"

I dug my cell phone from my pocket and passed it to him.

"Nope," he said after a minute. "And all I've got is the rifle under that blanket in the rear. What's the plan if there's trouble?"

"If things look hinky, we tell them the sheriff knows we're here and hope that's a deterrent."

"Plenty of cases where it hasn't been."

Jefferson was starting to sound a hell of a lot like Serenity Brook. "All right, Mr. Worst-Case Scenario. I'll turn around and park facing out. You get behind the wheel and keep the engine running. If they gun me down, don't be a hero, get to civilization and bring the cavalry."

He snorted in disgust, but didn't offer Plan B.

And, in any case, it wasn't necessary.

As I turned the SUV around with the intention of backing between a tractor and a vintage station wagon, a young woman came out of the house and trotted along the path, long hair waving like a small flag, two Australian Shepherds flanking her. "Are you lost?"

When she was a few feet away, I asked a question of my own. "Are you?"

She blinked.

"You're Angelina Vernon, right?"

"Uh." She backed up a few steps, reaching behind her as if feeling for a chair. The dogs crouched, whining.

"I'm Dan Stone. This is Jefferson Longyear." I held up the photograph from her file. "And this is you, four years ago. The last picture taken before you disappeared one Friday after school. Your parents used it to make posters to hang on power poles and bulletin boards."

"I . . . uh . . ." The dogs pressed against her and she gripped their collars.

"I work for the Ashokan County Sheriff's Department. My job is to close your case."

"My case?"

"You disappeared. Most everyone thought you'd been abducted, maybe killed."

She gasped, then swallowed hard. "I didn't . . . I didn't know. We don't have a TV."

As if that explained it all.

"While they were searching for you, your parents worked out their issues. They're together again. They always believed you were alive."

She released the dogs and twisted the tail of her work shirt. "I didn't think they cared. I didn't think they wanted me."

Jefferson tapped my arm. "Somebody's coming from one of the outbuildings," he whispered.

I turned a thumb up to him. "Listen, Angelina, I have no intention of trying to force you to go home—or anywhere. All I want to know is whether you could leave here if you wanted to."

"What? Why wouldn't I be able to leave?"

The way she asked made me wonder if she didn't understand what I was saying, if she didn't realize she was a prisoner, or if she'd been brainwashed to an extent where this was her entire world and she'd never thought of leaving.

"If you said you wanted to visit your parents, would anyone try to stop you?"

"No. Why would they? People leave here all the time, especially in the winter when there's not so much to do. Last year a bunch of us drove to Florida." She lifted her head to look past me and smiled. "It was fun, wasn't it, Sam?"

"Yeah." A lanky young man with sun-bleached brown hair and a gray T-shirt stained with grease gave a hand signal to the dogs that sent them racing away, then stepped to her side. "What's going on? These guys lost?"

"No." She tucked her hand into his and beamed a bright smile. "But *I* was. Or at least everyone thought I was." She tugged him closer to the SUV. "Sam, this is . . ."

"Dan Stone." I thrust out my hand. "Cold case investigator for the Ashokan County Sheriff's Department. This is my colleague, Jefferson Longyear."

"Sam Livingston." He gripped my hand, his fingers strong and rough. "Cold cases? What brings you up here?"

"Me," Angelina said. "He came to find me."

Sam released my hand and stared at her.

"I ran away from home four years ago." She toed the asphalt. "People thought I was dead. But not my parents."

"Parents?" He cupped her face in his hands. "You said—"

"I know. I lied. To you and Mark and everyone. I didn't know what else to do. I didn't want to get sent home."

She turned to me, hands outstretched, eyes pleading. "They were fighting all the time, fighting over everything, even me and how much time I'd spend with each of them after the divorce. They didn't ask me. They wouldn't listen. They kept yelling and my head hurt and my stomach hurt and I threw up all the time."

She swallowed and gazed at the barns and the fields beyond where the fence-menders and seed-planters were at work. "And then I came up here and it was so peaceful and everyone got along. And there were puppies. And I thought my parents would never miss me . . ."

For a moment we were all silent and then Sam asked, "Do you want see them? Your parents. We can go as soon as I change my shirt."

"I want to see them. I want you to meet them." She stood on tiptoe and kissed him. "And I want to tell them we're getting married in the fall. But . . ."

Jefferson nudged me. "Neutral ground," he whispered.

I nodded. "Your parents have learned a lot about loving and listening, but it will be a shock when you turn up." I plucked one of my cards from the ashtray, wrote the sheriff's number on the reverse, and passed it over. "Things might go better if you have Sheriff North lay the groundwork. Give him a call, tell him who you are, and ask if he can facilitate a reunion."

"That's a good idea, Angel," Sam said.

She took the card and headed for the house. "I'm calling him right now."

Sam watched her go, a look of stunned amazement on his face. "I thought I knew everything about her."

"It's a woman's mission to keep you guessing, son." Jefferson passed the picture of Angelina through the window to him. "Might as well get used to it before you take those vows. Makes for less aggravation later on."

I glanced in the rearview mirror as we rolled past the strip of meadow and saw Sam looking from the picture to the house and scratching his chin.

"Facilitate?" Jefferson said with a snort. "You're turning into a full-fledged bureaucrat before my very eyes."

"Ha. Ha." I shot him a glare. "If you drop that right now, I won't tell Mary Lou you used the word 'aggravation' when referring to married life."

"But in lighthearted way," Jefferson said.

We bumped across the cattle guard. "No doubt she'd see the distinction."

"On a good day, yeah."

He flipped the top of the water bottle he'd brought along. "On the subject of laying groundwork, you didn't think you should call the sheriff before she did?"

"Nah." I turned onto a paved road and sped up. "Let's keep him on his toes."

When I got home there was a message on the machine. "You trying to stop my ticker, son? Not that I'm complaining about you closing another case, but would it kill you to give me a heads-up? And what's with this 'facilitate a reunion' stuff? Last time you were in my office, was there a psychology degree on my wall?"

Laughing, I puttered around for a bit before I called him. "I was thinking it made for good press, you bringing them together."

"Yeah, yeah. Once I got over being poleaxed, I figured as much. Got one of my hand-holders working on it. She's thinking maybe an ice cream parlor or the duck pond in the park. I'll let you know."

"Why?"

"So you can be there, get credit."

"I don't—"

"And so reporters don't track you to your house."

I flashed on an image of Colden Cornell walking down my driveway last year, searching for a story, searching for the pup that survived when he killed Clarence Wolven and his dogs.

A match struck and North sucked at his pipe. "Two in two weeks. If you keep up this pace you'll have the decks cleared around the Fourth of July."

"Well, don't schedule news conferences in advance. I have a feeling all I've done is take the easy ones off the board. From here on out it will be slow going."

"Slow going still puts you miles ahead of Pallister and Eakins. Eakins was always a waste of oxygen, but Pallister . . ." He sucked at the pipe again. "Well, I guess he pretty much was, too."

He hung up, leaving me to think again about reality and appearance, about Genevieve Graham's clandestine calls and Micah Thielman's pretenses. Had Franklin Turner and Theresa Gilligan also kept secrets? And what about Judy Arnold?

Because I started with the oldest cases and then moved to the freshest, her case got shuffled to the bottom of the stack. I moved the folder to the top and promised her I'd review it the next day.

But as my grandmother used to say, "A man who makes plans should be prepared to change them."

First, Camille woke up late and left it to me to get Chance washed and dressed and then cart him to Pattie's house. Since floor-walking had excused me from morning preparations, I wasn't familiar with the process and moved at the speed of a geriatric sloth. As I was heading out, Sheriff North called to say the reunion was set for 11:00 at a pizza parlor and I better be there.

What with everyone telling their stories, reporters asking a thousand questions, photographers recording interviews and cover video, and the pizza parlor owner laying on a feed, the event rolled on for a couple of hours. Angelina's father gritted his teeth half a dozen times and her mother was white-lipped with contained anger more than once, but there were plenty of hugs and tears as well. When it was over, the Vernons followed the precedent set by Jeremy Yount and offered Sheriff North reimbursement before they accompanied Sam and Angelina up to Galloway Hollow Farm to start planning a wedding.

The next morning Julie and I headed to the storage unit I rented after Rachel Miller died last summer.

"Julie will know when she's ready to sort through it all," Camille had told me back then. And Saturday morning the time came.

Jefferson, Freeman, and Evan tagged along and, at Julie's direction, parceled out furniture, clothing, linens, small appliances, books, and pictures. We built piles bound for charity, Justin's house, or our garage.

"This smells like she did, like lilacs and roses." Julie held a deep blue dress against her face. "Before she got sick and smelled like medicine."

"If you put it in a box by itself you can keep the smell for a long time," Jefferson said. "Whenever you open the box it will seem like she's right there."

Julie hugged him, rubbing her face against his shirt to blot her tears.

After snacking on sandwiches at the store, we made the trek to Rachel's house and lugged several dozen boxes from the attic. Justin joined us and claimed his grandfather's wood carvings and tools, a hunting knife, a leather jacket, and a box of wool socks salted with so many mothballs the odor nearly knocked me over.

"You can never have too many wool socks." Freeman waved his hand to clear his nose. "But I'd let those air in a stiff breeze for half a century or so."

Julie collected more framed family photos, sepia-toned and faded. "Mary Lou will know who these people are. I'll write their names on the backs."

I couldn't imagine Julie putting the images of dour-faced ancestors on her bedroom walls beside bright watercolors and bulletin boards crammed with greeting cards and comic strips. I expected she'd pack them in another box and, when she had a home of her own, move them to another attic. The past was a carapace, a shell and a shelter.

Rachel had kept few reminders of her son, but tucked into a box of china knickknacks, we found a framed photo of Ronny by the lake, displaying a string of trout. "How old was he then?" Julie asked.

I studied the picture, seemed to have a vague memory of there being a companion shot of me with my own string of trophies—a string smaller than Ronny's because that's the way it was. "About eight, maybe nine. That's a new rod he's holding. He gave me his old one and I passed mine on to Willie Dean."

Julie shot me a teary smile and pressed the photo into Justin's hands. "You should put this up in the bait shop."

Justin shook his head.

"No, really," Julie said. "This is from . . . from way before."

From before malevolent rot ate away Ronny Miller's moral core. Before creeping evil, relentless as the glaciers that once overran these mountains, took control.

I thought of what Reverend Balforth said about praying he would recognize evil "as familiar as the sunrise," evil that had been among us all our lives. I'd recognized it in Ronny, but I'd denied and excused it. Perhaps if I hadn't, if I'd stood in his path years before, things might have been different for all of us.

"He was so happy then," Julie said.

Justin glanced at Jefferson and then at me. "Take it," I said. "No matter what he did, he was your father."

Chapter 31

That evening Brother Elijah's third revival rocked Hemlock Lake. Larger and louder, it drew visitors from New Jersey, Connecticut, Massachusetts, and Vermont. Stub, clad in an orange vest and his fire department cap and wielding a whistle the size of my fist, halted a stream of cars and waved us across the dam. A stocky young deputy shook his head when I signaled for a turn at the post office, then stopped traffic and waved me on. "Great job on those cold cases," he called as I rolled past.

Mary Lou and Jefferson had staked out the same tree-shaded plot and spread an old quilt to claim space for us. "What with Memorial Day and all, I didn't get a picnic organized," Mary Lou said.

"Just as well." Jefferson stood to rearrange chairs and make room for Chance's stroller. "Freeman and Evan won't come out of Bluestone Hollow until the holy rolling is over and the roads are clear."

"That might not be until dawn." Justin emerged from the grove behind us and sprawled on the quilt. "Cars are parked on both sides of the road all the way to the dock and beyond. If fire breaks out, Stub could never squeeze the tanker truck through."

"Be fun watching him try," Jefferson said.

I grinned, imagining Stub bulling the ancient fire tanker through a gauntlet of parked cars, ripping off side mirrors and crumpling fenders. "Could be Stub's finest hour."

"And maybe his *last* hour as fire chief," Camille added. "But he'd go out in a blaze of glory."

"So would the house he couldn't get to," Justin said in a baleful voice.

"You're right." Mary Lou patted his shoulder. "We shouldn't joke about fire."

Especially in front of the son of an arsonist and the woman he killed.

"Julie's enjoying those little kids." Camille pointed to the makeshift corral and the teenage girls herding a dozen toddlers. "I hope she doesn't lose her enthusiasm before Chance starts walking."

"I hope she doesn't decide she needs one of her own," Justin said, "before I'm ready to be an uncle. Which won't be for another dozen years."

"Is she still showing an interest in Isaac?" Camille asked.

Justin ran his fingers through brown hair an inch longer than his father would have tolerated. "Yeah, some. But that could be because he's the only game in town. And he's different."

"He's certainly quiet," Mary Lou said. "Never says a word more than he has to when he comes in to mail things for his father."

"The other day he bought a sack of split peas and an onion. Dither asked if he was enjoying living here and all he did was shrug, give her five dollars, take his change, and walk out." Camille turned to Justin. "Is he as quiet with you?"

"Yeah. But he sees and hears everything. He's like a deer in a clearing, sniffing the air, snapping his head around. He'd probably twitch his ears if he could." Justin leaned on his elbows. "The only thing he says more than a few words about is salvation."

"Well, that's natural," Mary Lou said. "He's been steeped in his father's views since he was born."

"Yeah, but he doesn't have the same take."

"In regard to renouncing things you like too much?" Camille asked.

"Mostly. I don't ask him for specifics because I don't want to get sucked in."

"Sucked into a discussion?" I asked. "Or into religion?"

"Both. I don't have much time for talk, especially pie-in-the-sky talk. I've got studying to do." Justin got to his feet. "He asked me to come tonight. I told him not tonight or any night, but he said he'd set a chair for me under the tent."

"I guess you have to admire his faith," Mary Lou said.

"Faith can be powerful," Jefferson said, "but I don't always admire what it can lead people to do."

We all slept late on Sunday, even Chance, and at noon were on the porch, working on a stack of waffles with Julie reporting on the revival. "Isaac says later in the summer when the water gets warmer his father's going to baptize people in the lake. He's gonna walk them to that sandy spot near the dock and dunk them. Isaac says his father says dunked all the way is what counts. If a minister only sprinkles you, then you're not saved."

She frowned and speared a slice of banana. "Did I get sprinkled or dunked?"

Camille shot me a glance that said this question was mine to answer. "I don't know. I was in Arizona when you were little."

"We could look in your baby book," Camille suggested.

"I already did. There's nothing there." Julie smashed the banana slice with her fork. "Does that mean I wasn't baptized? Am I going to hell?"

"Of course not." Camille kicked over her chair in a rush to hug Julie. "Maybe your mother got busy and forgot to write it down. We'll check the church records. And if you weren't—and you want to be—we'll see that it happens."

"But before that," I said, "I'd like you to read up on the history and purpose of baptism and what it means to the church *and* to the person being baptized. Read up on different religions, too. It's a big decision—a lot bigger than buying a car. And you've put hours into that."

"I guess," Julie mumbled against Camille's shoulder.

"Dan has a good point." Camille shot me a wink and chuckled. "And you know I don't say that often because I hate to be caught agreeing with him."

Julie giggled.

"Besides, it's not like he's asking you to write a term paper. You can probably find everything you need on the Internet." Camille righted her chair, topped off her coffee, then dropped into her seat. "When you've done the research, if you want Wesley Falton to dunk you in the lake, then go for it."

Julie nodded, loaded the smashed banana onto a piece of waffle, folded it over, and ate it like a sandwich. "What if I already got sprinkled by Reverend Balforth?"

"Well, this country was founded on freedom of religion," I said. "And that also means freedom to *change* your religion."

Julie glanced from me to Camille. "And lots of really good people don't go to church at all."

"But it's good to know we could go to a service." Camille threaded her fingers with mine. "It's good to know our options are open."

Later, while I was kicking back in a lounge chair on the patio with Chance asleep on my chest, Julie laid a towel on the picnic table and spilled out the contents of the jewelry box I'd brought home from Rachel's apartment the day she died. There wasn't much in it—thin gold bands, engagement rings with tiny diamonds, watches that no longer ticked, simple hoop earrings, a charm bracelet, and a braided silver chain with a crystal acorn dangling from it.

Julie stirred the collection with her forefinger. "Grandma used to go to church, didn't she?"

"Yes, she did."

Until her son killed his wife. Until she felt judged when she slid into her pew.

"I thought she wore a cross. A gold one."

"She did."

Until she decided to take her own life in her own time instead of leaving that to cancer.

I lowered my gaze so Julie wouldn't sense the secret Camille and I had sworn to keep.

"What about Mom? Did she have a cross?"

"She might have. I don't remember."

If she had, would it have saved her?

I put the brakes on that train of thought. "I *do* remember seeing your mother wear that acorn pendant."

Julie lifted the chain. "I kinda remember."

"You can check with Mary Lou, but I think she gave that to your mother after she took first place at a regional craft fair."

"Neat." Julie studied it for a few seconds, then set it aside and sifted through the heap of jewelry again.

Was she searching for what wasn't there? Could I persuade her to want what was?

"Mary Lou gave your mom that acorn because she didn't think a blue ribbon was enough. She could have given her a star because that's what your mom was. And she could have given her a heart because she loved her. But I think she picked out that acorn because it represented the woods and the little creatures she created. And a whole lot more."

Julie picked up the chain again. Sunlight struck the crystal acorn, scattering bits of rainbow across the patio stones. "Like what?"

"Like her strength and patience and determination." I sat up—no easy feat with a sleeping baby on my chest. "You know plenty of acorns never sprout and grow into oak trees, right?"

"Because squirrels eat them," Julie said. "And deer. And jays."

"Or because they land on a rocky spot."

Julie's eyes glistened and she blinked away tears. "My mom's spot was pretty rocky when she was little. Later, too."

"It was. But she made the best of it and grew as tall as she could and she sheltered you. And she never doubted your determination. She knew you'd roll or bounce or hijack a squirrel or launch yourself into a stream—whatever it took to get to the perfect spot to set your roots."

Julie swung the crystal, scattering rainbows. "So I'm like her acorn?"

"That's the way I see it."

I let her think that over while I pretended an absorbing interest in a chipmunk peering at us from beneath the barbecue grill.

"Do you think Mary Lou would mind if I wore this?"

"I think she'd be thrilled. Want me to hook it for you?"

She nodded, sat beside me, and lifted the hair from the nape of her neck. I hooked the clasp and she stood and stepped into a spill of sunlight. "How do I look?"

"Beautiful."

And so much like her mother my breath caught in my throat.

Chance cranked up for less than an hour that evening and, for the first time in weeks, I got a good night's sleep. That, however, had a downside in terms of time to call my own.

"Since you're so chipper, there are things that desperately need doing around the store." Camille handed me a tall cup of coffee and pointed to a pad of paper on the end of the counter. "A couple of shelves need more support, the hydraulic device that closes the door is giving out, and the metal edging on the counter is loose. Can we replace it with something we won't cut ourselves on?"

I dropped whole wheat bread into the toaster and checked the rest of the list. All small stuff. But small stuff had a way of leading to more small stuff or expanding into not-so-small stuff. Especially if Camille and Dither put their heads together and came up with a series of ideas starting with the words "one more thing" or "it might be better if" or "while you're there." And especially if the usual retired suspects came by to offer opinions and assistance.

Which they did.

No matter where Freeman and Evan stood, they managed to be in my way. By late afternoon on the second day I was at the frayed end of my rope. "Why don't you guys go help Stub at the garage?"

"No fun," Evan said.

"Yeah." Freeman settled himself against the frozen food case. "When he's under a truck, we can't see his face when he realizes he messed up. And his cursing lacks variety and polish. You're more inventive with vocabulary."

"Eloquent," Evan added.

"Must be because you went to college."

"Yeah. I grunted as I powered a screw into the brace for a sagging shelf. "Proficiency in profanity was a requirement for graduation."

Evan's eyes widened. "Maybe I should have matriculated."

Freeman snickered. "My mother told me I'd go blind if I did that."

They guffawed and nudged each other like a couple of kids.

"Maybe you could lend Jefferson a hand."

They glanced toward Mary Lou's domain in the post office. "Can't," Freeman muttered. "Last week there was, um, an incident."

"Unintentional," Evan added.

"Could have happened to anyone."

"Could have been worse."

"Varnish can could have been full."

"And next to the stairs."

"Besides, we're fine here." Freeman opened the sliding door to the freezer case and stuck his head inside. "Although I can't say much for the air conditioning. You got that on your list?"

Before I could answer, Evan snapped to attention and yelped, "Incoming. Take cover."

Freeman slammed the door and turned to face Camille. She wore a sweet smile, the kind that can give a husband cold sweats. "I've been talking to Alda and Pattie," she said. "They were *delighted* to hear that their husbands were so willing to assist a friend striving to complete the tasks on his list. But they were *dismayed* when they checked the lists they left for those same husbands and found not a check mark anywhere."

Evan gulped.

Freeman opened his mouth to speak, then apparently thought better of it.

Heads down, they shuffled to the door, mumbling "Catch you later."

When the door swung closed—thanks to the new device I'd installed—Camille slumped against the frozen food case laughing.

"You couldn't have saved me sooner?"

"I tried. But Pattie and Alda were so glad to have them out from underfoot that I didn't have the heart to send them home. The Shovel It Inn was closed yesterday and Mary Lou's house is off limits until Jefferson finishes the renovations. Maybe longer."

"Yeah, I heard there was an accident."

"Caused by not looking where they put their feet. Jefferson didn't rat them out. In fact, he tried to cover it up. And he might have succeeded if Mary Lou hadn't run home for a minute to get a recipe." Camille sighed. "They mean well."

I set the screwdriver aside and hugged her. "They're like mud in the spring and mosquitoes in the summer. They come with the territory. For an outsider, you've done a damn good job of adapting to the terrain."

She kissed me and snuggled for a moment. "Speaking of the terrain . . ."

"More jobs?"

"Just one. Julie has a project. It's a little above and beyond."

"Will there be a reward?" I pulled her close. "Will you be presenting it to me on an evening to be named later?"

"Definitely."

"Then sign me up."

And that's why I spent the rest of the week building backdrops for photographs to be taken at the prom. The theme was "A Cruise on the Nile" and several fathers had volunteered to create replicas of Egyptian landmarks. They were long on ideas, but short on tools and know-how, and in far over their heads. On the other hand, since they all had teenage girls approaching full meltdowns, they were motivated—highly motivated.

Friday afternoon, while we shuffled our feet, fingers crossed behind our backs, Julie and the rest of the decorating committee surveyed our efforts. "It's still a gym," she said. "But if we turn off most of the lights, this will work. Thanks, Uncle Dan, you rock."

High praise.

"Oh, and, um, a couple of the chaperones can't make it."

High praise with an agenda.

"You want me to chaperone? How will you have fun if I'm hanging around?"

Julie rolled her eyes. "The junior class has to do all the work so I won't have much time to dance." She lowered her chin and dropped her voice. "And the guy I wanted to go with asked someone else."

I felt that like a knife to the heart. I hadn't realized there were boys in Julie's galaxy except for the distant planet named Isaac. When she'd talked about preparations for the prom, it never occurred to me she might be hoping a boy would ask. And she hadn't told us her dream had been dashed.

I wrapped her in a hug. "As of this moment I am officially at your service as a prom chaperone and chauffeur and whatever else will make your day."

I felt her sigh. "Do you think Camille would come, too?"

"If we can get someone to watch Chance, you bet she will."

And that explains why I drove 20 miles to a costume shop, spent a small fortune in rental fees, and went to the prom in sandals and a black-and-gold outfit with a short pleated skirt.

"I hope there's something under that," Julie said as we entered the gym.

"And I hope there isn't," Camille murmured.

"If you don't make an asp of yourself, maybe you'll find out later."

Camille shot me a wicked smile, patted the rubber snake wrapped around her arm, and beckoned me to follow as she floated off in her long gown for a crash course on chaperoning.

Chapter 32

When Monday finally came around, I felt like I'd been away from the cold case files for a year. I checked the list of things hanging fire and noted that Fred Maddox had yet to send Theresa Gilligan's letters. I made another call to his charter service and left another message. Then I drank coffee and stared at the folder with Judy Arnold's name on it, trying to remember details beyond that she disappeared four years ago, she was in her twenties, her parents were dead, and she worked in a men's clothing store.

When I opened the file, I saw there wasn't much more. The original investigators had done a thorough job, but Harry Pallister hadn't busted his butt on the follow-up. Oh, there were notes and interviews with Judy's aunt and the owner of the clothing shop, his son, and two friends, but Pallister hadn't flung his net any wider than the original investigators. Or, if he had, he hadn't dredged up one new bit of information. No one saw Judy Arnold after she walked out the door of the shop on a Saturday evening. She was planning to meet a man for a drink, but no one knew where she intended to have that drink, and no one knew the name of the man.

The friends now lived in Texas and Utah, and the shop owner had died a year ago, leaving the shop to his son. I called Judy's aunt and she said she hadn't remembered anything new, but I could come by any time.

Emma Howe had a pottery studio in a ramshackle house off the main road to Ashokan City. She came out to greet me, wiping her hands on clay-smeared overalls that hung from slender shoulders and flapped around her ankles.

"Pardon my outfit. Everything gets so grubby that I don't bother to clean up until I'm finished for the day." She tucked a strand of wavy brown hair behind one ear and smiled as she stuck out a hand. "Judy used to badger me into dressing less like a train-wreck survivor. She loved clothes, loved putting outfits together—right from the time she started dressing herself."

I shook Emma's hand. It was small enough to belong to a child and softer than I expected. "I hope you're up for talking about her. I want to get more of a picture than I pieced together reading the file."

"There's nothing I'd like more—if you don't mind me working while we talk. I have a commission and I'm running behind."

"I don't mind at all."

I followed her into the studio where she wiped dust from a wobbly metal stool and pointed to a coffeepot on a TV tray in the corner. "Coffee's there if you need to stoke up."

"I'm good."

I sat, opened the satchel, dug out the file and my recorder, and watched her shaping a lump of clay into a bowl.

"This is for a company that sells specialty nuts and snacks. Corporate logo goes in the bottom so when you're finished pigging out you're reminded where the goodies came from."

"Good marketing technique."

"Only as good as what goes in the bowl. Fortunately, they make tasty stuff."

"Good to know." I tapped the file folder. "According to the men who worked this case before me, Judy wasn't involved with anyone."

Emma smiled. "Judy was 'involved' with everyone and everything. She had dozens of male friends, but as far as I knew she hadn't singled one out."

"And you'd know?"

"I think so. Judy and I talked about everything."

I let that ride. In my experience, "everything" usually meant "almost everything". People held things back, didn't think they were important, or saved them for another conversation. "Did she enjoy her job at the clothing store?"

"As much as anyone enjoys a job that involves doing something that isn't your own thing. Judy had unique tastes and strong opinions about fashion. Not everyone agreed with her."

"She had conflicts? With customers?"

"No. They loved her. She had a way of making them feel like her ideas were their ideas. She'd persuade men to take a little risk and try colors and styles they'd never considered before. It was her boss she had conflicts with."

"What kind of conflicts?" I tried not to sound too eager, told myself if the solution to this mystery was so simple, Harry Pallister would have seen it.

"Over what to stock, what to display. Judy recognized there was a growing market for clothing that was more casual. He was afraid if they tried to attract younger customers they'd lose the old ones."

Emma removed the bowl, carried it to a table already crammed with similar ones, and plunked another lump of clay on the wheel. "They never argued. Judy didn't operate that way. She'd take 'No' for an answer, but the next day she'd come up with another idea and another after that. She kept chipping away."

The wheel spun and the clay changed shape between Emma's hands. "She was working with a seamstress to learn all she could about fabrics and stitching, and she was saving to open a shop of her own, to make and sell her own designs. There's almost $20,000 in her account. Want to see some of her drawings?"

"Sure."

Emma abandoned the clay, wiped her hands on her overalls, and led me outside and to a cottage set behind the studio. I followed her through a living room large enough for a loveseat, two chairs, and a few low tables and lamps, then along a short hall to a narrow bedroom furnished with a single bed, a bookcase, and a drawing table. The stark white walls were plastered with drawings of men—men in all shapes, sizes, and ages, men in suits, men in jeans, men in jackets and casual shirts, and men in overcoats and scarves and capes. Most sketches were simply pen or pencil, but on others she'd added chalk or crayon or watercolor.

I turned to take it all in. "She had talent."

"She had a *ton* of talent. I'm not sentimental. I don't keep her room the way it was because I think Judy is coming home. She was smart and strong-willed. She'd be here by now if she was able to make it."

Emma waved a hand to take in the designs. "To me this is art, a display, a mini gallery. I come in here almost every day and see a detail I hadn't noticed before." She pointed to a drawing pinned above the door. "Like the pattern on that shirt."

Yanking a yellow bandana from a pocket, Emma wiped away tears. "I miss her. She moved in with me when her parents died. I was just a kid myself and struggling to get my business going, so I treated her like a little sister. I keep wondering if what happened was my fault, if I could have done better."

"Every parent thinks that." *Except those as cold-hearted as Paul Yount.*

I patted her shoulder. "Do you mind if I look around?"

"No." Emma stuffed the bandana into a rear pocket. "Should I stay?"

"No need. If I have questions I know where to find you."

The first detective on the case, a woman who'd moved on to a bigger city and a bigger paycheck, had searched Judy Arnold's room two days after she disappeared. She'd found nothing she deemed relevant. Harry Pallister had noted that he "looked around," but added nothing further to the file. I figured I wasn't in the same league with the first detective, but by now I knew I was a power hitter compared to Pallister. I went through the room as if no one had come before me.

The closet held a mix of jeans, casual blouses, and slacks and jackets Judy probably wore to work—all with unique touches like bits of embroidery and decorative stitching, buttons and linings I doubted came from the factory. There were scarves with swirling colors, wide belts, boots and sandals, and a stack of broad-brimmed hats. Her jewelry box held chunky pendants, earrings, and rings with enormous stones. Every item made a statement.

In the bookcase I found more designs—a dozen sketchbooks full. I sat on the bed and flipped through the pages. A young man in a bomber jacket looked familiar. So did an older man in a formal suit and a tall man in a cream-colored shirt with sleeves alternately puffed and gathered.

I glanced around and found all three of them displayed in different poses and outfits. Had Judy Arnold drawn these men from imagination and then duplicated their features in other drawings? Or were these men she knew? If so, could one of them be the man she intended to meet the day she disappeared?

I lugged the sketchbooks to the studio and asked Emma Howe if she knew any of the men in the drawings or if Judy had mentioned who her models were.

"No. Judy had an amazing imagination. I guess I assumed the drawings weren't of actual people."

"Did other investigators ask about the drawings? Ask if you knew any of the models?"

"No." She squeezed the bowl on her wheel back into a lump of clay. "I should have—"

"Don't go down that road. Don't take on blame."

She blinked back tears, then nodded and resumed work on the bowl.

After assuring Emma Howe I'd take good care of the sketchbooks, I made my way to the clothing store where Judy Arnold once worked. A blue and white awning arched above a door painted glossy red and the mannequins inside wore clothing Judy might have designed.

A young man carrying a few extra pounds—the model for many of Judy's sketches—emerged from behind a display rack. His hair hung to his shoulders and he wore a sunny yellow shirt and deep purple jeans. "Stanley Rudolph," he told me as we shook. "But I go by Lee. Not that there's anything wrong with Stanley, but I never thought the name was me."

I nodded. I was used to seeing the name on hand tools—screwdrivers and tape measures, hammers and saws. It didn't fit on him.

He gestured to a pair of chrome and leather chairs on either side of a three-panel mirror at the rear of the store. "Make yourself comfortable."

I handed over the first of the sketchbooks I'd lugged in. "I believe that's you on the fifth page."

He flipped to the drawing and grinned. "Yes. The raw material was pathetic, but she made me thinner and better looking. What a little piglet I was then." He made a show of sucking in his stomach. "Still love that pasta, but I'm getting my cravings under control."

"Do you recognize the others?"

He flipped pages. "Well, that's a guy we used to call 'Mr. White Shirt.' He never bought any other color, not even gray or beige." More pages riffled by. "And here's a guy she dated a few times. He went into the Army." He flipped a few more pages. "Here's the mail carrier. And the plumber. And here's Dad. Judy captured his stern look. Not a huge challenge. He wore it most of the time."

He traced the outline of his father's image, smiling, eyes focused on another time. "When I started working here after high school, Judy and I used to come up with the most outlandish ideas just to see his expressions."

"You liked Judy?"

"I adored Judy. So did most of the men who came through that door." He pointed to the front of the store. "It used to be gray. It was Judy's idea to paint it red. Dad wouldn't even consider it. But after he died . . . Let me show you something."

He set the sketchbook on the floor, launched himself from the chair, hustled behind the counter, and returned with a notebook. "Judy's marketing and promotion plan for the store. She presented it to Dad a week before she disappeared. He stuffed it in his desk—probably never opened it. But whenever he was out of the store, I did. And when I inherited this place I put her plan into action. Business is up 300%."

His smile collapsed. "But Judy's not here to see it."

"You said the men who shopped here adored her. Was that—?"

"Sexual?" He curved his fingers into claws and growled. "Judy had a way of seeing the inner beast. She'd tap into a primal desire and she'd play to that when she suggested clothing."

Laughing, he pointed at me. "You look as if you're imagining she'd try to dress a man in a loincloth and fur boots."

"That crossed my mind."

"Mine, too. But what she'd do is figure out what a man wanted—love, power, money, strength, respect—and she'd sell to that. Maybe she'd suggest a jacket that made his shoulders appear broader or a color she thought women would be drawn to, or a suit that screamed of success, or a style that made him look younger and more virile. Plenty of men came in for a shirt or a tie and left with slacks and a jacket, too. But they also left feeling better about themselves."

"Ah." I wondered what Judy would have suggested I trade my jeans and T-shirt for. "Did Judy have a lot of boyfriends?"

"Judy never lacked for a date if she wanted to go to a club or dinner or a movie, but she didn't have any serious relationships. Her dreams came first. She told me she wouldn't set them aside for any man."

Could that have been a motive for murder?

"What do you think happened to her?"

"Something horrible." He shuddered. "She's dead. Or a prisoner. Otherwise she'd call. She'd visit. We'd go to lunch."

He bowed his head and I gave him a moment before moving on to the next question. "Do you keep records of your customers?"

"Records, profiles, preferences." He pointed at a computer on the counter. "Thanks to Judy's plan, I have spreadsheets and financial charts and an e-mailing list longer than my arm."

"What about records from before Judy disappeared? Names and addresses? Dates of purchases?"

He shook his head. "Dad's record-keeping gave his accountant ulcers. And Dad didn't like to 'bother' his customers. That meant he didn't ask their names if they paid cash, and he didn't stir from the stool behind the counter unless someone specifically asked for assistance. Judy was the one who made personal connections."

He tapped the side of his head. "And as far as I know she kept it all up here. Judy was sharp."

If a customer abducted Judy, would he continue to shop here? Would he be on Lee's list? And if he was, how would I know?

That brought me to the sketchbooks again. "Would you be willing to go through Judy's sketchbooks and take a run at identifying her models?"

"Sure. But I doubt I'll know many names. Or even recognize all the faces. She might have drawn men she saw walking past, or on TV, or in a movie."

"That's okay. Write what you know on sticky notes. For example, you recognized the postman and the plumber. Make a second note if the sketch is of someone Judy showed a special interest in—or who showed more than usual interest in her."

"You mean like a stalker?"

I nodded. "Or anyone you had a strange feeling about. Anyone she didn't like to wait on. Anyone she might have said gave her the creeps."

"Got it. I'll start today." He picked up the sketchbook. "Hey, what if I e-mailed my list and asked if anyone who knew Judy wanted to help? I bet a bunch of guys will pitch in. That way we might get more names."

I pondered the pros and cons. If there was a lead in these books it might be the only one I got. But the man who abducted

Judy might volunteer to help in order to get rid of sketches that implicated him.

"I'll have these copied and get them to you tomorrow." I reached for the book in his hands.

"Tomorrow? But I want to start now."

"I appreciate that, but the originals need to be in a safe place."

His eyes widened, his lips went white, and he released the book. "You think the person who took her might . . ." He sagged into the chair, breathing hard.

"I'll understand if you don't want—"

"No." He shoved that idea aside. "I'm not brave, but I'm no coward. Judy Arnold was my friend. I'll do whatever it takes. Any chance you can copy them today? I close at 6:00, but I can stay later."

It was late afternoon when I finished making two sets of copies with numbered pages so Lee and I could coordinate. I carried the sketchbooks to Sheriff North's office and found him making red-pencil slashes on a sheet of numbers I suspected represented next year's budget. He shot a scowl at the sketchbooks and copies. "What's all that?"

"The basis of a long shot."

I explained while he flipped through one of the books. "She did a lot with a few lines, didn't she? No mistaking that the guy on the second page and this one are the same person." He closed the book and set it on the stack. "But whether one of them is a killer . . ."

"Like I said, it's a long shot."

"Well, you've scored on two other long shots so I won't be the one to tell you to forget it." He patted the pile of sketchbooks. "I'll get the originals locked up. You go on home.

That baby may be getting past the colic, but you look like you're a month behind on your beauty sleep."

I passed on three sarcastic replies and contented myself with wondering how Judy Arnold would have envisioned Sheriff North's inner beast. An aging saber-toothed tiger? A bear just out of hibernation?

What would she have designed for him to wear?

North slapped his desk blotter. "What are you grinning at?"

"Must be the thought of that beauty sleep. Couldn't be because you paid me a compliment a minute ago. I'm sure I imagined that."

"You're right." He bent over the sheet and slashed at another number. "You have a hell of an imagination."

Chapter 33

I spent part of the next day at Emma Howe's place, photographing the walls in Judy Arnold's bedroom, removing drawings, making two sets of copies, taking one set to Lee Rudolph, then restoring Judy's gallery. I spent a bunch of days after that settling into Chance's new routine, a routine that involved sleeping through the night and on into the morning. The first day found us checking his breathing, taking his temperature, and surfing the Internet for advice. But soon we accepted that this, like the colic, was normal. For now.

"He seems to be making up for all those nights he was awake." Camille toweled her hair and plucked fresh jeans and a blouse from the closet. "And I don't have the heart to wake him."

"I do." I gave her a fiendish grin and a laugh to match. "I want revenge."

"But he's so sweet, so happy." She bent over the crib and stroked his fingers. "I bet you looked like this when you were a baby."

"And I bet my father didn't let me sleep in."

"True," she said in a voice dripping with sarcasm, "and we all know you want to follow in his footsteps. So wake your son and get him on the floor for 50 pushups followed by a five-mile run and a brisk swim across the lake before heading into the woods to shoot something for lunch."

"My father wasn't that extreme." I feathered Chance's fine hair into a mini Mohawk. "But I get your point. When he wakes up, I'll bring him along."

So, what with cleaning up the breakfast dishes, checking my e-mail, and wrestling a mountain of laundry through the washer and dryer, I passed the time until Chance woke and I started on the round of chores necessary to get on the road. "I don't know how your mother got you washed and changed and still had time to eat breakfast and make it to the store so Julie could catch the bus."

Chance made a crowing sound and waved his arms and legs like a turtle trying to right itself. "Yep, she's a wonder. We are two lucky guys."

Nelson whined and I corrected my statement. "Three lucky guys."

If the plan didn't call for a run far afield, Nelson rode shotgun when I delivered Chance. Some days we checked in with Jefferson who was making good progress on Mary Lou's honey-do list without the "help" of Freeman and Evan. Other days we drove up to the Miller houses and watered plants or swept off the porches and walks. Martha Cutter had a "fish on the line" for Rachel's house, but warned me that the other place might sit on the market for a bit.

"Lots of buyers are squeamish about living in a house where there was a murder. They're scared it's haunted. I respect their views, but I don't believe in ghosts."

Two years ago I might have made the same statement. Now I wondered if the choice was ours. Did ghosts believe in us? Did they care whether or not we believed in them?

Clarence Wolven's ghost had hounded me to find his killer, and summoned the ghosts of others when Colden Cornell kidnapped Julie. And when their work was done, they departed—except for Clarence who Jefferson swore showed up as a hum in the air now and then. I hoped Lisa might return to help guide Julie but, although my memories of her were strong in the kitchen and on the lawn where I'd tried to resuscitate her, I felt no ghostly presence. As for Ronny, powerful as he'd been and hard as he died, I often expected to see him stalking my dock, but he never appeared.

At least not to me.

Every second or third day, Lee Rudolph called with a name to follow up on.

I'd come to think Lee had a better mind for organization than I had. In fact, Lee could give Serenity Brook a run for her money.

Undaunted by the number of sketches, he'd taped them to the walls of his home where he could walk among them and search for physical and facial similarities. Within a day he'd identified dozens of "models" who appeared more than once, and clipped those sketches together. Once he eliminated the ones he recognized and could name, he sent out a plea for help, offering coffee, soft drinks, and snacks to those who came to page through the remaining sketches stacked on a table in the rear of the store.

"A few retired guys are spearheading this," he told me late in June when he passed on the name of an electrician who appeared in four sketches. "They've been rounding up other guys, too, ones who aren't on my mailing list. Every time I think we've hit a wall we won't get past, someone else wanders in and says, 'Hey, I've seen him in the supermarket.' And maybe there's still no name, but the Spearheads—that's what I call them—get everyone out looking and sooner or later they find the guy and get a name."

"They're doing great. I wish I could pay them."

"Are you kidding?" Lee laughed. "I heard one of them say they ought to be paying you."

"At least let me spring for coffee and doughnuts."

"Forget it. I'm writing that off as a promotional expense. Since the Spearheads set up shop and got the word out, I'm selling clothing like I'm the only shop in the state—stuff they think Judy would have liked is flying out of here. I feel guilty about making money, but if anyone could see the irony and opportunity of this, it would have been Judy."

So I left him to the process of discovering names and I followed up on those the Spearheads identified—all the while wondering how I'd know if I came across the man who took Judy. After all, my track record was abysmal. I'd encountered two serial killers in the past two years and failed to recognize either of them. So, as I tracked down and interviewed the men Judy sketched, I was suspicious of everyone.

Some of the models—like the plumber and a delivery truck driver—were surprised and flattered that she'd captured their images and dressed them in styles they'd never considered. Several men asked for copies to show their wives and friends. At first I found that strange, almost creepy. But when more requests came—including one from a widow who wanted to remember the man she lost the way Judy saw him—I viewed it more as human nature.

But part of human nature was wanting more, envying, lying, and killing—for reasons other than survival.

So I thought a lot about the dark side of human nature, and what could have happened to Judy, and why.

Robbery gone wrong? Maybe.

Money? Probably not. Judy had only what she'd saved to open a shop. About $20,000. People killed for less, but the money was still in her account. And her aunt, presumably her heir, hadn't touched it and seemed happy with what she had.

Power? Doubtful. The only people who might have seen Judy as an obstacle to their power were Lee and his father—a man who could have fired her, but didn't.

Anger? Also doubtful. Lee's father resented changes Judy suggested but—back to the argument about power—he never fired her. Not that an angry and unbalanced man might not escalate to murder without considering other ways to get back at someone, but . . .

Love? Maybe. As far as Lee and Emma knew, Judy wasn't deeply involved with anyone. But that didn't mean someone didn't see himself as deeply involved with her. And if another woman wanted the man who was obsessed with Judy, envy and jealousy kicked in—maybe with mental imbalance thrown into the mix.

Love was a powerful force.

And corrupted love had a fierce negative energy.

On the last Saturday in June, Wesley Falton held another revival. Her new license in her wallet, Julie drove Camille's car into town to run the kid-watching corral. Camille and I stayed home, but got regular updates courtesy of Mary Lou.

The event was larger and louder than the previous one and featured music courtesy of four teenage boys with drums, guitars, and energy. After an hour of bombastic preaching, Falton led more than two dozen people to the lake to be baptized and called on everyone in Hemlock Lake to join him in the water soon. "He said our souls are in peril," Mary Lou reported in a can-you-believe-it? tone. "And his is the only way to salvation."

"That's not going to sit well with Reverend Balforth," Camille mused.

And it didn't.

Late Sunday morning Freeman and Alda drove up brimming with news.

"Haven't been to a service since Lou Marie passed." Freeman came up the porch steps wearing his go-to-meeting clothes: a pair of black slacks, a white shirt, and a gray jacket. A blue tie dangled from his pocket. "But after what Mary Lou told me Wesley Falton said last night, Alda thought there might be fireworks."

"And there were." Alda settled herself in the rocker, her forehead glistening with perspiration.

"How about lemonade?" Camille offered.

"I'll get it." Julie bounded to her feet. "If you promise not to start until I get back."

"Promise." Freeman tossed his jacket over the porch railing. "But only if you throw in a few cookies."

Camille glanced at her watch. "It's almost noon. Why don't you stay for lunch?"

Freeman patted his belly. "Talked me into it."

Alda shook her head. "We couldn't impose on—"

"No imposition, Alda." Camille motioned for me to sit in the swing and put Chance in my arms. "Especially not if you lend a hand making the sandwiches."

The steps of their social tango completed, Camille and Alda went inside and Freeman settled into the swing beside me. Chance seemed to track his motion, a look of concentration on his face. Freeman held out his forefinger to be examined. "He over the colic?"

"Seems to be." I tapped the arm of the swing, knocking wood. "Hope we never go through that again."

"We were lucky with our sons. Granted, they presented a fair share of problems later on, but we're all still standing."

"Is that how you determine parental success?"

"That's the measure I use." He pushed off with one foot, rocking the swing. "There's only one house in the world I'd trade mine for, and that's this one. I have a great view up in Bluestone Hollow, but I wouldn't mind being on the water."

"Even if the view includes Brother Elijah?"

Freeman canted his head and squinted at the house across the lake. "Narrow as the lake is at this end, if you wanted to get baptized, seems he could walk over and dunk you."

"Walk *on* the water?"

"Some think if he put his mind to it he could walk on water, in the clouds, or all the way to the moon. They might change their minds if they saw how he's keeping up that house and yard."

I'd been in the habit of intentionally not gazing at the house for more than a second or two. If the Faltons were looking this way, I didn't want them to think I was interested in their lives—although I was. I'd heard a mower start up ten days ago and later noticed it standing at the end of a single swath cut through tall grass. It was there still, but now the mown grass had made a comeback and all that was visible was the handle.

"Stub could fix that mower," Freeman observed.

"Unless it's not broken. Maybe Wesley Falton realized mowing the grass might demonstrate that he cared too much for his lawn."

Freeman guffawed. "Must be why he hasn't braced that trellis that's leaning over or cinched up the sagging clothesline."

"Maybe he's not handy."

"How handy do you have to be to tighten a clothesline?"

"Maybe he's too busy with saving souls and writing a book."

"Too busy for a ten-minute job?"

Julie came out with a stack of plates and silverware and dashed inside for glasses, a pitcher of lemonade, and two bottles of beer. In a moment, Camille and Alda followed with a platter of grilled cheese and tomato sandwiches cut into triangles, another platter laden with chopped vegetables, bowls of dip, and a bag of potato chips bigger than Chance. Nelson wandered up from the lake and took a position under the table, waiting for droppage or tribute.

"I love summer." Julie poured lemonade. "Eating on the porch and knowing I won't have homework until September."

"And strawberry shortcake for dessert," Camille said. "With wild strawberries."

"Wild strawberries." Freeman's eyes sparkled. "I haven't had wild strawberries for years."

"That's because it takes forever to pick enough to make it worthwhile." Alda gave him a sharp look. "Or so says the retired man who spends his days driving his neighbors crazy."

Freeman rolled his eyes and piled sandwich quarters on his plate. "Hurts my back to be bent over in a field searching those things out."

"Julie found the mother lode up by Rachel's place." I tucked Chance into one of the many contraptions we'd acquired for his lounging pleasure. "There's no searching involved."

"Strawberries took over Grandma's old garden." Julie opened the potato chips, rattled a few onto a plate, and slipped one to Nelson.

"It's weeds that are taking over *our* garden." Alda said.

"Hurts to—"

"I'll come over and weed for you," Julie said. "For all the work you put in finding a car for me."

"Haven't exactly found one yet. At least not the right one."

"And it's got to be right." Camille flashed me a smile. "Your first car is the one you'll always remember. Later you'll buy cars because they have cargo space or good gas mileage or a decent price. But that first car has to feel special." She turned the smile on Julie but the message in her eyes was serious. "It has to be safe, too."

"It'll be safe. We'll see to that." Freeman set his plate on the table and pointed at Julie. "But a car's not safe if the driver does stupid stuff."

"I'll leave that to the stupid kids." Julie dragged a carrot stick through a bowl of dip. "Now eat so you can tell us what happened in church."

So we devoured everything, down to the crumbs in the potato chip bag and the last bit of berry-stained whipped cream on the shortcake plates. Then Alda insisted we clean up and take a broom to the porch. Finally Freeman tipped his chair, put his feet on the railing, and turned to his wife. "You tell it."

Alda preened, brushing at her dress and patting her hair, then settled in the rocker and took in a long breath. "The church was warm. The windows were open, but the air was still this morning. Close. Heavy. Like it is before a thunderstorm."

"Had that waiting-for-something-to-happen feeling," Freeman added.

"Exactly. Well, the last chord of the opening hymn had barely wheezed out of that old organ and folks were still closing their songbooks when Reverend Balforth let the congregation have it with both barrels."

Chapter 34

"Both barrels and a grenade," Freeman added.

"He said Brother Elijah has set himself up as a false idol, that people came to his tent more to worship him than to learn about the teachings of the Bible and consider how they should follow them every day."

"And he said that's what Brother Elijah intended," Freeman added.

"And then he preached a bunch about vanity and pride and the deadly sins. He didn't come out and say it, but he made it clear as day that Brother Elijah has committed a bunch of them."

"Isaac says he yells at him," Julie said. "So maybe that's wrath. And he's not getting his book written as fast as he promised, so that could be sloth. But he's so skinny! How could he be guilty of gluttony?"

"Maybe it's a loose interpretation," Camille mused. "I've heard of people being called gluttons for punishment. Reverend Balforth might think Wesley Falton is a glutton for power or lusts for fame."

Julie twitched her nose, thinking that over.

"Anyway," Alda said, "Reverend Balforth went on about that for a good while. Then he got on the subject of dunking folks in the lake and he did something I never heard him do before—he started asking us questions like maybe he wasn't sure of the answers."

I remembered the conversation Jefferson and I had with him the night of the first revival. Were Balforth's doubts growing?

"Except I guess he didn't want us to tell him what we thought the answers might be," Freeman said, "because he didn't shut up."

Alda flapped her hand, shushing him. "He asked if we knew the purpose and symbolism of baptism, if we understood what water meant, if we thought that the amount of water was important, and if we thought getting dunked in Hemlock Lake would save us if we led sinful lives after the dunking. I tell you, I never saw such a confused bunch of people in all my days. Folks were paging through their Bibles, sneaking glances at each other, and judging the distance to the door."

"That was me," Freeman said. "And if I could have got out past Alda without tripping, I would have been gone."

"But he couldn't. And I wasn't going to stand up and draw attention to myself, not with Reverend Balforth telling us to think long and hard about the time we had left on this earth and what we wanted our children to say about us after we're gone."

Freeman rolled his eyes. "I already know. My sons will say if I'd spent as much time doing chores as I did finding excuses, then everything would have been finished before I kicked off."

"And they'd have a point." Alda crossed her arms and narrowed her eyes.

Freeman mumbled something under his breath and Julie giggled.

"Anyway, when Reverend Balforth was done with all the questions, he spread his arms in his black jacket so he looked like a giant crow on the wing, and he swore he wouldn't abandon us even if we abandoned him. And then he said he believed Brother Elijah had sinned, sinned beyond forgiveness or redemption, and he would be judged from above—an avenging angel would come from the sky and show no mercy on him."

"Didn't say when that angel was due, though," Freeman muttered.

Alda scorched him with a glare. "And then he pounded his fist on the pulpit, stalked down the aisle, pushed open both doors, got into his car, and drove off."

"First time the collection plate didn't get passed," Freeman said in a loud whisper. "I saved five bucks."

"No, you didn't," Alda informed him. "On the way home you'll stick it in the box by the door."

"Yes, dear. Whatever you say, dear."

Julie giggled again.

I shook my head. "Freeman's dug a hole, Julie. Don't encourage him to keep shoveling."

"Huh?" Julie blinked and turned to Camille.

"I'll explain later." Camille tapped Alda's wrist. "And then?"

"Well, we sat there, quiet as church mice, nobody knowing what to say or even if they should talk at all."

"And I kept nudging her," Freeman said. "Trying to get her to move."

"But I didn't want to be the first."

"And then Denny Balmer said, 'Well, hell.' And a couple of the ladies gasped and Denny got up and everybody followed him outside."

"And we stood there for a time." Alda rubbed her temples with her forefingers. "Everybody looking the way people do when they come from a funeral or see a wreck on the highway. People whispering among themselves trying to make sense of it."

"Not sense of the message," Freeman said. "That was pretty clear."

Alda nodded. "Yes, there was no doubt about that. But it was the force of Reverend Balforth's delivery that stunned us. You know how he usually talks. Well, today his voice rose and fell and he talked fast, like he knew time was running out and he wanted to get it all said."

The next week I went over the five cases on my desk, searching for anything I'd missed, hoping for another lead, another clue, for even a single nugget of inspiration. I left another message for Fred Maddox. I dropped in to see Lee Rudolph. I hung around asking Jefferson if he had ideas until he threatened to put me to work painting the linen closet. I even let Serenity Brook heap verbal abuse on me for half an hour in the hope that would stampede my brain cells into action.

Nothing worked.

The Fourth of July came and we followed last year's tradition of packing a picnic dinner and driving 30 miles to a fireworks show—picking up two of Julie's cousins on the way. The girls, one just into her teens and the other a few months shy of that milestone, were entranced by Chance and came along when we moved far from the staging area to protect his hearing.

Camille had done her homework and brought along soft pads to cover Chance's ears and the girls took turns holding their hands against his head to shield him further. He, in turn, seemed to thrive on the attention and paid no heed to the noise.

"I wish I could say the same about myself," Camille said. "Is it louder than last year or are we older?"

"Louder," I said, skipping over that trap. "Definitely louder."

On Sunday Freeman called to report that the church was packed with people on the edge of their pews waiting for Reverend Balforth to let loose once more. "But he was his old self and it was like he was phoning it in. Like he was saying religion wasn't about the show."

"But it's the show that gets them in the door," Camille said later as we sprawled on the dock eating ice cream and splashing each other to beat the heat. "If they don't *hear* the message, they won't *get* the message. It's a shame, because Balforth is a good man and he's always there for the community."

"You're not saying we should go to church next Sunday, are you?"

"No."

"That we should let him baptize Chance?"

She licked a drip of caramel pecan ice cream from her cone. "Maybe. After all, we don't *know* what's coming after this life."

I nodded to the house across the lake. "But we *do know* we don't want Wesley Falton dunking him."

"Or dunking Julie, either," she said in a steely voice.

"She hasn't mentioned that lately."

"That doesn't mean she's not thinking about it. Didn't you say you were going to check the baptismal records at the church?"

"I did. I will. Bible study's Wednesday evening so Balforth will be around."

Monday, without a better idea, I pursued the flimsy theory that, somehow, some way, the five cases on my desk were linked. With Nelson watching from a prone position on the cool concrete floor, I tacked a couple of white shower curtains to the wall of the garage. Last summer, before we finished the house, they had screened the outdoor shower I rigged up. I'd saved them as drop cloths, but figured they'd find a higher purpose as the canvas for a large-scale map of Ashokan, Buckingham, and Quarry Counties.

Using a thick black marker, I drew the outline of the counties and noted major towns and cities. It was a crude map at best, but it gave me a big picture of where my murdered and missing people had been in relation to each other, and where their lives might have intersected.

Filling in what I knew about where they lived, worked, shopped, and went to school took most of the hours left after I delivered Chance to Camille. The process also made abundantly clear what I didn't have, what I didn't know, and what I hadn't followed up on.

I didn't have the letters Theresa Gilligan wrote to Fred Maddox while he was serving in the Coast Guard. I didn't know where Micah Thielman met a mystery man for coffee. And I hadn't transcribed the recording I made the day I interviewed Franklin Turner's mother.

I made yet another call to Fred Maddox's machine and told him the letters could be crucial to the case and I was fast becoming willing to fly to Alaska and pry open his storage unit, or hire someone to pry for me.

The investigator who got the Thielman case had worked it hard. His notes indicated fliers had been tacked up around the campus and elsewhere. Those would be trashed by now so, with the blessing of the Buckingham County Sheriff, who still had his staff chasing a burglar, I made new ones with Micah's picture, a bit of biographical information, and my name, phone number, and e-mail. Armed with a stack of fliers, tacks, tape, and a stapler, I drove the roads between Micah's home and the college he'd attended, stopping at any place that sold coffee—restaurants, bars, taverns, diners, espresso stands, and mini-marts, bookstores, and even service stations with vending machines. "Meeting for coffee" didn't necessarily mean that they met in a conventional coffee shop.

The next day I dug out the recorder and listened to my interview with Natalie Turner, transcribing bits of it into my computer. Franklin liked swimming and tennis. I made a note to find the pool and tennis courts. He watched baseball. On television? Or at a local sports field? And he acted in a play at a summer church camp. Where?

I should have asked those questions when I met with Natalie. Sure, I'd been exhausted, but that was no excuse. I called the bakery but she wasn't there and didn't answer her phone. I left a message, outlining the information I wanted and saying I'd get back to her. Someone at a park or pool or church might remember Franklin and recall who he'd been with.

I shut it down for the day, checked the chore list on the kitchen counter, picked the assignment I hated the most, and went out to chop weeds among the rows of corn Camille swore would make good eating in August.

After dinner, carrying $20 to slip into the collection box by the door, I drove to the church, figuring to catch Reverend Balforth when he arrived, then escape before Bible study got underway. Balforth's car, as black as his suits, was parked at the side of the building. Another car, long, low, and white, anchored the opposite side. Wesley Falton's.

I coasted onto the grassy edge of the gravel lot, slid out, and closed the door with a soft nudge. Staying on the grass, I headed for the narrow porch and the open double doors.

What brought Falton here? Had he come to see about renting the building when weather put a stop to the tent-revival business?

Doubtful.

First, the building would hold only a tenth of the people Falton drew to his outdoor revivals. Second, it had been built by Mary Lou's ancestors and leased to a board of directors responsible for hiring a minister and keeping up the property. The board might find rental income attractive, but I couldn't see them crossing Reverend Balforth to get it.

What else would bring Falton here? Had he heard Balforth was preaching against him?

I halted at the base of the steps, listening to a hum of voices, telling myself this was none of my business. This was a private conversation.

But in small communities, what went on between two people—especially people in positions of leadership—often had a way of lapping over onto other lives and forcing choices and actions. And if what went on between these two escalated to physical conflict, it would be my business, if only because I was on the spot and in possession of a badge.

Their voices rose. Now and then a word formed in the thrum: obligation, respect, sin, renounce, redemption.

Still not my business.

Curiosity had me in its tingling grip. I eased to the tiny porch outside the double doors.

More words took form: evil, weak, judgment, smite, atonement.

The voices swelled to an incoherent stream of shouts.

Something fell with a thud that sent tremors through the floor.

Something shattered.

Now this was my business.

Chapter 35

I crossed the porch, passed through the double doors left open for a breeze, and strode across the vestibule.

Like chess pieces, one black and one white, Balforth and Falton faced each other in front of the overturned pulpit. Their fists were clenched, their eyes locked on each other, their breathing harsh and labored. Sunlight streaming through the stained-glass window splintered on the shards of a broken vase and on water droplets caught on the leaves of scattered roses.

For a moment they seemed oblivious to my presence, then Balforth's gaze flicked my way. "Dan. Something I can do for you?"

I went with a casual approach. "Yes, but I'll come back when you're not busy."

"Mr. Falton was about to leave."

Mr. Falton. Not Brother Elijah.

Falton smiled and raised his chin. A moment later, still smiling, he brushed by me. The smile, I noticed, didn't reach his eyes. They were flat. Empty.

Balforth knelt and bowed his head.

I watched until he reached for a piece of the vase, then I stepped to the tiny closet in the vestibule, got out a broom, a dustpan, an ancient galvanized bucket, and a couple of rags. "Hope that wasn't someone's favorite vase."

Balforth winced. "I expect it was. It's been here for years."

"An heirloom. Even worse." I swept bits of thick glass onto the dustpan and emptied it into the bucket. "I don't know if you're responsible, but I have a feeling you'll shoulder the blame. If I arrest you for destroying church property, you'll get some sympathy. As a bonus, the heirloom owner might simmer down while you're locked up."

He smiled. Granted, it was a wintry smile and faded in a few seconds. "Thanks. But if it's who I think it is, simmering will take the rest of her life."

He tossed a mangled rose in the bucket and blotted water from the blue runner. "I'm glad you came along. I prayed for patience, but I prayed in vain."

He didn't offer more, so I went after it. "Why was he here?"

Balforth stood and threw the wadded cloth into the bucket. It hit with a squishy clang. "He wants to use the building."

"Why?"

"He didn't say." He hung his head. "I didn't give him a chance."

He said that last sentence in a way that made me think he was referring to more than this afternoon's conversation. And he said it in a way that made it seem he was questioning himself, wondering if he should be asking forgiveness.

But then he squared his shoulders and stepped to the overturned pulpit. I got on the other side and wedged my fingers beneath it. Tall, broad, and crafted from mountain oak generations ago, it weighed as much as a small man.

Once it was in position and Balforth turned aside, I gave it a shove with both hands, testing the force it would take to topple it. The pulpit rocked barely half an inch.

Balforth—or Falton—had more strength than I imagined.

Or more rage.

"I should roll up this runner," Balforth said, "and carry it outside to dry so it doesn't damage the floor."

"I'll take care of that." I touched his arm. "No need to soil your suit."

"Thanks." He laid his hand over mine for a second, then fingered the black cloth of his sleeve as if he was considering a purchase. "My father wore black. And his father. They said it meant they were serious about their calling. And they claimed it wouldn't show dirt—although it does."

He frowned and released the sleeve as if it had burned him. His voice was querulous, his expression confused. "I don't like black. Why should I wear it?"

He gripped my wrist. "And why should Mr. Falton wear white?"

His hand was cold, but his face was flushed, his cheeks hollow, his eyes burning with fever.

"Is there something you know about Wesley Falton? Something I should know?"

He shook his head. "There's nothing that I *know*. There's only what I feel." He laid his hand across his chest. "I feel rot where his heart should be. I feel malignancy and putrefaction in his mind. And I feel evil, a monstrous evil."

I drove home pondering what Balforth said. Did he imagine he felt rot and malignancy and evil because he was jealous or threatened? Or were those feelings based on something more? I had always thought of Balforth as a contained man with inner strength and certainty. But the man I saw tonight seemed weak and wandering in a wilderness.

Camille was on the porch with Chance at her breast sucking his dinner. "Julie's out on the lake with Nelson."

"Meeting up with Isaac?"

"She didn't say." Camille reached for my hand. "I know you don't have positive feelings about him, but I think he's harmless. So does Justin. He says it's clear that Isaac likes Julie, but that's as far as it goes. And besides, as long as Nelson's with her, I'm not worried about a boy thinking that 'no' means the opposite."

True. Nelson had nearly given his life for Julie last summer. I had no doubt he'd do it again.

"I don't think Isaac is her type." I sat beside her. "And I'm not as worried about close encounters of the sexual kind as I am about Julie being sucked into Wesley Falton's whirlpool."

"Same here. Did you find out whether she was baptized?"

"She was." I unfolded the paper on which I'd copied details from the book Reverend Balforth kept in a cabinet in the vestry. "Rachel and Lisa were there."

"But not Buck or Ronny?"

"Hunting trip. Balforth remembers Lisa apologizing."

"Lisa apologized for a lot." Camille shifted Chance. "I often wonder how it might have gone if she hadn't made excuses for Ronny early on, if she'd stood up to him. If she was still with us, I think we'd be good friends."

"I know you would be."

She stroked the back of my neck. "You were a little in love with her, weren't you?"

I swallowed, feeling heat rise from my chest. "More than a little, when we were young."

"I'm glad. That's what makes you so good with Julie." Camille wove her fingers with mine. "You were gone longer than I expected."

"There was an incident at the church."

While I told her what I'd seen and heard, we studied the house across the lake. Wesley Falton's car was in the driveway beside his wife's, but neither of them was in view. Grass grew higher around the abandoned mower, the trellis leaned farther, and a downspout hung loose from its gutter.

"I never thought of Reverend Balforth as a man subject to the same frailties and temptations as the rest of us. But I suppose that's because he wears that black suit like a uniform and I see a minister, not a man."

"Maybe that's how he saw himself. Until lately."

"It's probably normal for a minister to have a crisis of faith."

I thought about Balforth's icy hand, the fever in his eyes. Was he suffering more than doubt?

"We should keep this to ourselves," Camille said. "There's enough talk already."

When I checked my e-mail the next morning, I found a message from Fred Maddox. "Boat problems. Sorry for delay. Should have box next week or week after."

Crap.

The longer those letters remained out of my grasp, the more I wanted them, the more I felt they were significant.

I kicked my desk.

And regretted that kick for the next two minutes while I hopped off the pain.

Resigning myself to being stalled, I dropped Chance with Camille late in the morning and decided to turn ground I'd been over before.

First stop, the men's store.

Lee Rudolph stood beside the triple mirror watching a white-haired man waffling over a fuchsia shirt. "You don't think it's years too young for me?"

"Judy would have liked it," a trio of male voices harmonized from the table at the rear of the store.

The man tugged at the cuffs. "My wife won't."

Lee shot me a wink. "Twenty percent off. Today only."

The man rolled his eyes. "Oh, all right."

"Slacks to go with it?" a voice from the rear asked.

"New belt?" another queried.

"Socks?" a third suggested.

"No. No. No." The man darted into the curtained dressing room muttering.

Lee grinned and turned to me. "Coffee?"

"Sure."

"That's all I've got for you."

I poured coffee into a mug, grabbed a chair at the table, and nodded to the three men Lee called the Spearheads. When they first got involved, the table had been awash in copies of Judy's sketches, but now the unidentified drawings were in plastic sleeves inside a fat notebook that lay open before them. I flipped the pages, marveling again at how Judy captured unique physical features with a few lines.

"Like to know who that is." The Spearhead on my left slapped a page. "She made a lot of drawings of that guy. And I know I've seen him somewhere."

"Me, too." The Spearhead next to him tugged at his earlobes and patted his cheeks as if that might joggle his memory.

I studied the sketch of a tall, lean man, hair brushing his shoulders. He wore a jacket broad at the shoulders and nipped in at the waist. It reminded me of the styles in old noir movies. I felt a tingle at the back of my brain, but in a second it was gone.

"She made us all look better." The third Spearhead tapped the page. "For all we know, this guy could be bald and dumpy."

"Good point." The first Spearhead tugged the notebook from my hands. "Let's go through these and imagine them fatter and older."

Lee gave a mock sigh of relief. "Glad we already took my sketches out—I'm feeling fat and old enough without the three of you adding pounds and years."

The second Spearhead waved him off and the three of them bent over the notebook, pointing and suggesting. I left them to it and left Lee rolling his eyes and straightening stacks of shirts in royal blue, lime green, and lemon yellow.

After several stops in Ashokan City to pick up what couldn't be found at the Hemlock Lake Store—organic cereals, cheese that wasn't Swiss or cheddar, various types of flour, sun-dried tomatoes, dog chews in bulk, lemon soap, and dozens of other items on Camille's list, I found a parking spot in the shade near the bakery where Natalie Turner worked. The air inside was warm and heavy and the mingled scents of vanilla and coconut made me think of tropical islands and crystal blue water. A teenage girl with freckles and stubby pigtails gave me a bright smile and spread her hands to draw my attention to trays of pastries and cookies. A swinging door behind her was propped open and I saw Natalie pulling pans of rolls from a mammoth oven and sliding them into a rack to cool. She glanced my way, seemed to struggle to remember who I was, then held up both hands, fingers spread.

Ten minutes.

I nodded, conferred with the girl behind the counter about what would be more like lunch than breakfast, and got pastry rolled around cheese, spinach, onion, and sausage. It impressed the hell out of my taste buds, so I ordered another plus two to go, and pulled a bottle of root beer from a cooler near the door. Then I made myself as comfortable as a good-sized man can get on a chair with spindly legs and a seat the size of a pie pan.

Three customers had come and gone and the second pastry was history when Natalie dropped into the chair across from me.

"My compliments to the baker." I saluted her with the dregs of the root beer. "The sausage roll was the best I ever had."

"Thank you." Her tone was as empty and exhausted as her expression.

"Sorry to bother you at work, but I was in the area and I'm anxious to get the information I mentioned so I can fill in a few blanks."

"It's okay. I was just finishing up."

"Is it all right if we talk here? We won't be in the way, will we?"

"No. Will it take long? I have a little more to do and I'm . . . I'm tired."

"Just a few minutes." I pulled a notepad and pen from my satchel. "You said Franklin liked to watch baseball."

"On TV. And at the park." She nodded to the east. "He really liked watching the little kids, the tiny ones. He liked their determination."

"Did he go with a friend?"

"No. Sometimes I went with him."

"Do you remember anyone talking with him? Waving to him?"

She shook her head.

"What about tennis? And swimming?"

"The courts and the pool are in that same park. He swam a lot when he was little. The last few years he'd go with me but never on his own." She pulled a napkin from a silver dispenser and shredded it. "He was self-conscious about his body because he was so thin and because he burned instead of tanning. I'm sure the other kids teased him, but he never said. He didn't like to worry me."

She layered shreds of napkin as if building a pie crust. "I think it was the same with tennis. He took his racket and a ball to the park when I told him he needed fresh air, but he never mentioned playing *with* anyone."

"But he could have."

"I suppose."

If he had, how would I find that person? Sure, I could stake out the courts and ask anyone who came by to take a look at Franklin's picture and tell me if they saw him playing here three years ago. But how likely was it that someone would remember him or anyone he played with?

"The church camp he attended, the one where he was in the play, where was it?"

"At that brick church about a mile that way." She pointed with her chin to the west and then frowned. "Strange. I don't know what denomination it is. I always think of as the big brick church."

"You didn't go there?"

"No. I didn't go to church *anywhere*. Neither did Franklin. I always intended to take him to several different churches and let him decide, but Sunday would come and we'd sleep late and . . ."

"But he went to church camp?"

"Yes, but not for the Bible study or the recreation programs. Just for the acting class." She scraped the woven napkin shreds into a heap and started again. "That wasn't run by the church."

I made the first notes on my pad: check on summer programs, find people who remembered Franklin. "Who was in charge of the acting class?"

"Someone from the community theater. I can't remember her name. She had long gray hair and always wore a scarf."

I made another note.

"Franklin went to the library a lot." Natalie scraped napkin scraps into a ball and packed it tight. "I forgot to tell you that. I'm sorry."

She said that not in the automatic way people do, but with deep regret.

"It's okay. You've helped a lot."

She glanced up and gave me a wisp of a smile. "It's kind of you to say that. But I should have held him closer, watched him better, paid more attention."

I set my pen aside and closed my hands around hers.

She nodded and we sat that way for a few minutes. Then she drew her hands from mine and stood. "If I think of anything else . . ."

"You have my number. Call any time. I mean that. Even the middle of the night."

She offered a smile so faint I wondered if it was my imagination, then retreated behind the counter.

I wanted to stop at the church right away, but I had cheeses to consider, so I contented myself with driving by. The parking lot and lawns were thick with kids of all ages. Cars lined the streets—mothers come to pick up children. If there had been as many enrolled in programs three summers ago, I'd be months tracking them down and asking if they remembered Franklin.

Then I remembered the Spearheads and what they'd accomplished in next to no time. The key was networking—in person, through e-mail, or on the phone. And I knew someone who was an expert at that.

Chapter 36

"Maybe I even know some of the kids there," Julie said after I laid everything out after dinner. "I can go tomorrow if Camille doesn't need me at the store."

"I'll be fine." Camille stretched out on the swing with Chance.

"Great." Julie plucked at my shirt, towing me into the house. "The first thing you'll want is a separate e-mail account."

"And I'll want that why?"

"Because you'll get a lot of mail."

So we set up an account, made fresh fliers with Franklin's picture, and hit the brick church the next morning. The building had an enormous white rotating cross on top of a spire, but nothing to tell me the denomination. Since I wasn't in the market for a place of worship, I decided I wouldn't put energy into digging for the information.

Julie gaped as I searched for a parking spot. "It's a lot bigger than what we have in Hemlock Lake."

I laughed. "Almost everything is."

"I know. And most of the time that's fine."

I squeezed the SUV into a slot at the rear of the building. "I see kids over there." Julie pointed to a group romping on playground equipment. "They're too young, but the counselors might have known Franklin. And the girl with the braids looks like a friend of Stephanie's."

She jumped out and peeled off with a wave.

"Keep me posted," I ordered.

She raised her hand and waggled her phone.

I found my way to a cluttered office and an angular woman in a crisp white blouse and navy blue skirt who told me she hadn't been around three years ago, but listened to what I had to say. When I finished, she groaned and tugged at short gray-blond hair. "Two summers ago, no problem, it would be in the computer. Every class, every instructor, every counselor, and every kid who registered."

She patted the laptop on the desk in front of her and then stood, opened a closet, and pointed like a game-show hostess to a stack of swollen boxes overflowing with papers. "But three years ago—and before that—this was the system. Some instructors rented space from us to run their programs, and others we recruited and paid. We have the records." She nodded at the stack. "Somewhere."

"Are there records of the kids who attended?"

"Maybe. Now they sign in every day on specific forms, but then there was no uniformity. They wrote their names on whatever the counselors had handy, including paper bags, hamburger wrappers, and even cardboard from the inside of a roll of paper towels. Half of the counselors didn't bother to put a date or the name of the activity at the top of the page. The word 'chaos' doesn't begin to describe it."

I joined her at the closet door. "Are those boxes arranged by year?"

"If only. When Jane retired—a step she didn't take by choice I might add—she 'cleaned up' the office for me. That meant stuffing everything in here, locking the door and taking the key with her. When I finally got it back, I thought I'd straighten things out, but halfway through the first box I came to my senses."

I doubted I would have made it that far and told her so.

"I'll make sure a flier goes up in every room and I'll make copies and pass them out to everyone who comes in." She laid a hand on my forearm. "I wish I could be more help. You're welcome to go through all this if you want, as long as it stays in the building."

I considered the stack, three boxes wide, two deep, and four high. "I'd like to try another approach first. Would there be any objection to me talking to program directors and instructors?"

"Not from me. And I expect not from them if you do it when they're not in the middle of something."

I assured her I'd be respectful of their time and she pointed me toward a long wing. "The swim class is at the park this morning, but most of the other activities are in rooms along that hall or in the basement. Drama may be in the small chapel. Prepare for a hike."

"I'll drop breadcrumbs so I can find my way back."

"You won't be able to *get* back if our custodian catches you dropping food of any kind. We've had an ant invasion and he's on the warpath."

I headed off along a long corridor, but as I peered into the first classroom, Julie rang in. "I found a counselor whose sister was here the year Franklin was. She says maybe some of the older counselors remember him. If we come at lunch, we can probably talk to most everybody."

"Sounds like a plan. Let's hit the library in the meantime."

The library was cool and quiet, but yielded nothing. One librarian thought Franklin looked familiar, but had no idea when she might have seen him or if he'd been with anyone. "We notice two kinds of children the most, those who are destructive or unusually loud, and those who come often and engage with the staff."

"I bet librarians knew you when you were a kid," Julie joked when we were in my rig. "The way you plow through books it would have been a full-time job to get them back on the shelves."

I rewarded her with a laugh and we made a quick stop for burgers, then returned to the church.

More kids swirled around the grounds than I'd seen yesterday. They overflowed the lawn, lining up at lunch stations, perching on playground equipment, squatting on curbs, and clustering in clumps of shade beneath trees while munching on sandwiches and chips and slurping milk from small cartons. Fliers in hand, Julie headed for a knot of kids her age at a picnic table.

When did she become so confident? So capable?

She'd been with us only a year and it seemed as if it had never been any other way. In another year she'd be off to college. Glancing over her shoulder, she frowned and pointed to the church, telling me to get to work. Armed with my clipboard and a stack of fliers, I headed for the community hall where instructors and program directors ate.

They were a mixed bunch, including three women in their twenties, one with paint in her hair, two young men wearing white shirts and serious expressions, an older man with bandages on two fingers, another with a tank top and bulging biceps, two middle-aged women having a conversation in sign language, and an older one with a calligraphy pen behind one ear. Time was short, so I tackled the whole group, stepping to the center of the room, holding up a flier, introducing myself, and getting right to it.

And netting next to nothing.

Except for Bandage Man—who helped kids build birdhouses and towel racks—and Tank Top Man, no one had been here three years ago. They didn't remember Franklin, but knew the drama teacher—and knew she died last winter from injuries suffered in a fall from a ladder while adjusting lighting.

I asked if any of them knew staff members from three years ago. Tank Top Man remembered a few first names—Lorraine, Chris, and Ed—but no last names to go with those.

Telling myself this was about what I expected, I trudged outside and found Julie with a tall boy with sun-bleached hair and sky-blue eyes. "This is Rick."

"Dan Stone." I thrust out a hand and we shook. His grip was firm and his gaze held mine.

"Rick teaches swimming here and goes to college in Maine," Julie informed me. "He took the drama class with Franklin Turner, only he can't talk right now."

"This won't take long," I said.

He nodded toward a mob of milling kids. "Sorry. I have to get my group to the park. And later on I have a . . . a thing I'm committed to." Rick cast a glance at Julie that said he wished that "thing" was with her. "And then I'm headed to Buffalo. My parents said if I don't go with them to visit my grandmother I can forget about tuition. But I'd go even if they didn't threaten me. My grandmother's tight. I could call tomorrow and tell you what I remember about Franklin."

I put a lid on my impatience and handed him a card. "I'd like to talk with you face-to-face. Call and we'll arrange a time to meet."

He aimed his gaze at Julie again. "How about I call you?"

"You could," she said in a teasing voice, "*if* you had my number."

Rick blushed and shuffled his feet. Julie pasted on an aloof and angelic smile. Rick's tongue twisted a stammer between his lips. "I . . . uh . . . could . . ."

Taking pity on him, I reeled off Julie's cell number.

He shot me a grin, punched it into his phone, and hustled off to join a pack of kids disappearing around the corner of the building.

"I was gonna tell him," Julie said.

"In my lifetime?" I headed for the SUV. "I know the unwritten girls' guide to guys says to make them suffer, but the unwritten guys' guide to females says we should help out when we see a young man skewered on a smile."

She blushed. "I wanted to see if he really wanted to call."

I put my arm around her shoulders. "He did, trust me. I'll bet you ten dollars he calls you tomorrow."

"What time tomorrow?"

I started my rig and hit the air conditioning, thinking about what I would have done at that age. "Not first thing, because he won't want to wake you up. But as soon as he can after that."

Julie belted herself in, then asked in a near whisper, "Did you like him?"

"Well, I like that he looked me in the eyes when we shook. And I like that he likes his grandmother. And I like that he got flustered and turned the color of beet juice. That shows he's not full of himself."

I pulled out of the lot thinking I really liked that he wasn't Isaac.

"All the counselors are gonna send their friends Franklin's picture and the information." Julie tucked her phone into the pocket of her shorts. "What do we do now?"

"Well, we've cast our lines into the water, so now we do the hard part—we wait."

The next night's revival brought a huge crowd to Hemlock Lake. Anticipating the traffic snarl, most residents decided to stay home. But then word got out that Reverend Balforth was standing in the field, facing the tent and Wesley Falton's platform. He held a sign that read: YOUR SIN WILL BE REVEALED. YOU WILL BE JUDGED. YOU WILL BURN.

Our phone rang. And rang. And rang.

"Doesn't say who will be judged," Jefferson said. "Maybe he means all of us, but my money says he means Wesley Falton."

"Reverend Balforth's face looks like it's carved out of rock," Alda reported. "He's as still as a heron watching a frog in a pond."

"A couple of people under the tent kept turning to look at that sign and getting real itchy," Pattie told me. "They finally got up and left."

I relayed everything to Camille. "You answer the next call. I'm going out on the porch to read."

"No, let's go to the revival." She gathered up Chance and the pack of baby gear we'd gotten in the habit of leaving on a chair in the kitchen. "If there's going to be a showdown, I don't want to be the only one in Hemlock Lake who misses it."

"You won't miss a thing. Someone will post it on the Internet before morning."

"That's not the same as being there."

"The road is probably snarled all the way to Bobcat Hollow. We might have to walk for miles."

"Not if we take the boat." She pulled a bottle of water from the refrigerator. "We can put in near Stub's garage and be almost there."

True. The air was still. The trip down the lake would be an easy one. But the return . . . "As long as we head home before dark."

"Julie has my car. If it gets late we'll come home with her and leave the boat."

Neither of us mentioned Susanna. But I knew Camille was also thinking of the night she died in the lake.

I called Nelson inside, locked up, and made sure Chance was belted into the tiny lifejacket Julie found for him. For once the motor started without complaint or hesitation and we chugged along, me vigilant for hazards in the form of logs or rocks, Camille on the lookout for floating litter. We kept a small net in the boat, and she used it to nab a plastic cup lid, a rubber duck, a champagne cork, and a couple of fishing bobbers.

"What kind of sin do you suppose Reverend Balforth means?" Camille mimed holding a sign. "What do you suppose he imagines Wesley Falton did? Commit adultery?"

"Falton wouldn't be the first religious leader to do that."

"Theft?"

"A lot of money comes through that tent, but it all goes to support Falton's ministry and projects, so he'd be stealing from himself."

"True. What if he ripped off someone's elderly aunt, took her life's savings in exchange for salvation?"

"Seems like a niece or nephew would be blowing the whistle on him and someone would have heard about it."

"Hmm." Camille scooped a soda can into the net and peered at me over her shoulder. "What about murder?"

Before I could answer, she laughed. "Listen to me. I've been reading too many mysteries. Who would Wesley Falton murder? And why?"

Recalling the rage and power behind toppling the pulpit, I didn't share in her laughter. Wesley Falton was a man on fire. How hot did he burn? Hot enough to take a life? Whose life? And why?

Chapter 37

I mulled those questions all the way to the tiny cove near Stub's garage. Partially screened by birches leaning over the water, it provided only a few feet of coarse sand on which to beach the boat. Camille leaped out, tied the painter to a stump, and waited for me to hand Chance to her. In a few minutes we'd threaded our way through the crowd and found Jefferson and Mary Lou in their usual spot.

"Thought you might decide to witness whatever Balforth is up to." Jefferson pointed at a couple of folding canvas chairs set up beside a cooler. "No charge for the seating service. Or the refreshments."

Cooing, Mary Lou took Chance from Camille's arms. "I brought fresh lemonade."

"And I brought something to splash into it." Jefferson held up a pint of dark rum.

"Plain lemonade for me," Camille said, "until Chance is weaned. Which will be the same day he sprouts his first tooth."

"I'll have her splash. But no more. We brought the boat." I held out a plastic cup. "What have we missed?"

"Nothing much. Wesley Falton's still in his little dressing tent. Reverend Balforth's still standing like he was cast in bronze. And people are still coming."

"And going." Mary Lou pointed at a couple walking away from the field, the woman taking short, quick steps, the man lagging. "Usually it's the man who's in a hurry to leave after he sees Reverend Balforth and his sign, but I guess this time she's the one with something to hide."

"We all have something to hide," Camille said. "And I thought that was the point of these revivals—that you get washed clean and start fresh."

"Maybe that woman doesn't believe." Mary Lou nuzzled Chance's cheek. "Or maybe she thinks she can't be forgiven—or shouldn't be."

"I've seen things I'd never forgive," Jefferson said. "And done things I—"

"That was in a war." Mary Lou took his hand. "And you were ordered to."

Jefferson looked to the sky. "I wouldn't put that on a list of reasons to show me mercy. Not when there were some who had the conscience to take a stand and object or leave the country."

"You were a different man then."

"No, I *wasn't* a man. Not then."

"It's a fascinating topic—what we can be forgiven for and what we can't." Camille held out her hands, palms up. "Maybe it's about balance. There's everything you did that's bad or wrong, and everything you did that's good or right—by whatever definitions you use. And maybe there's intention, as well. And maybe the specific situation is a factor."

She moved her hands up and down and I knew she was thinking about the day she killed the ex-husband who had come to kill her. "Do enough positive stuff to tip the scales and you might squeeze through the gates and get a harp and a halo."

"Jefferson will squeeze through," Mary Lou said.

"More likely he'll batter the gates off the hinges," I said.

"I will if they let Mary Lou in and tell me I can't be with her." Jefferson splashed more rum in his lemonade and stood to survey the revival tent. "Here comes that trumpet player. Brother Elijah must be about to take the stage."

Camille and I got to our feet and shaded our eyes against the gold glare of sunlight streaming through dusty air.

"I can't move," Mary Lou said. "Chance is drifting off. Tell me what's happening."

The trumpet sounded, echoing from the hills.

Jefferson cupped his ear with one hand, held his glass in front of his mouth and spoke in a deep voice, a parody of a TV announcer. "Ladies and gentlemen, welcome to another edition of *Your Soul's in the Line of Fire Tonight* coming to you live from Hemlock Lake. This evening's event is a battle between favorite son James Balforth and outsider Wesley Falton."

"Don't make light of this, Jefferson, or they'll reinforce those hinges," Mary Lou warned, "and I'll have to spend eternity without you."

Jefferson rolled his eyes, but lowered the glass and resumed his normal tone. "Isaac and Hannah are herding stragglers under the canopy, giving Balforth a wide berth, not looking his way. Falton's still in his little tent, but he's peeking out through a slit in the back."

The trumpet sounded again.

"Falton's coming out, bounding like a deer. And now he's on the platform and he's pointing at Balforth and smiling."

A hush fell over the crowd.

I stared at Balforth, wondering if he had discovered something about Falton and was acting out of concern for his flock, or if he had personal reasons. Would this escalate?

Mary Lou tugged at Jefferson's shirt. "What's happening?"

"Nothing. They're staring at each other. Balforth raised his sign a little higher. Falton's smiling so I can see most of his teeth. I wonder if that hurts his lips. Okay, now he's pointing at the guy with the trumpet."

The trumpet sounded again. And then Brother Elijah's voice rang out.

"We are warned not to pronounce judgment because by that we shall be judged. We are instructed if we shall be hypocrites we shall be measured by that."

Except for the occasional twitch of his eyelids, Balforth was still.

"When we forgive the sins of others, then we shall be forgiven. If we confess our sins, then we shall be purified. If we turn away from all that tempts us, we shall be as white as new snow."

On the word "white," Falton raised his arms in benediction, the sleeves of his suit pearly in the glow of the lights strung around the tent. "Now let us pray in silence, pray for the strength to forgive."

And so it went, Falton paraphrasing the Bible to his message, and Balforth standing like a statue.

"Like he was turned into a pillar of salt," Jefferson said. "Except he always wears black, so he'd be a pillar of pepper. Falton would be that spire of salt."

"Don't make light of this," Mary Lou warned again. "As serious as Reverend Balforth is, I have a feeling this won't end well."

The sun set, the stars came out, and Wesley Falton preached on and on.

"Trying to wear Balforth down?" I mused.

"Except he's starting to lose his voice," Camille said. "And Reverend Balforth is holding his sign a little lower, but that's it."

"Stillness like that, he could have been a world-class sniper," Jefferson said. "I'm starting to admire him."

"Enough to go to church tomorrow?" Mary Lou asked.

"If Dan does."

Camille chuckled. "Dan will stay home and wait for the report from Freeman—unless this revival runs right through church time tomorrow and there's nothing to report."

Wesley Falton's voice was a croak and he was drenched with sweat when the revival wound up with a few rousing songs and shouts of salvation. Leaping from the platform, he worked the crowd, shaking hands and kissing women and children. Families gathered chairs and coolers and trudged to their cars. Isaac and Hannah gathered garbage. Balforth stood like stone.

Julie crossed the field from the kiddie area, waving at Isaac as she came. After a glance in his father's direction, Isaac flipped his fingers in a miniscule salute, keeping his hand close to his body.

Julie didn't seem to notice. Smiling, she ran the last few yards and gave me a hug. "He called. Like you said he would."

Jefferson loomed over us. "Who called?"

"Rick. I met him yesterday."

"Seemed like a nice kid," I said.

Jefferson grunted. "Is he aware he'll have to get my approval before he does more than speak with you on the phone?"

Julie giggled, but after a second her smile faded. "You're serious."

"As a heart attack. I won't let you buy a car that isn't safe and I won't let you date a boy who isn't sane. Get him up here and let's see if he passes inspection."

Julie tugged at my arm. "Really?"

"I admit the concept is a shade old-fashioned, but Jefferson has a point."

She stomped one foot and spun to Camille and Mary Lou. "Seriously?"

Mary Lou patted her shoulder. "Jefferson loves you, dear."

"But no boy will *ever* pass *his* inspection," Julie moaned. "And while they're all flunking, I'll be dying of embarrassment."

"I don't know if that's medically possible," Camille said, "but I'll research it. In the meantime, since Dan wants to talk with Rick anyway, why don't we invite him over next Sunday? We'll have everyone over for a potluck barbecue."

"Everyone?" Julie whirled in a circle clutching her stomach.

"Sure. That way you can get the embarrassment over with all at once."

"Justin too?"

"Of course. We can't leave him out."

"But he hates all the guys I like."

"*All* the guys?" Jefferson asked. "Who are *all* these guys?"

Julie stopped whirling. "Well, mostly Isaac. And I don't like him like a boyfriend, just like a friend. Justin says he's got too many issues and he's way far under his father's thumb and he needs to figure out who he is and grow up."

"I vote with Justin on that one," Jefferson said.

Especially the last part, I thought. And Justin should know, given how Ronny once controlled his thinking.

"Then it's settled," Mary Lou said. "I'll bring potato salad and custard cream pie. I heard that's good for girls who are dying of embarrassment."

Julie groaned and twirled in another tight circle, then stopped and pointed at Reverend Balforth. "Look, he's moving."

"In slow motion," Camille said. "Like a mime."

"He's stiff." Jefferson rolled his shoulders. "I know the feeling well."

Balforth twisted his torso and flexed his joints. Then he turned his back on Wesley Falton. As he passed us, his gaze locked on mine. He nodded, but said nothing.

Camille leaned close and spoke in a low voice. "I already admitted I read too many mysteries, so feel free to ignore me, but I wish you'd look into Wesley Falton's background."

With Alda behind him dishing out apologies and proclaiming that they had no intention of inviting themselves for lunch this time, Freeman mounted the porch steps late the next morning. Julie hustled to make lemonade, I set aside a draft of a report on my activities for Sheriff North to present at a county budget meeting, and Camille went on snapping the ends off string beans picked that morning.

"Hot as it is, the church was packed." Freeman scratched Nelson's ears and dropped into the rocker. "Everyone jammed into the pews, even a reporter from the paper, all of us sweating and waiting for the explosion."

"You could have heard a pin drop when the organist stopped playing." Alda took off a miniscule straw hat and fanned herself with it. "And when Reverend Balforth walked to the pulpit, I heard his leather shoes squeak. I got goose pimples." She rubbed her fleshy arms. "The squeaking was so . . . I don't know, so odd. Maybe because I never heard his shoes squeak before. Maybe because it made him seem human. Does that make sense?"

"It does to me." Camille handed a bean to Chance and he went to work gumming it. "Because he's a minister, we tend to set him apart and above, so it's jarring when something makes us realize that he's the same as any of us, squeaky shoes and all."

"I never thought of it that way." Alda sipped lemonade. "But now that you mention it, I never thought of him cooking dinner or taking out the garbage or doing laundry like all the rest of us do." She patted Freeman's head on her way to the lounge chair. "Or like some of us do—the ones of us who aren't fortunate enough to be married to women who do it for them."

"Hey, I take out the garbage," Freeman protested. "When you remind me. And when I'm not busy."

"Like when a long commercial comes on TV," Julie whispered. "And there's time left when he's finished getting a snack."

"What happened to children being seen and not heard?" Freeman groused.

"Same thing that happened to men putting their wives on pedestals," Alda shot back.

Freeman turned to me for support, but I shook my head. "Give it up. Unless Chance learns to talk in the next few seconds, we're outnumbered."

Chance waved his string bean, but wisely kept silent.

Freeman rolled up his sleeves. "Anyway, Reverend Balforth stood there for a while, kind of staring out over our heads. And we tried to look innocent. The way kids in school did when someone put a tack on the teacher's chair."

"And then," Alda said, "it was like popping a balloon that's almost out of air. It was just a regular sermon—except he didn't go on as long as he usually does."

"Probably too tired after last night." Freeman mimed holding up a sign. "All he did was read something about driving people out. I wasn't listening much."

"What a change," Alda said. "Usually you hang on every word."

Julie giggled.

"Appears Alda's tongue is sharp enough to slice the pie she baked this morning, so we'll be leaving now." Freeman rocked forward and stood. "I'm assuming Reverend Balforth meant the

Faltons would be driven out of Hemlock Lake, but what I don't know is whether he intends to do the driving or whether he hopes the guy upstairs takes the hint."

"I'm in favor of choice number two," I said. "Or any other version that doesn't make paperwork for the sheriff."

Chapter 38

The next week crept along like a snail crossing the Sahara. I rolled into the sheriff's office and researched Wesley Falton's history with the law, turning up only a minor fender-bender of an accident several years earlier. He'd been cited for going too fast for conditions—darkness, fog, rain, and wind—on a winding road across the river from Ashokan City. He paid the fine promptly.

After asking me whether I didn't have anything better to do than waste her time, Serenity Brook turned up dozens of newspaper articles about his revivals. Sheriff North got wind of my search and, when I'd told him about the stand-off, said he hoped I wasn't billing him for time spent peeking into a preacher's past for no good reason except that another minister didn't like him.

When Rick called, I invited him to come on Sunday, casually mentioning that we'd provide dinner for his trouble and that he might persuade Julie to take him out on the lake for a little fishing or swimming. He said he'd like that and added that his mother would insist he bring something. He'd been learning to cook and was thinking his next project would be cheese straws. I allowed as how I hadn't had a cheese straw for a decade and didn't realize how much I missed them, then suggested he show up any time after 2:00.

E-mail messages trickled in from the network Julie set up. The gist was that Franklin was quiet, kept to himself, and didn't hang out with anyone. "We were all kind of together," one girl wrote. "But Franklin was off on the edge of the group. I can't remember if I ever talked with him."

On Tuesday, an offer came through on Rachel's house.

It wasn't a great offer, but it was a good one. I penciled it out for Julie and Justin that evening, showing them how much went to the real estate agent and how much for closing costs and legal and filing fees and what I projected they'd pay in taxes. "All that takes a chunk but the good news is that if you accept it, we don't have to fix or replace anything. Not even the chipped sink in the little bathroom. So you two split everything else."

I divided the final number by two.

Justin whistled. "That will pay you and Camille for what you put down on my house and the bait shop."

"And that's a bunch of money for college." Julie stared at the result, tears brimming in her eyes. "But I wish I could have Grandma instead."

"I wish we could have everyone here again." Justin crossed to her side of the table and hugged her. "And I wish we could fix what was wrong and start over and do better. But we can only go on from here."

"I know," Julie sniffled.

Justin shot me a crooked smile and tousled her hair. "Now, what's all this about some guy named Rick coming for dinner on Sunday?"

Julie groaned and pulled away from his embrace. "Does *everybody* know *everything* about *everyone* in this town?"

"Uh, yeah, mostly." Justin nodded toward the house across the lake. "Except for them. Nobody knows anything much about them."

"We know they don't eat anything they really like." Julie stroked Nelson's back with her bare feet. "Or have any pets."

"Or mow their lawn," I said. "Or fix that trellis."

"Or trim those bushes or sweep the porch," Justin said. "Would it mean they liked the Brocktons' house too much if they took care of it?"

Camille held up a hand. "If we're going to continue this discussion, let's steer clear of wild supposition and stick to what we actually know."

Chastened, we were all silent for a moment, then Julie said in a small voice, "I know Mr. Falton proposed on Valentine's Day. Isaac told me."

Justin narrowed his eyes. "How did that come up?"

"I was telling him about the fireworks on the Fourth of July and he said he'd like to see them sometime. Then we talked about other holidays and he told me about his father proposing." Julie frowned. "He said it was weird because now his father never buys his mother flowers or candy or even a card."

"Well, I'd miss the chocolates." Camille shot me a glance that said I better remember. "But I think some holidays have become too commercial. Perhaps his parents mark the occasion in other ways."

"Maybe," Julie said. "But it sure seems like they miss out on a lot of stuff. I mean, they don't watch TV. Not even educational programs."

"How's Isaac doing at the dock?" I asked Justin.

"Okay. He does his job."

"But nothing more?" Camille asked.

"Pretty much." Justin leaned on the railing. "Sometimes I think he doesn't notice stuff that ought to be done, and sometimes I think he notices but . . . It's like he's afraid to do anything more than the usual stuff."

"Sounds like he hasn't had a lot of leeway in his life," Camille said.

"And the ax falls if he gets off the path set for him," I agreed.

"I understand what it's like to have a father who wants things done his way," Justin said. "But even Dad wasn't always bullheaded enough to think that was the *only* way, or there might not be a better way."

I nodded, noting the word "always."

"It will be interesting to see what happens," Camille mused, "if Isaac tries to break away and be a person in his own right."

Sunday came around and the church was once again packed. Freeman called to report that Reverend Balforth seemed smaller, thinner, exhausted, and confused.

"He talked about loving our enemies and then he tossed out a whole bunch of questions again. 'How do you know who your enemy is? Why is your enemy your enemy? What does it mean to love? Can love drive out hate? Can love change your enemy or will it only change how you view him?'"

Freeman drew in a breath. "It wasn't like he wanted us to think about that stuff, it was like he didn't know. And he's supposed to know. Isn't he?"

"Sounds like he's mixing messages from the Bible and having a crisis of faith," Camille said when I told her. "It's eating away at him."

I speculated as we got the house spiffed up for the barbecue. From what he'd told me, Balforth didn't have a firm foundation of belief. A crisis of faith could rattle that foundation and rattle his congregation and the community.

"Maybe we should talk to him," Camille suggested.

"And say what?"

"I don't know." She tossed a sponge in the sink, sending a geyser of soapy water across the counter. "I can't say we support him in his crusade against Wesley Falton because there's no proof Falton has done anything worse than let his lawn go to seed. For all we know, Balforth's gut feeling could be a case of jealousy."

"Or indigestion," I said with a chuckle.

Camille retrieved the sponge, wrung it out, and mopped up her mess. "But I still feel like we should talk to him. Even if all we do is let him know he can talk with us."

I didn't look forward to a talk with Reverend James Balforth, but I couldn't deny Camille's urge to show support. "All right."

"I'll call him next week and— Is it 1:00 already? You better get that grill cleaned."

I hustled to obey, passing Julie who, as my grandmother used to say, was all atwitter, scurrying around the house with a duster, moving chairs an inch or two, plumping cushions, and rearranging photos on the mantel. When I came in from scraping, she cornered me in the kitchen and "suggested" that I change out of my faded red T-shirt.

"Why?" I asked with a straight face. "This has only two holes and those are under the arms."

"Come on, Uncle Dan, that shirt's old and ugly."

"So am I."

"No you're not. Please change into something nicer."

"But not too nice," Camille said. "You'll get grease stains or barbecue sauce on it and it will be ruined."

"How about that blue shirt with the green stripes?"

THE DEVIL'S TOMBSTONE

Julie made a gag-me motion and Camille rolled her eyes.

"Okay, the tan one with the red stitching?"

"And look like you work at a gas station?" Julie headed for the bedroom. "I'll find something."

"First date jitters," Camille said.

"So it's officially a date?"

"I'd say so." Camille held out a spoonful of salsa. "What does it need?"

I gulped, felt a burn spread across my tongue. "Needs beer to wash it down. Otherwise it's perfect."

"Good, because I hear the sound of tires on gravel."

Tires slowing, brakes squeaking.

"Must be Rick." Camille pushed me toward the bedroom. "You go change. I'll show him where to park and bring him to the library so you can interview him while Julie puts on another outfit."

"What? She's changed three times already."

"If you're smart, you won't mention that. Especially not to Rick."

I nodded and hustled to the bedroom where Julie was weighing the merits of a blue-on-blue Hawaiian shirt. "Rick's here."

"Eeeekkkk!" She dropped the shirt and raced for the stairs. "I have to change."

Shaking my head, I tore off my T-shirt, yanked on the Hawaiian shirt, and made it to the library seconds before Camille ushered Rick through the door, turning a thumb up behind his back. He wore moccasins, a pair of faded jeans, and a tan shirt a heck of a lot like the one I hadn't been allowed to wear. I bet Julie would like his just fine.

"Glad you could make it."

We shook, his gaze sliding from mine to take in the library. "Wow. Are all these books yours?"

341

They were now. Many had once belonged to Clarence Wolven. I bought them from his estate at a price above what was asked.

"All mine. All except those." I pointed to a stack of picture books Camille bought for Chance. "Those are Julie's. She's working her way through the one about the elephant but it's been slow going."

His eyes widened and then he laughed. "Good one. Julie told me she's taking advanced placement English."

"She lied."

This time his eyes narrowed before he laughed again. "Are you trying to embarrass me? Or Julie?"

I liked this kid better all the time. "Apparently all I've managed to do is embarrass myself, so let's get to what you remember about Franklin Turner."

I pointed to two easy chairs by a window, set the recorder on the table between them, and explained how going over old ground with new eyes sometimes turned up important details. Then I opened the file to the photo of Franklin. "I know it's been three years and memories fade, but tell me what you remember about Franklin. How would you describe him? What did you think of him?"

"He was shy. Stressed out. He bit his nails. Talented. Smart. Creative. But kind of afraid to offer his opinion." Rick crossed his legs and worried a worn spot on his jeans with his thumbnail. "You want everything I thought?"

"Absolutely. A little thing that seems like nothing to you might be the piece I'm missing."

He thought for a minute, then said, "All right. Well, it was only a feeling, and I don't want you to think I'm prejudiced or anything because I'm fine with it, but I thought he was gay. I felt like he was working up the nerve to come out, and trying to figure out how to do it without, you know, putting up a billboard or posting on the Internet."

"In other words, he was more subtle than a lot of teenagers."

Rick grinned. "Yeah. Most kids I know put it right out there."

I wondered how he'd feel about what Julie had to put out there—the losses and tragedies of her life. How he reacted would be a litmus test for the future of their relationship.

"Did you see Franklin showing a special interest in anyone?"

Rick shook his head. "Not in drama class. He was all about the play. And that's all he was there for. When everyone else lined up for chow, he left."

I nodded, then played the silence card. Rick worried the worn spot again, and chewed the corner of his lower lip. "There was one kid. Maybe a year or two older than Franklin. I saw them talking a couple of times after drama class—off on the far side of the parking lot. They had their heads close together. Once I saw him put his hand on Franklin's arm."

"How? Like he wanted him to stop? Or like he wanted to be closer to him?"

"I don't know. Is there a difference?"

"Sure, but could you tell from a distance? Probably not." I glanced past Rick and spotted Julie lurking in the doorway. She wore a nervous smile and one of the outfits she had on earlier—a pair of cut-off jeans and a blue-and-white-checked blouse. "Last question, can you describe the boy you saw talking with Franklin?"

"Tall. Skinny." He spread his hands. "Like I said, they were aways off and I was in a hurry to get lunch. Drama classes usually ran long."

343

"Then I'll cut this short." I stood, noted Julie had disappeared, and pointed to the door. "If you go out that way and across the porch, I bet you'll find Julie on the dock getting the boat ready. Tell her I said to take it slower than yesterday. If I have to replace one more motor she's grounded for the rest of the summer. And if she lets Nelson drive again she's grounded for life."

"Who's Nelson?"

"Our dog."

Rick did the eye-widening thing followed by a laugh, then headed for the dock. In a moment the motor fired up and the boat roared off up the lake.

The usual suspects arrived shortly afterward and we got busy at the tasks tradition dictated—men hovering around the grill or setting up tables, women bustling in and out of the kitchen with platters and bowls and baskets. Julie and Rick came up from the lake while the final burger was scorching, so there wasn't time for small talk before we lined up to fill our plates and find chairs on the shaded patio.

"Boy has a good grip," Jefferson said. "And he made some world-class cheese straws."

"He's got a good appetite, too." Mary Lou nodded at the mound of potato salad on Rick's plate. "I like that in a man."

"Good thing," Jefferson said, "or I'd be living in the woods again."

"The test will come with Marcella's macaroni salad. If he eats that without puckering like he's suckin' a lemon, I'll invite him again next Sunday."

"It's not to everyone's taste," Mary Lou agreed.

"It's not to *anyone's* taste," Jefferson said. "It almost makes me long for that gelatin salad Priscilla always brought."

Rick reached the macaroni salad and we held our breaths. He dug in with the serving spoon and built a pile on his plate.

"That's a lot of eating," Jefferson observed. "And he's *gotta* eat it. Marcella will have her eyes on him."

"Maybe he's fond of vinegar and onion," Mary Lou said. "Maybe it's the way his mother makes it."

"Then he's kinda immune." Jefferson picked up a plate and transferred two pork chops from a platter.

"Let's hope so." I grabbed a burger. "Otherwise Julie will never hear the end of it."

Chapter 39

Maybe Julie clued him in. Or maybe Rick was the best-mannered young man in Ashokan County. At any rate, he ate the macaroni salad without a flinch or a pucker, complimented Marcella, and claimed he'd have seconds except he'd missed Alda's baked beans on his way through the line and had to leave room for those. On his way to the buffet table, he stopped to tell Mary Lou he'd never had better potato salad, and informed Pattie that her cornbread was delicious.

"Boy's a born tactician," Jefferson said. "Scoped the terrain, read the situation, saw what he had to do, and did it."

"That won't work with Justin," I pointed out.

"He'll come up with a battle plan. You watch."

Julie set it up, suggesting they gather skipping rocks for a contest before dessert.

"I hope sedimentary rocks are okay," Rick said as they headed off. "But if you want me to hammer a glacial erratic to bits I'll do it for you."

Justin studied him with new interest. "You a geology major?"

"Chemistry. But Dad's a rockhound and I got caught up in the hunt when I was a kid."

"There are boulders at the end of the lake I'll show you sometime. Some believe they were set here when the earth was formed." Justin glanced toward the house across the lake. "But my money's on a glacier."

"One of those boulders has a story. A kind of creepy one." Julie led the way to the shore. "Maybe after dessert Mary Lou will tell it."

Jefferson stared in the direction of the Devil's Tombstone. "Wish I could convince myself whatever's there is my imagination."

I gripped his shoulder. "I felt it. It's dark. Cold. Should we haul Reverend Balforth out there to do an exorcism?"

"First let's see if he drives Wesley Falton out of Hemlock Lake. Come on, it's time to pitch a few horseshoes."

The moon was rising when Alda, Pattie, and Marcella gathered bowls and platters and herded their husbands to their cars. Mary Lou and Jefferson followed a few minutes later and, when I walked to the porch, I saw Rick saying goodbye to Julie, a process that involved standing close enough to signify that he wanted to see her again, soon.

When they broke apart, Rick shook hands with Justin, scratched Nelson's ears, thanked Camille for her hospitality, and asked me if we could talk for a minute in private. I steered him into the library and closed the door.

"I didn't want to distract you from the party, but while we were out on the lake I saw a guy who looked a heck of lot like the one I told you about." He tapped the Franklin Turner file on the edge of my desk. "The one I saw talking with Franklin."

I blinked.

What were the odds?

"He was aways down the lake," Rick said. "In an old rowboat. Not fishing, just sitting there, smacking one oar on the water. Julie waved to him."

Isaac Falton.

Isaac Falton knew Franklin Turner.

Part of my brain saw this as the end of the thread that might lead to an arrest. Another part of my brain said, "So what? So Isaac knew Franklin. So did plenty of other kids in the summer programs. So did Rick."

To take that a step farther, Rick could be casting suspicion on Isaac to steer me away from him.

I reminded myself to go slow, to assume nothing.

The next morning, after I dropped Chance off with Camille, I drove to the bait shop. Justin had left for school, and Isaac was alone, lugging a gas can and coming my way along the dock. He wore a pair of baggy khaki slacks, a white T-shirt, and a smile that didn't reach his eyes. I couldn't have asked for a better photo opportunity and snapped off several shots while he was intent on transferring the container to a trio of fishermen in an aluminum boat. When they roared off across the lake, I snapped on the recorder, tucked it in my shirt pocket, and approached, Franklin Turner's file in my hand.

"Good morning," Isaac said in a flat voice. "Can I help you?"

"Possibly."

I waited a beat, then opened the file and turned it so he could see Franklin's picture. "Know him?"

He gaped. "That's Franklin." Raising his right arm, he extended his hand by inches, and touched the picture with his forefinger. "That's Franklin Turner."

"Correct. This picture was taken shortly before he was killed. Stabbed to death. Stabbed more than two dozen times."

Isaac staggered and dropped to his knees. "I didn't know. I heard he died, but I didn't . . . we don't get a newspaper."

He seemed stunned, but I kept up the offense. "He was dumped in a ditch like a sack of garbage."

Tears brimmed in Isaac's eyes.

"It's my job to find the person who did that."

He trembled and swallowed hard. "You don't think it was me, do you?"

"I was told you were friendly with him."

"I . . . we talked a little. He was nice."

I kept the pressure on, kept my voice harsh. "How did you meet? You weren't in his drama class."

"No." He shook his head and got to his feet. "No. I'm not allowed to go to movies or plays, or be *in* a play unless it's a church play and Dad approves of it."

I'd bet my boat that a play about Huckleberry Finn wouldn't meet with Wesley Falton's approval.

"Franklin was in the hall," Isaac said in a soft voice. "He was practicing his lines by the water fountain, pretending it was one of the actors. I was early for Bible class and I stopped to watch. He was good, really good. He didn't see me until he was done and I clapped. Then he smiled and bowed."

"And you talked with him."

"A little."

"And the next day, were you early for class again?"

He flushed. "Yes."

"And Franklin was rehearsing again?"

"Yes."

"So you became friends."

"I guess, I mean. I *wanted* to be friends. He was smart and funny and he didn't seem to mind that I could only talk to him for a minute or two and only there, at that church."

He kicked at a boat cleat with the toe of one ratty sneaker. I bit back my questions, waiting, holding the picture of Franklin.

"How can you really be friends when you can't do things together or even call each other because you can only use the phone for church stuff and emergencies?" His voice rose. "When you can't go get a piece of pizza or play tennis or have anybody over for dinner or go to their house to spend the night?"

He sat, then rolled onto his side and curled into a fetal position. I fought the urge to sit beside him and pat his back to comfort him. If this was acting, then he was a master. If this wasn't acting, then he had strong feelings.

Franklin Turner's wounds spoke of strong feelings.

"The last time I saw him was when he was in the play. He was awesome." Isaac sat up and gazed out over the lake. "We were renting a house a few miles from the church that summer—we moved again at the start of September. We move all the time. I snuck out my window and walked to the church. In the rain." He rubbed his arms and peered toward his house. "Mom and Dad don't know. You won't tell them, will you?"

"I have no reason to. But if I find out you're lying . . ."

"I'm not. Honest, I'm not."

"Was there anyone else Franklin hung out with at the church? Anyone you saw him talking to?"

"Just kids in the drama class. He went home when it let out. Sometimes my class was over at the same time and I'd walk with him to the edge of the parking lot."

"I didn't kill Franklin." He got to his feet, clenched his fists and set his jaw. "I wish I knew who did. I'd kill *him*. Somehow, I'd kill him."

Back home I replayed the interview, made notes for the file, and thought about what I'd learned. Isaac Falton had feelings for Franklin Turner. Isaac might have expressed his feelings and Franklin might have reacted in a way that made Isaac angry or afraid. He might have lashed out.

But if that happened—and my gut told me it hadn't—how did Isaac transport Franklin's body from where he was killed to where he was dumped?

According to Julie, Isaac hadn't gotten his license until recently. When he went to see Franklin in the play, he'd walked. In the rain. If he killed someone, however, he might have been desperate enough to appropriate a car to dump the body. Or, if one of his parents discovered what he'd done, they might have helped.

Hannah, not only to protect him from the legal consequences of his act, but also from his father's wrath.

Wesley, to protect his own image.

I was still pondering when Camille and Julie came home and blew the horn—a signal that I was needed to carry in groceries. Reporting for duty, I found a bulging cardboard box with a return address in Alaska.

"It's heavy," Camille warned.

And it was. "How did you get it in the car?"

"Jefferson carried it."

"Complaining all the way," Julie added. "He says you owe him."

"There's no one I'd rather be in debt to." I lugged the box to the stone wall surrounding the patio and ripped at the sealing tape with my house key. Fred Maddox had used what appeared to be an entire roll to make sure the box—splitting at the edges, torn at the corners, and stained on the bottom—would survive the journey.

Julie zipped into the kitchen and returned with a knife. "What's inside?"

"Letters." I sawed at three layers of tape sealing the seam between flaps.

"Whose letters?"

"Theresa Gilligan's."

"She was killed a long time ago, right?"

"Twenty years. She wrote these letters to her boyfriend." I handed Julie the knife and pried at a flap, releasing the mingled scents of mildew and perfume. "Back in the dim and distant days before text messaging."

Julie laid her hand against her forehead and said in a quavering voice, "The very thought of that dark era makes me feel faint."

"Don't swoon with that knife in your hand. You might ruin the edge when it hits the patio."

Huffing an annoyed sigh, she set the knife on a table by the grill, and peered at the contents of the box. "There must be hundreds. Are you gonna read them all?"

"Yes."

Julie flicked aside bits of broken rubber band and plucked out a fat pink envelope. "Smells like dried flowers." She peered inside. "This one is four pages long. Wow. And her handwriting is tiny." She drew another from the box. "This one isn't as long, but the ink is faded. I could help you read them if you tell me what you're looking for."

"That's the problem, kid. I don't know that there's anything on those pages to look *for*. I'll have to read them all myself. But you could help put them in order—when you're not talking to Rick."

She blushed and ducked her head. "He only called twice today."

"Bet he calls twice more this evening."

Keeping her chin tucked, she asked in a whisper, "Did you like him?"

"I would have shown him the door if I didn't."

"Did Camille like him?"

"She didn't sic Nelson on him, did she? Not that Nelson would have gone for him, not after Rick fed him half a hamburger."

"You weren't supposed to see that."

"I'm a trained officer of the law. I have eyes everywhere." I patted my back pocket. "There's one now, watching my wallet."

Julie sniggered and I put my arm around her shoulders. "The important thing is whether *you* like Rick."

"I know, but if you and Camille didn't like him, it would be hard for all of us, wouldn't it?"

"Well, I guess that would all depend on *why* we didn't like him. Not liking him because he chews with his mouth open or licks the guacamole off a corn chip and dips the chip again isn't the same as not liking him because he thinks girls need to be slapped around."

"Rick's not like that. And if a guy tried to hit me, I'd walk away. Over his unconscious body."

I laughed and hugged her close. "That's my girl. Now let's haul this box to the garage and get these put in order."

Chapter 40

With a break for dinner, the process took several hours. A number of envelopes bore clear postmarks and most letters had dates, but Fred had failed to keep all the pages together. After the letters were spread out in order, we had more than three dozen loose pages left.

"Tomorrow." I massaged the small of my back with my fists. "We'll tackle it again tomorrow."

"It's like doing a jigsaw puzzle." Julie set the stack of spares on the workbench. "I want to keep going until all the pieces are where they belong."

"I know the feeling. That's why Camille made the rule about no puzzles with more than 200 pieces."

"It would be cool to do one of those giant ones." She opened the door a foot at a time, checking for wind that might play havoc with our array of letters. "But I wouldn't want to take it apart once I got all the pieces in place."

I went to work the next morning after I dropped Chance off. Yellow marker pen and notepad in hand, I took the first ten letters to the porch along with a giant cup of coffee, figuring if I found a page missing I'd search the misfit stack then.

Theresa's writing was tiny, but individual letters were fat, crowding against each other. She'd also had little use for punctuation. Words, phrases, and sentences ran together.

After two hours, my notepad was still blank. As I'd told Julie, I didn't know what I was looking for, but I knew it wasn't lengthy reports on the weather, a new diet, the latest hairstyles, perfumes, and nail polish colors, or how her cat barfed in her mother's closet.

When my eyes stung from the strain, I took a break and made a roast beef and Swiss sandwich on sourdough rye with sliced cucumber and tomato, spinach, horseradish, and mustard. As I ate, I considered whether I should skip ahead to the final few dozen letters, the ones written during the weeks before she died. That might save time.

And it might not. If there was nothing in those later letters that rang even a distant bell in my mind, I'd have to return to where I was now. The safe and sure way was the slow and plodding way.

But first, there were chores to be done, weeds to be pulled, laundry to be washed, bathrooms to be scrubbed, and sheets to be changed. It was almost enough to make me consider hunting for a full-time job and hiring a cleaning service.

Almost.

I'd grown to like the pace of my life and didn't mind paying a price to keep it. Besides, drudgery might make me eager to return to Theresa Gilligan's letters.

And it did.

Wednesday, accustomed to rounded letters and rambling sentences, I made faster progress. I read about different brands of lipstick, what a professional manicure involved, the pros and cons of highlighting hair, and the merits of pearl earrings. I learned Theresa preferred soap with moisturizing lotion and cotton sheets dried on a clothesline. I found out she loved the cowlick above Fred's left temple and thought he should wear red more often. I gathered she wanted to know more about Fred because here and there she asked questions about which side of the bed he preferred to sleep on and who he would vote for. And I gathered she worried about whether their marriage would be a success because she asked how he thought they might divide housework, how soon he wanted to have a baby, and whether she ought to read more books about sex.

Nowhere was there a clue about who might have killed her and why.

Thursday morning the phone rang just after dawn.

"I'm afraid something's wrong with Reverend Balforth." Mary Lou gulped air. "I heard the church bell ring in the night. Just once. I thought it was a dream. But when I got up I saw his car parked by the church. Seemed odd, so Jefferson went over."

She gulped air again and gave a little moan. "The car's covered with dew and the church is locked up and Jefferson couldn't hear anything. He took my key and his rifle, but he's waiting for you before he opens the door."

In 15 minutes I was by his side, wearing a pair of gloves and unlocking the door, senses tingling. I was hyper-aware of the summer morning sounds of Hemlock Lake: a car starting, a dog barking, a late rooster crowing. I smelled damp grass and frying bacon and brewing coffee. And, faint but close by, I caught the scent of death.

Reverend Balforth, wearing his trademark black suit, hung from the bell rope in the vestibule, his black shoes dangling a few inches from the floor, the organist's bench overturned nearby.

"Shit fire." Jefferson stepped back.

I did the same, closing the door and turning the key in the lock. "I'll call the sheriff and keep the area secure. You better tell Mary Lou."

Jefferson nodded. "Knew he was going off the rails. Never thought he'd take that jump."

"Neither did I."

Jefferson took off and I dialed Sheriff North's home number.

"I'm not in the mood for bad news at this hour," he said. "You better be calling to tell me you solved another cold case."

"Reverend James Balforth is hanging from the bell rope in the church."

"The hell you say."

Hell. Hell followed the pale horse.

"Suicide?" Sheriff North asked.

"Looks like it."

"You say that like you're not certain."

"It's not my job to be certain about cause of death. That's why you pay the experts."

He snorted. "Well, hold the fort until I get those experts to the scene. Give them a hand with the door-to-door if they ask."

I vowed to volunteer before they asked, vowed to make sure one of the doors I knocked on was Wesley Falton's. Never mind that it was seven miles from the scene of the crime.

Sheriff North hung up.

I hung around, thinking about Wesley Falton and that overturned pulpit and the sign Balforth brandished at the revival and our conversations about faith. I wondered if Balforth found something to believe in before he died.

Mary Lou brought coffee and a plate loaded with bacon, scrambled eggs, and buttered biscuits. "Seems wrong to be eating with Reverend Balforth in there like that. But I bet you didn't stop for so much as a glass of juice before you left home and going hungry won't help matters."

Jefferson followed with a mounded plate of his own and we sat in my rig, doors open. The air was already heating up, the sun sucking dew from the grass. "Gonna be the hottest day yet."

That didn't call for a response more elaborate than a grunt.

"Suppose he'll be buried on the hill?"

"Guess that depends on whether he arranged for a plot. The Bonesteels would know."

Jefferson stuffed scrambled eggs and bacon between the halves of a split biscuit. "Would anyone quibble if taking the jump was his idea?"

"No one did when my brother shot himself. And if there's a place on that hill for Ronny Miller, there ought to be a place for the reverend."

Jefferson bit into his biscuit sandwich, chewed with deliberation, swallowed, and washed it down with coffee. "Wonder who'll do the burying. Can't remember anyone ever filling in for Balforth. He never took time off."

"He might not have believed in his mission like he thought he should, but he dedicated himself to serving his flock."

"That he did. Be interesting if Balforth didn't spell it all out and Wesley Falton decides it's his place to do the dust-to-dust speech."

"I'm not sure 'interesting' covers it."

"Yeah. Whether they like Brother Elijah or not, folks will be up in arms if he steps in. And you can bet reverend Balforth will be spinning in his grave if he knows who's preaching over him."

"Well, there will be time to sort things out. Won't be any burying or preaching until after the autopsy."

As it turned out, I didn't have to knock on Falton's door. He drove up a few hours later and circulated among those gathered beneath the trees, offering his condolences and an unsolicited alibi. He'd been up late working on his book, dictating to Hannah. He didn't learn about Balforth's death until she went to the post office midway through the morning.

An alibi that hung on the word of a woman cowed into submission wasn't an alibi I'd accept without question.

I wrote up a report about the confrontation at the church and e-mailed it to the sheriff.

Sunday came and almost everyone in town gathered in the shade of the maple trees beside the church for prayers and an informal remembrance ceremony organized by Alda and Freeman. "After all the years I spent coming up with excuses to avoid services," he told me when he invited us, "I never thought I'd be calling for one. But life has a way of playing jokes on us."

Life also had a way of forcing us to walk away or rise to an occasion. And Freeman rose. In a clear and solemn voice he gave us a brief history of James Balforth's life—his education, his decision to serve in a rural area as a modern-day circuit rider, his dedication to his congregations and communities.

He didn't mention Balforth's silent confrontation with Wesley Falton and neither did anyone else. As they contributed memories, they spoke of the way Balforth stayed true to the old hymns and comforted the sick and dying. Camille spoke of how he'd presided at Clarence Wolven's funeral even though the two never met. Julie talked about how her grandmother told her to respect him because he cared how others would spend eternity.

When the last person had spoken, we bowed our heads in silence. Then everyone pitched in to set up tables and chairs and set out platters of fried chicken and salads and cakes and pies.

"Reverend Balforth would have loved this." Alda moved a platter a few inches to make way for a bowl of corn pudding. "He loved a good potluck."

"And this is a damn fine potluck," Freeman said.

"Would it kill you not to swear?" Alda asked. "Especially on a Sunday?"

"Damn? That isn't swearing." Freeman rolled his eyes in my direction, then admitted his defeat. "You're right, dear. I'm sorry."

"You certainly are. Now get everyone's attention and say grace."

Freeman did as he was told, stumbling only a little over words he hadn't said for years. Then we got to the eating and, between bites, to speculating about why Balforth left us the way he did.

"Science is a wonderful thing," Sheriff North said when he called Monday morning. "Science knows how far along James Balforth was with digesting his dinner. Science knows he had a pin put in his left leg 30 years ago. Science knows he had cancer in his pancreas. But science *doesn't* know whether he killed himself."

"No fibers? No defensive wounds? No indications his hands were tied?"

"Not a thing except four scrapes on the floor that might mean someone pulled that bench out from under him, or might mean he was the kind of man who would shove a bench aside instead of kicking it over."

"No prints on the bench, right?"

"Not a one that doesn't belong to the organist or the reverend himself."

"He plays when the organist is sick. Tell me about the cancer."

Paper shuffled and the sheriff's chair creaked. "Nasty. Spreading. Inoperable."

Had Balforth known? How could he not? Was it pain that spurred him to challenge Wesley Falton at the revival?

"And nobody saw anything? Heard anything?"

"Couple of folks heard the bell in the night, but that's it. No cars. No shouts. Nothing else."

"That report I wrote up about Balforth and Falton arguing at the church a few—"

"I passed it on to the investigators. They're looking at it."

Meaning I should stay out of their territory and let them do their jobs.

"You keep your ears open," Sheriff North instructed. "Ask Camille and Mary Lou and Jefferson to do the same."

I laughed. "They already don't miss a whisper, I can't imagine what they'd hear if they worked at it."

A week after he died, Reverend James Balforth was buried on the hill above Hemlock Lake. Members of his three congregations gathered at his grave. His father, a man with a bent back and an unbending will, conducted the service.

"Seems strange," Mary Lou whispered, "hearing someone else say the words."

"This is his son he's burying," Camille observed. "I thought he might go beyond the usual words. And at least show a glimmer of emotion."

"If he believes his son killed himself," I told her, "he might not want to share the emotion he feels."

"If he believes that, he's a fool. I know there's no proof that someone killed Reverend Balforth, but I know he didn't commit suicide."

"He had cancer," I reminded her. "Pancreatic cancer."

"Yes, but I don't think he knew it. I mean, he might have known he was sick, but if he knew how bad it was, he would have been making arrangements for someone to take his place."

Mary Lou nodded. "He wasn't the kind of shepherd who'd go off and leave his flock."

"Not much in the way of cold, hard proof there, Dan," Jefferson said. "But I vote with them. This was murder."

Chapter 41

Like everyone else in Hemlock Lake, Julie wrestled with the question of who would kill Reverend James Balforth and why. She considered theories ranging from the remotely possible to the paranormal, suggesting the deed was done by a developer hoping Balforth's death would prompt Mary Lou to sell the church, or by the ghost of the evil man who chased his wife to the Devil's Tombstone two centuries before.

Alone in the house late Friday morning, I realized she hadn't mentioned the elephant in the room—Wesley Falton.

Julie didn't know about the confrontation in the church, but she was aware of the challenge at the revival, and aware of Freeman's reports on Balforth's sermons. Had she left Falton off her list because he was a minister? Because a minister taking a life seemed more unbelievable than murder by a ghost?

And there seemed to be no strong reason for Falton to kill Reverend Balforth. Yes, they'd argued about Falton using the church. Yes, Balforth had challenged him, chastised him, preached against him. And yes, he'd driven a few away from Falton's revival. But all that had also raised interest and likely insured a larger turnout for the next gathering.

Balforth told me he had no proof, only suspicion. But suppose he'd discovered something since our conversation.

What?

And where had he come across it?

There was nothing in police records except that minor accident. Nothing in past newspaper reports.

What could Balforth find that I hadn't? And how?

Balforth had ministered to the members of three small congregations—300 people, tops, living on the hills and in the hollows of the Catskill Mountains. Did someone in one of those congregations know something about Wesley Falton?

If so, I doubted that person was a member of the Hemlock Lake congregation. Everyone in this town loved to gossip and, as dialed in as Mary Lou and Camille were, they would have heard whispers.

That left 200 people spread out around a town 12 miles south of Hemlock Lake and another 17 miles east. If I went to those churches on Sunday I could—

Waste time I should be spending on those cold cases. And maybe piss off the investigators assigned to Balforth's case. Piss off Sheriff North, too.

I poured the dregs from the coffeepot into my mug and took a fresh stack of Theresa Gilligan's letters out to the porch. I was within two months of her death, and the daily messages had developed a sameness that caused my thoughts to drift. So, before I took the first one from its envelope, I gave myself a lecture. "Theresa may seem frivolous, but she was barely 20, only a few years older than Julie. She lived a sheltered life. She bought into the happily-ever-after myth and thought she had to do everything exactly right to get there. The color of the nail polish she wore to walk down the aisle mattered to her. The least you can do is read about it without yawning."

Having told myself off, I settled in the swing and read about the ornaments she bought to set aside for their first Christmas tree together, how her father made the wrong kind of popcorn for stringing, her thoughts about whether chestnuts should be in the stuffing or roasted to eat with wine, and how hard it was not to have gravy on her mashed potatoes but she had to give it up or she'd never fit into her wedding dress. I read about a cold snap and the chains she bought for her car and how difficult it was to put them on and how she wished Fred had been there to help. I read about her meeting with the elderly minister who would marry them and his thoughts about the duties of a wife and husband, the importance of family, and how she thought Reverend Durant was behind the times but meant well. I read about what her friends Ginger and Linda thought marriage was all about and the views of a young man she met who was also meeting with Reverend Durant and planning to marry in the spring.

"He hasn't even asked his girlfriend yet," Theresa wrote, "and he's planning the music and flowers and colors. It seems kind of weird for a guy to be doing that instead of the girl, but it's kind of sweet, too. And Wes says he enjoys it and his girlfriend doesn't care as much about details as he does."

Wes?

I sat up with a jolt and stared at the house across the lake.

What were the odds?

Long.

As long as the odds of Isaac knowing Franklin Turner?

Longer?

Probably.

There were thousands of men named Wesley. For all I knew, the Wes Theresa referred to was named Weston or Westley or something else entirely.

Still . . .

I made a note—the first one since I started this project. Then I went for the file and the list of those interviewed 20 years ago. No one named Wes. No one with a name anything close to Wes.

Among the newspaper clippings in the rear of the file I found a story on Theresa's funeral that included a reference to Reverend Harold Durant presiding. I copied his name onto my notepad and checked the list again. Reverend Durant hadn't been interviewed.

Next stop, the computer. I plugged in Harold Durant and within a minute learned he'd been dead almost as long as Theresa Gilligan. Another search and I learned his church hadn't survived him by long. It burned a few months after his death. A deacon quoted in the article mourned the loss of the building as well as records, guest books, and diaries that went back more than 100 years. "We were setting up a committee to enter everything into a computer," he said. "Now it's too late."

I stewed for a few minutes, then called Fred Maddox. As usual, I got his machine. "This is Dan Stone. Got a few questions about Theresa's funeral. Do you know if anyone kept a guest book? If so, do you have any idea where it might be now? And do you recall whether a young man named Wes attended the funeral? If you remember anything about him—anything at all—call as soon as possible."

Knowing it might be days before Maddox called, I stewed some more and stared at the house across the lake. The grass was taller and turning brown. Only a few inches of the lawnmower handle showed. The trellis had fallen and the downspout had toppled.

In 20 minutes I could be knocking on Wesley Falton's door. Sooner if I took the boat. I could ask him if he received pre-marital counseling from Reverend Harold Durant and if he remembered meeting Theresa Gilligan.

Slumping to the steps, I reviewed what I had.

It wasn't much.

I had Reverend Balforth dangling from that bell rope. Balforth had a connection to Wesley Falton.

I had Franklin Turner at summer camp. Through Isaac, he had a connection to Wesley Falton.

I had Theresa Gilligan meeting a young man named Wes.

Was that more than simple coincidence?

If I went to his door, Falton, who hadn't appeared fazed by Reverend Balforth's silent challenge, would likely give me a blank stare. And even if he knew Theresa Gilligan 20 years ago, why would he kill her? What was the motive?

I thought about my dislike of Wesley Falton. What was that based on other than secondhand information or distant observation? Had I gone over to welcome him when he moved in? Had I invited him to join us for dinner? Had I even thought about doing either of those things?

No.

On the other hand, Wesley Falton hadn't so much as waved when he came and went. And he hadn't come into the post office or store to introduce himself. The only personal contact he'd had was with Evan when he rented the field for his revivals and with Reverend Balforth the night they argued. When he wasn't holding revivals here or in other towns, he kept to the house.

In a way, he was a modern version of the man who chased his young wife to the Devil's Tombstone. And that line of thinking, I realized, marked me as one of those who watched and speculated.

When I was a child, the tight communications network of those born and raised around the lake meant someone usually knew where I was headed when I crossed the dam on my bike. Someone knew about apples snitched from orchards or candy that could spoil my dinner. By the time I left for college I felt stifled, smothered. And now I was like the rest.

I paced the house, from the file on my desk, to the letters on the porch. Twenty years had slipped away since Theresa Gilligan left our time-bound world. Would 20 more see her case still unsolved? Would I become, like Jonah Umhey, an old man who couldn't let go?

If that's what it took, that's what I'd do.

Armed with a pack of sticky notes and the remainder of Theresa's letters, I returned to the porch and went on the hunt for further references to Wes.

That hunt was interrupted by everyday events, including Camille's decision that the room next to Julie's should be painted and outfitted for Chance. Last summer, unaware that Camille was pregnant, I'd painted it in one of what seemed like thousands of shades of off-white. Justin had occupied it briefly before we bought the bait shop and house, and now the challenge was to find a color scheme that meshed with Chance's personality.

"Feisty," Julie said as she set the table Friday evening. "Demanding. Determined. Strong."

I shuffled paint chips spread on the far end of the table. "And what color is that?"

"Not these." Camille pushed all the pastel shades into a heap. "And I don't want to go with the traditional blue."

"No blue." I shoved those aside. "Green?"

"There's so much green outside," Julie said.

"On the night Chance was born there wasn't," I groused. "That was a whiteout. Hey, what if we—?"

"No." Camille pushed all the white chips to the floor. "We're not leaving it white."

Can't blame a guy for trying.

But you *can* blame a guy for not being smart enough to know when to steer clear of a discussion where his opinion won't count. I retrieved a beer from the refrigerator, drained pasta, and made a mental list of outside chores that would keep me away from the paint chips until the great debate was over.

Saturday morning I got an e-mail from Fred Maddox answering all my questions with the same three word sentence: "I can't remember." I cursed for a full minute and kicked the desk a few times, then tackled my weekend chore list with a vengeance.

Rick took Julie to a movie in the late afternoon. They returned after dinner for a swim in the lake and pie and ice cream on the porch with the old folks. Hanging with us didn't seem to make either of them uncomfortable and Camille and I watched him drive off with feelings far more positive than we anticipated we'd have about Julie's first boyfriend.

Sunday morning brought rain showers followed by Freeman and Alda with the latest on the church. Alda ducked into the house and entered the paint chip debate and Freeman braved the drizzle to join me on the gentle slope beyond the patio where I was rigging a swing.

"Brother Elijah called last night," he said without preamble. "Wanted to deliver the sermon this morning. And next week and the week after."

"And you said . . . ?"

"That it wasn't up to me, that I'd have to put it to the board and they'd likely want to put it to the whole congregation."

In a community of strong-minded people, that was the safest way to see it done.

Freeman checked the knots that held the plank seat in place. "He didn't like that one bit. Reminded me I'm chairman.

Told me I should be able to make a decision without consulting every Tom, Dick, and Harry."

"And you told him . . .?"

"That maybe *he* didn't feel the need to consult anyone else on this green earth before he set a course, but I damn well do." He glanced at the house across the lake. "Turns out I might have been tarred and feathered if I said 'Come on ahead and preach.' When I put it to the group this morning, there was a lot of spirited talk—*none* of it in favor."

He glanced at Falton's house again, then lowered his voice. "I don't know what it is about that man, but I don't care for him. Neither does anyone else. Nobody wants him standing behind Reverend Balforth's pulpit. Not this week. Not ever."

"You gonna call and tell him that?"

"Hell, no. I'm no coward, but I'm no fool. I'll have Alda write a letter—she's better with polite words than I am."

He sat on the plank seat, testing the spring in the thick branch I'd secured the rope to. "Nice job. Forget about video games. Every kid should have one of these."

"I'm with you there."

He pumped his legs, swinging higher. "Last Sunday when we had that ceremony outside . . . Well, that was partly because it was stifling inside the church and partly because . . . Well, Pattie and Alda said he was still there."

"Reverend Balforth?"

"Yup. His ghost. Or spirit, or what have you. And they said he was mad."

I thought about my encounters with the ghost of Clarence Wolven, the angry buzzing that filled my head, the feeling that he was frustrated because I didn't understand what he wanted. "How could they tell?"

"When they went in to straighten up Saturday, they said the vestibule was cold in spite of it being so hot outside. Pattie brought a chair for the organist on account of the crime scene people took the bench. She set it where it belonged and when she turned her back to get flowers for around the pulpit, it crashed right over. She set it up again, and over it went again. And she screamed and Alda ran over to her and they were both right there when the organ gave out what they said was a groan. And that was it. They were out and locking the door in ten seconds."

He dragged his feet, stopped the swing, and put a hand on my arm. "Do you believe that?"

A man who died as Balforth had wouldn't slip easily from this world. No matter what the mind intended, the body had a way of fighting for one more breath. And a man forced to go before he was ready . . . "I don't disbelieve it."

"All right, well here's the rest." He gripped my arm tighter. "This morning I intended that we meet under the trees again, but the rain started and Denny Balmer said there was no point in getting wet when we could go inside. He's got a key because he's on the board, so he opened up and we trooped in and the vestibule was cold all right, but the chair was up by the organ like it should be. Well, Pattie and Alda said they'd stand in the rear where they could get out fast if something weird happened. And when I brought up the request from Wesley Falton, that vestibule got as cold as the North Pole."

Balforth's spirit hadn't liked that.

"Well, it got clear real quick no one wanted Wesley Falton in the church. Some said Reverend Balforth didn't like him and that's all they needed to know. And when Evan apologized for renting the field for the revivals and claimed he wouldn't extend his lease, why, everyone chimed in, 'Amen.' And right then the temperature in the vestibule went up to normal."

Freeman released my arm and stood. "So I think we got Reverend Balforth's vote, too. And what we decided was we wouldn't have *any* preacher—at least not for a time. We'd meet on Sundays and Wednesday nights and if someone had something to say they'd say it, and if someone wanted to pray they'd pray—out loud or to themselves."

"What about weddings and funerals?"

"We thought we'd make a list of ministers that might come when we need someone, you know, official. But otherwise we'd kind of do it ourselves."

In the independent tradition of these hills.

We gathered up the spare rope and the hammer and chisel I'd used to notch the board for the seat.

"And maybe if somebody was reading a good book or had some ideas about how to keep the deer out of the garden, we could talk about that." Freeman headed for the house. "Kids have the old schoolhouse. Why shouldn't we older folks have a good-sized place where we can get together besides the Shovel It Inn where Merle keeps interrupting to ask if you want to order something else?"

"Keep on like this and you'll be filling out the paperwork to make this into a real town instead of a wide spot in the road. Next thing you know Hemlock Lake will have a mayor."

"Never happen. We don't need campaigning and politics and promises nobody intends to keep. That kind of BS gets in the way. What we really need is to all work together."

Chapter 42

Monday I returned to Theresa Gilligan's letters. I read about an ice storm that knocked out power for two days, about a recipe for beef stew with beer she thought Fred would like, and her concern about tiny crows' feet at the corners of her eyes. I read lengthy accounts of her visit to a fabric store, the debate over throwing rice or birdseed, and the merits of long veils over shorter ones.

By the end of the afternoon my eyes burned, but I'd found another reference to Wes. Again, she encountered him at the church while waiting for her appointment with Reverend Durant.

"Don't get me wrong, Fred," Theresa wrote, "I feel that I can tell you anything. But it's easy to talk to Wes, too. Maybe because he has a girlfriend and I have you and so I don't wonder if he's flirting with me or if he might think I'm flirting with him. Not that I would flirt with anyone, because I love you, but sometimes guys—and girls, too—think you're flirting when you're not."

Tuesday I found another reference to Wes. Again, they ran into each other at the church. She'd come at a different time and on a different day, but as she was leaving he arrived to drop off a book he'd borrowed. He suggested they get a cup of coffee because he wanted her opinion about whether he should rent a tuxedo for his wedding or buy a good-quality suit he could wear on other occasions. "Fred, I know you say you don't care what you wear and you want me to make the decision," she wrote, "and that's okay. But it's fun to talk with a guy who knows about cloth and tailoring and cufflinks."

Wednesday I found another reference. She'd been walking from work to a diner a few blocks away to pick up a sandwich and spotted Wes peering into the window of a shoe store. He came along to the diner and then they went to the store so he could show her the shoes he was thinking of buying.

This was too coincidental to be coincidence.

Wes had been stalking Theresa Gilligan.

Had she been too naïve to see it? Had she been flattered by his attention and pretended for Fred's sake that they met by chance? Or had she been encouraging those meetings?

I called Jonah Umhey.

He answered in a whisper that splintered like old wood. "You got something?"

"I don't know." I laid out what I'd found and what I suspected. "There's no mention of anyone named Wes in the file. Does that name ring any chimes?"

"No." He was silent for a moment, then sighed, a hissing sound like a wave retreating across coarse sand. "No. And I've got damn few chimes left to ring and damn little time to ring them in. So you'd best get back to those letters and see what you can dig out."

By the end of the week I found three more references to Wes. The first two came with few details, but the third was illuminating. "After work today," Theresa wrote, "I went to a travel agency to pick up brochures for honeymoon destinations and ran into Wes doing the same thing."

By now I would have bet $10,000 she was complicit in this string of "coincidental" meetings. She might not have suggested they get together, but by mentioning her plans to Wes, she made it possible.

"We went to a restaurant and got a booth so we could spread the brochures out. I definitely want to go on a cruise, but Wes hasn't decided yet. He says it doesn't matter where he goes because the honeymoon is about getting to know his new wife more than seeing sights. And he's not nervous about the wedding night like I am. He has a friend who's older and she's explaining what to do and how to do it so it feels good and doesn't hurt his wife."

I read that last sentence again, nerve synapses firing.

An older female friend.

Genevieve Graham?

What were the odds?

Impossibly long if the Gilligan and Graham cases weren't connected.

But if they were . . .

I scrambled for my desk and the files, laid them out on the kitchen table, and flipped through the pages.

Theresa Gilligan disappeared on February 12th. Genevieve Graham was killed on February 13th.

Theresa Gilligan, engaged to Fred Maddox, became friendly with a young man named Wes who planned to marry soon and was friendly with an older woman. Genevieve Graham, age 48, may have been seeing someone in secret.

Knowing I was chasing my tail, I called Helene Cooper and left a message. Helene had said her mother was secretive. And years had passed—time for Helene to forget a name she might have heard whispered into a telephone only once.

I went back to the letter and read the next paragraph. "Wes says that counseling is fine when it comes to learning about respecting and listening. And he says books are okay. But books don't always answer his questions and he can't see asking Reverend Durant about sex, so he's glad to have a friend who isn't uptight and can fill in the blanks. I wish I had a friend to help me. I mean, I know you're my friend and you have more experience, and I know you'll be kind and patient, but I wish I wasn't so worried about my first time and making you happy."

And that was the last reference to Wes or wedding-night sex.

The next few letters seemed shallow and less personal. There was more about the weather and her job and less about wedding plans.

Had Theresa Gilligan been embarrassed by how much she revealed to the man she planned to marry? Or was she distancing herself from Fred because she was getting closer to Wes?

I went over the file and spotted my notes from my first conversation with Jonah Umhey. A friend had suspected Theresa was "stepping out" with someone, but didn't have a name. That friend, Ginger, had supplied nothing new when I called her weeks ago, but perhaps a name would jar something loose. I got her voice mail and asked her to think about the name Wes, think about the two months before Theresa died and whether she'd seen her in a diner or café or a shoe store, or anywhere, with a man.

After that I went out to the garage and marked Reverend Durant's church on my crude map. I stared at it for a time. Then I stood on the porch and stared at the house across the lake.

I told myself all I had was coincidence. I had to be objective, couldn't make an intuitive leap without a springboard of evidence. I told myself to hold my suspicions close so I wouldn't crash and burn.

Then I hauled the file and letters to my desk and vowed to spend the weekend away from them to clear my mind.

On Saturday I picked up sample cans of paint in a rainbow of colors, brushes in a variety of sizes, and painter's tape in every width available. Knowing how plans were apt to change, I didn't ask what Camille had in mind for Chance's room.

Rick took Julie to an outdoor concert with his parents and she reported they were nice, but not very exciting. I refrained from asking what Rick had told them about us.

On Sunday, Julie asked if Rick could come up to swim and stay for dinner. "It's fine with me." Camille looked up from sketching geometric designs on a sheet of paper. "If Dan can stand to have him around all day."

"I don't mind," I said. "As long as Justin doesn't."

"Oh, come on, it's not like I'm going to marry him!" Julie put her hands on her hips and stomped in a tight circle. "At least not until I finish college and get to see Australia and Easter Island and Scotland and the tippy end of South America. I'm not marrying anybody until after that."

"Good to know," Camille said.

"So, can I invite him? He'll be gone to college soon and it's such a long drive up here and I don't have a car yet."

"Yeah, your posse is letting you down."

"They're too picky. And they get all bent about the price, like things should cost what they did when they were young."

Camille laughed, then shot me the look that said I better leap into action.

"Jefferson's about finished with his renovations. I'll see if he can light a fire under the others."

"Thank you." Julie gave me a rib-cracking hug. "Do I really have to ask Justin if Rick can come?"

"No," Camille said. "Dan was kidding about that."

Julie scuffed a toe on the floor. "Does that mean you like him?"

"We like what we've seen so far." Camille drew something that looked like a ball with spikes. "But we reserve the right to change our minds."

Monday morning as I bundled Chance into the SUV, I brushed against the map I'd stared at on Friday and a cluster of brain cells connected. I recalled Isaac Falton saying the family moved often. If I marked the places where Wesley Falton had lived, would I see connections I didn't see now?

An hour later I entered Serenity Brook's lair, unfolded the usual sorry excuse for a chair, and pretended to get comfortable.

She wore a bright orange T-shirt, a pair of turquoise denim overalls with one shoulder strap unhooked, and no shoes. A streak in her hair matched the purple polish on her toenails. "Nice look," I said.

"Wish I could say the same to you."

"There's something wrong with jeans and a gray T-shirt?"

"Nothing a major infusion of color and style wouldn't fix."

"I had a pair of name-brand Hawaiian print swim trunks on yesterday."

"Well! That means you get a pass from the fashion police for the next month." She rolled her eyes. "To what do I owe the honor of this visit?"

"If I wanted to know all the places a person lived, going back 25 years or so, could you find that out?"

"Theoretically." She plucked a screaming orange tortilla chip from a bag and bit into it, releasing the aroma of toasted corn, cheese, and spicy seasoning. My salivary glands went into overdrive.

"As long as I have plenty of time to work my magic. And as long as that person had power or cable or a piece of mail now and then. If that person was sofa surfing, it's more of a challenge." She stuffed the last of the chip into her mouth. "Fortunately for you, I like a challenge. Who is this alleged person?"

I swallowed. "Wesley Falton."

"As in Brother Elijah?"

"The same." I snagged a chip. "You mind?"

"No. But are you sure that color works with your outfit?"

"I'll risk it."

"Brother Elijah," she mused as she tapped keys. "You thinking he got up to something he wouldn't want on his revival resume?"

"I'm thinking I want to know more before I go too far in the wrong direction."

"And you want this done without the whole world knowing?"

I nodded.

"But you're in a rush, a hurry, a swivet?"

I ate another chip. "A two-cylinder swivet. But the sooner the better. And I want everything you can find."

"Define 'everything' in words an old woman can understand."

"Where he lived, what he drove, where he went to school, phone records, jobs he held before he started his tent shows, how he spent his money, and if he ever owned a gun."

Her eyes sparkled. "You suspect the evangelist is no angel." She ate another chip. "Smart money says you suspect he's connected to one of your cold cases."

I shrugged.

She grinned. "Your secret is safe with me."

I liberated another chip from the bag. As I crunched it down, more brain cells joined the active roster. "Give me everything you can on his wife, too."

Chapter 43

I'd told Serenity Brook I wasn't in a world-class rush, so I had no right to complain when a week went by and I didn't hear from her. I did hear from Helene Cooper who told me she couldn't remember whether her mother ever mentioned someone named Wes, but her feeling was she hadn't.

And I heard from Freeman. "Man won't take 'No' for an answer."

"Wesley Falton?"

"Right. Called to tell me he got the letter and wouldn't hold it against me that I made a hasty decision. Said he'd be glad to discuss his offer when I reconsider my refusal to let him use the church."

"*When* you reconsider?"

"Yep. When."

I laughed. "He doesn't know Hemlock Lake men very well, does he?"

"Nope. When we take a stand we put down deep roots. It takes a mighty strong wind to budge us." Freeman laughed. "Unless and until our wives change our minds."

Saturday night Wesley Falton held another revival. Despite posters tacked up far and wide, fewer people came than before. And when he marched to the lake for a mass baptizing, only a dozen tagged along, trooping past our usual place beneath the trees at the edge of the field.

"Seems to be losing his touch," Mary Lou mused.

"Might be some folks think Reverend Balforth went up above to lay out his case and get that judgment and punishment underway," Jefferson said. "Might be they don't want to be standing too close when the smiting begins."

"Or maybe folks with complex lives and complicated problems are searching for guidance from someone with a broader message." Camille stood and settled Chance on her hip. "Right now I'm searching for guidance from a man who can get me home so I can put this baby to bed. Are you coming for dinner tomorrow?"

"Wouldn't miss it." Mary Lou stroked Chance's foot. "Will that young man of Julie's be there?"

"Yes." I fixed my gaze on Jefferson. "I've been made to understand that, because Julie doesn't have a car, Rick will be shoving his feet under our table so often I'll start to wonder if he lives with us."

Mary Lou sighed. "Jefferson, you know Julie needs a car when school starts. She can't be riding that late bus and getting dropped at the store for someone to pick up every time she has to stay after for a project. You get Evan and Freeman and Stub off their butts."

"But you told me to finish the upstairs before Labor Day."

"I didn't 'tell' you anything. I said it would be nice. And anyway, you couldn't do both?"

Jefferson growled.

I intervened. "We're one-thing-at-a-time kind of guys, Mary Lou."

"Well, I don't see why you—"

"Round over. Go to your corners," Camille said. "Right now Julie can use mine, so we have two weeks to line up a car. Meanwhile, it's flattering that Rick is willing to drive to the back of beyond, and it's a bonus we're getting to know him."

There was silence for a moment, and then Mary Lou said, "Are corn fritters okay?"

"Perfect." Camille kissed her cheek and headed for the SUV, calling over her shoulder. "Dan's cooking ribs."

That was news to me, but I nodded as if I knew it all along, picked up Chance's gear, and followed Camille.

I got through Monday without calling Serenity Brook only by reminding myself that she would eviscerate me with her rapier-like wit, then sentencing myself to weed the rose garden for even thinking about annoying her. Tuesday morning I was contemplating dropping by with a few dozen of the oatmeal cookies Julie made to impress Rick, when Lee Rudolph phoned.

"This might be nothing," he cautioned, "but the Spearheads identified another sketch model. They insisted I call and ask you to come by. No hurry. When you have time."

Time was something I had plenty of. I snatched up a bag of cookies, stuffed Chance into a fresh diaper and T-shirt, handed him off to Camille, and gunned it to the clothing store.

The Spearhead gang had expanded. Six men crammed around the table and three more stood nearby. They had a show-and-tell exhibit spread out for me that included several of Judy Arnold's drawings of a long-haired man and a poster printed on stiff paper. That poster was yellowed from sun and stained by rain. Its corners were torn as if it had been ripped from the staples that held it in place. But none of that affected the quality of the photo in the center—the photo of Wesley Falton.

"Imagine him with long hair," the Spearheads chorused.

Lee placed a sheet of clear plastic over the poster. A flurry of lines sketched on it became a shoulder-length hairdo. The resemblance to the drawings rocked me back on my heels.

"I spotted that poster yesterday," one of the Spearheads crowed. "Walked right by it and then did one of those double takes. Ripped it loose and brought it here. For a few minutes they thought I was crazy and then—"

"I don't remember ever seeing him in the store," Lee said. "But there were plenty of hours that I wasn't here. And from all the drawings Judy did, I'd say she was interested in him."

"Once you see it, you can't unsee it," a Spearhead told me. "It's him. It's Brother Elijah. I'd bet my place in line at the Pearly Gates."

While a few of the others guffawed and questioned whether he'd make it into the line let alone through the gates, I shuffled Judy's sketches. Now that the Spearheads pointed it out, the model couldn't be anyone but Wesley Falton.

My heart thudded.

What were the odds that he might be linked to another of my cold cases?

Enormous.

Perhaps she'd seen him on the street. Maybe she'd even gone to a revival. He had an interesting face, a unique way of moving. These drawings didn't mean she'd met him or was in any way involved with him.

On the other hand . . . The vibrant shirts Falton wore suggested Judy's influence. Had his wardrobe undergone a change four years ago? I vowed to go back through the articles about his revivals and check for photographs. In the meantime, I played it cool to quash unfounded hope. "It looks like him. But . . ."

The Spearheads leaned toward me like lilies turning toward the sun. I frowned. The Spearheads slumped.

"Good work spotting the poster and adding this." I waved the plastic overlay. "Believe it or not, Wesley Falton is renting a place near me. I should be able to catch up with him in the next few days."

I gathered up the sketches, dragging out the process, breathing deep, calming myself. I wanted to sound casual, as if this was another lead to nowhere. "It's possible they never met. Maybe she saw his picture in the paper and wondered how he'd look with long hair or puffy shirts."

The Spearheads nodded.

"She did stuff like that," Lee said. "One day she saw this slobby guy running for the bus with his pants dragging and she did three sketches in about ten minutes. One had him in a suit, but another had him wearing a woodchuck costume with a flap in the back and his butt hanging out."

They all laughed. I joined in, then shook my head at the material I'd gathered up. "I'll let you know if this goes anywhere." Implying they shouldn't hold their breaths.

"We'll keep at it on the rest of them," the Spearhead at the center of the table said. "It's slow going, but it beats sitting at home."

"Don't know what we'll do when you solve the case," another added.

"Maybe we'll form a team and rent ourselves out to other counties."

"Maybe the FBI will want us," one of them whispered in an awe-filled voice.

Without a hint of a smile, I handed over the cookies and left them to their dreams.

I wasn't exactly in the vicinity, but I was on the road and feeling positive enough to shrug off at least a few barbed comments, so I stopped by Serenity Brook's den. The room felt ten degrees this side of dank, but she was dressed for the beach in bright pink flip-flops, baggy gray shorts, and a toxic green T-shirt that matched a streak in her hair.

"Knew you couldn't stay away." She sipped from a bottle of something that smelled like it had been brewed up in a cauldron following the witches' recipe from *Macbeth*. "Don't know why you told me to take my time."

"If you remember, I told you to take *your* time, not take *my* time."

"Good one." She sipped again, then set the bottle aside. "Herbal energy drink. Supposed to lower my cholesterol and pep me up without caffeine. Tastes like it came out of the hind end of a moose."

I hooked a leg over the corner of her desk. "I won't ask how you conducted research to determine that."

She grinned, hit a couple of keys, and brought a printer to life behind me. "Wesley Falton is a nomad. That's what I have so far."

I pulled a multi-page spreadsheet from the printer tray. It went back 25 years and contained more than 30 addresses and at least a dozen blank rectangles.

"I'm working on those gaps. Sometimes he rents in a conventional way and sometimes it appears he gets a place for free and pays the utilities. Sometimes he gets mail at a fixed address and sometimes he rents a post office box separate from the one he has for his business." She made air quotes around that word to tell me she didn't consider what he did a business.

I skimmed the addresses, trying to visualize where they'd fit on my shower-curtain map, whether they'd intersect with the lines I'd drawn for victims' routes to work and school and shopping. There were only so many main roads in these mountains. For that reason alone, a number of his lines were bound to cross those already on my map.

She hit another key and the printer churned to life again, spewing a dozen pages. "That's a list of all the places I found where he held revivals."

"Way to go above and beyond. Anything on a gun?"

"Crap. I forgot about that." Serenity snatched up her venomous brew, took another sip, shuddered, rolled to the second desk, and set the bottle on the far corner. "I'll keep at it."

I shuffled the spreadsheets together and headed for the door. "So will I."

Back home, I checked through the articles on Falton's revivals and found only stock headshots in black and white. Refraining from kicking my long-suffering desk, I rolled up the garage door and went to work on the map, casting occasional glances at the house across the lake while I marked dots and dates. As I thought, Wesley Falton's many addresses coupled with the sites of his revivals, covered the map like a bad case of chickenpox. Routes overlapped and intersected.

When I was finished I had no doubt that it was possible Wesley Falton had encountered all five of my cold-case victims somewhere, sometime.

But I had no motives for murder.

Theresa Gilligan may have been falling for him. Genevieve Graham may have been the older "friend" coaching him in the art of love. Judy Arnold seemed fascinated by him.

Why kill them?

Why kill Franklin Turner?

And what about Micah Thielman?

What was I missing? What hadn't I seen? What was I overlooking?

The next day I read through all five files once more. I read everything and I read fast. When Camille and Julie came home my eyes burned and a thousand details ricocheted inside my brain. I put the files aside and we went for a swim and ate cheese and crackers and fresh cucumbers and tomatoes for dinner and followed that up with raspberries and ice cream.

In the morning, the thousand colliding details of the cases had drifted to the bottom of my mind leaving only one hanging. Micah Thielman had met someone on a regular basis to commiserate. Micah Thielman was the only one of the five I couldn't connect to Wesley Falton.

I couldn't see Micah seeking counseling from Wesley. But I *could* see him sharing his doubt and confusion with Isaac.

I kicked myself for not thinking of that when I linked Isaac to Franklin.

While Camille and Julie ate breakfast, I went to the garage to check my map and see whether the Falton family had lived near the community college Micah attended. There was no red dot within ten miles.

I went for the spreadsheets, checked the period during which Micah had met with someone, and found a blank rectangle. Serenity Brook hadn't found rent or utility or other records for that time.

I wouldn't need those records if I could fill the blank another way.

When he woke up, I rushed Chance through his morning bath, dried him, slathered on extra rash prevention cream, and slipped him into a T-shirt and diaper. Despite the hustle, it was close to 10:00 before I grabbed the Thielman file and headed out.

I wanted to talk to Isaac alone and away from his father's house. The college summer session was over, but business at the dock was good; Justin had kept Isaac on for a few hours every day so he could work on the house. As I carried Chance toward the store, Justin came out chewing on a strip of beef jerky. "Who's minding the dock?" I asked.

"Isaac. I've got to straighten out my fall schedule. I'm in Economics instead of Ecology. I spent an hour on hold before I figured I better drive up there and talk to a real person. If I can find one in possession of a brain."

I wished him luck, handed Chance to Camille, and headed for the dock. When the lake warmed up, fish fed early and late. I expected midday business would be slow unless someone turned up to rent a powerboat or one of the three canoes Justin had recently added.

Two teenage girls in bright orange life jackets were wobbling away from the dock in a red canoe while Isaac stood in the shade of the bait shop, making balancing motions with his hands as if that might help them. I parked and studied him for a few minutes. He appeared healthier than when he came to Hemlock Lake. He'd gained a few pounds and stood straighter, but he was still weedy.

When he retreated into the shop, I advanced along the dock, the Thielman file in my hand, recorder in my pocket. I was three yards off when he appeared in the doorway, taking a huge bite out of a candy bar.

"Good morning."

He nodded, jaw working.

"I have questions for you."

He swallowed and rubbed his neck. "About Franklin Turner?"

"No." I pulled Micah's photo from the file and held it a foot in front of Isaac's face. "About this boy."

Chapter 44

Isaac's summer tan faded to buttermilk white and he reeled against the door frame. "Micah," he whispered. "Is he dead, too?"

"No one knows."

He dropped the candy bar and shook his head. "What does that mean?"

"He disappeared. Drove off for school one morning and never came home."

"Do you think I . . . ?"

I ignored that and asked a question of my own. "When was the last time you saw him?"

"I don't know." He staggered into the shop and slumped against the counter. "I mean, I don't remember the exact day. It was a week or more before we moved."

"Moved from where?"

"From a house near the college where Micah went. We were staying with an old lady who was sick. Mom was taking care of her. And then her son came from California and told Dad we had to find someplace else. Right away."

That must have gone over well with Wesley Falton.

Isaac's eyes clouded, as if he was gazing into the past. "It was a really nice house. It had a huge yard and lots of books and three TVs. Except I couldn't watch them. I'm not allowed."

"How did you meet Micah?"

A spark lit the backs of his eyes and then they clouded again. "Dad went off to meet with his publisher and Mom told me to get some exercise. I wasn't supposed to go to the college, but I did. Micah stopped and asked me if I was lost."

He fingered the metal strip at the edge of the counter. "I told him I was just looking around and he took me through some of the buildings and bought me a cup of coffee with chocolate and whipped cream. I never had anything like that before. It was so good."

Which, according to Wesley Falton, meant it should have been cast aside.

I kept my voice low and soothing. "You liked Micah?"

"I liked him a lot. He understood about all I'm not supposed to do and how hard it is and how much I . . . miss out on." Isaac closed his eyes and smiled. "He said other people set boundaries for us all the time, but when we get older we can decide whether to stay inside their fences or break out."

"And you want to break out?"

Isaac's eyes snapped open. "You won't tell my father, will you? He didn't know about Micah. He'd be mad. And madder that I talked to you."

"I won't say a word if you tell me everything you remember about Micah."

"Okay, but . . ." He glanced out the door. "Can we stay in here? My father's going out soon and if he—"

"I understand." Isaac Falton didn't want his father to see him talking to me. "In here is fine."

Fine if what you wanted was a sweatbox, a sweatbox that, despite scrubbing and priming and painting, smelled of worms and fish and wet wood. Isaac untangled two ancient wooden folding chairs and centered them in the meager empty space between the counter and display racks. I set my recorder on the counter and clicked it on, then snapped off the overhead fluorescent lights. The door faced north and the window east, so the interior was dim. Wesley Falton would have to be a few feet away to see us.

For the next hour, Isaac talked about Micah Thielman, about coffee and ice cream, about the freedom to say what he thought and felt without being judged, about the joy of talking with someone who understood. He spoke the way people do when they're a little drunk or high, spilling sentences like water from a bucket, splashing out adjectives, splattering exclamations.

When he finished, flushed and panting, he took in a long breath, covered his face with his hands, and moaned. "I thought Micah trusted me, but he didn't tell me he was going away. Why?"

I clicked off my recorder and bet myself Micah hadn't told Isaac because Micah didn't know.

Isaac lowered his hands. "Franklin and Micah were the only friends I ever had."

Again, I didn't say what I couldn't prove—that they died *because* there were Isaac's friends. And somehow, for some reason, Wesley Falton was responsible.

"Will you find out what happened to Micah? Will you find out who killed Franklin?"

I gathered up the file, folded the chair, and set it against the wall. "I intend to do my damnedest."

Friday Serenity Brook called before I was out of bed. "I can't find anything to show Wesley Falton ever owned a gun, but I *can* tell you his wife's father was an avid hunter."

An avid hunter almost certainly had guns. All kinds of guns.

Serenity chomped on something that crunched and fractured and tore between her teeth like a sandpaper-wrapped bacon burrito. I held the phone away from my ear until she swallowed.

"Good work."

"There's more. Hannah got a hunting license when she was old enough to be legal. She had one every year until she married Wesley Falton twenty years ago."

Another crunching, ripping bite and Serenity disconnected.

I set the phone aside and gazed at the ceiling, listening to the thrum of the shower and the little sounds of contentment Camille made without realizing. Thuds and bumps from above told me Julie was awake and digging through her closet for a T-shirt or shorts or missing sandal. Nelson snuffled and rearranged himself beneath the crib. Chance slept with one fist against his cheek.

Hannah Falton.

Mousy, fearful, scurrying Hannah Falton.

I tried to picture her with a rifle, stalking a bear. The mental image that formed was of a bear stalking her.

Had she conditioned me—and others—to see her that way? Conditioned us by wearing drab clothing and using subservient body language?

Beneath the costume of compliance, was she a killer?

Again I came back to the why of it all, the motive.

Jealousy?

If Hannah was the girlfriend Wesley planned to marry, she might have made certain of the aisle walk. She might have taken out her rivals—Genevieve Graham and Theresa Gilligan.

And if, years later, Wesley showed too much interest in Judy Arnold, Hannah might have made her disappear.

But where did Franklin Turner and Micah Thielman fit in?

They were friendly with Isaac, not Wesley.

Had Hannah killed to keep her son from becoming more than friends, from committing what she viewed as a sin? Had she killed to protect him from his father's wrath?

Camille emerged from the bathroom, her skin damp and glowing. Except for a slight thickness around her waist, the baby weight was gone. I whistled in appreciation and she twirled about. "Swimming every night is paying off."

I whistled again.

She laughed. "I love a man of few words."

I flipped the sheet aside. "Want to show me how much?"

She smiled, then glanced at the clock. "We don't have much time."

"Then it's a good thing we have experience."

After I dropped Chance off, I went to see Sheriff Clement North. To his credit, he didn't scoff at my evidence—or lack of it. What he did was rub his bristly eyebrows with his thumbnail, nod, fill his pipe, and chew on the stem.

When I finished, he fished a match from his desk drawer, torched tobacco, and flipped on the exhaust fan. "It fits, but . . ."

"I know. It fits because I want it to and because that's how I laid it out. There's no hard proof." I laughed. "Hell, there's no *soft* proof."

"Which isn't to say you're not right about Hannah Falton. But speaking out against the wife of Brother Elijah without proof could create a shit storm of prodigious proportions."

I nodded.

"So before you say a word to anyone—even to that dog of yours—you better have your ducks in a row. And I mean a tight, straight row."

I shot him a mock salute and left. I wasn't worried about lining up those ducks once I found them. What worried me was where to look, where to find that elusive stuff called proof.

Saturday I had little time to think about metaphorical ducks. While Julie ran the store, Camille and I picked, peeled, and chopped tomatoes, sliced peppers, shredded zucchini, pureed basil in olive oil, and packed it all into the freezer in the garage. The work seemed endless, and only talk of spaghetti and lasagna in our future kept us going until we mopped up the last splotches and spills and retreated to the porch with a chunk of cheese, a box of crackers, a sliced cantaloupe, a tall glass of lemonade, and a bottle of beer.

"We got those tomatoes picked in the nick of time." Camille pointed at a roiling gray-black cloud rising like a volcanic plume above the mountains across the lake. "Hard rain or hail won't do the garden any favors."

"Well, it's the season for these boomers." Lightning spiked and I counted until I heard a faint grumble of thunder. "That one's more than two miles off. Might veer south and miss us."

"And it might not."

I clinked my bottle against her glass and chuckled. "Give birth once in a howling snowstorm and you turn into a pessimist."

"Not a pessimist. A realist with more respect than I previously had for weather spawned in these mountains."

Sunday brought another kind of storm to Hemlock Lake.

By late morning the air was steamy, the breeze sluggish, the temperature high enough for a sauna. I was near the top of the driveway, filling a channel cut by runoff from yesterday's downpour, and sweating like my body intended to rid itself of every drop of moisture it held. Nelson, offering his idea of assistance by searching for salamanders, cocked his head toward the main road and whined. I heard a car coming. Coming fast.

"Too early for Rick. And if Camille catches him speeding, he'll be apologizing for a week."

I gripped Nelson's collar and eased him behind a thick-trunked pine as the car came into view. Freeman was at the wheel, jaw clamped, leaning forward as if that would make the trip faster. Alda sat beside him, one hand across her eyes, the other braced against the dashboard. The tires flung rooster tails of dust and gravel, pebbles ripping into trees and brush along the drive like machine gun fire.

Nelson barked and twisted his neck, trying to escape from his collar. When the car was out of sight, I released him, surveyed the fresh damage to the driveway, and abandoned the project for now. Big news brought Freeman out here. Big news that likely had something to do with the church. And Wesley Falton.

When I reached the house, Alda was leaning against the car, fanning herself with one of her miniscule hats and lecturing her husband at the same time. "I don't know why you had to race like a snake with its tail on fire. You could have run over Nelson or hit Camille and Chance. There's no prize for getting here first with the news."

Freeman dug the toe of one shoe into the dirt, hung his head, and shot me a look that said if I was any kind of friend I'd take his side.

I kept quiet.

Camille emerged from the house with Chance on her hip. A baby to cuddle beat a tirade to deliver. Alda tossed her hat in the car, wagged her finger at Freeman one more time, smoothed her dress, and headed for the porch.

"Saved by the baby." Freeman hauled in a breath. "Wesley Falton's off the rails. He marched into church this morning and—"

"Come up here and tell Camille, too," Alda called. "No point in going through it twice."

"Yes, dear."

As Freeman and I climbed the steps to the porch, another car rolled down the drive. Jefferson and Mary Lou got out, he with a bemused expression on his face, she with lips clamped and shoulders stiff.

"Lemonade coming up," Camille said.

"I'll take mine with a shot," Freeman said. "Anything will do."

Alda didn't contradict him, and in a few moments we were seated with drinks in hand and a bottle of rum making the rounds, all of us staring at the house across the lake.

"You start," Mary Lou told Freeman and Alda. "I have a feeling my part of this story comes after yours."

Freeman gulped his drink and got to it. "We're in the church, maybe 20 of us, talking the way we decided we would, when the doors open—"

"With a bang," Alda interjected.

"And Wesley Falton comes down the aisle like he owns the place, gets behind the pulpit, and starts lecturing us."

"Telling us we're too proud," Alda said. "Telling us we're in love with ourselves and our heritage and our traditions."

Freeman nodded. "Telling us we're insolent and pretentious and a lot of other five-dollar words. Claiming we should cast aside pride before it's too late."

"Telling us we should put ourselves in his hands and he'd show us the way to salvation because otherwise we surely won't find it." Alda took a long sip of lemonade. "He was close to screaming before he was done. Pounding the pulpit. Red in the face. Spit flying from his—"

"There he is now." Freeman pointed to the far side of the lake.

Wesley Falton's long, white car drew up beside the house and he got out, slamming the door with a thud that echoed across the still water. He stood for a time, shading his eyes and staring in our direction. Then he raised both hands and tipped his face to the sky.

Alda put her hand over her heart. "Don't tell me he's asking for divine help to get us to change our minds."

Freeman snorted. "Asking ain't the same as getting."

"I take it you rejected his offer?" Camille filled Freeman's glass.

"Not in so many words," Alda said.

"Not in *any* words." Freeman topped off his glass from the rum bottle. "We all stared at him the way kids do when they're being lectured. Went on staring after he wound down. No one making a sound."

"And then he shook his head, disgusted like." Alda took the bottle from her husband and set it beside her chair. "And he said if we were so mule-headed we refused to see the light and ask him to lead us to salvation, then he'd pull the rug out from under us."

Chapter 45

"And that's when he came to see me," Mary Lou said. "To ask me to sell him the church."

"There was no *asking* about it." Jefferson scooped the bottle from beside Alda's chair. "It was all demanding and commanding. Until I showed him the door."

"Frogmarched him to the door," Mary Lou corrected.

"Nobody talks to you the way he did. I almost punched his eyes out."

Freeman chuckled. "*That* would make it hard for him to see the light he was jabbering about."

I glanced at Wesley Falton, still standing with raised arms. "Just out of curiosity, how much did he offer?"

"Twenty thousand dollars," Mary Lou said.

Alda gasped. "I hope you laughed in his face."

"She didn't, but I did." Jefferson splashed rum into his glass. "Especially when he said he'd put $500 down and pay what he could afford at the end of each month while she went on forking out for taxes and insurance and upkeep."

"I'd like to say I admire his nerve, but I don't." Mary Lou took the bottle and added a dash to her lemonade. "And I don't like being called selfish and negative and an obstacle to the spiritual salvation of the community."

Camille glared at the man across the lake. "He said that?"

"And more." Mary Lou capped the bottle. "If I thought for one minute that people wanted him in that church, I wouldn't hesitate to sell it to him."

Camille patted her hand. "I know you would. We all know you would."

"You might even give it to him," Alda said. "Like you gave the old schoolhouse to the community for the kids' club."

We all nodded in support of that.

Wesley Falton lowered his arms, pointed at us with both forefingers, then turned and marched up the weed-choked walk to the house.

"You'd think a man who makes out like he cares so much about our futures would worry more about his own," Freeman mused. "If he doesn't cut that lawn soon, it's likely to swallow him up."

Jefferson grinned. "That would be worth paying to see."

I nodded agreement. As long as I got some answers first.

Monday I started again, reading through the cases, hunting for a loose thread to pull. I read every word of the three autopsy reports, but there was nothing, no blood, no fibers, no DNA. I expected that from the older cases, but was again surprised that the person who killed Franklin Turner hadn't left a trace. Had the killer been careful? Lucky? Or both?

I called Serenity Brook and asked if she'd come up with more information to fill in the blanks on the address spreadsheet she'd created for Wesley Falton.

Her response didn't surprise me "What part of 'I'll e-mail you when I have something' don't you understand?"

Put in my place, I retreated to the garage and reviewed the list, double-checked the dots on my map, then stared at it for an hour.

Following that, I blanked my mind and combed the letters Theresa Gilligan wrote starting with the first mention of Wes. I read for new information and I read for tone and emotion, for what was on the pages and what wasn't. I concluded, as I had before, that she was drawn to him, fascinated by him, perhaps enough to waver in her commitment to Fred Maddox, and perhaps enough to pursue him and put herself in Hannah's sights.

Genevieve Graham had gone to great lengths to keep her relationship a secret. But what if Wesley Falton hadn't? What if Hannah discovered that Genevieve was "coaching" her boyfriend in the art of love?

Theresa Gilligan disappeared on February 12th. Genevieve Graham was gunned down on February 13th. And on February 14th, according to Isaac, Wesley proposed to Hannah.

Had Wesley Falton suspected Hannah in Theresa's disappearance and Genevieve's death? Had he feared what she might do if he didn't commit to her? Had he proposed to save his life?

Had he strayed again with Judy Arnold 16 years later? Or had Hannah suspected that he might and removed temptation?

And, later still, had she removed temptation for her son by killing Franklin Turner and Micah Thielman?

My theory fit the killings.

Unfortunately, plenty of other theories would, too.

Wednesday morning I borrowed the key from Mary Lou and went to the church. Sun streamed through stained-glass windows, lighting up dust motes liberated from the runner by a breeze through the open door. I walked to the pulpit and stood behind it, surveying the empty pews. Reverend James Balforth saw his share of those—more every year. But in his final days he gathered his flock, even if they came for the wrong reason, the way people do to see a wreck or a fire.

"What did you know?" I asked his spirit. "What did you know about Wesley Falton?"

I turned to face the cross. "I have no proof. I have nothing except suspicion and theory. That's not enough. Not for this age, this place on the earth."

Balforth's ghost was silent.

I walked to the vestibule and stood where he died. The bell rope was gone, taken to the crime lab. Since that single peal five weeks ago, the bell hadn't rung out. Freeman hadn't mentioned plans to replace the rope.

"I guess it's a tribute to you," I told Balforth's ghost. "A silent tribute."

I leaned against the wall for a bit, listening to the tiny sounds of the old building warming under the August sun.

"It's not easy, is it? Waiting for a sign. Did you get one before you challenged Wesley Falton? Did you die knowing what you were here for?"

If Balforth's ghost was with me, it was as still and silent as the bell.

"If anyone had the power and determination to linger here or to cross back over, it would be you. If you're here, give me something. Help me see justice done."

Silence.

I locked the door, returned the key to Mary Lou, and drove home, wondering again about ghosts. Did they make their presence felt because we believed in them? Or because they believed in us?

By Thursday afternoon I was ready to pack everything in a box and take it to Sheriff North along with my resignation.

When I told Camille at dinner, she laughed. "You can no more walk away from those cases than Nelson can fly. But I was about to suggest that you put them aside for a few days. Everybody's coming here on Labor Day and there's a lot to be done. On top of that, the boys have zeroed in on a few cars. Since you're in charge of making up the difference from what Julie has saved, you should ride along and check them out."

"Riding along with Freeman or Evan isn't an option. Freeman drives too fast and Evan would be hard put to pass an anemic tortoise on a downgrade."

Julie giggled. "Jefferson won't ride with them anymore, either. Besides, Stub will want to go to check out the engines. That's too many people for one car."

"Problem solved. We'll take two cars. If Stub isn't driving, he falls asleep after the first mile, so he won't care who he rides with."

True to form, Stub slept in the back of Freeman's car 20 miles in one direction, 15 in another, and 10 more in a third. Prodded awake, he checked oil and fluids, belts and brakes, listened to the engine rev up and settle, then huddled with Freeman, Evan, and Jefferson.

He eliminated the first car after a glance under the hood, but liked the second because it had low mileage, new tires, and complete maintenance records. Freeman and Evan agreed that it purred, but thought the price was too high and held it against the owner that she wouldn't dicker. Price didn't bother me if the vehicle was sound, but Julie hated the color and claimed it reminded her of what she found in Chance's diapers. Jefferson said nothing.

The third car had electric blue paint and was fitted out with a custom steering wheel and jungle-print seat covers. Julie loved it. Stub listened to the engine, bending closer and closer until finally he backed off and shook his head. Julie pouted. Evan and Freeman kicked the tires and shook their heads. Julie stomped to my rig, threw herself in, and burst into tears. "I'm never getting a car, am I?"

Jefferson growled low in his throat, flung open his door, and stalked to the trio beside the blue car. Talking in a low voice, he pointed at Freeman and Evan, then at Stub, then hooked a thumb toward Julie, then toward the highway. Stub smiled and nodded. Freeman and Evan shook their heads. Jefferson pointed at them again. Evan scratched his chin. Freeman tugged at one earlobe. Jefferson pulled his wallet from his hip pocket.

"What's he doing?" Julie sniffled.

"Bending them to his will."

She sat up straight and wiped her eyes on the hem of her T-shirt. "What does that mean?"

"It means he's done all the recon he needs and it's time for action."

"Huh?"

"You're getting a car."

"*That* car?"

"No. I trust Stub to know a death rattle when he hears one, no matter how faint. That car will leave you stranded."

Julie huffed. "But it's the perfect color."

Jefferson opened the door. "Lunch."

I turned the key and backed around. Freeman roared past and turned left onto the highway. "Should I follow them?"

"No." Jefferson clicked his seatbelt. "They're on a mission."

"What kind of a mission?" Julie asked.

"A mission that requires speed and stealth."

And that's all he said.

We found a café and he pored over the menu, cross-examined the waitress, ordered a sandwich, then lingered over a second cup of coffee and a slab of pie. Julie squirmed in her chair and tried to hurry him along, but he wouldn't be rushed. Finally he told me I could pick up the check, I told him I was honored by the privilege, and we headed out of the parking lot.

"Bank," he said.

"Right." By now I'd figured out what was what. I got a cashier's check and a few hundred in cash and we drove back to the second car. Freeman, Evan, and Stub stood beside it munching on hot dogs.

"Why are we here?" Julie wailed. "I don't *like* that car."

"You will," Jefferson said.

"I won't." Julie crossed her arms.

"Trust me, you will." Jefferson got out and flung wide the driver's door of the vehicle in question.

"Are those pink fuzzy dice and jungle bird seat covers?" I opened my door and hustled over for a look. "Does that steering wheel cover have jewels on it?"

"The car is still an ugly color," Julie called.

"That's why they make paint," Stub said. "I'm thinking metallic blue with silver racing stripes."

Julie pushed past me, threw herself into the driver's seat, and gripped the wheel. "How long will it take to paint it?"

Stub shrugged. "I know a guy I can take it to this afternoon. But the long weekend's going to hold things up. So, maybe a week."

"Think you can live that long without it?" Freeman asked.

"Barely." Julie hurtled from the car and delivered hugs all around with kisses on both cheeks for Jefferson. Then she dove into the car and tossed me her phone. "Take a picture so I can show Rick."

Julie was still bubbling when we got home. But Justin, sprawled on the porch steps, was at the other end of the emotional scale. He smiled and congratulated Julie and asked questions about the car, but he was clearly distracted. When Julie went up to her room to phone her friends, I found out why.

"I need advice. Isaac's acting weird."

"Hmmm." I settled in the swing. "Define that."

"He comes every day—not just the days he's scheduled. He knows I can't pay him, but he comes anyway and hangs around."

I studied the clouds billowing above the mountains to the west of the lake. "There's a fine tradition of hanging around in Hemlock Lake. But mostly it's a tradition followed by retired guys like Freeman and Evan."

Justin gave me a wince of a smile. "This doesn't feel like hanging around to pass the time before you go on to something else. This is like hanging around because there *isn't* something else." He stood and paced, eyes dark with worry. "When I reminded him his job would end in late October, he cried."

"Cried?"

"Sat on the dock and sobbed."

"Did he think you plan to let him go because he failed at the job?"

"I explained when I hired him that the job was only for a few months. When the fall color show is over no one will be around except the locals and a few hard-core fishermen who bring their own boats and gear. I reminded him of that. I told him I'd shut the place in November and wouldn't open again until spring."

"Did he understand?"

"Yes and no. He got the part about closing, but he begged me to let him stay. And I mean begged. On his knees. Said he'd live in the bait shop, buy food with the money he saved over the summer, wouldn't bother anybody."

Justin shook his head, slumped in a chair, and wiped his sweat-beaded forehead. "I told him the bait shop doesn't have a lick of insulation, no heat, and no running water. I told him the chemical toilet is all he'd have. He said he didn't care, at least he'd be in a place he liked, and he didn't want to move again."

"Move?" I glanced at the house across the lake. It was shadowed by the building clouds but dim light didn't hide creeping disrepair. A gutter hung loose, a window sat crooked in the frame. "The Faltons are moving?"

"Isaac says they can't afford to stay."

"What about collections from the revivals? And the book Wesley's writing? Won't there be money from the publisher?"

"Isaac says they already spent all they got and the book isn't finished and the publisher still doesn't like the beginning part." Justin spread his hands. "Isaac wants me to talk to his father and mother and convince them I need his help through the winter."

Warning bells clanged in my brain. I wanted to yell "Don't!" But that would telegraph my fears that Hannah or Wesley—or both?—had killed. Justin would wonder at my reaction. And I'd found it was better for both of us if I avoided a hard position, went slow, and asked questions that allowed him to clarify his thinking.

"And you don't want to do that?"

"I don't, but I feel bad. I mean, Isaac is a nice guy and he's done a decent job this summer, but there's no work over the winter, so I'd be lying about that. Not that I haven't ever lied, but never to a preacher. And I'm not sure I want to start with a preacher as scary as Wesley Falton."

Amen to that.

"I heard about what he pulled in church last week. That took a lot of nerve."

Or the courage of his convictions.

The thought made me sit up straight. For months now I'd viewed Wesley Falton as someone who was more about the spotlight, showmanship, and the contents of the collection plate, than about a desire to save souls. What if I was wrong? What if his confrontational attitude in the church and with Mary Lou was the result of genuine belief? What if he wanted what he thought was right for the congregation?

I reminded myself that definitions of "right" could be radically different. History was littered with examples of those who demanded or sanctioned slaughter in the name of what they thought was right.

"I don't want to feel guilty about Isaac living out in that shack. I don't want to cave and invite him to sleep on the sofa or even in the spare room when I get it finished." Justin stood and paced again. "I'd do that for a friend, sure, but . . ."

The last two boys who befriended Isaac were gone from this earth.

I swallowed, cleared my throat, and posed another question. "You don't think of Isaac as your friend?"

Justin pressed his lips together and nodded. "The thing is, we work together, but that's all we have in common. He doesn't watch baseball or football, he doesn't fish or hunt, he doesn't read anything that isn't the Bible. I feel sorry for him, but I like living alone. And I don't want to get between him and his father."

And I sure as hell don't want you to.

But I couldn't tell him why, not without breaking my promise to Sheriff North and possibly jeopardizing the investigation.

Justin toed a twig, lining it up with a crack between the planks of the porch floor. He kept his chin tucked as he spoke, but I saw color washing up his cheeks. "And I think Isaac has a different way of looking at friendship than I do. Friendship between guys."

"Ah."

"I mean, it's okay with me that . . . he wants whatever he wants . . . but I don't want him to think I . . ."

"I got it."

Justin glanced up, relieved, then ducked his head again. "I guess I should spell that out for him."

"It won't be easy to do that. But it will clear the air."

"Yeah." He smashed the twig into the crack, then toed it free again. "What do I do about the rest of it? Tell him there's no work and no place for him to stay?"

I checked the towering clouds, now shadowing half the lake, and heard a low rumble of thunder. "Well, there's no place with you, but there are folks who rent rooms to skiers and hunters. Some might put him up in exchange for chores. And the ones who head south for the winter might need caretaking done."

"Good idea. He could check that out." Justin scooped up the twig, stood, and tossed it over the railing. "He'll be gone all weekend at a revival down the river with his parents, but I'll talk to him Tuesday. Or maybe Wednesday. I'll tell him he's old enough to make decisions for himself and doesn't need me to make a case to his father and mother." His voice was light with relief. "His mother seems okay, but I'd rather find a copperhead under my pillow than cross Wesley Falton."

"I'd be tempted to steer clear of both of them until you know how they react."

"Yeah, they might decide I'm to blame. If I see them coming I'll get gone." He stuck out his hand. "Thanks, Dan."

"For what?"

He grinned. "For letting me think I'm figuring things out on my own."

I stood and we shook. "You are."

"Maybe. But I couldn't do it without you holding the compass." He gripped my hand harder. "I don't say it as often as I should, but without you and Camille and Jefferson and all the others, I don't know where I'd be."

"Probably here. Or on your way. Hemlock Lake is where you belong. You would have figured it out."

"But maybe not until I screwed up more." He released my hand. "Anyway, I'm glad you came back two years ago and I'm really glad you and Jefferson came hunting me last summer. You saved my life."

I gripped his shoulders and turned him to face me. "*You* saved your life, Justin. You made a good decision."

On Wednesday, he made another.

Chapter 46

The day was the hottest yet. By late afternoon the sun seemed to halt its march down the western slope of the sky, refusing to give way to the moon and cooling night. Clouds swelled behind the mountains. A storm would roll through the valley, but not for an hour or more. And it might not bring rain.

The lake was down, the shoreline several feet below the spring level. Striations on exposed shale marked the progression of the dry spell. Patches of gray mud had baked into random patterns.

Julie, having survived the first day of school, changed into a halter top and ragged cut-offs, waded out until water reached her knees, then flopped on an air mattress. As she talked on her phone, she sculled with one hand, sending out clusters of ripples. I half expected the wavelets to sizzle when they lapped at the rocky rim where Camille sat with Chance, dipping his toes in tepid water. Nelson found a patch of soft mud, rolled in it, then retreated to the shade of a laurel bush where he grunted with the effort of each breath.

I felt puffed up like a toad, as if I'd inhaled a deep breath and couldn't release it.

"Too much beer," Camille said when I mentioned that.

"One bottle is too much?"

"It is when you drink it on top of a grilled cheese and hot pepper sandwich, and all those barbecue potato chips and onion dip."

"Julie had the same thing. Except for the beer."

"Julie is a teenager."

"Ouch. Thanks for reminding me I'm pushing 40."

I headed for the porch, intending to sprawl in the swing, but my phone rang.

"We gotta do something," Justin shouted. "Wesley Falton took Isaac."

"Took him?"

"Punched him. Knocked him down. Dragged him to the car. Drove toward their house."

I shaded my eyes and peered at the house across the lake. Wesley's car wasn't there, but Hannah's stood beneath the draping branches of a hemlock on the north side of the house. "Are you okay?"

"Yeah. I had a boat in the shade out behind the bait shop, cleaning off fish guts. Wesley screamed for me to come out, but I kept quiet. Isaac told him I was out on the lake and I got low in the boat so Wesley couldn't see me if he came around. But he didn't. He yelled that Isaac was an abomination and so was I and we didn't belong on this earth. He said he'd pass judgment on Isaac and come for me later."

An abomination? Judgment?

I headed for the gun rack. "You did the right thing. Call the sheriff's office. Then get in your house, lock the doors, and stay there."

"What about Isaac? Deputies won't get here for—"

"Just call. Call now. I'll try to stop Wesley."

I disconnected, unlocked the gun rack, pulled down my old shotgun and Julie's rifle, loaded my pockets with ammunition, then sprinted to the lake and tossed my phone to Camille. "Wesley Falton took Isaac from the bait shop. He said he was an abomination, and he intends to pass judgment."

Camille stared with horrified eyes. "What can I do?"

"Call Stub—tell him to blow the siren. It might make Wesley think. Call Freeman and Evan—tell them to block the road at Bluestone Hollow. Call Jefferson—tell him, uh, just tell him what happened. He'll know what to do."

She thrust her chin toward the house across the lake. "You're going over there."

It wasn't a question.

She scooped up Chance, stood, and headed to the porch, punching in numbers as she went. I raced along the dock and untied the powerboat.

"Where are you going?" Julie called. "Why do you have my rifle?"

"There's trouble. Come out of the water and get in the house."

"What kind of trouble?" She turned onto her belly, tucked the phone in her back pocket, and paddled for shore. "What's happening?"

Before I could frame an answer, Wesley Falton's car shot into the clearing beside the Brocktons' house, barreled across the derelict lawn, and crashed into the corner of the porch. A support beam folded, bringing down a section of the overhang with a crumpling crash.

Julie stopped paddling and stared.

Isaac flung himself from the passenger door and stumbled toward the old rowboat tied to the Brocktons' tiny dock. Blood streamed down his face and onto his pale blue T-shirt. He wiped at it with the backs of his hands.

"He's hurt," Julie screamed. "Isaac's hurt."

413

Wesley Falton tumbled from the driver's door. He pointed at Isaac, bellowed, and bent to retrieve something from the car.

I stowed the guns and pushed off from the dock.

Julie screamed again and paddled for the boat. "Mr. Falton has a knife. He's after Isaac."

I yanked at the starter.

The engine delivered a lethargic cough.

"Hurry," Julie wailed. "We have to help Isaac."

"There's no 'we' about this." I yanked the cord again, got another cough and a hiccup. "You stay here."

"No." She flung herself over the gunwale as the engine caught.

"Get out. Stay here."

"No." She braced herself in the bottom of the boat, splayed like a starfish.

Isaac Falton reached the dock and squatted to untie the old rowboat. Wesley closed the distance, knife held high.

"Julie, he's got a knife."

"You have two guns."

And Hannah Falton might have at least one. "Get out of the boat. Stay here."

"No."

Isaac freed the rope, but Wesley was on the dock, slashing, screaming, the sharp sounds like ice in the blistering air.

I abandoned the argument and powered up.

Julie scrabbled to a sitting position and shrugged into a life jacket, then gripped her rifle and called over her shoulder. "Bullets!"

"No. Get down."

Isaac dodged a knife thrust and struck back with an oar. Wesley kicked out, connecting with Isaac's knee, dropping him to the dock.

The lake was narrow at this end, but shallow, especially on the far side. Rocks and snags drowned deep in winter now lurked close to the surface. I picked my way among them.

"Faster," Julie pleaded.

"We can't help Isaac if we slam into a rock."

"We can if I have ammunition."

I dug into my pockets.

Isaac rolled, his feet tangling with Wesley's, bringing him down.

Julie loaded the rifle.

Isaac flailed with the oar. Wesley slashed with the knife.

Where was Hannah?

I scanned the yard and house. No sign of her.

Isaac fended off another thrust, then lost his grip on the oar.

Wesley raised his arm.

Julie aimed at the mountains and fired.

Lightning flickered in bulging clouds now towering high into the sky and sagging onto the slopes to the west.

Wesley jerked his head toward us, then drove the knife down.

Isaac rolled. Then he was on his hands and feet, moving like a crab along the dock. Reaching the shore, he stood and hobbled for the woods at the north edge of the clearing, one hand clutching his side.

Wesley pointed at us and shouted something I couldn't make out, then leaped to his feet and pursued his son.

Julie clamped the rifle to her shoulder and tracked him.

I arced toward Dark Moon Hollow, paralleling the shore, threading the boat through narrow channels between exposed rocks.

Far down the lake the fire siren wailed. Stub was on the job. If Camille had reached Jefferson, he would be on the way. But to where?

I ordered myself not to think about that, to concentrate on what was in front of me.

"I can't see them," Julie cried. "They're too deep in the trees."

I let the boat drift, considering whether Isaac would return to the house and barricade himself inside, or try for the rowboat again.

Julie looked over her shoulder at me, her eyes dull with pain. "I wanted to shoot Mr. Falton. In the arm or leg. To stop him, you know? But the boat was wobbling and if I missed I might have hit Isaac. And if I didn't, I might have killed him."

"You did the right thing," I assured her. "Isaac will get away."

I had my doubts until he emerged from the trees and tottered along a rough beach of broken shale 50 feet away.

"Isaac," Julie screamed. "Come here. We'll help you."

Isaac took two steps toward the water, then shook his head.

"It's not deep." Julie set the rifle aside and hoisted a life jacket. "I can see bottom. I'll throw this. Get it and wade out to us."

Isaac took another step.

Wesley hurtled from the trees, his white suit torn and streaked with dirt, his face a mask of pure fury. "You can't escape judgment," he howled.

"Hurry, Isaac." Julie hurled the life jacket toward him and grappled for the rifle. "Hurry!"

Isaac took one more step, then turned and darted into the woods with Wesley close behind. Too close to risk a shot that might hit Isaac.

Their shadows flickered among the trees, following the curve of the shore. I eased the boat through the rocks, fighting waves kicked up by a gusting wind.

Isaac was young, but Wesley had the power of madness. Again I wondered about Hannah. What mother wouldn't respond to her son's cries for help?

The wind brought the wail of the fire siren, faint and thin.

A narrow ridge of rock, curving upward like the spine of a submerged water monster, loomed ahead. I throttled back and Julie stood, peering into the water. "It goes out a long way into the lake. And there are lots of rocks on the other side. It will take us forever to get around."

"Then we go ashore here. The storm's about to hit. It's not safe on the water anyway."

I angled between two slabs of rock until the bow scraped stone, then shut off the motor.

Julie shed her life jacket, grabbed the painter, and jumped out. "Nothing to tie to. It'll drift."

"Can't be helped. We'll find it later."

I set the safety, handed her the rifle and my shotgun, climbed out, and followed her along the spine of rock. A gun in each hand, she balanced like a circus performer on a tightrope, taking quick, sure steps with her bare feet. I moved with more care and less speed, tilting this way and that, my old running shoes slipping. Wind plucked at my T-shirt and lifted Julie's hair from the nape of her neck.

From here, low in the deep cove where Dark Moon Creek spilled into the lake, I couldn't see my house or the Brocktons' place. But I had a good view of storm clouds rolling along the ridges and filling the hollows. Lightning spiked from cloud to cloud and rumbles of thunder overlapped. We hadn't been safe on the water, but we weren't safe in the woods, either. We'd need to stay low and out of open spaces.

The rocky spine descended into a pool of shallow water. Julie leaped, guns held high, landed knee-deep, and slogged to shore. I took the pool in two long steps and headed for the woods. "Get into the trees as fast as you can. Stay away from clearings."

She sprinted for cover in a clump of young maples, the undersides of their leaves flashing silver in a pulsing updraft. "Do you see them?"

"No." I took the old shotgun from her grasp and loaded it, thought about ordering her to stay here while I searched, then abandoned the idea. She wouldn't listen. It was my blessing—and my curse—to be surrounded by strong-minded women.

Julie cupped her hands around her mouth and shouted. "Isaac. Isaac, where are you?"

A strangled scream broke from somewhere on the slope above us.

Julie pointed right. "That way."

I pointed left. "Sounded more like that way."

Julie shouted again, but her words were swallowed by wind whipping from the lake. A burst of chill rain came with it, thick drops rattling leaves above our heads. Julie shivered. Goose bumps rose on my arms.

I remembered the slab of leaning rock near the Devil's Tombstone. It wasn't much of a shelter, but it would break the force of the rain. "Come on."

I led the way north and west, angling across a ridge, Julie behind me, calling for Isaac. "Why doesn't he answer?" she wailed. "Is he dead?"

"Maybe he's keeping still so his father doesn't find him. Maybe he went up a tree. Stay close and keep looking around and behind you. If you see Wesley Falton, yell and drop."

"Okay, but I can't see very far."

Neither could I. Pine and hemlock grew thick on the south-facing slope and broke the force of the wind. Beneath their branches the air was green-gray, viscous, fevered.

I plodded on, testing my footing, conscious of Julie's bare feet. Wind mauled the branches high above us, tearing holes in the canopy that dark rain slashed through. Lightning sizzled and thunder cracked. The wail of the fire siren was only a memory, lost in the frenzy of the storm.

Julie tugged at my T-shirt. "Where are we going?"

"There's a rock like a lean-to near the Devil's Tombstone."

"I remember. I think it's farther west."

I eased along the face of the slope. "If we don't find it soon, we'll get low in a clump of trees and wait this out. We'll be wet and cold, but—"

"Not as cold as the night Chance was born."

"I hope never to be that cold again."

"And I hope I'm never that scared."

She said nothing else for a few moments, then tugged at my shirt again and pointed down the slope. "There's the Devil's Tombstone."

She gasped. "And there's Isaac."

Chapter 47

He lay curled in the depression on top of the boulder, his head tucked, his arms shielding it. The rock gave off an aura like dark flame.

Julie brushed past me, calling his name.

Isaac raised his head. His face was tight with pain. He lifted a bloody hand.

"Come down," Julie called. "We'll protect you."

Moving as if half his bones were fractured, Isaac inched to the edge of the rain-slick boulder, lowered his right foot, and felt for a toehold. His pants were streaked with blood. Leaves and twigs tangled in the laces of his shoes.

"I'll help you." Julie leaned her rifle against a log. "I'm coming."

She'd covered half the distance when Wesley Falton erupted from a thicket of oak at the top of the ridge. His suit and lavender shirt were blotched with blood and mud.

"Julie!"

I brought the shotgun to bear on Wesley.

He shot past as if he saw only his son, his knife, and his vision of judgment.

Isaac yelped and jerked his dangling leg, toeing the rock, struggling to get on top again. Shouting a jumble of words, Wesley jumped and stabbed at Isaac's ankle. Isaac kicked out, slipping closer to his father.

Keeping her eyes on Wesley, Julie edged out of my line of fire and toward her rifle.

"Wesley," I shouted. "Stop. Put the knife down."

Wesley stabbed again.

The air sizzled. My hair stood on end and my skin tingled. A bolt of lightning zigzagged through the treetops. Thunder shook the ground.

Wesley sprang again, the knife blade sparking against the rock an inch from Isaac's ankle.

Isaac squirmed and clawed, got his toes into a crevice, and inched toward the lake side of the rock. Twice he tried, but couldn't pull himself on top.

"Put the knife down, Wesley. Put it down or I'll shoot."

Would I? I wanted him alive, wanted the answers he might have about my victims.

Wesley spat a vicious twist of a language I couldn't understand. He stalked his son to the lower side of the rock, to that cold spot where nothing grew. Getting a fresh grip on the knife, he raised his arm high. "You won't shoot," he roared. "You can't judge me."

My finger tightened on the trigger.

Lightning ripped the sky.

Thunder cracked and rolled.

Wesley's knife hand shattered.

With a banshee's wail, he crumpled.

My finger hadn't moved.

Julie pointed to the lake. "Jefferson did that. He must be on the dock."

Risking lightning for us.

421

"Wesley's down. Get your rifle and watch him," I told Julie. "I'll help Isaac."

I raced through a barrage of rain to the far side of the rock and laid the shotgun beside the tree Julie used to climb down months ago. I was five feet up when Julie shouted. "He's coming."

Wesley Falton, the knife in his good hand, staggered toward me. "You cannot stand in the way of judgment. My son must die. He is an abomination. I removed temptation from his path twice and he continues to sin."

Up the tree to the top of the boulder?
Or down into Wesley's path?
Couldn't let Wesley get to the shotgun. Had to lead him away.

"You're insane." I jumped. "You're crazed."

"I am judgment."

"You're a killer."

Gaze locked on Wesley, I backed up the slope, feeling with my feet among slick leaves for a branch to parry a knife thrust. Wesley followed, ruined hand against his chest. Hail shredded leaves and beat against my head. "Franklin Turner and Micah Thielman were just kids."

"They tempted Isaac. I judged them. As I will judge Justin Miller before this day is done."

Julie screamed.

"Leave Justin alone," Isaac bawled. "He's my friend. My only friend."

"He tempted you to defy me, to plan to leave my house. *I will judge him.*"

The wind swirled, bringing the sound of a motorboat running hard. Justin? I risked a glance over Wesley's shoulder. Julie had her rifle raised.

422

"What about Genevieve Graham and Theresa Gilligan and Judy Arnold?" I moved sideways, circling back to the rock, to the shotgun, drawing Falton around to give Julie a clear shot. "Did you judge them, too?"

Wesley raised his blasted hand aloft, throwing a spray of blood into the lashing rain.

So much blood. How was he still standing?

"They were the devil's women," he screamed. "They lured me, tested me."

"And you failed the tests," I taunted. "So you killed them."

"I *judged* them."

The wind shrieked and thrashed through the trees. Thunder pounded like the hooves of a hundred horses.

"And Reverend Balforth?"

"He presumed to judge me."

"And you couldn't stand for that? Especially because there were five murders to judge you for. Where did you bury Judy? And Micah?"

"Where you will never find them. Never."

He lunged at me.

I jumped aside, stumbled, fell across a log, felt a slicing pain along my side.

Wesley laughed. "And now I will judge *you*."

"No." A woman's voice rang out. "Now *I* will judge,"

Hannah Falton stood a few yards away, a shotgun braced against her shoulder. Her lips were split, her cheeks bruised, and one eye puffed shut. "Put the knife down."

"You won't shoot me, Hannah." Wesley laughed, but took a step back. "You don't have the will. Obey me. Put the gun down."

Hannah didn't move.

Julie, in the line of fire, slipped behind a tree.

Wesley brandished the knife. "Obey me."

"Never again."

Hannah advanced.

Wesley retreated.

I lumbered to my feet, ribs blazing with pain.

Foot by foot Wesley gave ground.

Foot by foot Hannah followed.

He reached the blighted earth at the south end of the rock, came to a halt, and raised his shattered hand. "You will not judge me, Hannah. You do not have the power to judge me. No one on earth has the power to judge me."

Lightning crisscrossed the sky.

Thunder rolled.

Wind howled.

Then, in a second of stillness, a church bell rang.

And Wesley Falton was gone.

Chapter 48

Sheriff Clement North rubbed his bristly eyebrows and studied the Devil's Tombstone and the patch of earth surrounded by yellow tape. A crime scene technician scooped soil samples while Justin walked in widening circles, taking pictures and occasionally scratching something in a notebook. I guessed he was searching for a scientific explanation, and wondered what he'd come up with.

Yesterday Wesley Falton stood on that blighted ground and howled that he wouldn't be judged by anyone on earth. Today Falton was gone and pale green sprouts poked through soil no longer cold. A spring bubbled from the base of the Devil's Tombstone, nourishing those sprouts and sending a trickle of clear water into Hemlock Lake.

Had a lightning strike brought water from the earth?

Or had evil cancelled out evil to nurture new growth?

"I've got to admit, son," North said, "that this tops anything I've ever seen. Or heard about. You're sure you were watching when he disappeared?"

Julie and I nodded.

"I had the scope on him," Jefferson said. "And then he was gone."

"Maybe a wave joggled the dock and—"

"I was in the water. Standing on a rock."

North frowned. "Maybe you blinked."

Jefferson's eyes narrowed. North raised his hands. "Of course you didn't."

"Hannah and Isaac Falton were watching him, too," Julie said.

"I know, I know." North scratched at his eyebrows again. "It's not that I don't hear what you're saying, but I can't believe a man vanished into thin air."

"And neither does the prosecutor?" I asked.

"Yep." North smiled. "I'm glad he's the one who'll have to unsnarl this and decide how to proceed with those cold cases and Reverend Balforth's murder."

"We heard Wesley Falton confess." Julie kicked at a dead branch. "Four of us heard him."

"Judges tend to want a little more." North turned his gaze on me. "But now that we know who killed those folks, and now that we have Hannah and Isaac to lend a hand, maybe we can dig up a little hard evidence. Bodies, too."

Jefferson snickered. "Meaning *you* do the digging."

"Kind of hard for a man with three cracked ribs to shovel," I said.

North rolled his eyes. "Then sit on a stool and use a garden trowel."

I'd use a teaspoon if I had to. And I knew where I'd start searching—somewhere near the site of that fender bender Falton had been involved in.

Julie tugged at North's sleeve. "I haven't told any of my friends. Dan said not to. Not until—"

"Until we all get our stories straight?"

"Uh, yes. But does that mean we have to lie?"

"Only by omission." North patted her on the head. "Hannah and Isaac Falton will file charges for assault. They're willing to testify to abuse going back years. Justin witnessed part of the assault on Isaac, and you and Dan saw more of it. Wesley Falton chased his son into the woods and you followed. You found Isaac, but Wesley disappeared. End of story."

Julie shook her head in a way that said his explanation was pathetic. "Nobody will believe that."

"Why not? People disappear in these mountains all the time."

"People get *lost*," Julie corrected. "Most of them get found again."

"Well, let's just say the sheriff's office received information that Wesley Falton left the area last night. And until we get further information, we believe a search wouldn't be productive."

Julie rolled her eyes.

North chuckled, patted her head again, signaled Justin that he was ready to leave, and ambled to the shore and the boat he'd arrived in.

"Where do you think Wesley Falton went?" Julie asked as we crossed Dark Moon Creek on our way to my rig. "Do you think lightning fried him to nothing?"

Jefferson shook his head.

"Maybe there was a tornado that we didn't see and it carried him off."

I shook my head.

"Okay, maybe not a tornado, but a really fierce blast of wind. So much wind that it rang the church bell."

I shook my head again.

There was a lot I'd never know about what happened at the Devil's Tombstone yesterday, but one thing I was sure of—it wasn't wind that rang the church bell, it was the ghost of

Reverend James Balforth. And he was telling us judgment was nigh.

Carolyn J. Rose grew up in New York's Catskill Mountains, graduated from the University of Arizona, logged two years in Arkansas with Volunteers in Service to America, and spent 25 years as a television news researcher, writer, producer, and assignment editor in Arkansas, New Mexico, Oregon, and Washington. Her interests are reading, gardening, swimming, and NOT cooking.

Website: www.deadlyduomysteries.com

Blog: http://deadlyduoduhblog.blogspot.com/

Also by Carolyn J. Rose

No Substitute for Murder
No Substitute for Money
No Substitute for Maturity
Hemlock Lake
Through a Yellow Wood
An Uncertain Refuge
Sea of Regret
A Place of Forgetting

With Mike Nettleton

Drum Warrior
Death at Devil's Harbor
Deception at Devil's Harbor
The Hard Karma Shuffle
The Crushed Velvet Miasma
Sucker Punches

Made in United States
North Haven, CT
21 November 2021